Red Hot Chili Peppers FAQ

Red Hot Chili Peppers FAQ

All That's Left to Know About the World's Best-Selling Alternative Band

Dan Bogosian

Backbeat
Books

Guilford, Connecticut

Backbeat Books
An imprint of The Rowman & Littlefield Publishing Group, Inc.
4501 Forbes Blvd., Ste. 200
Lanham, MD 20706
www.rowman.com

Distributed by NATIONAL BOOK NETWORK

The FAQ series was conceived by Robert Rodriquez and developed with Stuart Shea.

Book design by Snow Creative Services

British Library Cataloguing in Publication Information available

Library of Congress Cataloging-in-Publication Data available

Names: Bogosian, Dan, 1988- author.
Title: Red Hot Chili Peppers FAQ : all that's left to know about the
  world's best-selling alternative band / Dan Bogosian.
Description: Lanham : Backbeat Books, 2020. | Series: FAQ | Includes
  bibliographical references and index. | Summary: "The Red Hot Chili
  Peppers are the best-selling alternative rock band of all time. This
  book tells their whole story in an easily digestible format for new
  fans, with the most interesting trivia and all the juicy details
  revealed for hardcore fans"—Provided by publisher.
Identifiers: LCCN 2019046413 (print) | LCCN 2019046414 (ebook) | ISBN
  9781617137228 (paperback) | ISBN 9781493051427 (epub)
Subjects: LCSH: Red Hot Chili Peppers (Musical group)—Miscellanea. | Rock
  musicians—United States—Miscellanea.
Classification: LCC ML421.R4 B65 2020 (print) | LCC ML421.R4 (ebook) |
  DDC 782.42166092/2 [B]—dc23
LC record available at https://lccn.loc.gov/2019046413
LC ebook record available at https://lccn.loc.gov/2019046414

To my parents, who supported me when I wasn't worth supporting: thank you, I love you.

To Emma, who believed in me when I had nothing to believe in.

To the QC, who were friends with me when I wasn't someone worth being friends with.

To Tara, who loved me when I wasn't worth loving.

I owe you.

Contents

Foreword

Ziplining and the Broken MP3s

I've never seen the Red Hot Chili Peppers live. Every time I've had an opportunity, one thing or another has come up that prevented me from attending the show. It's a shame that I hope to rectify soon, and I hope that this revelation doesn't discredit my appearing within the pages of this book.

I do remember the first time I heard the Red Hot Chili Peppers. It was late 2006 (that's right, I'm an actual child—get over it!), and I was sitting in the backseat of my babysitter's car listening to the radio, driving through the wintery suburban Northeast. In a fitting moment, "Snow (Hey Oh)" came pulsating out of the speakers. I perked up with the first speedy, plucked notes of the opening riff, and by the time we reached that chorus, I was utterly hooked. It was a melody and lyrical progression that quickly got stuck in my head and still has yet to leave it more than twelve years later.

At the conclusion of the song, the radio deejay announced that it was the latest single from the new album by a band called the Red Hot Chili Peppers. As I'm sure is common, when I become entranced with a band, I will fight to get my hands on whatever music they have available. Now, with digital streaming, this isn't a difficult task. In 2006, I asked my babysitter to take me to the public library, of which I was an excited, fresh new member. I checked out every Chili Peppers CD they had in stock (the checkout limit was a whopping fifteen items) and ripped them directly into my iTunes library. To this day, I still have broken MP3 files on my computers complete with skips and misaligned start/end times due to the scratched CDs I burned.

I was fascinated with the intricacies of the guitar licks, the slapping bass, and the imperative role the drums played in the building of their melodies. I grew up on punk rock; I had never heard anything like this before. Even as a kid, I found myself shaken to my core when Anthony Kiedis called out to former tour mate Kurt Cobain in the lines of "Californication."

More than a decade later, many of the bands that emerged alongside the Red Hot Chili Peppers have come and gone. Some of them have returned in recent years for the easy cash grab of a reunion tour. The Chili Peppers, on the other hand, have always been around, going strong. While their peers called it quits, Anthony Kiedis and company were headlining stadiums and festivals and consistently releasing new music.

Fans—myself included—feared the band's demise after the unfortunate departure of guitarist John Frusciante in 2009, taking his talents to work on solo music. However, Frusciante was quickly replicated in 2010 with touring guitarist Josh Klinghoffer, who at one point played drums in Frusciante's solo band and also briefly served as a session guitarist for Christina Aguilera.

In a pleasant turn of events for all parties involved, Klinghoffer actually served as a fitting replacement for the band's lost guitar legend when it came time to hit the studio for the follow-up to *Stadium Arcadium*. Klinghoffer brought his unique flare to 2011's *I'm with You*, providing the band with a rebirth of sorts. With the release of *I'm with You*, the Chili Peppers proved themselves an unstoppable force, recovering from a massive blow of a lineup change with an album that was received mostly positively by critics and resulted in one of the band's most successful tours to date.

The Red Hot Chili Peppers is a band that seems to effortlessly stand the test of time, even as their fan base grows older and more passive. Today, the music feels simultaneously nostalgic of a bygone era and also inventive, constantly pushing the envelope of what is considered to be "mainstream rock." More than their tendency early on to put socks on their appendages, the band's history is exceptionally rich, and—perhaps surprisingly for a band at this stage—the sky still seems to be the limit for what is to come next.

In the fall of 2017, I had the opportunity to interview Chad Smith for a piece on a TV special he was promoting. We didn't talk for long, but somehow we worked together to come up with a ludicrous plan to zipline from the Hollywood sign to the Troubador. I didn't tell him about his band's broken MP3 files that are still sitting in my iTunes library.

—Zachary Gelfand, *Rolling Stone, Uproxx* writer

Acknowledgments

I would never have survived writing this book if weren't for the total understanding of my coworkers at EMI (not the record label).

I was assisted more than I have the words to speak of by Hamish Duncan, who helped me with everything from finding photos to just being someone who understood what it was like to obsess over the Red Hot Chili Peppers and exactly how many songs they recorded exactly for *Greatest Hits*. (I wish I had a studio recording for "Rolling Sly Stone.") Duncan answered almost any questions I had and really helped me cross the finish line as I struggled in the final miles of the marathon. (Duncan also runs www.rhcpsessions.com, which was a major help toward the end.)

In particular, I owe many thanks to the Red Hot Chili Peppers, who gave my high school mind something to obsess over. Websites like http://theside.free.fr, http://thechilisource.com, and https://www.rhcpsessions.com provided me with scans of articles and places to feel sane as I spent hundreds of hours figuring out exactly how many tattoos each band member had.

Introduction

Me and My (Teenage) Friends

As a young teenager, I remember playing Virtua Fighter 4 with my friends Ian, Henry, and Dawson, marathoning as a group until we beat the fighting video game for PlayStation 2, but we kept the television on mute.

We played *By the Way* over it, and everyone besides me knew all the words. I liked what I heard, but I felt behind: I would listen to this band when I went home.

For Christmas on the year of its release, I got the Red Hot Chili Peppers' *Greatest Hits*, and I fell in love. Before I played bass guitar, I would read and reread Flea's and John Frusciante's liner notes for the compilation—largely ignoring Chad Smith's, who wrote no more than a paragraph, with little in the way of inspirational words for a teenager to cling to. They became gods to me—Flea, an untouchable demon with fingers, pick, and his thumb on bass; John Frusciante, a virtuoso on guitar hiding that he could shred or do anything on guitar, refusing to play the most impressive thing he could do but instead always playing just the right thing; and Chad Smith, who seemed to hit as hard as John Bonham did in Led Zeppelin but still ghost noted like a jazz or funk player with both his left hand on the snare and his right foot on the bass drum.

I loved Anthony Kiedis's lyrics, but I worshipped the sound of Smith's hi-hats, listening to "Sikamikanico" over and over just loving my life, thinking of how amazing it was that a human being could hit two sheets of metal with wood and make a slush that was so interesting and distinct. I lay in bed wearing headphones—cranked way too loudly, probably damaged my hearing more than going to rock shows—wondering how a silly bass line, a silly guitar part, and a silly drumbeat could combine to form something not silly at all, something beautiful and strange.

The band means different things to different people, and they mean something different to me now than they did when I was a kid. When I was young, they meant everything to me. As I grew up, they were the band I'd revisit every year, always surprised that I still knew all the words, always catching me off guard that I knew all the harmonies to songs I hadn't heard in years.

It would be too easy to call the Red Hot Chili Peppers important and leave it at that. They came out of the Los Angeles alternative scene before alternative was a genre; they played shows with Black Flag and the Minutemen and were comrades with the Circle Jerks before any of those bands became the punk

A Red Hot Chili Peppers poster that still hangs on the author's wall. *Author's collection*

pillars they're viewed as today. They survived the heroin epidemic of the 1980s to become one of the rock bands to help push hair metal out of the way, mixing the colors of race all the while with a guitarist who used to play for Parliament and a drummer who came from the Dead Kennedys.

They survived at a time where it was easy to die. Even in this day and age, they've gotten away with crimes and assault but not been taking down; their art has shone through it, for better or for worse. Their mythos is dark—vocalist Anthony Kiedis relapses over and over again like clockwork for the better part of a decade, while no guitarist seems to last for more than a tour for almost half that time. But they kept on fighting and came out the other side stronger.

I needed that then, and I love that now.

This book doesn't exist to tell the band's story—it is not a chronicle retelling of what happened to the band. There are reasons the band survived when so many others passed; primarily, they've had a different culture than their peers no matter what the era, and their musicianship was always at the top that people who are listening purely for the music clung to it and still continue to. Because of that, I divided the book into three parts: the first about the things beyond music the band is associated with and the second about the musicians and how they became these otherworldly figures to me. The third part is a nearly year-by-year guide; toward the end, sections on each song are included for easier reference.

This book has been a labor of love—it was far more labor than I thought it would be, and far more love came out than I thought I had in me. I hope any Red Hot Chili Peppers fans reading this know how much time went into it—several hundreds of hours.

I still love, with all my heart, anything I have ever loved in my entire life. The Red Hot Chili Peppers are but one of those things. Enjoy.

Part 1

The Culture and What Has Come to Define the Red Hot Chili Peppers

Getting into Music

Their Teenage Exploration

A Wide Array

It may seem like every past and present member of the Red Hot Chili Peppers has always embodied an incredible depth of knowledge of a wide array of music genres, but this isn't the case. Not only were some band members a tad uninformed when it came to particular genres, but, especially in the case of guitarists, some band members learned entire genres through the band's discography prior to their joining. That said, most members of the band began their exposure through each other in their teenage years, often gaining new musical tastes from friends, family, the radio, and each other.

The Los Angeles Gang

Hillel Slovak and Jack Irons were the first two future Chili Peppers to meet and were directly the reason they started playing music. The two of them talked about playing rock music together before either played an instrument, and they started to play within a year of the discussion. Together, they would start a band with Alain Johannes—then known as Alain Moschulski—that began the flow of musical ideas.

Slovak, Irons, Michael "Flea" Balzary, and Anthony Kiedis all went to Fairfax High School; after school together, they'd go to one another's home and play records. Those group listening sessions jump-started the band's eclecticism and taste: Defunkt was Kiedis and his friend Donde Baston's go-to music for starting a dance party and was openly a huge influence on the band's early sound for Slovak and Flea. (Flea even introduced himself to Thelonious Monster's Bob Forrest by telling him he was playing the wrong side of a single during one of Forrest's deejay nights, while Kiedis would name-drop the band on "Can't Stop.")

In Kiedis's autobiography, *Scar Tissue*, he credited Flea for playing a Miles Davis record starting a lifelong love of jazz. Kiedis was also lucky enough that by his junior year of high school, Donde Baston and he became friends, and

Boston had friends at record labels who let them hear albums from David Bowie and the Talking Heads before they were released. Flea also named Eric Dolphy's "God Bless the Child" as a record he and Anthony would listen to for five hours straight together.

Like Flea giving Kiedis jazz, Kiedis gave Flea punk rock. This was born out of necessity: Kiedis and Flea were kicked out of what was the hip Los Angeles rock club at the time, the Rainbow, when Flea drank too much and projectile vomited all over the club—all while, the duo were underage no less. They'd hang out at the Starwood and the Palladium, catching acts like Devo, the Germs, X, the Circle Jerks, and Black Flag, and go wild.

They all shared taste in New Wave and popular rock 'n' roll, with no clearer evidence than the sound of Irons, Slovak, and Flea's group with Johannes, What Is This? (which also went by the names Anthym and, before that, Chain Reaction). Johannes, Irons, and Slovak would go to three consecutive King Crimson shows when Adrian Belew was on guitar, later introducing the other peppers to obscure time signatures and rhythms. Flea later said Slovak got him into progressive rock like Rush and Yes.

Kiedis's father, Blackie Dammett, hung out with the hangers-on and groupies who spent time with David Bowie, Keith Moon, John Lennon, and Harry Nilsson, which didn't impress the other band members.

The Michigan Man's Teen Years

In Chad Smith's own words, the single largest influence on his musical taste was his older brother, Bradley. Bradley introduced Smith to the bands that lead to his natural drumming style as a heavy-hitting rocker with Black Sabbath, Deep Purple, Jimi Hendrix, and Led Zeppelin, among others.

Drumming along to the records in his bedroom—first air drumming, then with pillows and blankets before finally working his way up to a real kit—this was Smith's primary way of learning music: sneak a record away from his brother, dwell and obsess on it, and learn the drum parts.

The Start of a Direct Influence: John Frusciante

Frusciante's exposure to music came primarily through two sources: his family and the radio. As young as age ten, he would listen to the radio (primarily KROQ) and try to record everything from the punk of the Clash to the electronic disco of Donna Summers to the rock-pop of Elton John.

Frusciante was influenced heavily by founding guitarist Hillel Slovak—not just in terms of style but also in terms of how Slovak's playing interacted with

Flea's and in an urge to sound only like himself. Frusciante didn't learn funk directly, instead learning it via following how Slovak played and listening to the records that Flea later said Slovak loved.

From his family, he was given classic rock and progressive rock, name-dropping Steve Howe's playing on Yes's *Fragile* as a big influence.

Frusciante joined the band at age eighteen, allowing his taste to expand throughout his time in the group.

The Final Direct Influence: Josh Klinghoffer

Guitarist Josh Klinghoffer was influenced directly by Frusciante and Dave Navarro, who played only on *One Hot Minute*. Frusciante wouldn't play any songs off of *One Hot Minute* live in his tenure from 1998 to 2009 other than a group jam after Flea's solo number, "Pea," telling *Rolling Stone* that he has never listened to it and that "nobody's ever made a good case to me why I should."

On the other hand, Klinghoffer's first purchase of the Red Hot Chili Pepper's discography was *One Hot Minute*. Although they rarely play songs from that album, Klinghoffer cites it as an early favorite of his.

Much like Frusciante's learning directly in the Chili Peppers, Klinghoffer played guitar for the band's opening act on the *Californication* tour, The Bicycle Thief, at age nineteen. It was there where he met Frusciante, who would invite Klinghoffer to write and play on his solo albums and form the side project Ataxia together alongside Fugazi's Joe Lally. (In Ataxia, Klinghoffer played drums; on Frusciante's solo records, Klinghoffer would play drums, guitar, and bass and sometimes sing.) This closeness to the band and their direct influence on his style were key factors in why he was chosen to replace him in the Red Hot Chili Peppers.

What Is This?

The Chili Peppers' Original Band

What Was That?

The ideological basis for starting the Red Hot Chili Peppers is, at its core, a teenage exploration of music that never ended, but the reality is that three-quarters of the founding members played in a high school band together that predates the group that took them to fame: What Is This? (originally known as Chain Reaction, then Anthym) was founded by guitarist/vocalist Alain Johannes Moschulski, bassist Todd Strassman, and future Chili Peppers Hillel Slovak on guitar and Jack Irons on drums.

The band started out playing a few rougher originals and classic rock covers. Anthony Kiedis and Michael Balzary—predating his name as Flea by several years—saw the band when it was known as Anthym do a pretty solid set of Queen and Led Zeppelin covers in the late 1970s, but Kiedis thought it was silly because it was behind the times, and they were already into both New Wave and punk. New Wave would eventually become huge for the group but not before several lineup changes.

Flea Goes In and Out

By all accounts, the group took a huge leap forward when Slovak began to teach his friend Flea bass guitar with the intent of replacing Strassman. It didn't take long: Flea had a background in both jazz trumpet and some minor experience in drumming, both of which came in handy when learning the new instrument. By Anthony Kiedis's account, Strassman "wasn't a very good musician, [but] did provide the band's PA system."

Strassman wanted to become a lawyer and had no intent of pursuing music full-time. Flea joined and the group took off reasonably well, being popular around southern California. In 1982, less than three years after joining, Flea would quit but stay on amiable terms with all: he had gotten an offer to join the well-known punk group Fear, famous in hard-core circles for an appearance on

Saturday Night Live that got the likes of Ian MacKaye from Minor Threat and Henry Rollins from Black Flag onstage dancing and everyone involved causing damage to the studio.

The Tide Turns Both Ways

Flea was swiftly replaced by Chris Hutchinson, and keyboardist Michael Bocretis was added to the group, signaling the shift toward a different style: New Wave. Hutchinson had a simpler playing style but still held down grooves, and as the group moved into a more dance-oriented feel, they again began to grow in popularity.

Two weeks before the Red Hot Chili Peppers signed to EMI America, What Is This? signed to MCA Records. Irons and Slovak decided to quit the Chili Peppers, viewing that as the side project and Anthym as the band they'd been pursuing since high school.

Sound

What Is This? mixed wavy keyboard and watery and chorus-filled guitar sounds with Johannes's deeper voice for a different take on dance music and New Wave. As serious musicians since high school, they also had more progressive ideas, occasionally playing in 6/4 ("Days of Reflection") and other unusual time signatures.

Although their releases are not available in any major music stores, they can easily be found on YouTube. Only one studio album and two EPs exist for the band, all of which are now highly sought after for collectors. *Squeezed EP* came out in 1984 under both San Andreas Records and MCA; the EP shows flashes of brilliance and demonstrates why they would sign to a major label.

What Is This?, their self-titled release from 1985, came out after Slovak quit to rejoin the Red Hot Chili Peppers. It features Slovak on guitar for all except three songs, but Irons drums throughout its entirety. The most notable thing about the album is that Todd Rundgren produced it.

3 Out of 5 Live also came out in 1985 on MCA and featured three new live recordings, the *What Is This?* version of "Dreams of Heaven," and a new song, "I'll Be Around." Although "I'll Be Around" was labeled the "(Rock Edit)" version on vinyl, no other version of this song was ever commercially released.

Breakup and Future Endeavors

It didn't take long for What Is This? to end: midway through 1985, the group was over. Moschulski began going by his middle name instead of his last name, Johannes, and continued his pursuit of music in an unusual path: he and his future wife, Natasha Shneider, formed the band Walk the Moon, who also signed to MCA. (This is not to be confused with the band Walk the Moon, still around today, of "Anna Sun" fame.)

After Walk the Moon's demise in the late 1980s, Shneider and Johannes formed Eleven with Irons—after his time back in the Red Hot Chili Peppers but before his time in Pearl Jam. Although Irons would leave during the recording of their third album, *Thunk*, Eleven reached a higher amount of fame than its predecessors, opening for bands like Pearl Jam and Queens of the Stone Age.

Soundgarden considered them family, leading to multiple tours together. After Soundgarden's end, Schneider and Johannes formed the backing band for Chris Cornell's first solo release, *Euphoria Morning*. After touring with Queens, the two joined Josh Homme on *The Desert Sessions, Volumes 7 & 8*, which led to recording as guests on the band's *Songs for the Deaf* and joining as the touring band after *Lullabies to Paralyze*.

If that wasn't enough to fully dominate six degrees of separation, Johannes also acted as a sideman for Them Crooked Vultures, the supergroup featuring Queens' Homme, Dave Grohl from Nirvana and Foo Fighters, and Led Zeppelin bassist John Paul Jones. Johannes has also carved out a successful recording career, producing works by Jimmy Eat World, engineering No Doubt, and playing guitar for Kelly Clarkson, among others.

Bad Blood

Rivalries from the 1980s

Two Feuds: One Friendly, One Ferocious

The Los Angeles scene in the 1980s was smaller than you'd imagine: even across styles and genres, musicians knew who each other were. (One odd example: Juan Alderete was a well-trained bassist who listened to punk and hip-hop who became a member of speed metal band Racer X and eventually replaced Flea in the Mars Volta.) It was because of the shared comeuppance—rising with the same tide at the same time—that bands like the Red Hot Chili Peppers and Jane's Addiction got viewed as competitors, even though there was never any bad blood between the two.

On the other hand, the Chili Peppers—or at least Anthony Kiedis—had real issues with Mr. Bungle and Faith No More's Mike Patton. Most likely due to a misunderstanding, Kiedis escalated tensions rather than relieved them, but the feud turned very real after both bands insulted each other as people in the press in the early and late 1990s.

The Friends

From the outset, the Red Hot Chili Peppers were compared to Jane's Addiction and viewed as rivals. The truth is that both bands were friends: Flea would play bass on Jane's Addiction's first reunion (and on a few songs for the returning release, *Kettle Whistle*), and Dave Navarro joined the Chili Peppers for *One Hot Minute* and the ensuing tour. Flea actually asked original Jane's Addiction bassist Eric Avery to rejoin for the Jane's reunion and accepted the role as bassist for that band only after his failure to convince Avery. Jane's drummer Stephen Perkins even played percussion on a few *One Hot Minute* songs—perhaps contributing, along with Navarro's layered guitars, to the album's different sound.

Flea named original Jane's Addiction bassist Eric Avery one of his biggest influences, as did John Frusciante. (Frusciante went after Avery's sound at times on *Stadium Arcadium* but specifically after the "Three Days" bass line on "I

A photo of the band in Philadelphia from 1985.   *Photo by John Coffey*

Could Have Lied" on *Blood Sugar Sex Magik*.) Kiedis commented in 2016 and throughout his autobiography that the band's rivalry was unspoken and more about being the bigger, better Los Angeles alternative rock band than any hard feelings or negativity. They still always pulled for one another.

When Frusciante quit the Chili Peppers, Dave Navarro was everyone's first choice as a replacement. (After Navarro left the band, he lived on lyrically as the know-it-all referenced in the song "Scar Tissue.") Before joining, though, Navarro and Chad Smith became friends. They started a friendship that still exists to this day. Smith eventually played on Navarro's 2001 solo album *Trust No One*, and when Smith produced Glenn Hughes's 2005 album *Soul Mover*, he invited Navarro to play on two songs (as he also did on one song with Frusciante). Navarro received a lot of hate mail from Chili Peppers fans during his tenure, primarily via e-mail, in its early days. He often responded jokingly by telling fans to take it up with his employers—meaning that if he didn't fit in, then blame Smith, Flea, and Kiedis.

Frusciante was highly influenced by Jane's Addiction vocalist Perry Farrell as a person. When Frusciante quit the Red Hot Chili Peppers, he spoke of how Farrell personally guided him through the process and how the band helped him through hard times. Jane's Addiction's last show in California before their first breakup was the same night Frusciante originally tried heroin. In a fitting end, Farrell was eventually the person who took Frusciante to the hospital when he first tried quitting harder drugs.

Farrell was in charge of booking the first few Lollapalooza's—it was, after all, his festival. After Jane's Addiction headlined the first as their first farewell tour in 1991, the Red Hot Chili Peppers were handpicked by Farrell for the same slot for the second go-round in 1992. They've headlined the festival four times: 1992, 2006, 2012, and 2016.

The Foes

There was true bad blood between Faith No More vocalist Mike Patton and Kiedis. In 1989, Faith No More and the Chili Peppers were set to tour in Europe together. Faith No More was actually the more popular group in Europe at the time. Kiedis was already fearful of bands ripping off his musical style; he considered himself a fan of Faith No More and their album *The Real Thing* and privately thought Patton did some subtle stylings similar to himself.

Then the music video for "Epic" was released. When Kiedis saw it, he thought he was being mocked by Patton. "I watched [their] 'Epic' video, and I see him jumping up and down, rapping, and it looked like I was looking in a mirror," Kiedis told biographer Dave Thompson. After constantly getting asked by interviewers if he was tired of bands ripping off his style in Europe, one time became too many.

When *Kerrang!* asked, Kiedis asked what bands the interviewer was referring to, and the interviewer suggested Patton and Faith No More. Kiedis tried to turn his long-held thoughts into a joke that came off as feisty, saying Smith planned to "kidnap [Patton], shave his hair off and cut off one of his feet, just so he'll be forced to find a style of his own." The jab couldn't go unnoticed as the Red Hot Chili Peppers won the cover story and Kiedis's quip put to "Faith No More ripped us off! Like … GRRRR!" as the only description.

Response and Retaliation

This led to Patton getting asked about Kiedis's opinion numerous times, getting various responses both shrugging it off and insulting Kiedis back. He told *Hot Metal* that neither band was threatened by the other, celebrated the free press it generated to *Faces Magazine*, pretended to be Anthony Kiedis to *RIP Magazine*, and mocked the whole thing and blamed *Kerrang!* in the same magazine thirteen issues later.

Some nine years passed without any metaphorical punches thrown between the two bands. Then a coincidence may have revived it: Mr. Bungle's *California* and the Red Hot Chili Peppers' *Californication* were set for the same release date. To avoid confusion, one album would get postponed; as Mr. Bungle was the less popular band, *California* was pushed back six weeks.

That same summer of 1999, Kiedis threw more gas on the fire. On the *Californication* tour, the Chili Peppers were set to headline three festivals that one of Patton's projects, and Mr. Bungle—his original group predating Faith No More—was also set to play. On the same day, all three festivals called and pulled Mr. Bungle off the festival, saying it was requested by the Red Hot Chili Peppers and that the headlining band had the right to kick smaller bands off the bill written into their contract. This upset every member of Mr. Bungle.

Patton began to talk negatively about Kiedis in the press, calling him "pathetic" to *The A.V. Club* and pointing out that the Chili Peppers' manager had admitted that it was only Kiedis who caused the cancellations. Shortly after, Mr. Bungle took it another step up, pretending to be the Red Hot Chili Peppers for their Halloween show outside of Kiedis's hometown of Pontiac, Michigan, and mocking the most sensitive areas for Kiedis: they quoted and mocked previous Kiedis interviews and made insensitive comments about overdosing, with one member dressing up as the ghost of Hillel Slovak and miming heroin usage. (Guitarist Trey Spruance incorrectly remembered the show as being in Ohio.)

Post-Feud or Still Continuing?

In its aftermath, Kiedis denied getting the band kicked off of any festivals except for Big Day Out, and Kiedis credited Mr. Bungle's Halloween show actions as the reason to biographer Dave Thompson. There are two major problems with Kiedis's story: he must've done it in order to take credit for why he did it, and the Halloween show occurred in October 1999 while the Big Day Out in question was September 1999.

Kiedis hasn't spoken about it since 2004 and left all mentions of it out of his autobiography, though the Red Hot Chili Peppers and Kiedis teased a cover of a pre–Patton Faith No More song "We Care a Lot" in 2014. Patton's last remarks came in 2011, when he told *Bizarre* magazine, "I've no idea what it was about then and I don't know now. But I bet we'd have a warm embrace if we saw each other now." The feud briefly gained mainstream coverage again in 2016 when a Fox News host referred to the Red Hot Chili Peppers as "the poor man's Faith No More."

4

Inked

The Band's Tattoos and Their Meanings

The Asterisk All Over

The Red Hot Chili Peppers' logo appears to be an asterisk, but according to the autobiography of Anthony Kiedis (who drew it on a whim for record executives in 1984 when asked to create a logo), it is "an angel in heaven's asshole as view from earth" and is referred to as the "Star of Affinity." Part of its appeal may come from the asterisks' meaning, which is a complex conjugation of controlled chaos. Both Kiedis and guitarist John Frusciante have the asterisk tattooed on them, though Frusciante's is in far worse shape.

All the other notable members of the band throughout history are covered in tattoos—with one powerful exception: Josh Klinghoffer doesn't have a single one.

Anthony Kiedis

The front man has at least ten tattoos. When the Chili Peppers began, Kiedis had none; his first came sometime after their August 1987 performance on the *Arsenio Hall Show*, where his arms are visibly bare, but before Slovak had departed, as there are video performances showing the ink from that time. The tattoo is of Hunkpapa Lakota holy man Chief Sitting Bull.

The second tattoo was his final before Hillel Slovak's death, as it's noticeable in their appearance at PinkPop 1988. The second is of another tribe leader, Chief Joseph, on his right shoulder. (Sitting Bull is on his left.) The third tattoo he started took the longest to complete: started after PinkPop 1988 in Holland, the giant tribal bird design on his back was not completed until sometime in the 1990s. That marked the beginning of a long relationship with Hank Schiffmacher, a Hell's Angels associate also known by both Hanky Panky and Henky Penky whom Kiedis has tried to visit each time he passes through Europe. Kiedis would take Chad Smith for a tattoo that would also take two visits—but more on that later.

Fourth was the band's logo—which Kiedis got around the same time John Frusciante got his, possibly even together, as they got identical tattoos in identical places: on the right wrist. Frusciante's is noticeable as the back cover of *Blood Sugar Sex Magik*; Kiedis's is less prominent but still easily viewed anytime his arm is shown. Fifth came shortly after, a Celtic-style armband on his upper right arm inked in February 1990.

Several years passed before Kiedis got another one. By February 1996, Kiedis got a dagger that was a Maori design symbolizing love. Another Celtic band on his upper left arm followed, then another dagger-like design on his right arm came in 1998. His ninth was a tiger on the inner right forearm as an ode to his Chinese birth sign, the tiger, and the Chinese tradition of tigers bringing protection to their wearers. His tenth was a koi carp on the inner left forearm. There were rumors he got another around the time of the birth of his son, but the carp appears to be the last one, dated two years before his Everly Bear Kiedis's birth (2006 versus 2008).

Chad Smith

The story behind Smith's first Hanky Panky tattoo started in 1990 but ended in 1991. Smith got a hernia operated on in January 1990 but didn't let it hold him up and went straight to touring. Introduced to Kiedis's favorite tattoo artist, Smith wanted to let him run free with a big piece and asked for a tribal octopus; Hanky Panky whipped up the design and got to shaving Smith's leg.

The operation hadn't fully healed—perhaps since he had been playing drums every night—and Hanky Pank refused to ink Smith, believing that if he did he would give Smith gangrene and that the leg would eventually have to be removed. About a year later when the band returned to Amsterdam, Smith got the tattoo done. Frusciante also has an octopus tattoo, but it is nowhere near as stylized as Smith's.

Smith also has a tribal badge of a totem-style eagle on his left arm, a scorpion on his right arm, and Chinese symbols representing the names of his children on the inside of both arms and a dolphin on his left leg.

Jack Irons

Original drummer Jack Irons too went to Hanky Panky for his first tattoo. In the winter of 1998, the whole group planned to go—it is probable that Hillel Slovak got tattooed there too, but it's impossible to know, and Irons had never gotten a tattoo before. He wanted to get a tattoo of Bozo the Clown but couldn't find a picture of Bozo to show the artist. Panicking, he didn't want to give the artist nothing; he looked at a shirt he liked with sea life on it and had Hank customize it.

In the six years that followed, Irons got a new tattoo once every two months.

Dave Navarro

Dave Navarro was known for his tattoos, ultimately leading to his role on the television show *Ink Master*. He got his first tattoo with original Jane's Addiction bassist Eric Avery and found himself constantly adding ink to his skin. He has his mother's name tattooed on his lower back ("Constance"); she was mysteriously murdered (until an episode of *Unsolved Mysteries* helped crack the case). He also has a "CE" for his ex-wife, Carmen Electra. He also has a tattoo that says "Love Fades"—a heartbreaking line from the Woody Allen film *Annie Hall*.

Navarro pledged to never get any tattoos removed, believing his skin was like a walking diary: what goes on reflected a period of time and the state of mind he was in.

John Frusciante

Frusciante also went to Hanky Panky and got his octopus tattoo there on his upper right arm. Additionally, he got a Native American flash from him on his left upper arm. His left wrist has a similar style to the upper left arm but was done by a different artist.

The asterisk on the right wrist was gotten around the same time as Kiedis got his, but Frusciante's borders a red and blue design that, when viewed from a certain angle, is clearly a man and a woman having sex.

Frusciante is notable for how his tattoos now appear versus how they originally appeared: he injected cocaine rather than snorted it, shooting up almost every five minutes at the height of his addiction, leaving a large amount of scars (and some areas that have gotten skin grafted) that have altered several tattoos, including the whole of his right arm. He may have gotten more on his back or since leaving the band, but since he does not make public appearances anymore, those tattoos are what is known.

Flea

Although it may not seem like it, Flea has had the most tattoos of any Chili Pepper, past or present, other than Jack Irons. On his left shoulder, he got a portrait of Jimi Hendrix tattooed, as Hendrix was Flea's biggest rock musical idol; just below on his left arm is an armband of elephants and below that an abstract pattern that looks like an X.

His Hanky Panky tattoo is of a tribal bird on his right inside arm. What is the oldest known Celtic symbol representing the three stages of man (birth, death, and eternity) is inked on his right pectoral muscle. The design originated from the "Triskell" design that predates Christianity in Ireland by thousands of years. His right arm has a snake that slithers around a pair of dolphins and a dragon that appears in an S shape, something *Kerrang!* theorized was a tribute to Hillel Slovak.

He got a couple tattoos relating to family: on his left arm, the name of his first daughter, Clara, and on his left pectoral, his ex-wife's name, Loesha, who gave birth to Clara. In October 2011, he got a tattoo of a drawing by another one of his daughters, Sunny Bebop. (He tweeted afterward, "All the best tattoos are drawn by five year olds!")

His back tattoo is tribal. The design included a gap-toothed grin much like his own. The two oddest tattoos he has gotten are on his knuckles on both hands, he has tattooed "Love," and on his head, only visible when it's shaved, is his own nickname, "Flea." It's entirely plausible he has others, but those are what has been photographed and tweeted about. Several of these tattoos are more visible than normal in his role as a robber in the 2017 film *Baby Driver*. He talked about the nature of his tattoos—the finger tattoos especially—on *Late Night with Conan O'Brien* in 1998.

5

Death, Drugs, Rock 'n' Roll

Overdoses, Deaths, and Near Misses from Alternative Rock's Biggest Drug Survivors

Anthony's Early Drug Use

While Kiedis wasn't an addict from the start; he began drug usage far earlier in life than most. By the time he lived with his father, he was already pursuing sex, smoking hash, drinking, and even doing quaaludes, writing about doing some right before his twelfth birthday in his autobiography. His father passed him a joint in the kitchen while still a preteen.

Not all of Kiedis's drug use was stemming from his father—he first injected cocaine was at age fourteen, and by eighth grade one of his friends was growing and selling marijuana with a career-level income—but his father's drug trade proliferated the young boy's life. Once, at age twelve, Kiedis smuggled in $30,000 in cash after a drug-dealing trip with his father in Kenosha, Wisconsin. According to his autobiography, Dammett himself told the BBC, "It wasn't so unusual that I let him take a little bit of acid or a little bit of marijuana."

Kiedis Almost Gets Kicked Out

As written about in *Scar Tissue*, Kiedis skipped a show to score drugs. The rest of the band had Keith Morris from Black Flag and the Circle Jerks fill in for the show—where he improvised and yelled gibberish lyrics throughout, not knowing any Red Hot Chili Peppers songs—and began to practice without Kiedis before eventually letting him back in within a few weeks.

Morris doesn't agree on what led to the fill-in, believing that Kiedis was arrested for jaywalking that night. What is agreed on is that Morris's performance was fueled by a gram of cocaine and that it was at the Olympic Auditorium.

Hillel's Death, Irons's Leaving, and Kiedis's Sobriety

A founding member's death would be enough to tear apart many other bands. Hillel Slovak was trying to get sober when he relapsed and died of an overdose from speedballing heroin and cocaine on June 25, 1988. It immediately caused a huge difference in the band's career: founding member Jack Irons quit the band, afraid that remaining in it would lead him to eventually see a similar fate for Anthony Kiedis. Kiedis immediately reacted with the thought that it should've been him instead, decided to quit drugs, and vowed to never shoot up again. He went to rehab and remained sober until 1994, where he relapsed before the making of *One Hot Minute*.

Kiedis's Near Miss as an Adult

Anthony Kiedis was dating Claire Essex (born Yohanna Logan), also a drug addict, and the two were taking hits of cocaine. She convulsed and stop breathing at a hotel in San Francisco during the *Californication* tour. Kiedis called 911, but midway through the call, Essex woke up and began breathing again. Kiedis hung up and went back to getting high, even as the front desk called to see what the emergency was about and even after police eventually showed up at the door. (The police eventually left after recognizing Kiedis, and Essex greeted them to prove she was alive.)

Kiedis relapsed several additional times as well, once going on a bender shortly after Frusciante rejoined the band for an entire weekend, and then realized he was putting the band at risk and maintained sobriety again for some months. Kiedis eventually got sober (and has remained sober since) December 24, 2000, when he attended a Narcotics Anonymous meeting for the first time.

Frusciante Leaves the Band to Do Drugs and the Fan Club Starts

John Frusciante was only a teenager when he joined the group and had been exposed only to alcohol and pot. Within a few years, he was a heroin addict and a junkie—something he wasn't ashamed of but proud of. Frusciante entered a deep depression and left the band as they were on the verge of superstardom, using his newfound riches to fully explore his drug addiction.

In October 1993, John Frusciante and River Phoenix went on a drug binge that lasted nearly the whole month and eventually resulted in Phoenix's overdose and death on Halloween night. (Flea accompanied Phoenix in the ambulance ride to the hospital.)

In 1994, the same channel that had previously made two full-length documentaries on the Red Hot Chili Peppers did one on John Frusciante. He had lost an unhealthy amount of weight, sold most of his valuable equipment, and played his current songs on a classical-style acoustic guitar that was wildly out of tune. It is painful to watch and listen to—his eyes look sleepless, and his voice has dropped to a low, dry growl.

The same year, the band fired Shannon Chaiken, who started the band's fan club, the Rockinfreakapotamus. Chaiken started the fan club as a newsletter in 1990. Anthony Kiedis's father, Blackie Dammett, took over the job when his mother recommended him for it.

By December 1996, the *New Times LA* noted that he had lost most of his upper teeth, that he had rotten gums, that his skin was covered in cigarette burns, and that he spent most of his time reading, writing, painting, playing guitar, and shooting up. His arms were terribly scarred from improperly shooting up heroin and cocaine and the buildup of scar tissue that resulted. He released his second solo album in 1997 for the pursuit of drug money by his own admission.

Frusciante's Pursuit of Sobriety

In December 1996, Frusciante gave up heroin but struggled to give up crack cocaine and alcohol. In fact, his mind-set was to quit heroin and compensate with marijuana and alcohol and briefly tried to keep doing speed and crack. After a year of that struggle, at Bob Forrest of Thelonius Monster's urging—himself now famed for celebrity rehabilitation—Frusciante checked into a clinic and began recovery. Shortly after, Anthony Kiedis and Flea visited him in his new home in Silver Lake and asked him to rejoin the band. If Frusciante ever relapsed since, it was not public knowledge.

Navarro's Dark Time

Dave Navarro has attributed his drug usage to the loss of his mother, who was brutally murdered when he was only fifteen years old in 1983. Her death lead to an episode of *Unsolved Mysteries* about it (which eventually helped catch the murderer), and the story was told from Navarro's point of view in his documentary *Mourning Son*.

He relapsed in June 1997, telling MTV that he started experimenting with drugs again, and made no comment besides that drugs can kill you to *Rolling Stone* in March 1998. According to his brother, the drug usage ended six years of sobriety. His drug usage was a part of why he was fired from the band but

A collectible from the Rockinfreakapotamus fan club. *Author's collection*

not the sole reason—it contributed to his not showing up, not jamming, and not writing and recording his guitar parts, but it wasn't the only reason, as Navarro was not used to jamming and the whole package was why he was fired from the band.

Summations

Between their vocalist having multiple near-death experiences and relapses, the original drummer quitting for fear of drug usage, the founding guitarist dying of a drug overdose, and two subsequent guitarists having drug addictions, few (if any) bands have successfully steered through the depths of darkness that drug use can bring like the Red Hot Chili Peppers. It's worth noting that Josh Klinghoffer is the only guitarist in the band to record on more than one album to not be a heroin addict at some point in his life. As of this writing, every member of the band is sober.

6

Hollywood

Examining the Red Hot Chili Peppers' Acting Careers

Lights, Camera, Action

Both Anthony Kiedis and Flea pursued acting to various extents, with Kiedis trying out first in his childhood. Kiedis's father, Blackie Dammett, was an actor of middling success; before Kiedis got any roles, his dad appeared on an episode of *Charlie's Angels* ("The Vegas Connection" as Freddy), multiple episodes of *Starsky and Hutch* ("Murder Ward" as Charlie Deek, "Huggy Bear and the Turkey" as Sugar, and "Dandruff" as Ellis), and a supporting role in a made-for-TV-movie (*Nowhere to Hide* as John).

Anthony to Hollywood

Originally named John Kiedis, Anthony's father legally changed his name to Blackie Dammett to further his career, combining the first and last names of his favorite author, Dashiel Hammett. Being his son and idolizing his father, Kiedis decided that when he pursued acting, he would use a name that made sense as the son of Blackie—hence, he was billed as Cole for his child acting work, fulfilling a bit of a joke: Cole, son of Blackie.

"Cole" found himself cast fairly often in advertisements, often portraying a badass or a rough teenager. Without so much as an audition, he was cast as Sylvester Stallone's son in the film he did after *Rocky*, *F.I.S.T.* This brief dive into acting as a child ended after his father got them to play essentially themselves in *Jokes My Folks Never Told Me*, where he told a relatively dirty joke for someone his age.

No acting roles followed for years as music took over his life. His next two roles had him playing himself in band performances—both in the *Freaky Styley* era of the band featuring Hillel Slovak and Cliff Martinez. These two films were *Thrashin'*, where they played "Blackeyed Blonde" (and the song later appeared on the sound track), and *Tough Guys*. *Tough Guys* is notable for its inclusion of a song, "Set It Straight," that was recorded but never released after the film never made a sound track—but more on that in chapter 10.

Only two more roles appeared in Kiedis's lifetime: in *Point Break* as Tone, where his character's primary role was to threaten Keanu Reeves on the beach and then get his ass kicked, and *The Chase*, where he and Flea portrayed some far-out idiotic stoners in a jeep. Kiedis eventually sold the film rights to his autobiography, *Scar Tissue*, to HBO, and plans were made to turn it into a series called *Spider and Son*; in 2011, FX bought the rights, but it hasn't made any progress since.

Mike B. the Flea, the Actor

Flea's first acting performance came in a music video for the Barnes & Barnes song "Pizza Face." (Another Barnes & Barnes song, "Fish Heads," was given a brief nod of a joke in the film *Wayne's World*.)

Another acting role didn't come until after the Red Hot Chili Peppers had formed, playing Razzle in *Suburbia*, where he was billed as Mike B. the Flea. *Suburbia* was directed by Penelope Spheeris, who later cast him in *Dudes* as Milo and included the Red Hot Chili Peppers' song "Sikamikanico" on the sound track to her most prominent film, *Wayne's World*. Alongside his performances as himself in *Tough Guys* and *Thrashin'*, his 1980s acting occurred as Jester the Alien in *Stranded* (no relation to the Chili Peppers song of the same name), as Floyd in *The Blue Iguana*, and as Marty McFly's boss and nemesis, Douglas J. Needles, in *Back to the Future Part II* and *Part III* (Needles got McFly fired in the original future). Flea told the VPRO filmmakers he was unhappy with the two films and his performances in them and referred to the first sequel as "a multi-million dollar piece of trash." He has, however, made it a point to say that Michael J. Fox was very kind to him.

The 1990s saw his acting take an upturn in terms of frequency, quality of roles, and quality of films. Alongside Kiedis in *The Chase*, he played Dale, again exaggerating all sorts of California mannerisms, making the film a must-see for Chili Peppers diehards. He played Nihilist Number Two in *The Big Lebowski* and a simple musician in *Fear and Loathing in Las Vegas*, both in 1998, as well as Bob Summerfield in the remake of *Psycho* the same year. The acting became so prominent that he was interviewed on *Late Night with Conan O'Brien* in 1998 for his acting, where he complimented the Coen Brothers and called them some of the most talented filmmakers.

The most interesting role was as the voice of Donnie on *The Wild Thornberrys* television show (and its corresponding movies). The feral boy spoke entirely in gibberish on the show, with a frantic and manic energy. Flea's first attempt to be the star of a film came in 1999 for *Liar's Poker*; he loved the book and was the third-biggest role in the movie. When doing *The Wild Thornberrys*, he got to meet Tim Curry, someone he loved in *The Rocky Horror Picture Show* as a kid. Flea's mansion used to look down on Curry's, and Flea and Curry would exchange waves from time to time.

In 2014, Flea and Kiedis helped produce the film *Low Down*, which Flea also starred in. This marked his return to acting for the first time in more than a decade. Since then, he has had a few notable bit roles, including as a voice in the Pixar film *Inside Out* and as a criminal in Edgar Wright's *Baby Driver*. He starred in one episode of an Amazon Prime pilot that did not get renewed, *Highston*, where the title character sees his imaginary friends as real, but the imaginary friends are also all celebrities. (The pilot episode had him seeing Shaq and Flea everywhere, the two acting as an odd couple that help Highston through his predicaments.)

Flea helped make or appeared in many documentaries. He helped produce *Jaco*, the documentary about legendary jazz bassist Jaco Pastorius, alongside Robert Trujillo—the two were the main producers and did a press tour together to help promote the film. Flea often appears in documentaries about punk music due to his history playing in Los Angeles punk band Fear and his mainstream appeal from the Red Hot Chili Peppers.

Filmography (Excluding Red Hot Chili Peppers Music Videos)

Anthony Kiedis

F.I.S.T. (1978)—Kevin Kovak (credited as Cole Dammett)
ABC Afterschool Special (1978)—Jimmy Plummer, episode "It's a Mile from Here to Glory" (credited as Cole Dammett)
Jokes My Folks Never Told Me (1978)—Student (credited as Cole Dammett)
Tough Guys (1986)—himself
Thrashin' (1986)—himself
Less Than Zero (1987)—Musician #3 (credited as Cole Dammett)
Point Break (1991)—Tone
Ice Cube music video for "Wicked" (1992)
The Simpsons (1993)—voice of himself, episode "Krusty Gets Kancelled"
The Chase (1994)—Will

Flea

Barnes & Barnes music video for "Pizza Face" (1980)
Suburbia (1983)—Razzle (credited as Mike B. the Flea)

Tough Guys (1986)—himself
Thrashin' (1986)—himself
Dudes (1987)—Milo
Less Than Zero (1987)—Musician No. 1
Stranded (1987)—Jester the Alien
The Blue Iguana (1988)—Floyd
Let's Get Lost (1988)—documentary as himself
Back to the Future Part II (1989)—Douglas J. Needles
Young MC music video for "Bust a Move" (1990)
Back to the Future Part III (1990)—Douglas J. Needles
The Idiot Box (1991)—Mugger, Episode 2
Motorama (1991)—Busboy
My Own Private Idaho (1991)—Budd
Roadside Prophets (1992)—Two Free Stooges
Ice Cube music video for "Wicked" (1992)
The Ben Stiller Show (1992)—various small roles
Rhythm & Jam (1993)—documentary as himself
The Simpsons (1993)—voice of himself, episode "Krusty Gets Kancelled"
Son in Law (1993)—Tattoo Artist (uncredited)
24 Hours in Rock and Roll (1994)—documentary as himself
The Chase (1994)—Dale
Just Your Luck (1996)—Johnny
The Crow: City of Angels (1996)—Cameo
Duckman: Private Dick/Family Man (1997)—various voices
The Decline of Western Civilization Part III (1998)—documentary as himself
The Wild Thornberrys (1998–2004)—voice of Donnie Thornberry
The Big Lebowski (1998)—Nihilist No. 2, Kieffer
Fear and Loathing in Las Vegas (1998)—Musician
The Lionhearts (1998)—voice, episode "Singin' in the Maine"
Psycho (1998)—Bob Summerfield
Liar's Poker (1999)—Freddie
Three Days (1999)—documentary as himself
Goodbye Casanova (2000)—Silent
Gen¹³ (2000)—Voice of Grunge/Edward Chang
MADtv (2000)—small role on one episode
The Wild Thornberrys: The Origin of Donnie (2001)—voice of Donnie Thornberry
Rising Low (2002)—documentary as himself
The Wild Thornberrys Movie (2002)—voice of Donnie Thornberry
Rugrats Go Wild (2003)—voice of Donnie Thornberry
All We Are Saying (2005)—documentary as himself
We Jam Econo: The Story of the Minutemen (2005)—documentary as himself
American Hardcore (2006)—documentary as himself

Too Tough Too Die: A Tribute to Johnny Ramone (2006)—documentary as himself

Joe Strummer: The Future is Unwritten (2007)—documentary as himself

Patti Smith: Dream of Life (2008)—documentary as himself

Life on the Road with Mr. and Mrs. Brown (2009)—documentary as himself

The Simpsons 20th Anniversary Special: In 3-D! On Ice! (2009)—voice of himself

Everyday Sunshine: The Story of Fishbone (2010)—documentary as himself

The Other F Word (2011)—documentary as himself

Bob and the Monster (2012)—documentary as himself

Lexicon Devil (2012)—documentary as himself

Boardwalk Empire (2012)—episode "The Rise and Fall of the Medical Kush Beach Club"

The Art of Punk: Black Flag (2013)—documentary as himself

Die Antwoord music video for "Ugly Boy"

Jaco (2014)—documentary as himself

Low Down (2014)—Hobbs

Sheriff Callie's Wild West (2014)—Milk Bandit

Inside Out (2015)—voice of Mind Worker Cop Jake

Highston (2015)—himself

Baby Driver (2017)—Eddie No-Nose

American Dad (2016)—voice of the orderly, episode "Stan-Dan Deliver"

Family Guy (2017)—voice of himself

7

Reinventing the 1990s

Why the Red Hot Chili Peppers Outlasted the Grunge Boom

The King of the 1990s

The 1990s began still ruled by hair metal and pop artists: the biggest seller of 1990 was Janet Jackson's *Janet Jackson's Rhythm Nation 1814*, and the biggest seller of 1991 was Mariah Carey's *Mariah Carey*. When Nirvana "broke" in 1991 with *Nevermind* and the radio takeover of "Smells Like Teen Spirit," it brought alternative rock to the forefront.

But by Kurt Cobain's suicide in 1994, the so-called grunge boom was over, and boy bands and disco took control of mainstream radio, while rock radio was controlled by post-grunge bands like Bush and friendly acts like Fastball and Third Eye Blind. How did the Red Hot Chili Peppers outlast this wave?

Early Beginnings

While many factors contributed to the band's staying popularity, the fact that they predated the grunge boom worked highly in their favor. They gained new fans with newfound radio play, but they had already gotten onto MTV's regular rotation with their cover of Stevie Wonder's "Higher Ground" from *Mother's Milk*. Additionally, they had been touring hard for years, playing seventy-four shows in 1987 and eighty-three in 1988 despite Hillel Slovak's death, Jack Irons quitting, and DeWayne "Blackbyrd" McKnight getting fired after three shows.

Catching the Right Tide

Many bands took off with the alternative boom that both predated it—in addition to the Chili Peppers, Jane's Addiction and Soundgarden are two notables that had preexisting careers only heightened by the time—but few shared the

A poster of a tour with Nirvana.

Author's collection

same unison with the exact timing of Nirvana's prominence. Three prominent American acts released major albums on September 24, 1991: A Tribe Called Quest put out *The Low End Theory*, Nirvana released *Nevermind*, and the Red Hot Chili Peppers released what might be their magnum opus, *Blood Sugar Sex Magik*.

Even their singles were closely timed: "Give It Away" was released six days before "Smells Like Teen Spirit" that September, and "Under the Bridge" hit radio eight days after "Come As You Are" in March.

Their tour openers in those years also became stadium acts and were starting to grow right at that time. For the *Blood Sugar Sex Magik* tour, the original openers were Pearl Jam and the Smashing Pumpkins. When the record label urged a more successful band to be the opener, Pearl Jam was replaced by Nirvana—but then because of Billy Corgan of the Smashing Pumpkins and Kurt Cobain of Nirvana's shared history dating Courtney Love, the Pumpkins dropped, and Pearl Jam returned. For nine dates starting at the end of 1991, Nirvana opened for the Red Hot Chili Peppers, with Flea playing trumpet for the "Smells Like Teen Spirit" solo on occasion.

Continued Radio Play after the Grunge Era

The band was lucky (or unlucky, depending on your view) enough to not release two albums in the heyday of grunge, touring heavily off of Blood Sugar Sex Magik for long enough that Kiedis talked in interviews about how most bands had already released follow-ups to their breakthrough when they were still sorting through their guitarist situation.

The Red Hot Chili Peppers are literally the most successful band in alternative rock radio history. According to *Billboard*, they have the most top ten songs on the *Billboard* Alternative Songs chart at number twenty-five, most cumulative weeks at number one at eighty-five, and the most number one singles at thirteen. They've also done this over four different decades, which is truly the cause of their continued success: their first top ten song on the U.S. "Alternative Songs" chart was "Knock Me Down" in 1989, which reached number six. Their most recent to hit the top ten on that chart is "Dark Necessities" from *The Getaway*.

Sound Tracks, Film Works, and Some Brief Video Game Appearances

Many bands get a boost of success from appearing on a sound track—especially in the 1990s, the era that saw record sales hitting their highest—but cassette sales were relatively low, and people were unable to burn CDs or download yet, so the variety of artists that appear on a sound track had a certain appeal. The Red Hot Chili Peppers appeared on the sound tracks for *Say Anything* (1989), *Pretty Woman* (1990), *Wayne's World* (1992), *Coneheads* (1993), *Mighty Morphin' Power Rangers: The Movie* (1995), *Twister* (1996), *The Beavis and Butt-Head Experience* (1993), and *Beavis and Butt-Head Do America* (1996).

In the original video game *Guitar Hero*, an interpretation of the Red Hot Chili Peppers' version of "Higher Ground" is one of the playable songs. (All the songs on the first *Guitar Hero* are cover versions with the exception of Primus's "John the Fisherman," but as it is a guitar game, it's very much the Chili Peppers' song and not the Wonder original.) They also make an odd cameo in *Tekken 4*—not in appearance, but there is a mini-game called "Tekken Force," where four of the enemies are Anthony the Assassin, John the Assassin, Chad the Assassin, and Flea the Assassin, named as an homage to the band's lineup at the time (2001).

Virtually no one will know Anthony Kiedis best from his acting roles, but it's entirely possible that certain children raised in the 1990s will know Flea more for being the voice of Donnie in *The Wild Thornberrys* than they would his bass playing. (It's also possible that his odd work portraying musicians or nihilists in films like *The Big Lebowski* would give him more recognition—for more on this, see chapter 6.) The group also benefited from immortalization in *The Simpsons*, albeit with a lineup that did not last very long. (For more on this, see chapter 13.)

What Time

In a purely music and lyrical sense, the Red Hot Chili Peppers are about as timeless as it gets. Even if their cultural context is stuck with a certain era, their music combined 1970s funk with 1980s independent ideas and a mixture of genres from every era: a punk energy that's still around and a melodic pop sense that's still prominent without ever becoming pop punk. This is likely why they are not pegged as a "90s act" even if most of their hits have come from that decade.

It's also likely that since Kiedis never sang about the things that bands back then would sing about (something he joked about with Rick Rubin as "girls and cars" in the *Funky Monks* documentary), his lyrics get to stay more relevant, even at their most gibberish. Because he is very rarely making dated references beyond personal inside jokes and self-reference to his band's other songs (see the "True Men Don't Kill Coyotes" reference in "Mellowship Slinky in B Major"), rarely do we have to look at Chili Peppers lyrics and feel like they are stuck in their time. The obvious exception to this is when Kiedis objectifies women or romanticizes lust—but the most meaningful and personal songs remain unharmed.

8

Too Much, Too Loud

The Red Hot Chili Peppers, the Loudness Wars, and What You May Not Have Heard

A Brief History of the Loudness Wars

Since seven-inch singles took prominence in the 1940s, the music industry has tried to release music as loud as it can, typically gaining volume with each additional generation. This hit its peak with the invention of the compact disc (CD), when the digitalization of music allowed for things to hit a clear maximum amplitude. During this time—particularly before digital stores like iTunes or streaming applications like Spotify took off—CDs compressed audio waves to be louder without clipping, sometimes even allowing more and more clipping to happen than any fan would reasonably want to hear.

One of the best-mixed CDs in terms of not falling for the "loudness war" is *Blood Sugar Sex Magik*. One of the worst—and a famous example used by everyone from *Stylus Magazine* to Austin 360 to *TV Tropes*' list of the worst victims of the loudness war—is *Californication*.

A Matter of Volume

Californication is particularly harsh, still clipping even after the volume is lowered 5.6 decibels. *Greatest Hits* is also incredibly harsh, increasing the volume on songs that were once mixed better ("Under the Bridge" and "Breaking the Girl") and even on songs that were already flawed ("Scar Tissue"). This is why, when listening on headphones at higher volumes, all the words that start with "s" hurt the ears when Anthony Kiedis sings them: the volume on the mastering was intentionally cranked beyond what is reasonable.

There is an "unmastered" version of *Californication* online, featuring different, unedited versions of songs (it won't take long to notice how the mixing engineer chopped up Flea's "Around the World" verse bass lines in Pro Tools to build up more, for example) with different mixes (done from a prerelease mix tape given to the band) and with a more reasonable mastering. Even if one were to buy officially released material, the best option would not be the original release on vinyl, which used the same mix as the CD, but rather the rerelease, which suffered from a similar mix but was a much better master.

By the Way's mixing was also bad enough that John Frusciante talked about it at length in the U.K.-only *Guitarist* magazine:

> To tell you the truth, I've had a really hard time accepting that *By the Way* is actually finished. . . . Rick really mixes the vocals high and pushes anything that matches the vocals' power back so it doesn't come anywhere near it. I can't even listen to our last record because of that; the mix just drives me so crazy.

Frusciante also talked about how Rubin let him into the mixing process but still had his final say. The guitarist wanted any new instruments and interesting or different instruments louder in the mix, but Rubin put vocals at the max. Frusciante also wanted the volume and clipping lower overall, but Rubin had final say.

The next album after that interview would be *Stadium Arcadium*, a loud album but nowhere nearly as compressed nor featuring as much clipping as the prior three. Frusciante's feelings about the *By the Way* mix got to the point where for the single versions of "Can't Stop" and "Universally Speaking"—which ironically ended up on *Greatest Hits*—had different mixes directly approved by him because he could not stand to hear the album versions anymore. Some fans interpreted that to mean he did the actual remixing, but the mixing was actually done by engineer Jim Scott, the same man who mixed the album version. The Frusciante-approved mix features louder bass, better mixed backing vocals, and a more noticeable soprano backing vocal that appears only in the third verse. It was the version used in the official music video.

A List of Sounds and Sights Easily Missed and Differences between Versions, Organized by Album

The Uplift Mofo Party Plan

- During "Party on Your Pussy," someone can be heard shouting "party" right before the band comes in.

Blood Sugar Sex Magik

- The end applause after the guitar solo of "If You Had to Ask" is obvious. More subtle are the hand claps that appear during the guitar solo itself, most prominently right at its beginning. It then becomes less frequent before disappearing entirely just before the synthesizer jumps in for a brief melody.

- During the end of "I Could Have Lied," the lead guitar returns one beat before it starts soloing again. It slides down right as the snare hits, giving the snare some extra power.
- "Mellowship Slinky in B Major" is actually in B Mixolydian, with a key signature of E major.
- "Give It Away" is mastered at an incredibly higher volume on *Greatest Hits*.
- On the right channel during "Give It Away," there is some light screaming right before Kiedis begins to rap.
- "Under the Bridge" is mastered differently on *Greatest Hits* and is both louder and longer as they include the full harmonic that on *Blood Sugar Sex Magik* is considered part of "Naked in the Rain."
- All versions of "Under the Bridge" feature acoustic guitar and piano in the background during the outro that is barely audible.
- In the drum fill before the bridge (where Frusciante begins to sing "la la"), Chad Smith can be heard screaming. The scream is Smith's and recorded from his drum performance; it's his voice bleeding through the drum microphones.
- At higher volumes, one can hear traffic driving by during the performance of "They're Red Hot."

One Hot Minute

- Just before the drums come in, Flea's voice can be heard saying "yeah, aw yeah."
- The baby crying during "One Big Mob" was Dave Navarro's little brother, James Gabriel Navarro. At the time, James was fourteen months old.
- If listened to closely, you can hear the tape of James's crying rewind and start up again.
- There is extremely quiet harmonica during the chorus of the title track.
- "Falling into Grace" has an incredibly quiet acoustic guitar part.

Californication

- "Around the World" originally featured the "Asian" gibberish during each chorus instead of just the final version, as can be heard on the unmastered version.
- The bass line to "Around the World" was heavily edited in Pro Tools; all the fills are played by Flea, but in a different order than he played them, as can be heard on the unmastered version.

- "Scar Tissue" has noticeably less clipping on the vinyl rerelease than the original CD, while the version on *Greatest Hits* has noticeably more clipping.
- An additional backing vocal is added to each chorus of "Scar Tissue."
- "Otherside" features three guitar parts, including one that jumps in just before the final chorus; in every mix, it is muddy and easy to overlook.
- Someone says "woah" at the end of "Californication."
- "Emit Remmus" is "Summer Time" backward.
- "This Velvet Glove" features louder backing vocals on the vinyl rerelease than CD.
- Similarly, "This Velvet Glove" has a piano during the chorus that is difficult to hear unless one is trying to hear it.
- The versions of "Californication" on *Californication* and on *Greatest Hits* are wildly different; the organ comes in at different times (including a false start on *Greatest Hits*), and the first chorus is twice as long on *Greatest Hits*, making the song eight seconds longer on the collection than it is on the album. The 2012 vinyl rerelease has the chorus structure of *Californication* but the organ part from *Greatest Hits*.
- The vinyl version of "Easily" has additional outro vocals.
- The vinyl version of "Savior" also has additional outro vocals.
- Kiedis's vocal microphone picks up room noise before the full band kicks in for "Right on Time."

By the Way

- Every backing vocal part across the entire album done by Frusciante is doubled.
- A xylophone quietly follows the vocal melody during the second verse of "Universally Speaking."
- During the guitar solo of "Don't Forget Me," synthesizer vocals sound out the chord progression (A minor F C G) alongside the bass, sounding almost like a choir.
- During the second half of the same guitar solo, Kiedis sings, doubling the guitar melody.
- During "Can't Stop," an additional backing vocal is added after each verse. The least clear one and most easily distinguished between the single version and the album version is the highest backing vocal "ooh" added during the final verse after the guitar solo.
- "Can't Stop" has two different mixes: one from the album and one for the single and music video. The single and music video version was remixed by Frusciante; in addition to the previously mentioned vocal mix difference, there is more clarity of the bass guitar.

- The drum machine during "The Zephyr Song" is the first time the Chili Peppers used a drum machine since their debut album, *The Red Hot Chili Peppers*.
- A heavy synthesizer is mixed incredibly quietly on just the left side of "Midnight."

Stadium Arcadium

- The verse guitar part of "Charlie" is in 3/4 time, while the verse bass part is in 4/4, creating a polyrhythm that will lock up right before the chorus.
- "Especially in Michigan" features an entirely different guitar solo on vinyl than CD and digital stores.
- Kiedis sings throughout the outro of "C'mon Girl," which is barely audible on CD but more prominent on vinyl.
- "She Looks to Me" has layers and layers of vocal harmony by Frusciante; it is more noticeable in the vinyl mix than the CD version.
- Someone sings the instrumental introduction of "21st Century," and it can be heard in the final version.
- "Turn It Again" has quiet congas for its second verse.
- Flea says "whoa" at the end of the song "Death of a Martian" and thus at the end of the album, too.

I'm with You

- Kiedis's vocal part is doubled, one of which has intense reverb, on "Factory of Faith," but only when he says "Factually, I."
- One of the Peppers can be heard shouting before the final chorus of "Ethiopia."

The Getaway

- Kiedis can be heard clearing his throat about two minutes into "The Hunter."

9

Around the World

What the Band's Touring Is Like

An Active Road Act

From the outset, the Red Hot Chili Peppers hit the road hard. From 1983 to 1989, they played 504 shows (or an average of seventy-two per year); the 1990s was no different, completing 586 shows in the decade despite an absurd amount of cancellations and time off mid-decade due to guitarist changes and the personal health needs of various band members.

Flea's Chronic Fatigue Syndrome

Flea is perhaps the member most musically active outside the Red Hot Chili Peppers, but at one point, he was the reason for a year off of touring. In 1993, Flea was diagnosed with chronic fatigue syndrome as a result of their heavy touring (they played ninety shows in 1992), and the band had to cancel all touring for the year after, playing only six shows. The band may have been able to return to touring earlier, but the doctor's orders coincided with Arik Marshall's firing from the band, and they took the year off.

Anthony Kiedis talked about this negatively while it was ongoing. He told *RAW* magazine in 1994 that "the hardest thing about touring for me is the guys who aren't into it. Flea doesn't like touring—period. He'd like to tour for a maximum of two weeks at a time because he has a kid and it pains him to leave her."

Other Cancellations

The 1990s saw an insane amount of canceled tour dates from the Red Hot Chili Peppers even beyond Flea's chronic fatigue syndrome. John Frusciante quitting led to an abrupt end to the *Blood Sugar Sex Magik* tour, canceling the Australian area shows. After Dave Navarro joined, dates were consistently postponed or canceled: an entire winter run was moved because Chad Smith broke his

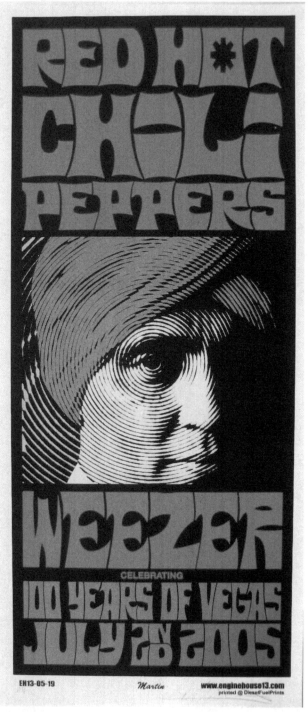

A live poster from 2005.

Author's collection

wrist playing baseball on November 9, 1995. About half of the group's summer dates in 1996 were canceled for unstated reasons. Half a year later, all except one show—July 26 at the Mount Fuji Festival—would be canceled because both Navarro and Kiedis relapsed on heroin. They publicly claimed to be working on a new album instead of touring—which was also true but wasn't the primary reason for getting off the road.

Splitting into Legs

The Red Hot Chili Peppers have toured in legs since *Californication*. The primary member behind this is Flea—similar to his bout with chronic fatigue syndrome, he burned out on the road after joining up with Jane's Addiction and expected to feel poor touring endlessly on the album. Flea proposed to Anthony Kiedis that the band do three weeks on, ten days off, and repeat until their touring was completed.

The band has done that on every tour since then, with mild variation in the length of a tour "leg" and the break between them. It made the cost of touring higher for the band but has always remained profitable.

Give It Away

The same time the tour-leg conversation happened, Flea proposed giving 5 percent of the band's touring income to charity. Sometimes, this has included donations to Flea's Silverlake Conservatory of Music, but it is not always the case.

Set Lists

Set lists are famously always chosen and written up by Anthony Kiedis. Ultimately, he was the reason why songs from *One Hot Minute* were rarely if ever played live, though in the John Frusciante era, he was not alone: Frusciante never listened to that album and told *Rolling Stone* that "no one ever made a good case to me why I should."

That said, Kiedis can be lobbied into including other things; *One Hot Minute* was the first Red Hot Chili Peppers album Klinghoffer ever bought, and it was his lobbying that enabled "My Friends" and "Aeroplane" to return to the band's performance rotation. (Smith has referred to *One Hot Minute* as the "bastard album," while Klinghoffer has dismissed that take and stated he enjoys it.)

Kiedis handwrites out copies of the set list and gives them to each band and crew member before the show. The handwritten set list can be seen as the track listing on their international live album *Live in Hyde Park*.

Set lists tend to fall into patterns across a given tour: while they are almost never the same each night, there's only a handful of songs that open on a tour and a lesser handful that close, while encores are also only a shared group of songs. Some songs tend to appear every night—"Give It Away" has been played at virtually every full-length concert by the band since its release as a single.

When Frusciante was in the band, he typically sang and played one (or sometimes two) solo songs each night; Kiedis sometimes asked what song Frusciante wanted to play and then stuffed them in with smaller handwriting into the set list. Sometimes, the rest of the band jumped in on these performances, like during Frusciante's cover of Fugazi's "Latest Disgrace" as seen on the *Live at Slane Castle* DVD or during the band's cover of Elton John's "Tiny Dancer" from PinkPop 1990, while other times they wouldn't join, like the same 2003 Slane Castle performance of the Chantels' "Maybe."

Tour Warm-Ups and Preshow Rituals

Flea has always done musical warm-ups and runs through the specifics of his routine on his instructional video. If he plans to slap that night, he will play triplets in a pattern of slap-slap-pop on every fret of the bass at increasing tempos; every night, he warms up by running through scales at progressive speeds. He does these warm-ups for about an hour, then literally runs around the arena—he is a marathon runner, after all—and then he meditates and prays.

Anthony Kiedis maintains a special diet, eating three hours before the show, and has an exercise routine that sometimes encompasses yoga. The diet often included kombucha tea on the *Californication* tour. Often, this means doing a quick jog or many push-ups; the end goal is to get his blood pumping so that the excitement of the show doesn't make him go full speed without being ready for it. He also does vocal warm-ups that he learned when he took vocal lessons.

He then writes the set list and gives band members a chance to lobby or cancel songs. This can be witnessed in the *Greatest Hits* DVD, where, in Asia, Frusciante pulls "Otherside" out of the set for the night because he cannot hit the high note in his backing vocals that evening.

John Frusciante's preshow ritual was often playing scales and running through songs and his vocal parts with an unplugged electric guitar. He also did a strict and challenging yoga routine, some of which can be viewed on the *Greatest Hits* DVD but all of which is ingrained in former guitar technician Dave Lee's memory. Lee said that Frusciante could "fold himself backwards. Like in half."

When Frusciante was in the band, he'd decide on the music that played backstage as Flea and Frusciante warmed up on guitar. Kiedis would do his vocal warm-ups while making tea for everyone, then, after having tea, they'd perform a few songs from the set list that night together with all their instruments unplugged.

Josh Klinghoffer warms up his voice before the show but also tries to play his guitar continuously throughout the day so that he is always ready to go. He tries to minimize visits from friends before the shows, as he finds entertaining them exhausting of the energy he needs to give the Red Hot Chili Peppers' performance his all.

As a group, they listen to music together to get in a unified mood to prepare for each show.

Bed Bunking

The band uses two buses for the four members, giving each member a little bit of privacy without going so far as to isolate everyone entirely. The members rotate who sleeps where to avoid playing favorites and maintain bonds across the band.

Band Members to Spare, and Everyone Gets a Tech

The band's touring lineup changed throughout the years, originally working only as a four-piece before expanding to include a horn section after *Freaky Styley*. The group then shrank to a four-piece as live performers until Navarro joined and required a second guitarist live. (For more on this, see chapter 13.)

From 2011 to 2014, after Klinghoffer joined, the live group included percussionist Mauro Refosco of Atoms for Peace, who played percussion in studio on *I'm with You* and played the "Sir Psycho Sexy" marimba part live. The band has used a live keyboardist since *Stadium Arcadium*—on that tour, it was Josh Klinghoffer who played keyboards. At present, Chris Warren and Nate Walcott both do. During performances of "Go Robot" and "Encore," Flea has switched to piano, and assistant tour manager Samuel Bañuelos III has played bass guitar.

Warren has served primarily as Smith's drum technician over the past twenty years. Flea's bass technician has been Tracy Robar since at least 2012, though he has had others before that. Flea's live rig remained largely unchanged from when he got sponsored by Gallien-Krueger amplifiers until his switch to Acoustic amps on the *I'm with You* tour; Chad Smith has changed his drum set fairly constantly every tour, even switching from four toms (two mounted, two floor) to three (two mounted, one floor) to three (one mounted, two floor). He has also switched his cymbals multiple times, most notably from Zildjian Ks to Sabian AAXs in the 1990s. For more on the band's live rigs and instruments, see the chapters in part 2 on each individual musician.

Jams

From the outset, musical improvisations and jamming played a major role in the band's live show. (Factually speaking, the band's first song was nothing more than a jam with Kiedis's rap over it, and that songwriting process and manic live energy remained their primary form for the majority of the 1980s.)

The length of jams reached their longest point when John Frusciante was in the band. Shows often closed with a hit song or a cover that would turn into a ten- or even twenty-minute jam session. For example, "Give It Away" on *Live in Hyde Park* clocks at thirteen minutes, thirty-seven seconds; "Yertle Trilogy" from a 1998 Buenos Aires performance crosses twelve minutes in length; and the *Off the Map* performance of "Search and Destroy" is twelve minutes, fourteen seconds, despite originally being a song less than three minutes in length.

Jams happened when Dave Navarro was guitarist, but they were more preconstructed. Some famous bootlegs exist in the tours that followed *One Hot Minute*—most notably *Flea's Birthday Gig* from October 16, 1995, where they performed multiple David Bowie covers—and these bootlegs show an extreme similarity in Navarro's improvisations, as they follow a set path and act more as planned links between songs or constructions with room for improvisation than as the pure creativity that spun out when Frusciante was in the band.

Klinghoffer's time as guitarist saw more frequent jamming than the band did with Navarro, but the improvisations haven't gone as long as they did with Frusciante. The longest jam the band has ever done included both Klinghoffer and Frusciante: the Federation Square jam from 2007 that was nearly a half an hour long.

Covers

While American audiences receive them less frequently than their international counterparts, the Red Hot Chili Peppers have constantly thrown in covers of well-known songs into their sets. "Tiny Dancer" from PinkPop 1990—complete with a series of ludicrous punk-rock references—made it into an EMI covers release that also included the studio versions of covers of Stevie Wonder's "Higher Ground" and Sly and the Family Stone's "If You Want Me to Stay."

Live, the band's already diverse repertoire expanded: everything from David Bowie's "Suffragette City" to an instrumental cover of Dr. Dre's "Ain't Nuthing

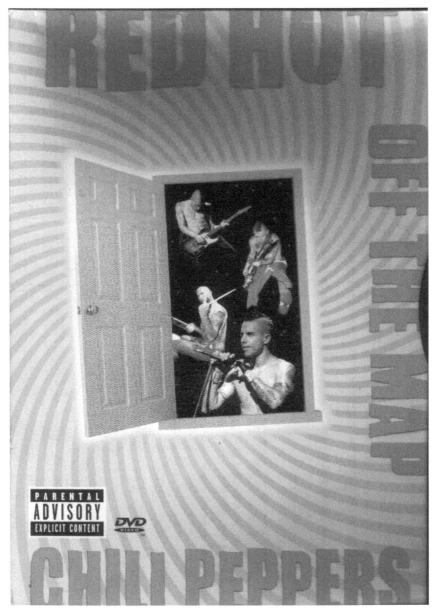

The cover of the *Off the Map* DVD.   *Author's collection*

but a G Thang" from Black Sabbath and Black Flag to the Spice Girls. They've usually chosen covers based on location—for example, "Ça Plane Pour Moi" in France—and context—for example, when an artist passes away or when at a tribute ceremony.

10

Greatest Hits and Misses

An Examination of Their Unreleased Recordings

Remastered with More

The Red Hot Chili Peppers possess an eleven-album studio discography: *The Red Hot Chili Peppers, Freaky Styley, The Uplift Mofo Party Plan, Mother's Milk, Blood Sugar Sex Magik, One Hot Minute, Californication, By the Way, Stadium Arcadium, I'm with You,* and *The Getaway.* Excluded in this are several other releases that possess studio recordings on them: the pun-titled *I'm with You* collection of B-sides, *I'm Beside You,* the early box set *Live Rare Remix Box,* the demo collection *Out in L.A.,* and the two greatest-hits collections from two different record labels: *What Hits!?* and *Greatest Hits.*

On every album, other songs were demoed or officially recorded; on almost every album, some of these songs have remained elusive. Several came out for the first time on their 2003 EMI album remasters. The demo for "What It Is [aka Nina's Song]" came from *The Red Hot Chili Peppers* and was released accordingly (alongside the demo versions of "Get Up and Jump," "Police Helicopter," "Out in L.A.," and "Green Heaven," all notable for being the first Chili Peppers recordings to feature Jack Irons and Hillel Slovak). The *Freaky Styley* remastered edition featured demos and songs that were previously released on *Out in L.A.*: the demos of "Nevermind" and "Sex Rap," the original longer version of "Freaky Styley" with Slovak taking a massive guitar solo, and the original composition "Millionaires against Hunger." *The Uplift Mofo Party Plan* rerelease featured no extra tracks.

Mother's Milk received the most extensive rerelease: "Pretty Little Ditty" jumped from one minute, thirty-five seconds, in its original form to three minutes, seven seconds, on its remaster, which now featured an extended trumpet solo from Flea and a repeat of all its instrumentals, including what became the basis for Crazy Town's "Butterfly." It included two live covers of the *Jimi Hendrix Experience*—"Castles Made of Sand" and "Crosstown Traffic"—as well as longer versions of "Knock Me Down" and "Sexy Mexican Maid" and a new instrumental: "Salute to Kareem."

As mentioned in chapter 6, the band appeared in the film *Tough Guys*, performing the song "Set It Straight." They never intended to release "Set It Straight" on an album, playing it just for the movie and recording it solely for the film's sound track. Since the sound track was never released, the music exists but hasn't ever been released. Several other songs with this lineup were recorded and never officially released but can be found online: "Bone," "Dum Chuck a Willie," and "Prince of Sadness."

Blood Sugar Sex Magik and iTunes Rereleases

The Red Hot Chili Peppers didn't release their music to digital stores until 2006. When they finally did, iTunes received previously unreleased bonus tracks available only when you purchased the albums in full. With *Blood Sugar Sex Magik*, this meant studio versions of two *Jimi Hendrix Experience* covers: "Little Miss Lover" and "Castles Made of Sand." The other B-sides from the *Blood Sugar Sex Magik* era that have been formally released are "Sikamikanico," which appeared on the *Wayne's World* sound track and *Live Rare Remix Box*; "Soul to Squeeze," which appeared on the *Coneheads* sound track and *Live Rare Remix Box*; their cover of the Stooges' "Search and Destroy," which appeared on the sound track to *Beavis and Butt-Head* and the *Live Rare Remix Box*; and an instrumental ode to Fela Kuti called "Fela's Cock," which appeared only on the *Live Rare Remix Box* (but can also be heard in the documentary *Funky Monks*).

Interviews with the band from the era to *BAM* and *Musician* magazines indicated that they recorded either twenty-seven or twenty-five songs. Between the seventeen album songs on *Blood Sugar Sex Magik*, the two iTunes songs, and the four from *Live Rare Remix*, that's still only twenty-three songs—leaving between two and four songs unreleased. One of these songs might be a cover of Hendrix's "Bold as Love"; Flea mentioned doing a studio version of it in his interview with *Musician* magazine, but it's possible he was confusing it with "Castles Made of Sand" from the same album.

An unknown song may have appeared on the VH1 documentary *Ultimate Albums: Blood Sugar Sex Magik*; the Red Hot Chili Peppers have soundboard live recordings from those days, and other music in the film consists definitively of live improvisations from the Dave Navarro era. Thus, even though some fans consider it a "holy grail," it may just be a jam.

One Hot Sequel

One Hot Minute got a similar treatment to *Blood Sugar Sex Magik*, with the iTunes edition getting an extra three songs: "Let's Make Evil," "Stretch (You

Out)," and "Bob." "Bob" was actually the first song written by the band with Dave Navarro and features a very laid-back song against a (fittingly) Eric Avery–esque bass line from Flea. Another song, "Melancholy Mechanics," appeared on the sound track to *Twister* and the Japanese edition of the album.

A few weeks before the album was to come out, the track listing was changed in a very major way. Originally, "Stretch (You Out)" was to follow "One Big Mob" and then be followed again by a short song called "Blender," which was never released. Flea mentioned a song named "The Intimidator" that was influenced by Miles Davis's "On the Corner" in this time frame to *Guitar World*, too; that song was never released. Chad Smith also spoke of something tentatively titled "Slow Funk"—though in both cases they may have been working titles, Smith indicated that "The Intimidator" was not going to be released on *One Hot Minute*, while "Slow Funk" may have ended up as another song. (He also indicated to *Modern Drummer* that both songs were just drums and bass at the time.)

The band also entered recording sessions for an album following *One Hot Minute* with the same lineup. This album obviously never saw the light of day with Navarro leaving the band and Frusciante rejoining. From those recording sessions, an *MTV News* report stated that only one song was completed, while an interview with *Bass Frontiers* said that "a few songs" were. This one definitively completed song was "Circle of the Noose"—still formally unreleased, but it leaked online and was published as widely as *Rolling Stone* in February 2016. The song was a tribute to Nusrat Fateh Ali Khan and sampled some of his work.

Frusciante's Return and the Mother Lode of *Greatest Hits* Sessions

Californication saw the return of John Frusciante and the longest-lasting lineup of the Red Hot Chili Peppers ever. With that, their output remained steadfast, and some songs were worked on across sessions: "Fortune Faded," released as one of the two new songs on *Greatest Hits*, started during *By the Way*, as did one of its B-sides, "Eskimo." (Another, "Bunker Hill," originated in the *Californication* sessions and was reworked during the *Greatest Hits* recordings.)

Californication's iTunes release saw it get "Fat Dance," "Over Funk," and "Quixoticelixir," the only truly new song of which was "Quixoticelixir," as the others were previously released as B-sides. The Japanese edition of the album includes "Gong Li," a song that was written for Flea's first attempt at a solo album in the 1990s—an album that got canned when Frusciante returned to the band, according to *Bassist*.

Other songs came out purely as B-sides—"Instrumental #1" came from "Scar Tissue," while "Instrumental #2," known as "Blondie" in prerelease interviews, came out as an Australian bonus disc. "How Strong" came out as part of the

"Otherside" single. The *By the Way*–era B-side "Slowly, Deeply" accompanied "Universally Speaking."

One song from this era, "Trouble in the Pub," has leaked online but has never seen a formal release.

Interviews from the era indicate wildly different numbers of songs: a *Sound on Sound* article said that thirty were recorded during the sessions, while a *Rolling Stone* article suggested twenty-eight. With twenty-five songs known or released (as mentioned in this chapter), that leaves between three and five songs without so much as a title to go off of.

Similarly, *By the Way* saw a massive recording output that would flow into the *Greatest Hits* sessions. "Time" came out on the "By the Way" single, as did a cover of "Teenager in Love." The single for "The Zephyr Song" had four B-sides on it, essentially acting as its own EP with "Body of Water," "Someone," "Out of Range," and "Rivers of Avalon." "Havana Affair" came from these sessions but was released on Rick Rubin's tribute to the Ramones: *We're a Happy Family: A Tribute to the Ramones*.

Three songs have leaked in rough mix format but remain unreleased: "Fall Water," "Goldmine," and "Rock and Roll." Another one or two have been referenced: "Upseen," a ten-minute-long jam, and "Strumming in D on J." They may be the same song, but since neither is released, it's impossible to know.

The real treasure trove of unreleased songs would be the *Greatest Hits* sessions. In the liner notes, the band spoke of not even knowing which two songs would be included, indicating it wasn't up to them. Only four songs are known to have come from these sessions, though fifteen were recorded. Those four are the two that came out on *Greatest Hits*—"Fortune Faded" and "Save the Population"—and two songs that came out as iTunes extras for *By the Way*—"The Bicycle Song" and "Runaway."

Two instrumental, unmixed songs from these sessions leaked online in October 2014: "Starlight" and "50Fifty." It's probable they still have vocals and exist somewhere in mixed form, as the band referred to everything from the *Greatest Hits* sessions as done. Assuming that "Eskimo" and "Bunker Hill" were worked on during these sessions, that keeps seven more songs from having hit the public ear. The rest is fan supposing: several songs from that era of touring would logically have had studio versions, and the *Hits* sessions came at the right time, but there's no way to confirm whether those songs were recorded at those sessions.

The songs in question are ones that appear on the non-American live album *Live in Hyde Park*: covers of "Brandy" and "Black Cross" and originals "Rolling Sly Stone" and "Leverage of Space." This also includes "Mini-Epic (Kill for Your Country)," something that fans claim the band intended to release for an anti–Iraq War compilation album organized by Rick Rubin that never saw the light of day, but neither a Chili Pepper nor Rubin has ever confirmed that.

A fan interview had Flea claiming they were all recorded during the *Greatest Hits* sessions, along with a heavier song called "Desiree."

It is unconfirmed as to whether it is from the *Californication* era, but in a *Kerrang!* interview from 2000, Chad Smith referenced that the band recorded a cover of Bachman-Turner Overdrive's "Taking Care of Business" with Cameo. (He also stated that it was the song he'd least like to ever hear and that it would never be released.) Red Hot Chili Peppers author Jeff Apter claimed the cover was recorded during the *Mother's Milk* era.

The Abundance of *Stadium Arcadium* Extras

The band claimed to have recorded thirty-eight songs for *Stadium Arcadium* to interviewers. To date, thirty-seven songs from these sessions have seen the light of day. In addition to the twenty-eight songs on the album itself, "Million Miles of Water," "Lately," and "Whatever We Want" came to light on the "Dani California" singles; "A Certain Someone" and "Mercy Mercy" came from "Tell Me Baby"; "Funny Face" and "I'll Be Your Domino"—a ska song—originated from the "Snow (Hey Oh)" single; and "Joe" and "Save This Lady" came out as B-sides for both "Desecration Smile" and "Hump De Bump."

Perhaps more interesting, the vinyl version of the album featured an entirely different guitar solo on "Especially in Michigan."

Klinghoffer Era

There were fifty songs recorded for *I'm with You* according to *New Musical Express* (*NME*). Fourteen songs came out on the actual album; an additional seventeen were released as B-sides and then collected on the Record Store Day release *I'm Beside You*. It is unknown whether the other twenty-nine songs were totally finished and whether they'll ever see the light of day.

It's unknown how many songs were recorded with Danger Mouse for *The Getaway*, as they scrapped most of their preproduction work when they began working with him. Nonetheless, Klinghoffer wrote of at least two songs in an e-mail responding to a fan published on his website: "Kaly" and "Outer Space." These sessions came to be known as the Fancy Demos by fans.

Teatro Sessions

This all ignores another set of studio recordings: the Teatro sessions. Before *Californication*, the band laid down basic demos for the album in Daniel Lanois's

El Teatro studio in Oxnard, California. A jam called "Teatro Jam" and a version of "Parallel Universe" originated from these sessions, and both were released as part of the "Around the World" single; nothing else from these sessions has ever been released in any official capacity. Nonetheless, everything else is out there in rough demo form. Several new songs are from here, including "Plate of Brown," "Tellin' a Lie," "Mommasan," "Andaman & Nicobar," "Sugar Sugar," "Trouble in the Pub," and "Boatman." Others were awkwardly different versions of songs that would get reworked later. In *Scar Tissue*, Kiedis talked about how he had the lyrics to "Californication," and Frusciante worked out several different versions before the final one was settled on. The version of "Californication" from the Teatro sessions is a very rough reggae song. "Purple Stain" is also wildly different, though the outro is the same jam.

Unreleased Red Hot Chili Peppers Studio Recordings

Freaky Styley Sessions

- "Bone"
- "Dum Chuck a Willie"
- "Prince of Sadness"
- "Set It Straight"

Blood Sugar Sex Magik Sessions

- Between two and four songs, possibly including a cover of the *Jimi Hendrix Experience*'s "Bold as Love"

One Hot Minute–era lineup

- "Blender"
- "The Intimidator"
- "Slow Funk"—may have been a working title that ended up as another song
- Potentially others from a follow-up to *One Hot Minute*

Teatro Sessions

- "Andaman & Nicobar"
- "Boatman"
- "Mommasan"
- "Plate of Brown"
- "Sugar Sugar"

- "Tellin' a Lie"
- "Trouble in the Pub"

Californication Sessions

- Between three and five other completed songs

By the Way Sessions

- "Fallwater"
- "Goldmine"
- "Rock and Roll"
- "Strumming in D on J"
- "Upseen"

Greatest Hits Sessions

- Potentially "Black Cross"
- Potentially "Brandy"
- Potentially "Desiree"
- "50Fifty"
- Potentially "Leverage of Space"
- Potentially "Mini-Epic (Kill for Your Country)"
- Potentially "Rolling Sly Stone"
- "Starlight"
- Between three and nine other completed songs

Stadium Arcadium Sessions

- Potentially one more song

I'm with You Sessions

- Twenty-nine songs in various states of completion

The Getaway Sessions

- "Kaly"
- "Outer Space"

11

Funky Crime

The Band's Run-Ins with the Law

Civil and Criminal

Many bands have careers altered by court cases, but few have had as many notable cases and not had them damage their course in any meaningful way as the Red Hot Chili Peppers. They've gotten accused of stealing songs (though never sued for it), sued a television show for taking their ideas, been sued by former members for damages, and been convicted of the most serious of crimes. (John Frusciante even got a restraining order against a fan for stalking him.)

A Criminal Battery

On April 21, 1989, Anthony Kiedis touched a woman's face with his penis after making sexually disparaging comments. The woman, a student at George Mason University in Virginia, served on the university's programming board and may have been partially responsible for booking the band. She sued him and won in April 1990, leaving Kiedis guilty of sexual battery and indecent exposure. She also tried to sue the band's management, but the common negligence rule that people do not owe duties to foresee or prevent the tortuous or criminal conduct of third parties found the management innocent.

According to the case, Kiedis denied ever doing that, but another unnamed band member admitted to United Press International that he encouraged him to do so, and several people claimed to have witnessed the event. In the end, he served no community service or jail time but was fined $2,000 and lost an AIDS prevention ad campaign featuring him supporting the use of condoms.

A Second Battery

Anthony Kiedis has rarely commented on his battery conviction, but Flea talks openly (and negatively) about his, a moment that was filmed in Daytona Beach,

Florida, for an episode of MTV's *Spring Break* in 1990 when the group was to lip-synch "Knock Me Down." As they had done in most lip-synching situations, they put down their instruments and danced, trying to turn the synch into a joke rather than a fake performance. (This happened for MTV years earlier and had the band switching instruments for an ultra-fake performance.) Flea was on Kiedis's shoulders when he fell.

He then picked up a woman whom Chad Smith proceeded to spank. Flea spun around, and she fell off, launching her away. Flea reacted by yelling obscenities. (Flea's version of the story was that he grabbed anything in his reach to stop the fall, and that happened to be the woman.) Two days later, the police arrested Flea for battery, disorderly conduct, and solicitation to commit an unnatural and lascivious act and Smith for battery. (Apparently, they were quite the obscenities.) Both members appear to regret it and admit their wrong-doings but insist they were not trying to commit any sexual acts or solicit anything but were just being dumb and playful. The most they've spoken about it was to *Rolling Stone* in 1992. Flea told *By the Way* author Dave Thompson that he tried to apologize.

It's worth noting that in 2016, a former record executive for Epic alleged sexual harassment against the band. She didn't name specific members, writing only that "they pressed up against me," but noted that the band had a reputation for lurid conduct, harassment, and assault long before they were convicted of it. The reputation is arguably well earned: Kiedis can be seen making unwanted advances multiple times in the *Funky Monks* documentary and across interviews in the 1980s and 1990s and was written about harassing a writer for *Creem* in 1990. He even outright showed his penis on the 1988 *VPro* documentary by Bram van Splunteren.

The Sherminator

On March 12, 1993, Jack Sherman filed suit against the Red Hot Chili Peppers— or, at least, the corporate entity of the Red Hot Chili Peppers—but specifically made allegations of verbal abuse against Flea and Anthony Kiedis. In Sherman's original allegations, he accused Kiedis and Flea of firing him via running into his house laughing and saying, "You're out of the band, bye." A Warner Bros. spokeswoman noted to *Entertainment Weekly* that Sherman had no complaints about the supposed abuse until the band became famous. The full court case named Michael "Flea" Balzary, Anthony Kiedis, and Chad Smith as defendants as well as then guitarist Arik Marshall, the band's then manager Lindy Goetz, and their lawyer Eric Greenspan and his firm, Myman Abell Fineman & Greenspan.

Anthony Kiedis wrote a slightly different account of the firing in *Scar Tissue*, though he did constantly portray Sherman in a negative light (calling him a "nerd" in the first sentence, mentioning him and saying he was easily the least cool candidate throughout his first page). He believed that he, Flea, and then drummer Cliff Martinez went to Sherman's house, discussed who would fire him, and began laughing out of nervousness. In Kiedis's account, they never made it inside the house, instead telling Sherman right at the door, "It's over. We're firing you. You're not in the band anymore." Shortly after that, they recruited Hillel Slovak to rejoin the group.

Flea noted in the liner notes for the rerelease of *The Red Hot Chili Peppers* that Sherman "alleged emotional abuse or some bullshit." He also at one point told *Guitar* magazine that he'd "like to go on record as saying that the one guy that played with us on our first record, Jack Sherman, was a non-creative asshole that had nothing to do with anything."

Factually, Sherman charged that his terms of the partnership were violated, specifically that he wasn't given the contractually obligated ten days' written notice of his firing; that the only money he ever received from the band was a $1,700 check on his dismissal; that he never received his share of the $30,000 publishing advance the band received for *Freaky Styley* (Sherman received writing credits for half of the songs on the album); and that he hadn't received a dime from the sales of *The Red Hot Chili Peppers*.

On his own brief investigation when he called the royalties department at Capitol Records, he was told the band had purposely been withholding his money to support their own touring.

Superior Court Judge Stephen Lachs dismissed the case just over a year later on March 22, 1994, ruling that it had exceeded the statute of limitations. Sherman was owed nothing additional and has been, by and large, deleted from the band's account of history.

Greenspan made a similar appearance in Sherman's life decades later when the Chili Peppers were elected into the Rock and Roll Hall of Fame. On entry, only current members of the band and former members who played on more than one album were included—leaving Sherman to feel mistreated and left out. Greenspan issued a public statement saying it was up to the Hall, not the band, after Sherman had complained in the press several times, including to *Billboard*.

Dream of *Californication*

In the most lighthearted of their court dealings, the Red Hot Chili Peppers sued Showtime over the name of the show *Californication*—an obvious recognition point because of their album, *Californication*, on November 19, 2007. Although the band never copyrighted "Californication," they made the argument that the series was "likely to cause a likelihood of confusion, mistake, and deception as to source, sponsorship, affiliation, and/or connection in the minds of the public," according to MTV. The show used plenty of references to the band, even referring to a character as Dani California.

The case was settled out of court in 2011, according to *The Wrap*.

12

Breaking the Girl

Anthony Kiedis's Relationships with His Dad, His Son, Women, and His Hypersexuality

Starting Young

The same way Kiedis's father, Blackie Dammett, introduced a young Anthony to harder drugs, he also got the boy pursuing sex at an incredibly early age. Dammett, as a young thirty-something, dated an eighteen-year-old named Kimberly; at age eleven, Kiedis propositioned her for sex, and Dammett brokered a deal to have his girlfriend and his son have sex. While Kiedis doesn't remember a ton of specifics about it, as the memory is a blur, he does remember feeling that his father was a little too present for comfort the whole time.

After losing his virginity, Kiedis had no sexual interactions for more than a year. He got high, did quaaludes, and fooled around with a twenty-four-year-old named Becky while in eighth grade, with her providing a sexual education on how to please and be with a woman. The first time he had sex with someone his age was also in eighth grade, with someone named Grace: the two made up a reason to get out of class, started fooling around in a men's room when someone else walked in, found a better place to do it, and had sex, and then he received oral sex.

Like Father, Like Son: Part 1

Blackie himself had a parade of girlfriends. While he wasn't physically abusive to them, it set a tone for the rest of his life; it doesn't take an amateur psychologist to see how his father's sexual pursuits and use of women as objects taught Kiedis to be the same way.

At a young age, Kiedis noticed his father didn't get too attached to women and would cycle through them to pursue the next one if things went awry or became too difficult. At first, this seemed like the path: an unconscious pattern he modeled his own life after. Eventually, Kiedis noticed the problems with it—but more on that later.

Sexual Military Dynamics

This isn't to say it was entirely his father's fault: Kiedis has throughout his lifetime demonstrated a poor understanding of respect for other sexes and a willingness to use power dynamics in his favor—be it dating and sleeping with fans, using his celebrity to woo women, or dating women decades his younger. He often recognized this himself: in the band's official fan book *Red Hot Chili Peppers: Fandemonium*, he wrote that he "fell in love and had sex with [his] first fan," something that a modern understanding of relationships would recognize as overly empowering.

The fan in question was German punk singer Nina Hagen. Although they wouldn't date long, her importance to Kiedis can be spotted throughout the band's lyrics: she is the Nina in question from the extended version of *The Red Hot Chili Peppers*' "What It Is [aka Nina's Song]"—a song she herself would later cover. (Kiedis had a writing credit on her 1991 song "Nina 4 President" as well.) It was also her attitude of giving rather than getting that gave the idea to "Give It Away," but their entire dating relationship took place in 1983.

Not only this, but Kiedis has possessed morally unethical tastes in women: as recently as 1994, he bragged to *Rolling Stone* that he was dating someone in high school, talking about how her senior photo had been taken when he was thirty-one.

He also was found guilty of sexual assault (for more information, see chapter 11) but also undoubtedly did it other times but was never charged, as written about in a *Pittsburgh Post-Gazette* show review claiming Kiedis stuck his unwanted naked butt into a woman's face.

During the making of *Blood Sugar Sex Magik* as witnessed in *Funky Monks*, Kiedis tried to get every woman who entered the mansion they recorded in naked. He succeeded with most, but his actions—to the point of complimenting the bosoms of the boom girl during a press interview—were grossly inappropriate and definitely constituted harassment.

Jennifer Bruce's Mohawk and Cheating

Kiedis was madly in love with—and cheated on—Jennifer Bruce from 1985 to 1987. Their relationship revolved around a mutual affinity for shooting up, something his father took note of and would write about in his autobiography.

His father paid a particularly close eye to Bruce over most girlfriends because he had introduced her to Kiedis. Things got worse as Kiedis toured more but hit high tension when he moved in with another female drug addict, Kim Jones, and cheated on Jennifer on tour with the titular Catholic schoolgirl referenced in "Catholic School Girls Rule."

After a night of loud sex and fighting before a tour, Kiedis's neighbors called the police for alleged domestic violence; the police arrived. Bruce was mad at Kiedis and let the cops in to find drug paraphernalia and discover outstanding warrants for Kiedis. After leaving for the tour, Bruce began seeing Chris Fish from Fishbone, and Kiedis dumped her. The two would reconnect over drugs on Kiedis's return and see each other until the Chili Peppers and Fishbone shared the stage for a charity benefit. Fish asked Bruce to do backing vocals onstage for Fishbone, and she agreed; Kiedis pulled an attractive woman onstage during a cover of "Foxy Lady" to do his version of retaliation, and Bruce hotheadedly attacked her, something that can now be seen on YouTube.

Bruce was forever immortalized in band lore when Kiedis wrote about this and talked about his attraction to how she shaved her pubic hairs into a Mohawk. (Kiedis would reference this over twelve years later on the *Californication* tour, still cracking jokes about her "Mohawk . . . downstairs" on a performance recorded for the *Off the Map* DVD.)

The Bearer of Bad News

Kiedis swooned heavily upon meeting Ione Skye, the daughter of folksinger Donovan. Skye was the one who had the unlucky task of telling Kiedis that Slovak had died of a heroin overdose. She had, by and large, accepted his drug usage for most of their relationship, but as it got worse and worse, she left him because of his drug abuse.

She went on to marry Beastie Boy Adam Horovitz.

A Pattern Is Established and "Breaking the Girl"

By the 1990s, Kiedis's sex and dating life fell into a pattern: he would sleep with women on tour and at home, hit a period of loneliness, search for meaning, and then fall in love at first sight of someone attractive and unrelentingly pursue her until they dated for a long time. Things would get in the way—be it drugs, cheating, or something else—and then the relationship would end, and the process would repeat itself. Nowhere is this stated more clearly than with Carmen Hawk, a model whom Kiedis dated in the 1990s.

In Japan, he slept with a girl the night before and received a message from her when Hawk walked in, and he instantly fell in love with her, not leaving her alone until she became his girlfriend. He believed it was destiny.

Despite this, he slept with a woman named Karen in London before he returned to Los Angeles and dated Hawk again. Hawk and Kiedis were volatile enough that Kiedis funded her a flight to model in Italy to safely end their relationship.

Both Kiedis and Dammett have written about how "Breaking the Girl" stemmed directly from lessons Kiedis learned after Hawk. In *Scar Tissue*, Kiedis wrote about how it also stemmed from how he didn't want to be like his father anymore after the relationship with Hawk. He questioned if he was echoing his father's inappropriate behavior and if he would end up feeling even more empty than his father did. He knew it felt exciting in the moment but wrote the song about how the feeling was temporary.

Sinead O'Connor

One of the more famous people Kiedis ever dated, Sinead O'Connor is most famous in the Red Hot Chili Peppers' world for directly inspiring "I Could Have Lied." The Chili Peppers and O'Connor shared the stage together, where Kiedis rather insensitively and inappropriately dedicated "Party on Your Pussy (aka Special Secret Song Inside)" to her (and, later, insensitively and inappropriately called said dedication "retarded" in his autobiography).

Having a huge crush, he and Flea hung out with her backstage for a while after her performance, and after her tour manager forced her to make a quick exit, Flea wrote and handed her a love letter. They ran into each other again months later and (in his mind) briefly dated before she suddenly left him a voice mail saying not to call her. The two have never really addressed the breakup but have remained polite to each other in public meetings since.

It's worth noting that she insists they never dated and that the end went down the way it did because he never understood that. She has outright said that they never had a relationship, only spent a little time together, and that she "cannot bear [the Red Hot Chili Peppers]."

Other Famous Girlfriends (Who Actually Dated Him)

Kiedis's longest-lasting relationship with another celebrity was with Sofia Coppola, lasting somewhere between 1992 and 1994, as they appeared in a film by *Details* magazine together saying they were in a relationship throughout 1993. He went on one date with Madonna after their performance of "The

Lady Is a Tramp," according to Kiedis's father, and also spent some time dating Melanie Chisholm—commonly known as Sporty Spice of the Spice Girls—in 1998. Chisholm became the "English girl" referenced in *Californication's* "Emit Remmus."

Heather Christie and Everly

In 2004, Kiedis started dating Heather Christie, a model much younger than he. Although he knew on paper it should not work, he found himself wanting to be with only her, bragging to *Blender* about how happy he was with her. The two broke up for a while in the mid-2000s but began dating again within a year, and she became pregnant with his child, Everly Bear Kiedis.

Christie is twenty-four years younger than Kiedis and became the inspiration for the song "She's Only 18" on *Stadium Arcadium*. The reasons for their split were not made public, but the parents remain amiable, sharing custody of Everly and still hanging out together as friends—something he, by and large, hadn't done with any other ex-girlfriends.

Like Father, Like Son: Part 2

Kiedis's relationship with women and the world at large (much like his relationship with drugs; for more details, see chapter 5) changed after the birth of his son Everly on October 2, 2007. Kiedis told the *Sun*, "As every heroin addict will know, temptation is always there. But becoming a father has given me a reason to live and stay clean for good . . . my son makes me very thankful that I am [sober]. I feel very lucky."

In the same interview, he communicated the parallels between the dynamic between him and his son and the dynamic he and his father possess. Kiedis believes that Everly and he communicated a lot better than he ever did with Blackie, and the love of his son has led to more forgiveness and being appreciative. It was after the birth of Everly that the Chili Peppers' lyrics became less sexually objective: beginning with *I'm with You* and continuing on *The Getaway*, Kiedis's songwriting was less and less about sex and drugs and wanting to mate and more family oriented (albeit still full of his typical style, down to California references and tongue-tied gibberish).

His views toward women have improved though remain imperfect: he publicly commented that he feels insulted when people imply that he views women as objects to *Rolling Stone*, revisions of Kiedis's autobiography have changed some language to be kinder toward women, and his actions in public have gone from the sexual assault days of the 1980s and 1990s to that of a proud father.

While his problems may have stemmed from his father, the solution for Kiedis appears to have been in wanting to provide a better example for his son.

Every day Kiedis is with Everly Bear, they have breakfast together. While Everly was a boy, Kiedis would create and tell Everly stories throughout breakfast; if the story wasn't good, Everly would reject it. While he was young, Everly didn't watch television. Kiedis played hide-and-go-seek with him and focused on stimulating his imagination while being an active father in his life. It's likely that this has helped Kiedis mature away from his more selfish and objectifying earlier days.

Occasional Moments Fighting for Women

Despite these negatives, Kiedis has occasionally been on the correct side of an antisexism battle. In the early 1990s, he was scoffed at for fighting to get more women on the bill of Lollapalooza when it was still a traveling music festival. He actively fought to get L7, an all-female rock band, on the bill but was scoffed at by the festival and the band's booking agent. He tried to reach out personally to Perry Farrell, the Lollapalooza creator and front man for Jane's Addiction, but was given instructions to fax Farrell by way of his booking agency.

Part 2

The Musicians and What Makes the Band Special

13

Sticking to the Six Strings

The Complete History of the Red Hot Chili Peppers' Guitarists and Drummers

The Original Lineup and Its Replacements

Anthony Kiedis's bombastic rapping and boyish charisma were always appreciated by his musician friends, but it took some time for him to join along in music. When offered to open a show for Gary and Neighbor's Voices based on his humor, Kiedis put together a band. Originally called Tony Flow and the Miraculously Majestic Masters of Mayhem, the ragtag group featured Kiedis on vocals and his three closest musician friends supporting: Flea on bass, Jack Irons on drums, and Hillel Slovak on guitar. After a handful of shows, they renamed to The Red Hot Chili Peppers—originally with a capital T, later renamed to just Red Hot Chili Peppers. A whirlwind of shows later, the Chili Peppers signed to EMI, which forced Irons and Slovak to choose: pursue their existing band, What Is This?, who were already signed to MCA Records, or stay with the Red Hot Chili Peppers. Both quit the Peppers for What Is This?—a precursor to the endless parade of guitarists and drummers the Red Hot Chili Peppers went through.

Flea, having been one of the most active punk musicians in Los Angeles from his time in the band Fear, quickly recruited two musicians from the Weirdos—Cliff Martinez on drums and Dix Denney on guitar—to join. It worked out well with Cliff Martinez, as their bond was quick and natural, but faltered with the guitarist. Denney auditioned and even had a few rehearsals, but the musical chemistry wasn't there. Several guitarists were recommended by various friends of Flea's, but it came down to two: Mark Nine and Jack Sherman, neither of whom the rest of the band knew anything about. The group viewed Nine as an art school reject and Sherman as a dork with guitar chops—an image Sherman would never overcome.

Although he went on to record with everyone from Bob Dylan to George Clinton, Sherman had no album credits predating his debut on *The Red Hot Chili Peppers*, having a reputation as a sturdy but uncredited studio guitarist.

After a few jam sessions, Sherman won out, making him the second guitarist to officially play in the Red Hot Chili Peppers. Both made their Red Hot Chili Pepper debut on July 3, 1983—a mere fifteen days after the band's last performance with Irons and Slovak. This lineup made the band's recorded debut: *The Red Hot Chili Peppers*.

Sherman felt like an oddity from the start: he had no bond with the band outside of the music. He'd clean and polish his fret board before and after every show, which—wisely or unwisely—Kiedis took issue with. The front man thought of the Chili Peppers as a fun band leading an endless party, and the uptight musician who took time to polish his gear rather than participate drove him mad. It was a matter of time before the honeymoon ended. Kiedis even gave his fair share of verbal and physical abuse leading up to the firing, kicking him around on stage, and bossing him around off it. Sherman was canned in early 1985; shortly after, What Is This? broke up, and Hillel Slovak was able to rejoin, making both sides happy for the recording of *Freaky Styley*.

The band did a handful with Chuck Biscuits from Black Flag and the Circle Jerks on drums as a fill-in when Cliff Martinez couldn't make a few shows in 1985. When EMI gave the band $5,000 to record demos for their follow-up to *Freaky Styley*, Slovak and producer Keith Levene set aside 40 percent of the money explicitly for heroin and cocaine. (Levene was also a member of Public Image Ltd, who Flea was a big fan of.) After that, Martinez's heart was no longer in the group—but he was still unwilling to quit. After months of deliberation, Flea and Kiedis gave Martinez the ax, making him the first of many Chili Peppers to leave the band for drug-related reasons. With What Is This? no longer around, founding drummer Jack Irons was able to return, making *The Uplift Mofo Party Plan* the only album with the original four.

This lineup had the saddest end of all. Slovak died of a heroin overdose on June 25, 1988, a mere three weeks after his last show with the band. Irons quit almost instantly because he didn't want to be in a group where his friends died, and he ultimately thought it was a matter of time before Kiedis also died of an overdose.

The Classic Lineup and Its Replacements

After a period of mourning, Kiedis entered rehab for the first time. He and Flea eventually decided to carry on, seeking out two musicians who briefly made the band half white and half black: former Parliament guitarist DeWayne "Blackbyrd" McKnight joined on guitar, and Dead Kennedys drummer D. H. Peligro played drums. This lineup recorded one song together: "Blues for Meister," an ode to Flea's recently deceased cat first released on the collection *Out in L.A.* (It's also one of two songs with Flea on lead vocals, the other being "Pea.")

McKnight played only three shows with the group before he was unceremoniously fired—something he would never forgive them for. The reason for the firing? Flea met a quiet, teenage virtuoso guitarist by the name of John Anthony Frusciante.

Having met the teenager through a mutual friend, Flea wanted Frusciante in the band after one jam. (That first jam together—before Frusciante was even in consideration to become a Chili Pepper—would become the basis for "Pretty Little Ditty" and thus also the basis of "Butterfly" by Crazy Town, which sampled "Pretty Ditty Little Ditty.") Flea took Kiedis to where Frusciante was auditioning to join Thelonious Monster, Bob Forrest's then current rock band. As Thelonious Monster was about to offer Frusciante the gig, Anthony and Flea offered Frusciante the Red Hot Chili Peppers job. The Chili Peppers were his favorite band—so John accepted with childish glee.

That lineup did a few shows, including a bizarre television appearance where they lip-synched "Me and My Friends" in a bowling alley. Peligro was suddenly the odd man out but not for musical or even personal reasons: his drug usage was scaring everyone else. They fired him, leading Peligro to a depressive spiral and a grudge against the group. That grudge would die down when Kiedis helped Peligro on the path to sobriety.

Without a drummer in the band, they recorded "Taste the Pain," using Fishbone drummer Philip "Fish" Fisher to fill in. (In an odd move, Peligro still received a songwriting credit.)

For the first time, the group used open auditions to find a new musician. With advertisements in *L.A. Weekly* and flyers around town, more than 100 drummers were auditioned, but no one stood out. A mutual friend, Denise Zoom, set up an audition for a mullet-wearing giant from Detroit named Chad Smith, who was the very last person to show up on a day full of auditions.

Arriving later than scheduled, Smith showed up to the audition wearing a Metallica shirt and his hair frizzed up like a supermodel's, turning off the three Red Hot Chili Peppers the moment he appeared. Once he sat down on drums, things swiftly changed. While other drummers were getting eaten up following Flea's fast slap chops, Smith not only kept up—he turned the tables, leading the jam the whole way, speeding up and slowing down and impressing everyone with his sneaky use of ghost notes. Frusciante broke a string during the jam and urgently changed his strings, excited to keep playing with the drummer.

The band offered Smith the job but told him he could have it only if he showed up the next day with a shaved head. Smith was going bald, knew it, and was insecure about it, so he showed up the next day with his hair unchanged. The other members interpreted that as a bold move showing how badass he was, so they still let him join.

The Chili Peppers never played with another drummer again, even when Chad broke his arm before the *One Hot Minute* tour. During that time, they canceled most of their shows, but he played one handed during their performance of "My Friends" on the *Late Show with David Letterman*. This lineup recorded both *Mother's Milk* and *Blood Sugar Sex Magik* together, garnering them their first big hits on MTV and radio and turning them into one of the most popular rock bands in the world.

Despite the popularity—or, arguably, because of it—Frusciante abruptly quit on May 7, 1992, before their show in Omiya, Japan. The other three convinced him to play that night's show, but without a guitarist, they were forced to cancel two remaining dates in Japan: Tokyo and Nagaokakyo.

Searching for a Replacement

Australian performances were scheduled for the week after, forcing the Chili Peppers to find someone to fill in for the remainder of the tour. Another former member of the Weirdos, Zander Schloss, was flown out to Australia, and two-a-day rehearsals began instantly. After four days, Schloss was playing all the right notes, but no one thought he had the right fit. The rest of the group decided to cancel the tour and fire Schloss. Schloss was heartbroken, acting as if he had been in the group forever, not a total of eight practices and zero shows. (Schloss, fittingly, had also played with Thelonious Monster and would go on to record in Bob Forrest's solo project.)

Although they wanted Dave Navarro to join, his group, Jane's Addiction, was still together, rendering him an impossible choice. (According to a clipping from Smith in *Rhythm*, Navarro's response when asked to join was "I'd love to do it, and I am probably the only guy who could do it, but I have to say no.") A major summer tour as headliners for Lollapalooza was already planned; with a quick search around the Los Angeles scene, the Peppers settled on Arik Marshall from the band Marshall Law on guitar. Marshall previously played in a band named Trulio Disgracias with Flea.

Although he never recorded with the group, Marshall was in the band long enough to make three vital visual appearances: the "Breaking the Girl" music video (despite not playing on the song), the "If You Have to Ask" music video (despite not playing on that song either), and *The Simpsons* episode "Krusty Gets Kancelled," where he says all of one line of dialogue.

> **Krusty:** Now boys, the network has a problem with some of your lyrics. Would you mind changing them for the show?
>
> **Anthony Kiedis:** Forget you, clown.
>
> **Chad Smith:** Yeah, our lyrics are like our children, man. No way.

Krusty: Well, okay. But here where you say "What I got you got to get and put it in you" [these are not accurate "Give It Away" lyrics, but that's what Krusty says], how 'bout just "What I'd like is I'd like to hug and kiss you"?

Flea: Wow. That's much better!

Arik Marshall: Everyone can enjoy that!

Marshall bonded well with the band musically but was introverted and kept to himself. When they started working on the next album, Kiedis called Marshall several times to work on songs the way he would with Frusciante—with the guitarist writing music and melodies to Kiedis's lyrics—but Marshall never picked up or called back. It was a matter of time before Marshall was fired, leading to another fruitless series of open auditions, this time for a guitarist. (Even Buckethead auditioned, but he didn't get the job.)

During that time, Anthony Kiedis watched alternative band Mother Tongue and recruited guitarist Jesse Tobias to join the Red Hot Chili Peppers—which he did but not for long. Although the chemistry was there, Flea felt like Tobias's technical skills weren't good enough. Chad Smith, who remained friends with Dave Navarro through the years, told the rest of the band that since Jane's Addiction had broken up, Navarro might be ready to join. Sure enough, Dave Navarro replaced Tobias in September 1993 and made his live debut at the madcap headlining slot of Woodstock '94. Tobias joined Alanis Morissette's touring band and remained there from 1999 to 2005.

Dave Navarro Joined for a *Hot Minute*

The Navarro lineup lasted a few years, recording an album that is often overlooked due to its neighboring album's successes in *One Hot Minute* and the song "Melancholy Mechanics," first released on the *Twister* sound track. Anthony Kiedis began to play second guitar live, though it was mostly for show: he played octaves during the "Give It Away" guitar solo and nothing else. Their former opening act Rob Rule played second guitar on a handful of *One Hot Minute* songs live but not consistently throughout their touring. It was during this era that Alanis Morissette's producer recruited Flea and Dave Navarro to do their own arranging to her a capella vocal track on "You Oughta Know"; the final product was a top ten hit in the United States.

Flea joined Jane's Addiction for their reunion tour in 1997, leading Kiedis to feel less close to Navarro than Smith or Flea. Even though Navarro made attempts at helping Anthony get to rehab, they stayed on opposite planes: Kiedis relapsed during Navarro's sobriety, and Navarro relapsed right after Kiedis got sober. When Navarro's drug use got in the way of working on a follow-up to *One Hot Minute*, Flea and Kiedis decided they had to fire Navarro. Flea, depressed through his own divorce and relationship woes, wanted to quit when he dropped a bomb on Kiedis: he had been talking to Frusciante and wanted to offer him the Red Hot Chili Peppers guitar job back.

Kiedis couldn't fathom carrying on with a guitar player other than John Frusciante.

The Classic Lineup Returned

They offered Frusciante the position; he cried when he accepted it, reportedly telling the two that nothing would make him so happy as returning to the Chili Peppers. Navarro remains friendly with the band to this day despite a handful of jabs thrown his way—some lyrical, some not.

This lineup lasted for almost another decade, only briefly fluctuating when the *Stadium Arcadium* tour added Josh Klinghoffer—formerly of Bob Forrest's then current group, the Bicycle Thief, on second guitar (primarily for the harmonies in "Snow (Hey Oh)" and "Dani California") and keyboard (occasionally getting a chance to jam with the group on the instrument, like the Federation Square 2007 performance). After a mammoth amount of touring, they took a nearly two-year hiatus at the end of 2007.

The Klinghoffer Lineup

Frusciante quit during said hiatus in 2008 but didn't go public with his departure until December 2009. The group made no effort to convince Frusciante to stay; as Frusciante veered further away from pop music in his solo materials, exploring ethereal guitar playing and oddly timed electronic music, it was clear he was unhappy being a Red Hot Chili Pepper.

Josh Klinghoffer formally joined the band after getting a phone call offering the gig at a Los Angeles Dodgers game—he would hang up, watch the game and consider it, and call back to accept it two weeks later, leaving the three other Peppers to sweat for fourteen entire days. Although he said yes in July, his first formal practice with the band as a full-time songwriting member was October 12, 2009.

Klinghoffer had opened for the Chili Peppers in the Bicycle Thief, played guitar and drums with Frusciante on his solo albums and drums in the side project Ataxia, and had played live with the group on tour as a sideman. When he joined, it gave Chad Smith a new energy: he had a second drummer in the band to bounce ideas off of, who also wanted the drums more to the forefront in the mixes. Occasionally, they toured with percussionist Mauro Refosco, who played percussion in Thom Yorke's group with Flea, Atoms for Peace. Smith's drum technician, Chris Warren, replaced Klinghoffer as live keyboardist. That was the lineup until Frusciante's return on December 15, 2019.

Timeline

Bass

Flea (1983–present)

Vocals

Anthony Kiedis (1983–present, with one gig covered by the Circle Jerks' Keith Morris in 1986)

Drums

Jack Irons (1983, 1986–1988)
Cliff Martinez (1983–1986)
Chuck Biscuits (1985, 1986)
D. H. Peligro (1988)
Chad Smith (1988–present)

Guitars

Hillel Slovak (1983, 1985–1988)
Jack Sherman (1983–1985)
DeWayne "Blackbyrd" McKnight (1988)
John Frusciante (1988–1992, 1998–2009, 2019–present)
Zander Schloss (1992)
Arik Marshall (1992–1993)
Jesse Tobias (1993)
Dave Navarro (1993–1998)
Anthony Kiedis ("Give It Away" second guitarist, 1993–1998)
Rob Rule (touring guitarist, 1996)
Josh Klinghoffer (touring member, keyboard and guitar, 2006–2008; full-time member, 2009–2019)

Miscellaneous

Keith "Tree" Barry—saxophone, violin, backing vocals (touring member, 1987–1990)

Rain Phoenix—backing vocals (touring member, 1995–1996)

Acacia Ludwig—backing vocals (touring member, backing vocals 1995–1996)

Lenny Castro—percussion (uncredited on *Californication*, 1999)

Marcel Rodriguez-Lopez—percussion (touring member, August 2006–January 2007)

Chris Warren—keyboards, drum synthesizer, percussion, backing vocals (touring member, 2007–present), drum technician (1989–present)

Mauro Refosco—percussion (touring member, 2011–2014)

Nate Walcott—keyboards, trumpet (touring member, 2016–present)

Samuel Bañuelos III—bass on "Go Robot" and "Encore" (touring member, 2016–present)

14

Rocking in the Flea World

The Evolution of Flea's Sound

A Punk Plays Funk

The stereotype of Flea is someone on bass with jazz chops playing funk music at punk tempos. While this is more or less true and explains a lot of his melodic, harmonic, and rhythmic choices, it doesn't even touch on his constantly evolving gear and literal sound. From the 1980s to the present, Flea has played dozens of different basses live and on record, often switching because of a dispute with the manufacturer rather than a problem with the instrument's sound.

The Beginning

The first bass guitar known to be used by Flea was a cheap Squire bass, either a Precision or a Jazz. This was exclusively before the *Red Hot Chili Peppers* came out. By the time of the band's recorded debut, he moved on to using a Music-Man Cutlass 1 bass occasionally backed up by MusicMan Stingrays. His primary bass was the Cutlass 1; covered in stickers of various punk bands, its image can be seen in the photos included in Anthony Kiedis's autobiography, and its look inspired Flea's "Punk Bass" that would come nearly twenty years later.

When *Freaky Styley* hit, Flea began to use multiple basses. He would often use a MusicMan Stingray for when he could play only one bass for an entire set but would switch between using a Fender Precision bass (or P-bass) for non-slap songs and the Stingray for slap bass.

A Specter in the Night

After *Uplift Mofo Party Plan*, Flea switched to Kramer Spector basses. A Spector LV and NS2-JA were used on *Mofo*, while an NS-2 was used for *Mother's Milk*. While the Spector was his studio bass, a MusicMan Stingray remained his live

Flea rocking out.   *Photo by John Coffey*

favorite; he can be easily seen with the Stingray on the *Psychedelic Sexfunk Live from Heaven* performance released on VHS. Although other live moments from this era had the NS-2, they were less common. He owned but likely didn't record with a Tiesco NB-4; it can be seen in the videos for "Taste the Pain" and "Higher Ground."

Blood Sugar Sponsorship Magik

Flea played most of the songs in *Blood Sugar Sex Magik* on a Wal Mach II, a custom-made bass from the United Kingdom that costs thousands more than even the most expensive of typical retail basses. The exceptions to this are the songs that require a low B string, which were played on a MusicMan Stingray five-string: "Funky Monks" and "The Righteous and the Wicked." Some people believe Flea played the Stingray on "Under the Bridge" as well; this cannot be confirmed or denied, but people infer this from the performance in the music video, which doesn't reflect what the band actually recorded with. (Similarly, John Frusciante played a Fender Jaguar in the music video, but that was not what he recorded the song with.)

Around this time, Flea received free gear from Ernie Ball MusicMan (previously MusicMan). He felt odd about this, making a point to say so in his instructional video from 1992 to River Phoenix, pointing out that once he could afford to buy a nice instrument, companies started sending him free instruments.

One Hot Minute between Sounds

Flea switched to an Alembic Epic for recording *One Hot Minute* on all except two songs. A MusicMan Stingray was used on "Aeroplane" (providing what is one of the best examples of the Stingray slap sound), and a Sigma Acoustic bass was used on "Pea." The "My Friends" video features a MusicMan Sterling, but Flea did not record with that bass.

Shortly after *One Hot Minute*, Flea began to pursue getting a signature bass. He originally wanted Ernie Ball MusicMan to do it, but they refused—as they have with virtually every artist—to do a signature model bass, feeling that their bass guitars are known entities and speak for themselves. Flea ended up getting a signature model from Modulus, where its specs were almost like a souped-up Stingray. He also owned a Treker Louis Johnson Signature four-string that Johnson himself gave Flea. Flea wrote "Aeroplane" on this bass but did not record with it.

The Modulus Flea Bass

Flea ended up with Modulus when both parties were mutually interested in working with each other. (In Flea's own words in a 1998 issue of *Bass Frontiers*, "it was a combination of my bass technician looking around to find someone to build me a Flea bass and Modulus being into it.") Modulus released two versions of the Flea Bass, one four-string model (FB4) and one five-string (FB5).

When Flea's deal ran out, the basses would remain unchanged but now be called "Funk Unlimited," or FU4 and FU5. Because Flea would later start another company called Fleabass, the Modulus will be referred to as the Funk Unlimited for clarity's sake.

The Funk Unlimited Flea played featured a double-cutaway body, thirty-four-inch scale, and Satin finish body and neck. It had twenty-two frets—one more than typically featured on a Stingray—and a Phenolic fret board. The neck was a bolt-on made of graphite, a material that players often found worse (or at least different) sounding but wouldn't require as many adjustments from climate changes, as the graphite didn't expand and contrast the way wood does with humidity alterations.

When on sale, the Funk Unlimited came by default with a Hipsot A-Style bridge and Seymor Duncan Custom Shop MusicMan pickups, but these were not what Flea used. Flea used original Lane Poor pickups—something that is no longer produced (though reproductions have finally started up again in the 2010s after a nearly ten-year absence)—and a BadAss II Bass Bridge. Flea also had an Aguilar preamp.

Flea had more than one of these basses. His go-to was a two-tone sunburst that looked more yellow than anything else, and his technician, Tracy Robar, claimed he used it on "pretty much 99% of all songs" in an interview with *Mixdown* magazine. Flea and Robar taped the EQ knobs in place so they wouldn't move during the set. His main bass for playing in Drop D for years was the "Aboriginal Bass," a Modulus that had an Australian aboriginal pattern on it. (Its primary appearance was during performances of "By the Way.")

Another one of his main basses was the Modulus "Punk Bass," a bass covered in official and unofficial band stickers, notably an unlicensed Fugazi sticker (as there are no officially licensed Fugazi stickers). The "Punk Bass" became his main bass for the *By the Way* tour.

Other basses owned by Flea include a Fleabass with custom art from Damien Hirst, a Modulus with custom art from Hirst, a more recent Fender Precision bass that has never been played live by the Red Hot Chili Peppers, and a Fender Bass VI that Josh Klinghoffer plays when Flea switches to piano during live performances of "Happiness Loves Company."

Non-Modulus Basses in Those Years

On *Californication*, Flea used his signature bass on all except "Easily," where he used his Fender Jazz, which would eventually become his main instrument, and "Road Trippin'," where he used a Taylor acoustic bass guitar. He used the Fender Jazz on a handful of songs on *By the Way*. It isn't known which songs specifically, but the Jazz is used in the "Can't Stop" music video, and it's likely it was used on that song, as it was recorded much later than the rest of the sessions.

By the Way Basses

In a 2002 interview with *Bass Player*, Flea outlined every bass he used on *By the Way*. He played a fretless bass, either a MusicMan or a Fender Jazz, on "I Could Die for You." He played his 1963 Fender Jazz on some B-sides but not the album material. Apart from playing John Frusciante's 1960s Vox bass (with a capo) on "Cabron," the rest was his Modulus bass.

Stadium Arcadium and Beyond

Flea recorded all of *Stadium Arcadium* on his 1961 Shell Pink Fender Jazz bass. For the tour after, he used the two-tone sunburst Modulus, feeling the Modulus could take more of a beating on the road. However, by the time *I'm with You* came out, the Fender Jazz was his go-to both live and in the studio.

When he started his own company to provide a quality, affordable bass guitar, he opted to use his likeness, and hence Fleabass was started. It was never his main bass—it was a cheaper, entry-level instrument—but it made Modulus rebrand the Flea Bass as the Funk Unlimited. (It's worth noting that several other A-list bass players used the Funk Unlimited when its name took after Flea, most notably the Dave Mathews Band's Stefan Lessard.) Fleabass started in 2009 but closed in 2011 after Flea stated he didn't enjoy the business side of the operation.

In this era, Flea also received a new Fender Jazz that became his main bass: a Custom Shop jazz bass built by Jason Smith with an active Modulus Lane Poor pickup and an Aguilar OBP-1 preamp. Once again, his EQ knobs are taped into place and there's a graphite neck. The easiest way to spot the new Jazz versus the old 1961 is that the 1961 has been defaced with a sticker of D. Boon's face from the Minutemen.

Atoms for Peace

With Atoms for Peace, Thom Yorke's project featuring Flea on bass, Flea played an instrument he owned for a long time but hadn't recorded with or used live before: a Höfner 500/1. The reasoning for this was that Flea felt it sounded better for imitating a synthesizer when going high up on the bass's neck.

Amplification

In the 1980s, Flea used a Trace Elliott AH500X amplifier into a Trace Elliot four-by-ten or an Ampeg VB4 into an Ampeg eight-by-ten for his live setup. Some video performances from this era feature an eight-by-ten from Peavey, but its usage was less common.

For *Uplift Mofo Party Plan* and *Mother's Milk*, Flea used a Mesa Boogie rig, using mainly a Buster Bass 200 into two-by-ten and two-by-fifteen cabinets. He switched over to Gallien-Krueger during *Blood Sugar Sex Magik*.

For a long time, Flea was sponsored by Gallien-Krueger and used only their amplification and cabinets. (As his need for volume increased, he began to bring a slew of GK amps; on the *I'm with You* tour, he played out of five Gallien-Krueger 2001RB heads into 410RBH four-by-ten and 115RBH one-by-fifteen cabinets.) For the *I'm with You* tour, he switched over to Acoustic USA, using an eight-by-ten and a USA 360 head but went back to GK midway through it, not completing an entire tour without GK. It's probable that his switch to Acoustic came from his love for Jaco Pastorius, as his amp selection matched that of Pastorious.

Strings

At the start of his career, Flea used Ernie Ball Roundwounds gauged at G50 D70 A85 and E105. He switched over to GHS on their sponsoring of him; he has had his own line for years that is virtually identical to the regular GHS Bass Boomers but has used the GHS M3045F Flea Signature Bass Boomers Strings since their release. They are gauged at G45 D65 A85 E105.

Setup

It may seem obvious, but Flea has always kept his bass strings long and light, as it enables fast playing. (One of the reasons he enjoyed graphite necks was that they allowed the action to get closer to the neck with less buzz.)

Pedals

This is where things can get fuzzy. Flea has never used a consistent pedal board, switching pedals in between tours and never keeping the same effects. For this reason, the chapter will end here with a complete list of pedals used and when they were used.

DOD FX25B Envelope Filter—never used live or studio, played on *Flea* instructional video

Electro-Harmonix Bassballs—eventually replaced by the Nano version of the same pedal, was used to write but not record "Coffee Shop"

Boss AutoWah—unknown model, used across *One Hot Minute*

Boss Dynamic Filter—unknown model, used during the recording of "Coffee Shop"

Boss ODB-3 Bass OverDrive—his primary form of distortion during the *Californication* era, featured prominently during "Around the World"

Electro-Harmonix Bass MicroSynth—*Stadium Arcadium* era

Electro-Harmonix POG Polyphonic Octave Generator—*Stadium Arcadium* era, likely replacing his previous octave pedals

MXR M-133 Micro Amp—a mainstay on his pedal board since *Stadium Arcadium*, used for clean boosts of lead lines

T-Rex Engineering Squeezer Compressor—*Stadium Arcadium* era

Boss GE-7 Equalizer—unknown era

Digitech Whammy—unknown era, was used in rehearsals for Atoms for Peace but disappeared from his pedal board when the band went on tour

Electro-Harmonix Big Muff Pi—unknown era

Electro-Harmonix Original Q-Tron—unknown era, but his primary envelope filter

Moog Moogerfooger MF-103 12-Stage Phaser—unknown era (The bass sound on "Sir Psycho Sexy" is his bass played through a shorting-out Moogerfooger pedal from the *Blood Sugar Sex Magik* era.)

Dunlop Crybaby 105Q Bass Wah—a mainstay on his pedal board since its release

Electro-Harmonix Bassballs Nano—a mainstay on his pedal board, used for recording some sounds on *Stadium Arcadium*

Malekko B:Assmaster Distortion—a mainstay on his pedal board since *I'm with You*

15

You Oughta Know

The Complete History of Flea's Session Work

Early Output, RHCP and All

During the band's early years, Flea did not do a ton of session work. Although he played with Fear, he never recorded with them, lasting in between the band's "Fuck Christmas" single and the album *More Beer*.

The First Credited Session

Of all things, Flea got his first paid and credited session work for Warren Zevon because of his connections to Parliament and George Clinton. The Red Hot Chili Peppers' guitarist at the time, DeWayne "Blackbyrd" McKnight, was requested because he was the guitarist for Parliament and Funkadelic during their most recently recorded album; George Clinton was also the arranger for the song and in charge of the session. The two knew that Flea was more than capable, and he got his first work for "Leave My Monkey Alone." From there, Flea became one of several bassists Clinton would reuse over the years.

It's worth noting that according to interviews in *Loaded* and Q magazine, Flea was offered the bassist spot in John Lydon's Public Image Ltd but declined it.

Don't Just Stand There, Bust a Move

The first notable session came when Flea was called to do some bass playing for Young MC. The lack of fair pay altered Flea's perception of session work forever, and he fought to get paid fairly and credited properly after it; odds are that Flea had been used in other sessions before, but after "Bust a Move" became a number one hit and Flea never saw an extra dime, he made it a point to get his name out there.

He held onto the grudge for the lack of fair payment for years, bringing it up in European interviews in the late 1990s and in a *Bass Player* interview in 1996. "The bass line I wrote ended up being a major melody of the tune, and I felt I deserved song-writing credit and money because it was a No. 1 hit. They sold millions of records, and I got $200!" he said.

The Jewel of the 1990s

Flea met Jewel in 1992 in San Diego, California. She was living out of her van and performing locally as an undiscovered artist; Flea felt sick one day and was just searching for something to do, saw Jewel, and took it as a sign. They talked and became friends, and then Jewel played her music, and Flea was surprised to find it enjoyable. When she later made it big herself, Flea joined her in performing "You Were Meant for Me" live on the *Late Show with David Letterman*, collaborated with her on a cover of the Germs' "Media Blitz" for a tribute album, and appeared on select songs on her album *Spirit*.

Alterative Rock Toots Flea's Horn

Trumpet was the first instrument Flea was good at, and he maintained his chops throughout the years, playing horn on Red Hot Chili Peppers songs "Taste the Pain" and "Torture Me." Because he was a well-known figure in the Los Angeles alternative scene even before the scene took off, he was the go-to trumpet player for alternative rock bands, beginning with trumpet on Jane's Addiction's *Nothing's Shocking* in 1988.

Flea's Brief Tenure as Guitarist

Flea was never a guitarist and could never play the instrument beyond rudimentary chords. That said, he did write the music to "Tearjerker" and "My Friends" on guitar, showing Navarro the basic guitar parts for him to expand on. He also played additional guitar on "Dosed" from *By the Way*, according to its credits listed on the international single.

Porno for Pyros into Jane's Addiction

Flea was never a member of Porno for Pyros (and neither was Dave Navarro). That said, after Dave Navarro and Perry Farrell made peace, Navarro was invited to play guitar on a few Pyros tracks, both of which Flea ended up playing bass guitar on. One of these songs made Porno for Pyros' final album, while the other would end up on Howard Stern's *Private Parts* sound track alongside a new version of LL Cool J's "I Make My Own Rules" that featured Navarro, Flea, and Chad Smith on the musical performance side.

From there, Flea joined Jane's Addiction as a full-time bassist during their first reunion. While he never played on an entirely new studio release, he did play bass on a handful of tracks on their first rarities release: *Kettle Whistle*. (He would go on to play bass for one song on Farrell's mid-2000s project Satellite Party.)

Red Hot Chili Peppers Session Work

Because the Red Hot Chili Peppers were known for their musicianship, the band was often called in for session work as a group. Sometimes this would be because the band was in the same studio as a pop artist needing session musicians; other times, they were selected because they were the Red Hot Chili Peppers. One time, two different lineups of the Red Hot Chili Peppers converged for one session: during Tricky's *Blowback* sessions, Anthony Kiedis sang backing vocals, and John Frusciante played on "Girls." On another album track, "#1 Da Woman," Frusciante played guitar and sang chorus vocals, Flea played bass guitar, and future Chili Pepper guitarist Josh Klinghoffer played drums on the song.

Random work where each of the Chili Peppers musicians would be credited individually would come throughout time: LL Cool J's remake of "I Make My Own Rules" for the *Private Parts* sound track came when Dave Navarro was in the band, Queen's two remixes of "We Will Rock You/We Are the Champions" and "No-One but You/Tie Your Mother Down" feature Chad Smith on drums, among others. It wasn't until after *Blood Sugar Sex Magik* that Flea became a name-brand session bassist and started to see constant work.

Rocking with Alanis

Perhaps the most well-known case of Flea playing in someone else's session was done with Dave Navarro for Alanis Morissette's "You Oughta Know." Flea was friends with her friend and engineer, a producer named Jimmy Boyle, and was recruited by him to play on it. Morissette had written the song with wildly different instrumentation; Boyle gave Navarro and Flea the vocal track and constructed their own musical sequence to it.

A Name Brand

Once Flea was well known for his bass playing, work took off. He would earn songwriting or performer's credits beyond pure session payments (as recognized through a "featured" spot in the title) throughout the years, often putting him on the same level as featured singers. This includes random, record-label-thought-up supergroups, like the one behind the cover of Edwin Starr's "War" for the *Small Soldiers* sound track: the vocals are by Bone Thugs-N-Harmony, and the music is performed by Henry Rollins, Tom Morello, and Flea. (Similar things helped Tom Morello become a recognizable name himself, as he was the producer and bassist on "Come with Me" by Puff Daddy featuring Jimmy Page for the *Godzilla* sound track and guitarist for the supergroup doing Pink Floyd covers for *The Faculty*'s sound track: Class of '99.)

According to *Bass Player*, his favorite session works were with Cheikha Rimitti on *Sidi Mansour*, his playing with Ziggy Marley, and Greg Kurstin's Action Figure Party or when he got to play with Bill Withers on Mick Jagger's "Use Me" off of *Wandering Spirit*.

Solo Work, Abandoned and Pursued

In the 1990s, Flea tried to do a solo album but opted against it. This came after he started learning guitar after being gifted one from Rick Rubin before *One Hot Minute* but before sessions for a second album with Dave Navarro began. Some of these recordings would eventually see the light of day: "Pea" ended up on *One Hot Minute*, while "I've Been Down" got released and credited as Flea for a sound track.

Flea told *Bass Player* in 2006 that he wanted to do a solo record but that he didn't want it to revolve around bass and did want it to focus more on songs and melody while using the sax player from the Lounge Lizards: John Lurie. He explained that the record never came out because he considered himself a bad singer—someone able to hit the notes but not sound good doing so.

Eventually, Flea released a solo album: *Helen Burns*. The release was used to fund Flea's Silverlake Conservatory of Music at a pay-what-you-want download price and eventually released on vinyl. Recorded with the help of drum technician and keyboardist Chris Warren, it does not sound like the solo work from the 1990s. Flea's early solo stuff is all vocals and guitar or all vocals and bass; this was more of a jam-oriented, produced record that featured a cowrite from Patti Smith and was mostly instrumental.

The cover of Flea's solo opus, the *Helen Burns* EP.   *Author's collection*

Flea's Complete Non–Red Hot Chili Peppers Discography

Warren Zevon—"Leave My Monkey Alone" (1987)—bass guitar
Jane's Addiction—*Nothing's Shocking* (1988)—trumpet
UK Subs—*Japan Today* (1988)—bass guitar
Keith Levene—*Keith Levene's Violent Opposition* (1989)—bass guitar
Young MC—*Stone Cold Rhymin'* (1989)—bass guitar on "Bust a Move" and "I Come Off"
The Weirdos—*Condor* (1990)—bass guitar on "Shining Silver Light," "Cyclops Helicopter," "Tropical Depression," "Terrain," "Something's Moving," and "Living Thing"
Peace Choir—*Give Peace a Chance* (1991)—bass guitar
Queen—"We Will Rock You/We Are the Champions (Remix)" (1991)—bass guitar

George Clinton—*Hey Man, Smell My Finger* (1993)—bass guitar
Andre Foxxe—"Reputation" (1993)—bass guitar
Mick Jagger—*Wandering Spirit* (1993)—bass guitar
Street Military—*Don't Give a Damn* (1993)—bass guitar
Jon Hassell—*Dressing for Pleasure* (1994)—bass guitar
Pigface—*Notes from Thee Underground* (1994)—bass guitar
Sir Mix-a-Lot—*Chief Boot Knocka* (1994)—bass guitar
Bam—*Rough Z'aggin Bible (Pray at Will)* (1995)—bass guitar
Flea—"I've Been Down" (1995)—everything, appeared on *The Basketball Diaries* sound track
Andre Foxxe—"Hanging Around" featuring Flea (1995)—bass guitar
Janet Jackson—"What I'll Do (Dave Navarro Remix)" (1995)—bass guitar
Alanis Morissette—"You Oughta Know" (1995)—bass guitar
P—*P* (1995)—bass guitar
Cheikha Remitti—*Sidi Mansour* (1995)—bass guitar
Mike Watt—*Ball-Hog or Tugboat?* (1995)—lead bass on "E-Ticket Ride," pocket trumpet on "Sidemouse Advice"
Aleka's Attic—"Note to a Friend" (1996)—bass guitar
Johnny Cash—"Spiritual" (1996)—bass guitar
Cheikha Rimitti—*Cheika* (1996)—bass guitar
Pornos for Pyros—"Freeway" featuring Flea and Dave Navarro (1996)—bass guitar
Michael Brook—"Ill Wind (You're Blowing Me No Good)" (1997)—bass guitar
Flea—"Tantric Sex" (1997)—everything, appears on *Schooloaf (Everything but the Crust)* compilation
Jane's Addiction—*Kettle Whistle* (1997)—bass on "Kettle Whistle," "So What!," and "My Cat's Name Is Maceo"
Jewel—"You Were Meant for Me (Live at Letterman)" (1997)—bass guitar
Livin' Illegal—"Married to the Game" (1997)—backing vocals
LL Cool J featuring the Red Hot Chili Peppers—"I Make My Own Rules" (1997)—bass guitar
No Doze Funkmob—*Hooded Figures* (1997)—bass guitar
Porno for Pyros—"Hard Charger" featuring Flea and Dave Navarro (1997)—bass guitar
Queen—"No-One but You/Tie Your Mother Down (Remix)" (1996)—bass guitar, drums
Jimmy Scott—"Love Will Keep Us Together" featuring Flea (1997)—bass guitar
Bone Thugs-N-Harmony—"War" featuring Henry Rollins, Tom Morello, and Flea (1998)—bass guitar
G-Rap—*Military Mindz* (1998)—bass guitar
Jewel—*Spirit* (1998)—bass guitar

Joe Strummer—"It's a Rockin' World" featuring Flea, Tom Morello, D. J. Bonebrake, Benmount Tench, and Nick Hexum (1998)—bass guitar

Banyan—"Grease the System" (1999)—bass guitar

The Doors—"Roadhouse Blues" featuring John Lee Hooker, Jim Morrison, Robby Krieger, Ray Manzarek, John Densmore, D. J. Bonebrake, Flea, Gregg Arreguin, John "Luke" Logan, and Ralph Sall (2000)—bass guitar

Fishbone—"Shakey Ground" (2000)—bass guitar

UK Subs—*Europe Calling* (2000)—bass guitar

Action Figure Party—*Action Figure Party* (2001)—bass guitar

Cliff Martinez—*Traffic* film score (2001)—bass guitar

Gov't Mule—"Down and Out in New York City" (2001)—bass guitar

Tricky—"#1 Da Woman" (2001)—bass guitar

UK Subs—*Mad Cow Fever* (2001)—bass guitar

Alanis Morissette—"Narcissus" (2002)—bass guitar

Johnny Cash—*Unearthed* (2003)—bass guitar

Ziggy Marley—*Dragonfly*—bass guitar on "Rainbow in the Sky" and "Melancholy Mood" (2003)

The Mars Volta—*De-Loused in the Comatorium* (2003)—bass guitar on every song except "Televators"

Axis of Justice—"(Free Jam)" featuring Flea, Brad Wilk, and Serj Tankian (2004)—bass guitar

John Frusciante—"The Slaughter" (2004)—upright bass

Incubus—"The Oydssey" (2004 and 2006)—trumpet

Jack Irons—*Attention Dimension* (2004)—bass guitar

The Mars Volta—*Frances the Mute* (2005)—trumpet on "The Widow" and "Miranda, That Ghost Just Isn't Holy Anymore"

Joshua Redman—*Momentum* (2005)—bass guitar

Bob Forrest—*Wednesday: Modern Folk and Blues* (2006)—bass guitar

Patti Smith—*Twelve* (2007)—bass guitar

Satellite Party—"Hard Life Easy" (2007)—bass guitar and a songwriting credit

Mina Caputo (formerly Keith Caputo)—"Bleed for Something Beautiful" (2008)—bass guitar

George Clinton and His Gangsters of Love—"Let the Good Times Roll" featuring the Red Hot Chili Peppers and Kim Manning (2008)—bass guitar

John Frusciante—*The Empyrean* (2009)—bass guitar on "Unreachable," "God," "Heaven," "Enough of Me," "Today," and "Ah Yorn"

Jane's Addiction—*A Cabinet of Curiosities Box Set* (2009)—bass guitar, trumpet

Bryan Ferry—*Olympia* (2010)—bass guitar

Slash—"Baby Can't Drive" featuring Alice Cooper, Nicole Scherzinger, Steven Adler, and Flea (2010)—bass guitar on "Why You Wanna Go and Do a Thing Like That For," "I Gotta See," and "Spoonful"

Ron Wood—*I Feel Like Playing* (2010)—bass guitar

Tom Waits—*Bad as Me* (2011)—bass guitar on "Raised Right Men" and "Hell Broke Luce"

Flea—*Helen Burns* (2012)—everything

Rocket Juice & the Moon—*Rocket Juice & the Moon* (2012)—bass guitar

Atoms for Peace—*Amok* (2013)—bass guitar

Flea—"Djebala Hills" featuring Falu, John Zorn, and Billy Martin (2013)—bass guitar

Antemasque—*Antemasque* (2014)—bass guitar

Bryan Ferry—"Avonmore" (2014)—bass guitar

Yelawolf—"Punk" featuring Travis Barker and Juicy J (2017)—bass guitar

16

Schooled

What Makes Flea a Great Musician

We Don't Need No Education

For years, Flea avoided musical instruction on bass guitar—he took one lesson when he began, but after his instructor tried to get him to learn a piece by the Eagles, he walked out and vowed to never take lessons again. His path to near virtuosity on bass guitar was unusual and distinct and remains evolving. Two weeks to the day after he picked up the instrument, he was playing it in a battle of the bands in Hollywood.

Flea has been named one of the best bassists of all time, coming in thirtieth on a 2017 *Bass Player* ranking and second in a *Rolling Stone* reader's poll from 2009, behind only John Entwistle from the Who.

Flea as a Multi-Instrumentalist

His first instrument was drums. While he never became a practical drummer, it did give him a feel for rhythm from the outset. The instrument he first became good at was trumpet. His first love was jazz, and he put in time and effort even before his teenage years to becoming a jazz trumpeter. As recently as 2006, Flea told *Bass Player* that the trumpet shaped his bass playing to the point that he still did not picture the fret board when hearing notes on bass but instead visualized the trumpet fingerings. He eventually worked through the Jamie Abersold books on trumpet, wildly considered the standard for learning melodic techniques on a given instrument, and mentioned that he may one day do them on bass guitar.

Flea also mentioned in his instructional video that, when he wanted to get good at slapping, he practiced drum rudiments on bass guitar. He doesn't display this in the video, but it's likely that he practiced a typical sticking routine with his thumb and finger to improve his slap technique.

For years, he wanted to learn upright bass; in the early 2000s, he began to work on this until he reached a point where he felt adequate. He gave up the practice when he returned to school, feeling he didn't have the time to focus on so many different instruments.

Early Techniques

The thing Flea was best known for in the 1980s was his hard, aggressive slap chops. He would often slap so hard so often so fast that his fingers bled, and he was recognized as a top bass player for the difficulty of such slap lines as "Get Up and Jump" and "True Men Don't Kill Coyotes" from *The Red Hot Chili Peppers*. His impressive slap technique continued throughout the 1980s, in Flea's mind peaking with what he told Reddit was his most difficult song to play, "Nobody Weird Like Me," and started to do it less beginning with *Blood Sugar Sex Magik*. On that album, he intentionally tried to play simpler and more melodic, as he had decided that it would make him a better bass player.

He told Bootsy Collins in *Bass Player* in 2006 that slap had turned into a show of masculinity and it turned him off. "All these rock bands had guys who played slap bass and were beating the hell out of it. It became this macho thing and the art wasn't really in it. I didn't do it for a long time, and instead I got into James Jamerson, playing these flowing lines."

Using a Pick

Flea did not use a pick with the early Red Hot Chili Peppers material. However, when he was in Fear, Flea was commanded by front man Lee Ving not only to use a pick but also that all playing had to be done picking downward "because that was the way to play punk rock," according to an interview with *VPro* in 1988.

He began to pick again when he joined Jane's Addiction for the "Relapse" tour. It carried over during the recording of *Californication*, as "Parallel Universe" called for a pick. For *By the Way*, the pick was arguably his preferred method of playing, happening on "Don't Forget Me," "The Zephyr Song," and "By the Way," among other tunes. He said it was because he was "ready to do something different."

Fingering It Out

Regardless of era, Flea's primary method of playing in the Red Hot Chili Peppers has been finger style. It was long argued whether Flea played with three fingers, but he has always used only two, even in the fastest parts: if you watch the "Right on Time" performance on *Off the Map* slowed down, it can be seen that even playing octave sixteenth notes at 128 beats per minute, Flea used two fingers. This ability to play inhumanely fast while keeping a simple technique has helped him excel. "Right on Time" is the fastest Flea played on record—128 beats per minute with sixteenth notes is approximately eight and a half notes in a single second—but he has other notable bass lines for more than just speed.

"Around the World," created by Flea after Frusciante brought in the corresponding guitar part, was the first thing played to it, using a Mixolydian sound jumping two octaves throughout. Its inane and start-stopping rhythms give it a funk feel, while Flea's use of chromaticism against Frusciante's droning riff give it a distinct interaction. (They used this technique again and again throughout the years, with one holding a melody and the other changing chords, notably on the bridge to "Charlie" from *Stadium Arcadium*.)

Regardless of guitarist, Flea often played a different rhythm for the majority of a riff before breaking into a unison with the guitarist for the end of one phrase. A prominent example is during the guitar solo of "Dani California": during an extended repeat of a three-note lick by Frusciante, Flea busts into a unison, building up and eliminating tension.

Sometimes, Flea will play against improvisations entirely, taking influence from his New Wave idols by repeating a phrase entirely nonstop as the guitarist and Chad Smith go wild. This happens during the outro of "Purple Stain"—Flea's bass line never changes.

When Flea began to slap more sporadically, it remained in his toolbox for bridges and brief solos. By *One Hot Minute*, it could be the focus of a song again, but on *Blood Sugar Sex Magik*, the only slapped bits are the bridge to "The Power of Equality," the open Es during the chorus of "Suck My Kiss," and the verses of "Naked in the Rain."

Back to School

Flea went to the University of Southern California for music beginning in the late 2000s. He didn't pursue a bachelor's degree but took classes on music theory, composition, and jazz trumpet as well as piano lessons. He also studied with his theory teacher, Professor Neal Desby, individually in private. Most of that time was spent examining classical chorales, particularly those from Bach, who swiftly became his favorite composer and one of his all-time favorite musicians along with Charlie Parker and Jimi Hendrix.

At the university, Flea spent his time focused on trumpet more than bass guitar. In his own words, he could focus on playing only two instruments well at a time. While at school, that was trumpet and piano. Once done with school, it became bass guitar and piano; that is why the trumpet parts on *I'm with You* are played by Mike Bulger.

Jams versus Riffs

While most of the music in the Red Hot Chili Peppers originates from jams, occasionally members bring in a riff, and everyone constructs their part around it. In the case of Flea, he brought in the riffs to "If You Have to Ask," "Suck My Kiss," "Mellowship Slinky in B Major," "The Righteous and the Wicked," "Give It Away," "Naked in the Rain," and "Apache Rose Peacock." He wrote the riffs to "The Righteous and the Wicked," playing bass while watching the film *Taxi Driver*.

Harmonic Selection

The actual music Flea plays on bass is often incredibly distinctive. When *Bass Player* did a lesson on the interval of minor sevenths, "Give It Away" and its famous bass line was chosen as one of the examples. In terms of note and interval selection, Flea often chooses notes outside of the chord being played that are not dissonant, providing him with a distinct flavor and feel. Another example of this is in the bridge of "Sir Psycho Sexy," where on the repeat of the bass line, he slides the top note of an arpeggio into a major ninth and returns to the octave, making it melodic but still keeping the groove in place.

When soloing on record, Flea typically stayed in pentatonic scales, be they the major pentatonic like in "Naked in the Rain" or minor pentatonic like in "Coffee Shop." Sometimes, he'd mix the major and minor modes; the most prominent example is the bass solo and outro line to "Aeroplane," which uses Aeolian with a major third added for its entirety.

Big Influences

His first influence was his stepfather, who played upright bass in a bebop band and kick-started his fascination with trumpet. His jazz favorites growing up were Miles Davis, Jaco Pastorius, Charlie Parker, Duke Ellington, Dizzy Gillespie, Louis Armstrong, and John Coltrane. He made it a point to say that Armstrong showed the value of playing a single note and how one note alone could be full of meaning, eliminating the need to play too much.

Mike Watt, bassist and sometimes singer for the Minutemen and fIREHOSE, was always a big influence. Flea has appeared on Watt's *Watt from Pedro* radio show, while the band as a whole dedicated *Blood Sugar Sex Magik* to Mike Watt. During multiple interviews for *Blood Sugar Sex Magik*, Flea praised the Meters bassist George Porter Jr., in particular for shaping the sounds that came out on "Apache Rose Peacock."

After *Californication*, Flea began to be more influenced by electronica and goth rock, singling out the Cure, Joy Division, and Siouxsie and the Banshees. At one point, he formed a live group with Stella Mozgawa, then future Chili Pepper Josh Klinghoffer on drums, and then current Chili Pepper John Frusciante on guitar, where they covered Aphex Twin's ".000890569."

Many bassists have been named Flea's top influence at one point or another. In addition to the melodic bassists like James Jamerson Sr., who played as an in-house session musician on the majority of Motown recordings (and whose bass line on Marvin Gaye's "What's Going On" blew Flea's mind), and Paul McCartney, whose work with the Beatles showed Flea that a rock bassist could play tastefully, he has specifically named dozens of others. He singled out former Sly and the Family Stone bassist Larry Graham as an influence inspiring him to slap but has also conceded that his two favorite Family Stone bass lines were not played by Graham. Both "If You Want Me to Stay" and "Thank You (Falettinme Be Mice Elf Agin)" were played by Sly Stone, though "If You Want Me to Stay" was credited to guitarist Rusten Allen, and "Thank You" was credited to Graham.

In the *Greatest Hits* booklet alone, Flea named John Paul Jones from Led Zeppelin, Jah Wobble (whose work with Public Image Ltd has been named in other interviews specifically), Bootsy Collins from Parliament and Funkadelic, Eric Avery from Jane's Addiction, Aston "Family Man" Barrett from Bob Marley and the Wailers, Andrew Weiss from Pigface, Henry Rollins, Peter Hook from Joy Division and New Order, and all the bass players from Fela Kuti and Ween, among others. He claimed that he "repeatedly stole" from those listed.

After going to school for music, Flea said that he had spent a lot of time in Africa and in particular Ethiopia, where each night he would try to jam with new musicians and learn something from them. (He explained to *Bass Player* that this was how "Ethiopia" got its name, even though he conceded it did not sound like an Ethiopian rhythm.)

Jimi Hendrix was always a big influence, leading to Flea getting the likeness of Hendrix tattooed on his body. Hendrix's melodic phrasing can be heard throughout Flea's playing; the way Flea slides through a major triad before doing a phrase above it originates with Hendrix. (Also notable is that in live performances and the studio version of the Red Hot Chili Peppers cover of "Castles Made of Sand," Flea played the chorus guitar part, note for note, on bass guitar.)

He told *Guitar* that his two favorite albums for bass lines were Marvin Gaye's *What's Going On?* featuring the bass playing of James Jamerson and the Minutemen's *Double Nickels on the Dime* featuring the punk bass work of Mike Watt.

17

Drive **On**

Cliff Martinez's Film Sound Tracks

Oddly Early Beginnings

Cliff Martinez was in several bands local to Los Angeles before he joined prominent punk group the Weirdos in 1980. Thereafter, he played with Lydia Lunch in 1981 and Captain Beefheart in 1982, then the Red Hot Chili Peppers. (After the Red Hot Chili Peppers and while film composer, he played drums for the Dickies on four albums: *Killer Klowns from Outer Space*, *The Second Coming*, *Locked N' Loaded Live in London*, and *Idjit Savant*.) The Weirdos were mentioned by Flea during John Frusciante's performance of "Tiny Dancer" during PinkPop 1990, later released on the *Under the Covers* compilation.

Martinez's connection to the Red Hot Chili Peppers was Flea; the two went to local punk shows and knew the prominent regional acts of the day. Martinez's sound track work stems from the Red Hot Chili Peppers. The whole band was friends of the director of an episode of *Pee-wee's Playhouse*: Stephen Johnson. He was slated to do a video for the band, and Martinez ended up asking him if he could score an episode of the show in exchange. He told *VICE Noisey*,

> I just realized that it was, A, the highest paying job I ever had, and B, it was just really fun to do what was, then, really experimental music for me and to fit to picture. That is when I became really interested in the idea of writing music for films.

The First Few Films

After scoring the episode pf *Playhouse*, a demo reel of Martinez's compositions ended up in the hands of Steve Soderbergh, who hired him to score his first theatrical release: 1989's *Sex, Lies, and Videotape*. He remained Soderbergh's go-to composer, doing the scores for 1991's *Kafka*, 1993's *King of the Hill*, 1995's *The Underneath*, 1996's *Gray's Anatomy* (no relation to the television show), 1996's *Schizopolis*, 1999's *The Limey*, 2000's *Traffic*, 2002's *Solaris*, and 2011's *Contagion*. (He would also compose for Soderbergh's television show *The Knick*.)

After *Sex, Lies, and Videotape*, he scored 1990's *Pump Up the Volume*. The scores made Martinez notable: rather than having one distinct style, Martinez showed experimentation in substance and styles. *Playhouse* gave him free reign to do anything he wanted; with other acts like the Residents and Stanley Clarke scoring episodes, he knew he was allowed to do what he wanted. Soderbergh gave him open chance to do what he wanted, but Martinez took a more minimalist and ambient approach.

Work with Nicolas Winding Refn, Collaborations, and Video Games

After working with Nicolas Winding Refn, Martinez's brand and notoriety took off. Beginning with 2011's *Drive*, Martinez has scored all of Refn's films: both the thriller *Only God Forgives* and the horror movie *The Neon Demon*. *Drive* originally was scored by Johnny Jewel of Desire and the Chromatics; the film studio hired Martinez to do it instead. (Some of Jewel's music was used in the score, but it is composed mostly by the former Chili Pepper; the bulk of Jewel's unused music was used as *Themes for an Imaginary Film* for his project Symmetry.) *Drive* and its score were critically heralded, leading to the score being pressed on vinyl and giving Martinez a new level of recognition.

He has also collaborated with a handful of artists—in addition to the previously mentioned Jewel, he composed with Skrillex for 2012's *Spring Breakers*. He has done the score for two video games—Ubisoft's *Far Cry 4* and Maxis's *Spore*—where he composed the main theme and a handful of other, unspecific compositions. The rest was done by Brian Eno, who collaborated with him on the theme.

New Instruments, New Approach, and Video Games

Martinez has typically stuck to the same synthesizers and sounds but consistently has tried to dabble with new things to keep moving forward. He has sometimes used acoustic instruments but sometimes not; for example, his score for *The Neon Demon* was all synthesizer, and the score for *Drive* was software that emulates synthesizers from the 1980s. On the other hand, he used a Crystal Baschet—a modern acoustic instrument played by rubbing its keys—on Robert Redford's *The Company You Keep* and Soderbergh's *The Knick*.

His fascination for synthesizers may have stemmed from his fear of drums being replaced by drum machines; to this day, he rarely uses artificial drum sounds and talked in 2016 of still keeping a drum set in his spare bedroom. Occasionally, his playing has appeared on his own works.

Only a Handful of Influences

Martinez has rarely named film composers as influences. Instead, he has mentioned minimalist composers like Philip Glass, older jazz musicians like Louis Armstrong, and experimental music like Captain Beefheart as his go-to listens in interviews with *VICE Noisey* and *VICE Thump*.

18

Iron Man

Jack Irons's Skills and Setup

The First Drummer

Jack Irons was the first drummer for the Red Hot Chili Peppers but had only a short tenure, as he was replaced by Cliff Martinez when they signed a recording contract. He rejoined and truly worked on only one studio album after the first album's demos: *The Uplift Mofo Party Plan*. Nonetheless, the years that followed were some of the heaviest for touring, and Irons had a huge influence on the band's early sound, being one of the four high school friends who put the band on the path to music.

Irons played for the drum line in high school but struggled. He admired other drummers on the line who could nail the cadences of performance even at faster tempos; he focused on it and was able to perform at that level after high school but told the *VPro* interviewers in 1988 that in high school, he thought the people who performed at that level were the real drummers.

Still Relevant, Post–Chili Peppers

No one else has been similar to Irons in the Chili Peppers story in the way that he was more notable in alternative rock after his time in the Red Hot Chili Peppers than he was during or before it. He was friends with the members of Mother Love Bone and stayed in touch with them and had their instrumental tape; he would give it to a friend of his whom he played basketball with, Eddie Vedder, who moved to Seattle to audition and later join the band. That band became Pearl Jam, a group Irons would eventually join for several tours and three albums with one song on *Vitalogy* and the complete drumming for both *No Code* and *Yield*.

The first musical act he joined after the Red Hot Chili Peppers was Joe Strummer; he became the Clash's former front man's go-to drummer beginning in 1989.

Irons has released three solo albums and has started his composing with the beat rather than with melody or lyrics.

Tribalism

The former Chili Pepper's sound was distinct and notably tribal even after leaving the band. His work with Pearl Jam was noted as difficult to replicate by his replacement, Matt Cameron, who altered the songs during live performances to be an almost entirely different beat. Pearl Jam used his beats as the basis for a few songs, notably "In My Tree" and "Who You Are," something that was rarer before his joining. Irons learned from the woes of the Chili Peppers and put Pearl Jam on a happier path, with producer Brendan O'Brien telling *SPIN* that "everybody was on their best musical behavior around [Irons] ... [he was] a big spiritual influence, if not the biggest."

Irons had a distinct style across all of his projects. Vedder even commented to *DRUM!* magazine that "no one plays like him. There's some kind of wild card, the way he hears things and the way he plays things that's completely his own." Irons was influence by everyone from funk artists to the jazz drumming of Max Roach, who specifically influenced "Who You Are" with his limb independence. He has recognized that he isn't that jazzy and that he has never thought he had particularly strong chops but knew he could play anything he heard on the radio and put his heart into it. He has put feeling ahead of technique, leading him to some strong rock drumming to funkier backbeats.

Setup

Jack Irons has used an unusual setup for the majority of his drum career: in his youth, he played on Pearl fiberglass drums. In the Red Hot Chili Peppers days, he can be seen most often playing with two mounted toms and one floor tom, a pretty common occurrence. The drum kit he used on *No Code* was a DW kit of this variety. Most of his career he played Vistalites and stainless-steel drums. After that, though, he typically used one mounted tom and two floor toms: a twelve-inch mounted, a sixteen-inch floor, and an eighteen-inch floor; that has been his sound since the early 2010s. (His snare was always fourteen inches and his bass drum twenty-two.) As of 2011, he used a pair of Zildjian fourteen-inch A Custom Mastersound hi-hats, a nineteen-inch A Custom Rezo Crash, twenty-one- and eighteen-inch A Custom Rezo Rides, and a twenty-inch K Light Flat Ride with rivets for his cymbals.

Irons's drums of choice were Masters of Maple in Lavender Storm Fade as of the 2010s. He has remained by Pearl Hardware throughout his career; he has used a Pearl Powershifter Eliminator double pedal for at least a decade, but it is unpublished whether he played double pedal when in the Chili Peppers.

Unlike many drummers, Irons has been unafraid to mix drums differently on each drum and use effects across the drums. He has often added reverb in postproduction to give only a specific drum a particular flair.

Notable Chili Peppers Beats

Although Irons did not appear on *Freaky Styley*, he did get cowriting credit for "Nevermind" and "Sex Rap," songs that were written when he and Slovak were originally in the band. He also played on *The Abbey Road E.P.*'s "Fire," which would later appear on *Mother's Milk*—the first album released after he had left the band. His take on "Fire" would prove influential, putting Mitch Mitchell's jazz-rock stylings at a punk-rock tempo, something the next drummer, Chad Smith, claimed as one of his favorites to play.

From *The Uplift Mofo Party Plan*, Irons had a few interesting drumbeats: "Skinny Sweaty Man" had him in lockstep with every note of a wild Flea slap bass line, bass drum on each slap and snare drum on each pop, actively plowing through an entire song in a minute and fifteen seconds, and "Behind the Sun" was one of the group's first efforts to go softer. Irons and previous drummer

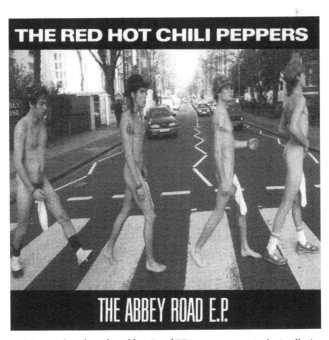

Jack Irons played on the *Abbey Road* EP.   *Author's collection*

Cliff Martinez had different tastes, though both had experience with punk and dance; Irons used faster and more prominent stickings, doing fills with paradiddle and paradiddlediddles, while Martinez tended to do more single and double strokes. (Irons still played these more straightforward fills, but his "jungle" feel stemmed from the offbeat and weak-hand accents he used.)

Mini Reunion

On June 25, 2017, Irons played with the current Red Hot Chili Peppers lineup in Grand Rapids, Michigan, on the anniversary of Hillel Slovak's death at the Van Andel Arena. Flea introduced the song they chose with Irons—"Fire"—by commenting as such. Irons had played with Flea since leaving the band—occasionally with Eddie Vedder in the Pearl Jams but also at infrequent Los Angeles jams. Irons also opened up for the Red Hot Chili Peppers on tour as a solo act and played on Flea's *Helen Burns* EP.

Video footage of the performance has floated online since.

Jack Irons's Complete Performance Discography

What Is This—*Squeezed* (1984)
What Is This—*What Is This?* (1985)
What Is This—*3 Out of 5 Live* (1985)
Red Hot Chili Peppers—*The Uplift Mofo Party Plan* (1987)
Red Hot Chili Peppers—*The Abbey Road E.P.* (1987)—"Fire" and "Backwoods"
Joe Strummer—*Permanent Record: Music from the Original Motion Picture Soundtrack*—"Trash City," "Baby the Trans," "Nefertiti," "Nothin' 'bout Nothin'," and "Theme from *Permanent Record*" (1988)
Walk the Moon—*Walk the Moon* (1988)
Keith Levene—"Some" (1989)
Joe Strummer—*Earthquake Weather* (1989)—"Gangsterville," "Slant Six," "Shouting Street," "Sikorsky Parts," "Jewellers and Bums," and "Ride Your Donkey"
Red Hot Chili Peppers—*Mother's Milk* (1989)—"Fire"
The Buck Pets—*Mercurotones* (1990)
Eleven—*Awake in a Dream* (1991)
Michelle Shocked—*Arkansas Traveler* (1991)
The Buck Pets—*To the Quick* (1993)
Eleven—*Eleven* (1993)
Sun-60—"Mary X-Mess" and "Tell Me Like You Know" (1993)
Ethan Hawke—"I'm Nuthin'" (1994)
Pearl Jam—*Vitalogy* (1994)—"Hey Foxmophandlemama, That's Me"

Red Hot Chili Peppers—*Out in L.A.* (1994)—drums on all but five songs

Eleven—*Thunk* (1995)—all but four songs

Carole Pope—"Kiss the Ground" (1995)

Pearl Jam—*Merkin Ball* (1995)

Neil Young—*Mirror Ball* (1995)

Pearl Jam—"Leaving Here" (1996)

Pearl Jam—"Gremmie Out of Control" (1996)

Pearl Jam—*No Code* (1996)

Pearl Jam—*Yield* (1998)

Pearl Jam—"Whale Song" (1999)

Pearl Jam—*Lost Dogs* (2003)—"All Night," "Don't Gimme No Lip," "Black, Red, Yellow," "Leaving Here," "Gremmie Out of Control," "Whale Song," and "Dead Man"

Eleven—*Howling Book* (2003)

Jack Irons—*Attention Dimension* (2004)

Eleven—"Stone Cold Crazy" featuring Josh Homme (2005)

Satellite Party—"Milky Ave" (2007)

Spinnerette—*Ghetto Love* (2008)

Spinnerette—*Spinnerette* (2009)

Hole—*Nobody's Daughter* (2007)

Jack Irons—*No Heads Are Better Than One* (2010)

Jack Irons—*Blue Manatee* (2011)

Mark Lanegan—*Blues Feneral* (2012)

Flea—*Helen Burns*—"333" and "Lovelovelove"

19

My Lovely Man

Hillel Slovak's Guitar Playing

Slim Beginnings

Hillel Slovak was always viewed as intelligent by his peers and family, joining an excellency program at an early age and maintaining good grades even after his family moved. "Slim" got his first guitar on his thirteenth birthday at his bar mitzvah. The guitar was an inexpensive Telecaster knockoff with a cream color to it.

According to his brother, James (who published Hillel's art and diaries in *Behind the Sun*), Hillel started with guitar lessons; he shared the same teacher as Alain Johannes, Robert Wolin, which is how the two met. One time after a lesson, he came home exclaiming that he "had it" and "got it" and never returned to lesson. Something internally had clicked, and the Israeli guitarist was proud to share it.

As a child, he played everywhere he went and kept the guitar with him at nearly all times. From an early age, he was compared to Jimi Hendrix, his favorite guitarist. The other Chili Peppers expanded his taste in music—but after Slovak's passing, the rest of his family viewed them, especially Anthony Kiedis, as enemies, with the belief that Kiedis was the one who got Slovak into drugs.

According to the *Guardian*, the way Slovak met Anthony Kiedis and Flea was purely chance: in 1978, Kiedis and Flea were hitchhiking to a water park on the other side of Los Angeles. They swam, smoked marijuana, and then realized they would struggle to get home. They spotted a member of their geometry class who lived down the street—Slovak—and waved him down; Slovak gave them a ride in his Datsun B210. Both were pleased to discover that Slovak already played guitar and was in a band; in their very first conversation, Slovak encouraged Flea to start playing bass guitar.

Influences and Influenced

Slovak's favorite bands as a teenager were KISS, Led Zeppelin, War, Aerosmith, Sweet, and Earth, Wind & Fire. Slovak and drummer Jack Irons started playing their instruments the same year but had previously talked about becoming rock musicians before that—a dream come true for both of them. After high school, Slovak took more to post-punk, like the Talking Heads, and 1980s David Bowie. Slovak himself believed that Jimi Hendrix and Gang of Four's Andy Gill were the two biggest influences on his playing. One of his favorite bands was Defunkt, who were one of the primary reasons he and Flea started writing music and getting into funk as a whole.

He became obsessed with progressive rock before the Chili Peppers formed, practically worshipping King Crimson and seeing them three consecutive nights in the 1980s. Additionally, he was a large fan of reggae and was an avid fan of jazz, ripping out jazz standards in between takes during the recording of *Freaky Styley*.

The biggest musician influenced by Slovak was clearly John Frusciante. Frusciante admitted as much on arrival in the Red Hot Chili Peppers, admitting to biographer Jeff Apter that all he knew about playing with Flea and playing funk music came from studying Slovak's playing. The Red Hot Chili Peppers have written several songs about or dedicated to him, spanning well after his immediate death, including "Knock Me Down" on *Mother's Milk*, "My Lovely Man" on *Blood Sugar Sex Magik*, "This Is the Place" on *By the Way*, and "Feasting on the Flowers" on *The Getaway*.

Outside the Red Hot Chili Peppers

Slovak has few recordings outside the Red Hot Chili Peppers and What Is This?. What Is This? was a very 1980s group; it was post-punk throughout all of its recorded history (despite starting as a classic rock cover band) and progressively fell more into typical pop clichés even as the guitarist and band members flirted with flashes of punk and jazz syncopations. After one album with What Is This?, Johannes believed that Slovak knew he wanted to leave the band to rejoin the Red Hot Chili Peppers. He told *Premier Guitar* that he "noticed that Hillel really started to focus on his songs in a hurry. . . . Once he'd gotten all the overdubs to the songs the way he wanted them, that was when he sat us all down and told us he was leaving."

A photo of Slovak in the early days of the Red Hot Chili Peppers.   *Photo by John Coffey*

Inside the Red Hot Chili Peppers

The *Freaky Styley* album artwork on both CD and vinyl includes "Wanted" posters for each member of the band. Slovak lists his aliases as "Slim, Slim Billy, Long Daddy Slow, the Monster, Maimbee," referred to his nationality as an Isrealie instead of an Israeli, and stated that he had the star of David over his left nipple as a birthmark, a mole in the shape of the Messiah on his body, and a red mark that he gave himself shaving. It's likely that all these things were untrue (other than his Israeli heritage), but this should give a good sense of his place in the band and his sense of humor.

Slovak's Styley

Slovak was an enigmatic guitarist, often flipping between fast shredding more typical of metal players and switching back to a single-note rhythm line after the solo with immediacy seldom seen before. Particularly on *Uplift Mofo Party Plan*, Slovak used soul-style guitar solos and slick single-note fills but calmly locked in with Irons and Flea when it was time to play a rhythm part.

Although he started on a Fender Telecaster, Slovak's second guitar was a Musicraft Messenger—loaned from Johannes. He had possession of a Gibson Flying V guitar, as seen in the "True Men Don't Kill Coyotes" video, but it was not something he ever played live. He used two guitars as his main instrument during the time with the Red Hot Chili Peppers: a Gibson Les Paul and a sunburst Fender Stratocaster. Throughout his entire career, he played through a Marshall Super Bass.

The Israelite used a talk box throughout his time, but he used it more often before the Red Hot Chili Peppers signed a major label deal. His most prominent usage came from the demo of "Green Heaven," available on the remastered rerelease of *The Red Hot Chili Peppers*.

Slovak did not play to a click. On *Freaky Styley*, the band's only source of timing was George Clinton's hand claps. He told the *Guardian* in 1985 that he wanted his and the band's sound to be described as "bone-crunching mayhem funk."

He often played only two notes of a full chord and strummed eighth or sixteenth notes—a common idea in funk. He was known to do little in way of variation unless it locked with what everyone else in the band was playing. In the studio, he often overdubbed these with lead lines, like in "Skinny Sweaty Man"—a song Kiedis wrote about Slovak—but live, he switched between rhythm and lead.

20

Strip My Mind

John Frusciante's Guitar Skills

True Beginnings

John Anthony Frusciante was born to musical parents: his father, John Sr., was a Julliard-trained pianist (and disciplinarian judge), while his mother, Gail, was a talented, trained vocalist whose choir group sang the studio version of the outro of "Under the Bridge." By the age of nine, he was obsessed with punk rock, and by age ten, he learned several songs on guitar, including most of the Germs' discography. He studied classic rock guitarists before his teenage years, obsessed with players like Jimi Hendrix, Pink Floyd's David Gilmour, and Led Zeppelin's Jimmy Page.

He was reportedly first introduced to the Red Hot Chili Peppers when his guitar instructor auditioned for the band in 1984—though given the time line, it is unknown whether his instructor was Jack Sherman, Dix Denney, Mark Nine, or someone else on the Los Angeles scene not previously mentioned as an interviewee. (For more information, see chapter 13.) He also learned at the Guitar Institute of Technology and first saw the Peppers in 1985 at the age of fifteen, swiftly learning their entire discography on guitar—idolizing the recently rejoined Hillel Slovak.

Early Influences

In addition to Slovak and the Germs, Frusciante learned guitar primarily through punk music at first: Pat Smear, Greg Ginn, and Joe Strummer were his original heroes before he moved to the post-punk of Public Image Ltd, the Smiths, XTC, and Siouxsie and the Banshees. When he got into classic rock, Hendrix was the primary force, providing him his core as a rhythm guitarist and lead player. He often commented to interviewees that he felt lead playing never progressed beyond Jimi Hendrix, and almost all rock music lead playing was still rehashing Hendrix's ideas, including on the *Stadium Arcadium* DVD.

As his skills progressed on guitar, he got into more eclectic music, studying the works of Frank Zappa heavily, followed by an obsession with Zappa's friend Captain Beefheart. (Frusciante would perform works by both artists when with the Chili Peppers, including the notoriously difficult-to-play "Inca Roads" by Zappa at PinkPop 1990.) At one point, Frusciante planned to try out for Zappa's band but opted not to while in the waiting room to an audition. He decided he wanted to live the life of a rock star, pursuing drugs and sex, and that wouldn't happen if he were a musician in Zappa's notoriously drug-free outfit.

Later Influences

While in the band in the *Blood Sugar Sex Magik* era, he told *Guitar World* that his biggest influences were D. Boon of the Minutemen, Frank Zappa, James Williamson from the Stooges, Eddie Hazel from Parliament, Robert Johnson, Snakefinger, Lightning Hopkins, Leadbelly, Tom Verlaine, Keith Levene from Public Image Ltd, Danny Whitten from Crazy Horse, Syd Barrett, Hillel Slovak, and Carlos Santana. Ironically, he also told *Guitar Player* that Dave Navarro influenced him as well as Zander Schloss from Thelonious Monster, who was the first person to try to replace Frusciante on a tour of New Zealand.

Meeting Slovak

It is widely talked about among fans that Frusciante met Slovak backstage at least once several months before Slovak's overdose, and Slovak noted that he didn't want the band to become too popular. It likely had some influence on Frusciante's decision to leave the band later but wasn't its sole reason. According to an interview with *RAW* magazine in 1994, the meeting went as follows:

> Hillel asked me, "Would you still like the Chilis if they got so popular they played the Forum?" I said, "No. It would ruin the whole thing. That's great about the band, the audience feels no different from the band at all." There was this real kind of historical vibe at their shows, none of the frustration that runs through the audience when they jump around and can't get out of their seat. I didn't even watch the shows. I'd get so excited that I'd flip around the slam pit the whole time.

Possible Synesthesia

It was never stated that Frusciante had or has synesthesia, the perceptual phenomenon in which an individual involuntarily experiences sounds as a different medium—most often experienced as sound becoming colors, like Jimi Hendrix or Frank Ocean. However, in an interview published after he left the Red Hot Chili Peppers for the first time (but published while he was no longer in the band), Frusciante commented to *RAW* magazine that people listen to his music and guitar playing "as a colour." He tried to compare it to soaking up a flower but did not clarify what he did when he soaked up a color other than bask in the imagery.

Joining and Changing in the Early Peppers

Within a year of meeting former Dead Kennedys drummer D. H. Peligro, Frusciante was jamming with him regularly and became one of his favorite musical partners. Peligro was connected to Flea and invited him over for a jam with Frusciante, and Flea recognized the musical chemistry right away, allegedly playing "Nobody Weird Like Me" and "Pretty Little Ditty" that first day of playing together. After Slovak's death and Jack Irons's leaving, Peligro and DeWayne "Blackbyrd" McKnight joined, making the band half black and half white for a limited time. Flea and Kiedis auditioned Frusciante behind McKnight's back and swiftly fired him after they agreed Frusciante was the one. (Frusciante received the call, saying he was in and ran around his house literally jumping with joy and admitted to *Behind the Music* that he evidently left permanent boot marks on his walls.) He had auditioned for Thelonious Monster and was set to join but much preferred the Chili Peppers—similar to how Klinghoffer would later start in the Bicycle Thief and eventually join the Red Hot Chili Peppers.

Frusciante showed a swift growth in his early Chili Peppers days; he told *RAW* magazine that the Chili Peppers were his favorite band and originally felt like four separate people but became one eight-armed entity. On *Mother's Milk*, Frusciante largely imitated the playing of Slovak rather than play his own way. Producer Michael Beinhorn wanted a heavy metal guitar tone, forcing Frusciante to play his Les Paul and having him layer his guitar parts against his own will. At the time, the guitarist did not know much funk music beyond Slovak's playing and was taught those ways throughout his early touring with the group. When asked about it, Frusciante told *Guitar World* during the *Blood Sugar Sex Magik* era that "*Mother's Milk* doesn't represent the type of guitar player I am. I'm a bit embarrassed by the album, really. I don't even want to talk about it."

The Frusciante Style

Although considered a virtuoso, Frusciante always placed an emphasis on the song, the rhythm, the melody, and the tone rather than a true display of force.

He often shaped the sound of the band: on rejoining with *Californication*, he didn't feel adept enough to play flashy, leading to the album's minimalism. After studying vocals and harmonies, *By the Way* came out very melodic. When he wanted to display more prominent guitar work, *Stadium Arcadium* happened.

He possessed an unusual sense of rhythm, often employing polyrhythms while doing something minimal with the actual chords. The most prominent example is in "Charlie," where Frusciante plays in three as the rest of the band plays in four during each verse. On the *Stadium Arcadium* DVD and an interview with *Guitar World*, he noted that most guitarists play in rhythms that fall strictly onto a sixteenth-note grid, especially while soloing; this led him to consciously choose different rhythms in his later career and also layer lead guitar parts slightly ahead or slightly behind the beat to give his playing a more human feel.

His sense of using partially voiced chords was unusual—he often claimed strong influence from Jane's Addiction bassist Eric Avery; he admitted as much on the *Stadium Arcadium* DVD while adding that he loved the sound of two "seemingly unrelated notes" when referring to the spacing between a root and the tenth of a chord.

Two great examples of partial voicings are in "Can't Stop" in the first time through the verse riff on the studio recording, where on the third chord the D melodic note includes a third that is never played again, and throughout the verses of "If You Have to Ask," where he is playing only the top three strings on his guitar and adding subtle melodies throughout.

In the 1990s, Frusciante was practicing clarinet more than guitar and believed it shaped his taste in note choices.

Guitars

Early Days

During his first stint in the band, Frusciante played a wide array of guitars of high quality though mostly a lower quality than what he would play on rejoining the band. For electric guitar, this included a 1965 Fender Jaguar in green and a 1962 Jaguar in blue, multiple Stratocasters (including one in black, a 1968 in sunburst and a similar one also from the 1960s, and one in red), a 1986 Kramer Pacer Custom II, an Ibanez RG 250 DX, an Ibanez RG760, a 1970s Gibson Les Paul Black Beauty, a 1990s golden Gibson Les Paul classic, an early 1960s Rickenbacker 365 Deluxe, and a fretless Stratocaster as played on the bridge to "Mellowship Slinky in B Major." He told *Guitar World* in 1991 that his favorite guitar was one of the two Fender Jaguars and said that most of the basic tracks on *Blood Sugar Sex Magik* were recorded on a Stratocaster but the Jaguar came in for most of the solos and overdubs.

He used guitars and instruments that weren't his on certain songs, like an electric sitar on "Blood Sugar Sex Magik" and a Gibson lap steel for the solo on "The Righteous and the Wicked."

Acoustic Guitars

For his acoustic guitars, his first stint relied on a twelve-string Martin D12-28 as featured on "Breaking the Girl" and a Martin D-28 as played on "I Could Have Lied." When *By the Way* was being recorded, producer Rick Rubin pushed John to try things other than Martins; as such, every acoustic guitar on the album is a Taylor. They were mostly rented and may not be guitars Frusciante actually owned or owns.

Later Years

While away from the band, he sold all of his guitars to get money for drugs except for one 1962 Fender Jaguar, according to Kiedis's writing in *Scar Tissue*. During his second stint in the band, he got even high-quality and more expensive guitars, including a sunburst 1962 Stratocaster and what he thought was a 1957 Stratocaster (*Vintage Guitar* editors suggested it was actually a 1955) and a 1961 Olympic white Stratocaster that was briefly used as his primary live guitar in 2001. (Yet another Stratocaster was a 1962 in red fiesta.)

He also had a 1960s Telecaster in sunburst, used for the solos of "Scar Tissue" and much of *By the Way*, that has been sourced as both a 1963 and a 1965—but it refers to the same guitar. One of his most valuable is a 1955 Gretsch White Falcon, which Frusciante idolized from the guitarist of BowWowWow and Malcolm Young from AC/DC. A 1961 Gibson SG was never played lived but was used in the studio for a more humbucker sound, like the solo and outro of "Otherside" and the more distorted parts across *Californication*.

Also used on *Californication* was a 1956 Gibson ES-175D, primarily for the solo in "Get on Top" and across "Porcelain." He continued to purchase more Stratocasters, buying a 1961 in candy apple red and a 1963 in white shortly before *Stadium Arcadium*. He acquired another Black Beauty 1969 Gibson Les Paul Custom, this time used for "Readymade" and live playing of "Fortune Faded." He possessed a Yamaha SBG, which he used on his more recent electronic-based solo albums, and a Gibson ES-335, which he believed made him play in a style that wasn't his own, so it was rarely ever used.

Some guitars have been seen in his possession via photo shoots but were never known to have been recorded with, like his 1960s Fender Duo-Sonic, his

1960s Bartell St. George XK12, and his 1964 Fender Mustang—a guitar he considered great for practicing and playing but not recording.

Amps

Frusciante's amplifiers were always typically Marshall. With the recording of *Blood Sugar Sex Magik*, he played through Marshall cabinets but switched between a Marshall guitar head and a bass head or played through both at the same time. For a practice amp in that era, he used a Fender H.O.T. For clean sounds, he went directly into the soundboard. A 200-watt Marshall Major was his primary amp throughout his entire Chili Peppers career.

Pedals

For years, Frusciante kept his pedal board simple. On *Blood Sugar Sex Magik*, he used only an Ibanez WH10 wah pedal and an Electro-Harmonix Big Muff. On *Stadium Arcadium*, he used a Boss Chorus Ensemble, an Electro-Harmonix English Muff'n, and an Electro-Harmonix Poly Octave Generator and processed many of his guitars through modular synthesizer and keyboard equipment. He has also used Boss Distortion pedals, occasionally a DS-1 but mostly a DS-2.

The WH10 in particular is something Frusciante is known for—the original models were made out of plastic, while the reissues—something not available for most of his time in the band—are more sturdy and made of metal. Frusciante would break them regularly, with his guitar technician buying all the used WH10s he could find in southern California. According to *Guitar World*, Eddie Van Halen ended up selling his to Frusciante via the guitar technician; Van Halen gave him the advice to not tell Frusciante it was his last pedal, as Van Halen was more careful with his gear when he thought it was the very last one.

Strings

He never explained why, but he told *Guitar World* he often recorded songs with broken strings still on the guitar, though he also said the harmonized guitar sound on "The Righteous and the Wicked" came because a string broke midway through the recording and made an additional overdub necessary.

The Spiritual World

Frusciante believed that music stemmed not from consciousness but rather from subconsciousness and, literally, spirits floating around in the world around him. He talked about this at length in interviews as far back as the early 1990s—including both VPro videos he was in, the *Funky Monks* documentary, and the 1994 interview with *RAW* magazine—and as recently as 2008 in an hour-long interview about creativity.

21

Going Solo

A Look at John Frusciante's Work outside the Chili Peppers

A Marathon of Art

John Frusciante has released more albums outside of the Red Hot Chili Peppers than he did as a member of the group. Under his own name, he has released eleven solo albums and four EPs as well as two albums with Joe Lally and Josh Klinghoffer under the name Ataxia and an electronic EP under the name Trickfinger. His most recent output under his own name combined the rock guitar work of his early solo material with the programmed drum machines and beats and modular synthesizer work of his Trickfinger and his electronic career.

Starting Solo

His first solo album was *Niandra LaDes and Usually Just a T-Shirt*. The album is effectively two separate shorter albums combined: *Niandra LaDes*, where songs have complete titles, *Usually Just a T-Shirt*, where songs are referred to as their track number or T-shirt number, such as "Untitled #3" or "Usually Just a T-Shirt #3."

The first half, *Niandra LaDes*, was recorded while he was in the Red Hot Chili Peppers, concurrently with *Blood Sugar Sex Magik* and its preparation. The second half, *Usually Just a T-Shirt*, was written and recorded shortly after his leaving the band while he was beginning to get deeper into heavier drugs but not fully a heroin addict yet. He recorded material by himself throughout his early years but never thought of it until several friends—notably Flea, Johnny Depp, and Perry Farrell—encouraged him to release it to the public. Some songs are blatantly about the Chili Peppers: "Blood on My Neck from Success" is about his guilt from and dislike toward the band's situation.

Although he wasn't yet a heroin addict for much of its recording, all of the album was recorded under the influence of drugs—at a minimum, marijuana. He told *High Times* in 1995, "The whole point of recording all of this stuff was just to smoke pot and trip out. I was stoned for every single note I played on [*Niandra LaDes*]."

Due to his record contract with the Chili Peppers, he was originally unable to release any solo material unless it was through Warner Bros. records. Because of the album's unmarketability and because Frusciante was reclusive, the label gladly handed it over to Rick Rubin, who released it on his own American Recordings. The album had only one pressing on CD in November 1994 before being released again briefly in 1999; both CDs are out of print, and the album is no longer available in digital stores or on Spotify. However, a first pressing on vinyl happened in the summer of 2017. What few critics heard it were generally pleased with it; *Rolling Stone* gave it a positive review, and it was "twisted, cool stuff" but also "a mess."

The album was one of his most creative, with most of *T-Shirt*'s instrumental featuring forward and backward guitar, layered harmonies and soloing, and melodies and countermelodies interacting more than any of his material in any other group ever did. His singing is still rough, and his pain sounds completely genuine; it is often an uncomfortable listen but perhaps is his most powerful work in his solo material.

On the *Californication* tour, Frusciante often played "Usually Just a T-Shirt #3," as seen on the *Off the Map* DVD.

Deeper into Drugs

His second solo album, *Smile from the Streets You Hold*, was recorded and released exclusively to finance his drug habits. It came at the end of his drug addiction, released on August 26, 1997. Some of the music was rejected material from *Niandra LaDes*, and some of it was all new; one track, "A Fall thru the Ground," was recorded in 1988.

A prominent moment displaying Frusciante's belief in the spiritual world happened in the recording of this album. (For more information on his beliefs in the spiritual world and creativity, see chapter 20.) While recording *Smile from the Streets You Hold*, he told *Guitar Player*,

> I was having a verbal communication with the spirits . . . and I started crying at the end of it. The spirits give you ideas for things, and what's important to them is what's important to me. I'm much more concerned with my fame in their world than with my fame in this one. That's why it's been difficult for me to adjust to being alive at all.

River Phoenix, who died nearly four years before the album's release on Halloween 1993, played on two songs: "Height Down" (which is also known as "Soul Removal" when viewed as a *Niandra* B-side or bonus track) and "Well I've Been" (which similarly was formerly known as "Bought Her Soul"). It is unknown if Frusciante chose to exclude those songs from *Niandra* because of Phoenix's passing.

"More," "Estress," and "I Can't See until Your Eyes" were recorded via boom box directly to a cassette in 1996. Nowhere is Frusciante's deteriorated health more clear than on "Estress," where his voice sounds like he has smoked a lifetime of cigarettes shortly before recording. The album is well known among Frusciante fans for being removed from record stores on his rejoining of the Chili Peppers, as he was ashamed of it and uncomfortable with its being available to the public. It was never rereleased but is easily found as a download online.

Early Integration of Electronica and the Internet

The aptly titled *To Record Only Water for Ten Days* marked the beginning of Frusciante's exploration into electronica and synthesizers. It was still primarily a singer-songwriter album, but its instrumentation includes drum machines, synthesizers, guitars, and programming on almost every song. It was recorded shortly after kicking his heroin addiction and while working with the band on *Californication*.

The album was recorded not in ten days but over two months. Frusciante's distrust of digital equipment stems from the mixing of *Water*; he hated how it ended up sounding and largely blamed the digital equipment. (That viewpoint would change within the decade but lasted for years.)

That same year, Frusciante released the Internet album *From the Sounds Inside*. Available only as a free download on his website, it included many unfinished or unmixed songs. It was entirely songs that didn't make *To Record Only Water* and included no song titles; any song titles listed online were assigned by fans.

Colliding with Klinghoffer

Three years passed between *To Record Only Water for Ten Days* and Frusciante's next solo release, *Shadows Collide with People*. (It was also a busy time for the Chili Peppers as they worked on *By the Way*.) It was the first album where he spent a good amount of money to produce it, with rumors suggesting he spent

Frusciante live during the *By the Way* era.

Fabio Diena / Shutterstock.com

around $150,000 to get it made. It is the only one of his solo albums to feature Chad Smith.

More notably, *Collide* began Frusciante's collaboration with future Chili Pepper Josh Klinghoffer. Klinghoffer cowrote two songs: "Omission" and "-ooGhost27." Both Klinghoffer and Frusciante sang lead on "Omission." That same song features the two dueling on lead guitar in what is a notable high point in Frusciante's solo material. Klinghoffer and Frusciante had met when Bob Forrest's band opened for the Chili Peppers on the *Californication* tour; the two hit it off and stayed in touch, and Klinghoffer became his most frequent collaborator beginning with this album.

Six (or More) Recordings in Six Months

Frusciante recorded six different musical workings in six months, which were mostly released in 2004: *The Will to Death* on June 22, *DC EP* on September 14, *Inside of Emptiness* on October 26, and *A Sphere in the Heart of Silence* on November 23. Another was released under a different band name: *Automatic Writing*, under Ataxia, a group that had Josh Klinghoffer on drums, Frusciante on guitar and vocals, and Fugazi bassist Joe Lally on bass guitar. (*Automatic Writing* was the first half of a single recording session; the second half was released on May 29, 2007, as *AW II* but came from the same sessions.)

Ataxia wasn't the only release that featured Klinghoffer: *A Sphere in the Heart of Silence* is credited to both of the guitarists. It is mostly electronic music, marking Klinghoffer's deepest foray outside of the rock realm thus far. This familiarity with Klinghoffer made him the first choice for the band's touring keyboardist on the *Stadium Arcadium* tour, where he also provided harmony guitars on "Dani California."

The sixth recording from that period was *Curtains*, the most straightforward of all of the releases from the six months. The *DC EP* is titled as such because it was recorded quickly in Washington, D.C., and produced by Minor Threat and Fugazi's Ian MacKaye. The guitar tracks from *DC* were done through Fugazi guitarist Guy Picciotto's Marshall JCM 800, famous to Fugazi fans for appearing on the cover of *Red Medicine*. (Frusciante loved Fugazi, having appeared in a *Blood Sugar Sex Magik*–era promo photo with a bootleg Fugazi shirt on and doing lead vocals and guitar with the Chili Peppers when they covered *Red Medicine*'s "Latest Disgrace" as an intro for "Parallel Universe" on the *Live at Slane Castle* DVD.)

In 2004, in the midst of his sprint of recordings, Frusciante also contributed five songs to the sound track of the independent film *The Brown Bunny*.

This period of solo work enabled Frusciante's creativity when it came time to record the next Red Hot Chili Peppers. He told *Guitar World* in 2006 that "the experience and freedom of doing my solo records gave me the ability to approach [*Stadium Arcadium*] with an experimental outlook."

The Empyrean

The Empyrean was John Frusciante's last solo release while still a Red Hot Chili Pepper. It came while the band was on hiatus after *Stadium Arcadium* but still features Flea on bass guitar on several songs as well as his then future replacement Josh Klinghoffer. The Sonus Quartet played strings on the album, while the Smiths and former Modest Mouse guitarist Johnny Marr played guitar on several songs.

The opening song, "Before the Beginning," was Frusciante's interpretation of "Maggot Brain" by Funkadelic; it was the same chord progression and harmonic rhythm and opening melodic lick but doesn't feature its two lines of lyrics. Funkadelic was not credited. The album artwork was a reference to the tree of life.

The Japanese release of *The Empyrean* features two extra songs: "Today" and "Ah Yom."

Solo Work after the Red Hot Chili Peppers

The last recorded work Frusciante did as a member of the Red Hot Chili Peppers was when the group contributed to George Clinton's cover album *George Clinton and His Gangsters of Love,* where the band did the music to his cover of "Let the Good Times Roll." Since leaving the rock quartet, Frusciante has released two albums, a compilation, and three EPs under his own name: 2012's *Letur-Lefr* EP and *PBX Funicular Intaglio Zone,* 2013's *Outsides* EP, 2014's *Enclosure,* and 2015's *Renoise Tracks 2009–2011* collection. This is on top of his three releases under the Trickfinger name: 2012's *Sect in Sgt,* 2015's *Trickfinger,* and 2017's *Trickfinger II.*

His Trickfinger material is all acid house music; the albums were all originals, while the two-song EP of *Sect in Sgt* is mostly sampled music reworked. The material under his actual name shows the influence of synthesizers, electronica, and acid house but still prominently features his guitar play and has some sense of rock music—particularly the *Renoise Tracks* compilation. Critics panned all of these works, going especially hard on the first few releases after leaving the group; Pitchfork said about *Trickfinger* that it had "flatulent bass runs" and that there was "not much more of interest going on than capable pastiche."

Work with Omar

Frusciante was fast friends with Omar Rodriguez-Lopez from At the Drive-In and the Mars Volta. When Rodriguez moved behind the board to produce the Mars Volta, his choice for a guitarist to simply play the parts was Frusciante; Frusciante played guitar on 2006's *Amputechture* (except for the acoustic Latin guitar on "Asilos Magdalena"), 2008's *The Bedlam in Goliath*, and 2009's *Octahedron*. He also took the first two guitar solos on *Frances the Mute*'s "L'Via L'Viaquez" and did additional guitar and synthesizer on *De-loused in the Comatorium*'s "Cicatriz ESP." (Flea played bass guitar on all except one song on *De-loused*.)

Frusciante has appeared on six Omar Rodriguez-Lopez solo records, some of which were unspecific recordings that were scrapped Mars Volta opuses. These albums are 2004's *A Manual Dexterity: Soundtrack Volume One*, 2007's *Se Dice Bisonte, No Búfalo* and *Calibration (Is Pushing Luck and Key Too Far)*, 2010's *Omar Rodriguez Lopez & John Frusciante* and *Sepulcros de Miel*, and 2016's *Arañas en la Sombra*. *Omar Rodriguez Lopez & John Frusciante* is credited to both John Frusciante and Omar Rodriguez-Lopez; it is unknown why the hyphen is included in Rodriguez-Lopez's name but not the album title.

Work with Other Groups

Frusciante was part of the short-lived Speed Dealer Moms, who released their self-titled album in 2010. The band consisted of Frusciante, Venetian Snares' Aaron Funk, and Chris McDonald of the Alison Project. It is similar to Frusciante's late solo material in that it has elements of rock music, but the creativity in the programmed beats is the main focus.

Frusciante's ex-wife Nicole Turley was a member of the band Swahili Blonde. He contributed to two of their albums: guitar and backing vocals on "Red Money," a David Bowie cover on *Man Meat*, and guitar work across *Psycho Tropical Ballet Pink*. "Red Money" also appeared on their *Covers* EP.

Swahili Blonde, Bosnian Rainbows, and Dante Vs Zombies collaborated on an odd supergroup called Kimono Kult that Frusciante was briefly a part of, playing guitar on two tracks from their release *Hiding in the Light*: "La Vida Es Una Caja Hermosa" and "La Cancion De Alejandra."

His only true foray into hip-hop was as a producer for the Wu-Tang Clan affiliate Black Knights; he produced 2014's *Medieval Chamber*, 2015's *The Almighty*, and 2017's *Excalibur*. The Wu-Tang Clan featured Frusciante on lead guitar on "The Heart Gently Weeps," where George Harrison's son Dhani played the chord progression to "While My Guitar Gently Weeps" and Erykah Badu sang. It wasn't Frusciante's first time working with Erykah Badu; Macy Gray's

"Sweet Baby" had Badu on vocals and Frusciante on vocals as well. Wu-Tang's RZA had Frusciante on guitar for "You Can't Stop Me Now" and "Up Again" from 2008's *Digi Snacks*; on the former, he also received a production credit. RZA and Frusciante would work again on N.A.S.A.'s "Way Down."

His first work as a studio musician was guitar on "Slave to My Emotions" by Kristen Vigard, where he also received a songwriting credit. Both he and Flea played on *Give Peace a Chance*, a compilation that Lenny Kravitz organized. The two, along with Jane's Addiction's Stephen Perkins, were known as the Three Amoebas; recordings existed of the group, but Frusciante lost them in a fire. That collaboration led to Frusciante's appearance in Perkins's jam band Banyan and their album *Anytime at All*. Perkins later played drums on Perry Farrell's *Rev*, where Frusciante and Rage Against the Machine's Tom Morello shared guitar duties on the new material.

After befriending them when they opened for the Chili Peppers, Frusciante recorded with Bob Forrest's band, the Bicycle Thief, on 1999's *You Come and Go Like a Pop Song*—his first recorded appearance with Josh Klinghoffer.

The instrumentalists to the Chili Peppers appeared on a cover of the Temptations' "Shakey Ground" for a Fishbone compilation in 2000. When Flea laid down bass lines for Tricky, Frusciante played guitar; the two had separate studio careers but often would get calls for both. The Red Hot Chili Peppers did a cover of "Havana Affair" for *By the Way* that ended up on *We're a Happy Family: A Tribute to the Ramones*; Frusciante contributed a cover of "Today Your Love, Tomorrow the World." Frusciante played on Ziggy Marley's "Rainbow in the Sky" that same year (2003) and did guitar work on the *Underworld* sound track.

Two covers Johnny Cash did on *American IV: The Man Comes Around* featured Frusciante: "Personal Jesus," originally by Depeche Mode, and the standard "We'll Meet Again," written by Ross Parker and Hughie Charles. (Chad Smith and Flea also played instruments for Cash's cover of Neil Young's "Heart of Gold.") When Depeche Mode's Dave Gahan did a solo album in 2007, Frusciante played guitar on "Saw Something."

When Chad Smith produced for Glenn Hughes starting with 2006's *Music for the Divine*, Frusciante contributed guitar and backing vocals on "Nights in White Satin." (Dave Navarro also played guitar on that album.)

His most mainstream appearance after leaving the Red Hot Chili Peppers was either playing guitar on Duran Duran's *Paper Gods* on four songs or playing mellotron on "Billie Holiday" by Warpaint; fittingly, this came at the time Klinghoffer played drums for them. After that, he has done guitar on six songs by Nicole Turley, guitar on BIG DOXX's "Indigenous Rhythm," piano on Amanda Jo Williams's *You're the Father of My Songs*, and guitar and synthesizer bass on "My Half" by Le Butcherettes and assisted with *The Album* by AcHoZeN.

John Frusciante's Complete Performance Discography

All contributions are guitar unless otherwise noted.

Red Hot Chili Peppers—*Mother's Milk* (1989)—guitars, vocals on "Knock Me Down," backing vocals

Kristen Vigard—"Slave to My Emotions" (1990)

Nina Hagan—*Divine Love, Sex, and Romance* (1991)

Peace Choir—*Give Peace a Chance* (1991)

Red Hot Chili Peppers—*Blood Sugar Sex Magik* (1991)—guitar, backing vocals, synthesizer on "If You Have to Ask," percussion on "Breaking the Girl"

John Frusciante—*Niandra Lades and Usually Just a T-Shirt* (1994)—vocals, guitar, bass, piano, banjo, clarinet

John Frusciante—*Estrus* (1997)—guitar, vocals, bass

John Frusciante—*Smile from the Streets You Hold* (1997)—vocals, guitar, piano, bass

Banyan—"Grease the System," "La Sirena" (1999)

The Bicycle Thief—"Cereal Song" (1999)

Perry Farrell—"Rev" (1999)

Red Hot Chili Peppers—*Californication* (1999)—guitar, backing vocals, keyboards

Fishbone—"Shakey Ground" (2000)

John Frusciante—*To Record Only Water for Ten Days* (2001)—vocals, guitar, synthesizer, drum machine

John Frusciante—*From the Sounds Inside* (2001)—vocals, guitar, synthesizer, drum machine

John Frusciante—*Going Inside* (2001)—vocals, guitar, synthesizer, drum machine

New Order featuring Moby and Billy Corgan—"New Dawn Fades" (2001)

Tricky—"Girls," "#1 Da Woman" (2001)—vocals, guitar

Macy Gray—"Sweet Baby" (2001)

Johnny Cash—"Personal Jesus," "We'll Meet Again" (2002)

Red Hot Chili Peppers—*By the Way* (2002)—guitar, backing vocals, piano, modular synthesizer, one line of bass guitar on "Don't Forget Me"

David Bowie featuring Maynard James Keennan—"Bring me the Disco King" (2003)

The Mars Volta—"Cicatriz ESP" (2003)—guitar, synthesizer

Ziggy Marley—"Rainbow in the Sky" (2003)

Red Hot Chili Peppers—*Greatest Hits* (2003)—guitar, vocals

Red Hot Chili Peppers—"Havana Affair" (2003)

Ataxia—*Automatic Writing* (2004)—guitar, vocals

The Brown Bunny Motion Picture Soundtrack (2004)—vocals, guitar, bass, piano

Ekkehard Ehlers—"Grisaisse 1" (2004)

John Frusciante—*DC EP* (2004)—vocals, guitar, bass

John Frusciante—*Shadows Collide with People* (2004)—vocals, guitar, synthesizers, bass, piano, mellotron

John Frusciante—*The Will to Death* (2004)—vocals, guitar, piano, synthesizer, bass

John Frusciante—*Inside of Emptiness* (2004)—vocals, synthesizer, guitar, keyboard, bass, sound design

John Frusciante and Josh Klinghoffer—*A Sphere in the Heart of Silence* (2004)—programming, white noise, guitar, vocals, synthetic strings, drum treatments, synthesizer, bass, piano, sound design

Red Hot Chili Peppers—*Live in Hyde Park* (2004)—guitar, vocals

Omar Rodriguez-Lopez—*A Manual Dexterity: Soundtrack Volume One* (2004)—Minimoog, Doepfer A-100

John Frusciante—*Curtains* (2005)—vocals, guitar, bass, melodica, piano, string ensemble, mellotron, synthesizer, treatments

The Mars Volta—"L'Via L'Viaquez" (2005)

Bob Forrest—"Dying Song" (2006)—guitar, vocals

Glenn Hughes—"Nights in White Satin," "This Is How I Feel" (2006)—guitars, vocals

The Mars Volta—*Amputechture* (2006)

Red Hot Chili Peppers—*Stadium Arcadium* (2006)—guitar, backing vocals, keyboards, synthesizer, mellotron, mixing

Ataxia—*AW II* (2007)—guitar, vocals

Dave Gahan—"Saw Something" (2007)

Omar Rodriguez-Lopez—"If Gravity Lulls, I Can Hear the World Pant" (2007)

Omar Rodriguez-Lopez—"Glosa Picaresca Wou Men" (2007)—vocals, lyrics

Satellite Party—"Hard Life Easy" (2007)

Wu-Tang Clan—"The Hart Gently Weeps" (2007)

George Clinton and His Gangsters of Love—"Let the Good Times Roll" featuring the Red Hot Chili Peppers and Kim Manning (2008)

The Mars Volta—*The Bedlam in Goliath* (2008)

RZA—"Up Again," "You Can't Stop Me Now" (2008)—guitar, production

John Frusciante—*The Empyrean* (2009)—vocals, guitar, keyboards, piano, Bass VI, drum machine

The Mars Volta—*Octahedron* (2009)

Warpaint—"Billie Holiday" (2009)—mellotron

Omar Rodriguez-Lopez and John Frusciante—*Omar Rodriguez Lopez & John Frusciante* (2010)—guitar, bass, synthesizer

Omar Rodriguez-Lopez—*Speulcros de Miel* (2010)

Speed Dealer Moms—*Speed Dealer Moms EP* (2010)—creative, drum programming, synthesizers

Swahili Blonde—"Red Money" (2010)—guitar, vocals

Swahili Blonde—*Psycho Tropical Ballet Pink* (2011)

John Frusciante—*Letur-Lefr* (2012)—vocals, synthesizers, guitar, samples, drum machine

John Frusciante—*PBX Funicular Intaglio Zone* (2012)—vocals, synthesizers, guitar, bass, keyboards, samples, drum machine

Nicole Turley—"I Wanta Go," "The Golden Corale," "Indigenous Rhythm" (2012)

Trickfinger—*Sect in Sgt* (2012)—all instruments

John Frusciante—*Outsides EP* (2013)—guitar, vocals, keyboards, synthesizers, drum machine, sequencer, samples

John Frusciante—"Wayne" (2013)

Amanda Jo Williams—*You're the Father of My Songs* (2013)—piano, organ

Nicole Turley—"H (heart) G" (2013)

Black Knights—*Medieval Chamber* (2014)—producer

John Frusciante—*Enclosure* (2014)—guitar, bass, vocals, keyboards, synthesizers, drum machine, sequencer, samples

Kimono Kult—*Hiding in the Light* (2014)

Sexual Castle—"Flip the Scrip" (2014)

Black Knights—*The Almighty* (2015)—producer

Duran Duran—*Paper Gods* (2015)—"What Are the Chances?," "Butterfly Girl," "The Universe Alone," "Northern Lights"

John Frusciante—*4-Track Guitar Music* (2015)—guitar, bass, vocals, keyboards, synthesizers, drum machine, sequencer, samples

Le Butcherettes—"My Half" (2015)—guitar, synthesizer bass

John Frusciante—"Fight for Love" (2015)—guitar, drum machine

John Frusciante—"Medre" (2015)

John Frusciante—*Renoise Tracks 2009–2011* (2015)—guitar, bass, vocals, keyboards, synthesizers, drum machine, sequencer, samples

Trickfinger—*Trickfinger* (2015)—all instruments

John Frusciante—*Foregrow* (2016)—Roland TB-303 and MC-202, Yamaha DX7 synthesizer, Electro-Harmonix Microsynthesizer, Elektron Monomachine, MIDI guitar, samples, vocals

Omar Rodriguez-Lopez—*Aranas en la Sombra* (2016)

Black Knights—*Excalibur* (2017)—producer

Trickfinger—*Trickfinger II* (2017)—all instruments

22

Nothing's Shocking

Dave Navarro's Guitar Style

Freak Off a Leash

Dave Navarro was born David Michael Navarro on June 7, 1967. He attended Notre Dame High School in Sherman Oaks, California, where he was a member of marching band and close friend with future Jane's Addiction drummer Stephen Perkins. The two would discuss music as friends and grew as musicians together, similar to how Slovak, Irons, and Flea did at Fairfax High. In March 1983, Navarro's mother was murdered by her ex-boyfriend; the case was featured on *America's Most Wanted*. Navarro later made a documentary about this named *Mourning Son*. The incident gave him a dark worldview, pushing him into drugs and into music.

Navarro took guitar lessons for less than a year before he (and his family) felt he had become a better player than his teacher.

First Developments

Navarro's first primary influence—similar to Flea and John Frusciante—was Jimi Hendrix, saying on his instructional video that he heard a song at the age of seven at a skate park and found it impossible to believe that all those sounds came out of one guitar. He was heavily into rock music as a preteen and early teen but abandoned listening it very early on. He loved Cream, Led Zeppelin, Grateful Dead, Pink Floyd, and Van Halen and knew most of their songs and would bust them out on request from friends—including Van Halen's "Eruption" in an era where it was considered the most difficult guitar performance—proving himself to be a showman at an early age. By age sixteen, all he listened to were classical music and talk radio. Despite that, he still played rock music and was the guitarist for the metal band Dizastre with future Jane's drummer Stephen Perkins.

Navarro played in jazz band and could sight-read music fairly well. "Thank You Boys" from *Nothing's Shocking* was designed to be something the band did while Jane's vocalist Perry Farrell briefly left the stage to put on his guitar; Perkins pulled a jazz sheet at random, and he, Navarro, and bassist Eric Avery played it. When Farrell strolled back in, he would say, "Thank you, boys!" and that was the song every night.

Later Influences

While Navarro was a classical music fan from a young age, he started piano lessons only in the 1990s. He was able to play two- and three-part inventions by Bach and Claude Debussy's "Clair de Lune" with proficiency. He struggled to read on piano but had a fine number of chops.

Definitive Synesthesia

Navarro has had synesthesia—the condition where he sees colors when he hears music—his whole life. It has greatly shaped his taste in music and can be used to explain his decision making in the Red Hot Chili Peppers. If he couldn't see colors as he made music, he wouldn't get into it. He admired John Frusciante's and Hillel Slovak's playing from a musical perspective, but the style of percussive guitar and funk they often played didn't activate his synesthesia, and as such, he didn't pursue their style very much even as he got more into funk music. He told *Guitar Player*,

> I see music when I hear it. When I don't see colors, I'm not into the music. A lot of bands that people really like, I don't, because I don't get the colourful vibe from them. Even old Chili Peppers—I truly respect Hillel, and John is one of the greatest guitar players around. His ideas, technique, and talent are incredible. But even though I'm blown away by him, I don't really enjoy music like that from a listening standpoint. It's too dry and percussive, as opposed to the saturated and warm sounds I like.

At age twenty-seven, Navarro named his favorite guitarists to *Guitar World* and *Guitar Player* as Daniel Ash from Bauhaus and Love & Rockets and Robert Smith from the Cure. He also added he found AC/DC boring. He said to both magazines multiple times that Perry Farrell ended up being one of his largest influences.

Navarro's Style

In Jane's Addiction, Navarro often shadows Avery's simple but melodic bass parts, playing octaves or power chords over them, such as in "Mountain Song." He would expand and go wild with Perkins as Avery held down the groove very simply and tightly on bass. He used unusual voicings and chord extensions for rock music to give an otherwise simple chord progression a different feel. His three favorite songs to play with Jane's were "Three Days," "And Then She Did," and "Ted, Just Admit It"; he consciously let the sound of those three in particular and their wandering, spacey, and ambitious qualities guide his guitar choices in the Chili Peppers.

Once in the Red Hot Chili Peppers, he used more overdubs than before. Virtually every song on *One Hot Minute* features two or more guitar tracks, which is why the Red Hot Chili Peppers had a second guitarist for the *One Hot Minute* tour. Navarro felt uneasy when joining the Red Hot Chili Peppers—not just because of how different of a guitarist he was than the man he replaced, John Frusciante, but also because he had never so much as owned a record from the Red Hot Chili Peppers before. Navarro and Flea struggled to gel musically until they stopped trying to meet each other in the middle and decided to go for something other than the old Chili Pepper sound.

Navarro and drummer Chad Smith became close during their time together in the Red Hot Chili Peppers, even doing a one-off side project as a duo, Honeymoon Lords, where they released one song—a cover of Joy Division's "Day of the Lords."

Throughout both bands, Navarro played very atmospherically. On a *One Hot Minute* song, Navarro slapped the back of his guitar neck to make the strings and feedback ring out, then shaped the sounds further with his wah pedal.

Beginning with *Nothing's Shocking*, Navarro intentionally tried to mix 1980s post-punk texture and atmosphere with 1970s rock bravado.

No Funk

Many Chili Peppers fans took issue with Navarro's aversion to funk. Navarro himself wasn't shameful about this; in a 1995 interview with *Guitar*, he said, "I'm not a funk guitarist and I don't like funk. It makes me feel dumb and I can't relate to music that makes me feel dumb." He added he liked everyone in the Red Hot Chili Peppers and liked being in the band, so he would play funkier when it was absolutely called for.

A Frusciante–Navarro Collaboration?

While in the Red Hot Chili Peppers, Navarro wanted to make a collaboration album with John Frusciante. Navarro bought a home close enough that he could see Frusciante's home from his window; Navarro wanted both of them to put their guitar amps on top of their homes, record them to digital audiotape, jam, and make a record that way. It was never attempted, but Navarro spoke about it to both *Guitar Player* and *Guitar World*.

One Cold Minute

While Josh Klinghoffer loved *One Hot Minute* and John Frusciante never gave it a full listen (for more details, see chapter 1), Navarro himself loved most of the album but hated a few songs on it. He specifically told *Guitar World* that "Tearjerker," "Walkabout," and "One Big Mob" were songs he would probably skip, depending on his mood, if he listened to it on a CD.

Guitars

The guitarist used many different guitars, going for his own sound most of the time but imitating previous guitarists' choices when playing older Chili Peppers songs in the band. Obviously, he most often played Fender Custom Shop Stratocasters when playing songs from *Blood Sugar Sex Magik*—he eventually commented that "Suck My Kiss" was his favorite Chili Pepper song to play live—and a Stratocaster-like guitar made by Modulus for some other songs. He played a Parker Fly Deluxe during live versions of "My Friends," as he believed its piezo-electric pickups were the closest an electric guitar could come to sounding like an acoustic guitar when playing venues of that size.

During the early days of Jane's Addiction, Navaro played a Black Beauty Gibson Les Paul. By 1988, his primary instruments were Ibanez RG guitars; one had a custom paint job of the *Nothing's Shocking* album artwork as seen in the music video for "Stop" and the film *Gift*. During the tour that followed, he switched to a single-cutaway gold Ibanez before switching to PRS guitars during the first Lollapalooza. PRS has since introduced a signature Dave Navarro model with a custom twenty-four-fret neck and a Brazilian rosewood fret board, mother-of-pearl bird inlays, a tremolo, gold hardware, and a carved maple top with a mahogany back. Since its release, that has been Navarro's primary instrument.

He has used a custom white Ibanez RG modeled after his signature PRS since 2008, but it has been his backup instrument. He also played a Kramer Van Halen signature, a Fender Telecaster, a Takamine twelve-string acoustic, and

Navarro never became a huge fan of playing Stratocasters.   *txking / Shutterstock.com*

a Squier Hello Kitty Stratocaster given to him by his ex-wife Carmen Electra, though none of them have appeared live or in studio with regularity.

Amps

Throughout his time in the first iteration of Jane's Addiction, Navarro's amp was a Marshall JCM800. He has since switched over to two Marshall JCM900s that he has dubbed "Tangerine" and "Peach" and that he plays out of two four-by-twelve straight cabinets and a Marshall Mode 4 for clean tones. In studio, he has sometimes used a Vox AC30 for clean sounds and a Bogner Uberschall for grittier ones.

Strings

Navarro has played Dean Markley .009 for years but was never very picky with strings. Markley merely was the first company to send Navarro free strings, so he kept using them. The only tunings Navarro played in with Jane's or the Chili Peppers are standard, drop D, or standard with the high E tuned to D-sharp for "Power of Equality."

Navarro stopped paying attention to his strings and setups once he got a guitar technician. He has often lied and joked with people about his gear specifications because he finds it largely unimportant compared to the notes and the guitarists themselves.

Pedals

Navarro has been an endorsed artist from Boss and has appeared in many of their print advertisements. From Boss, he has used an OC-2 octave pedal, two DD-3 digital delays, a BF-2 turbo flanger, an NS-2 noise suppressor, a CH-1 Super Chorus, a PSM-5 Power Supply and Master Switch, a TU-12 tuner, and an OD-2 Turbo Overdrive. Additionally, outside of Boss, he used a Dunlop Jimi Hendrix Cry Baby pedal for wah sounds.

He sometimes used an E-Bow, an electronic device meant to make a guitar sound like it's being bowed like a violin or cello. The best example with the Red Hot Chili Peppers is in the solo to "Falling into Grace," though he used it again for the middle part of "One Big Mob." He used a Heil Talk Box on "Falling into Grace" and hasn't used it much since.

Dave Navarro's Complete Performance Discography

All contributions are guitar unless otherwise noted.

Jane's Addiction—*Jane's Addiction* (1987)
Jane's Addiction—*Nothing's Shocking* (1988)
Jane's Addiction—*Ritual de lo Habitual* (1990)
Deconstruction—*Deconstruction* (1994)

Honeymoon Stitch—"Day of the Lords" (1995)—vocals, guitar, bass

Janet Jackson—"What'll I Do (Dave Navarro Remix)" (1995)

Alanis Morissette—"You Oughta Know" (1995)

Dave Navarro—*Rhimorse* (1995)—guitars, vocals, bass, songwriting

Nine Inch Nails—*Further Down the Spiral*—"Piggy (Nothing Can Stop Me Now)" (1995)

Red Hot Chili Peppers—*One Hot Minute* (1995)

Red Hot Chili Peppers—"I Found Out" (1995)

Red Hot Chili Peppers—"Love Rollercoaster" (1996)

Red Hot Chili Peppers—"Melancholy Mechanics" (1996)

Ugly Meets the People Soundtrack (1996)—score, guitar with Chad Smith

Jane's Addiction—*Kettle Whistle* (1997)

Marilyn Manson—"I Don't Like the Drugs (But the Drugs Like Me)"

Guns N' Roses—"Oh My God" (1999)

P. Diddy—"Bad Boy for Life" (2001)

Perry Farrell—"Song Yet to Be Sung" (2001)—guitars and percussion

Dave Navarro—*Trust No One* (2001)—guitars, vocals, bass, songwriting

Christina Aguilera—"Fighter" (2002)

Jane's Addiction—*Strays* (2003)

Gene Simmons—"Firestarter" (2004)

Glenn Hughes—*Soul Mover* (2005)

Tommy Lee—"Tired" (2005)

Dead Celebrity Status—"We Fall, We Fall" (2006)

Jane's Addiction—*Up from the Catacombs—The Best of* (2006)

The Panic Channel—*(One)* (2006)

Jane's Addiction—*A Cabinet of Curiosities* (2009)

Jane's Addiction—*The Great Escape Artist* (2011)

Nine Inch Nails—"Burning Bright (Field on Fire)" (2016)

23

The Rhythm Method

Chad Smith's Drumming

The Drum Machine

Chad Smith began playing drums at the age of seven but never took any drum lessons. He practiced on his drum kit by playing along to music with headphones on and gained non-rock experience by playing in every single band at school: marching band, jazz band, symphonic band, and concert band. He became adept at reading sheet music by the time high school was over.

His first experience on drums was picking up a pair of Lincoln Logs, setting up ice cream cartons stolen from a Baskin-Robbins by his father, and playing along as if they were actual drums. When he continued to do this, he moved on to a cheap set from K-Mart with terrible cymbals.

Early Influences

As a teenager growing up in Michigan, Smith listened to classic rock bands like Led Zeppelin and the Doors, punk like Iggy Pop and the Stooges and MC5, and funk and soul like the output of Funkadelic and what came from Motown.

His father raised him on country music; his first response was to rebel against it, playing KISS, Alice Cooper, Black Sabbath, and other hard rock, but he became an adept drummer for country music, though he could not play it as good musicians who truly loved country.

Although he loved many varieties of music, his first three drum heroes were John Bonham from Led Zeppelin, Mitch Mitchell from the Jimi Hendrix Experience, and Keith Moon from the Who.

Later Influences

Smith left school and began a life as a full-time musician without touring; he earned roughly $150 a week playing six out of every seven nights in more than

A poster sold at malls across America circa the *By the Way* era.   *Author's collection*

one group. One of these groups, a funk band named Pharaoh, included Larry Fratangelo, a former member of both Parliament and Funkadelic. Fratangelo taught him about the proper way to perform ghost notes on snare and how much playing was too much and how much was just the right amount. Smith credited Fratangelo with proper dynamics and song structure. Fratangelo used "What Is Hip?" by Tower of Power as a peak example of a drummer listening to the rest of the band to add an extra something to a song.

Fratangelo has since toured with Kid Rock—which is how Smith ended up playing on one of Kid Rock's records.

Joining the Red Hot Chili Peppers

In 1988, Smith auditioned for the Red Hot Chili Peppers and was the last drummer scheduled to audition. The rest of the band was tired, with Flea later insisting that none of the other drummers were able to keep up with him, and was expecting another disappointment from Smith, who looked more like a hair metal fan than a Chili Pepper.

Smith later admitted that he wasn't a knowledgeable fan of the band going in. He had heard that they were cool and that they rocked out hard from fans who were Smith's friends. Once he went into the audition and jammed, he loved it:

> Flea and I were just screaming at each other—"Come on, man! Fucking come on!" We just jammed, and Anthony was laughing hysterically. We hit it off musically, definitely, right off the bat, and everyone was really excited.

Smith later told a radio interviewer that John Frusciante broke a guitar string during that first jam and that he had never seen anyone change strings so fast to get back to playing. John Frusciante conceded that he was never so excited to get back to playing music. The video of the interview was posted on YouTube.

Style

Smith openly talked about how his style changed within the Red Hot Chili Peppers. He believed that as musicians gain more experience, their taste is refined and their confidence level goes up, and as they play with each other, their chemistry improves.

He often syncopated single kick notes while doing a constant stream of quarter or eighth notes on the hi-hats or ride. Smith gained this ability by playing straight four on the hi-hat and doing triplets with his kick or vice versa.

He was not known to play polyrhythms often but has found ways to make the other members' polyrhythms seem normal, like in "Charlie" on *Stadium Arcadium*. He changed the accents on the hi-hats to emphasize (or deemphasize) Frusciante's off-tilt guitar work. Similarly, Smith would flip his groove around on songs where Flea or Frusciante repeated a riff; a good example of this is in "Readymade," where the otherwise repetitive verses were made fresh by Smith's ability to split it into two different feels.

With regard to his snare drum ghost notes, he believed that opening up the possibilities with them came from practicing more than one way to do them. When he would see a large space between snare hits, unless it required emptiness, he intuitively tried to fill them with snare ghost notes. In contrast to his ghost notes, he was always known for hitting hard but with a certain amount of delicacy, once being compared to a chef who slaved over every meal as if it were a masterpiece.

Smith did not play with a click track in the Red Hot Chili Peppers. To make sure he used the right tempo, he recorded with a guiding vocal track; often, all the instruments were recorded live together, so members slowed and sped up together. (The recording of a guide vocal track for "Sir Psycho Sexy" can be watched on *Funky Monks*; he talked about the inconsistency of the tempo on "Mellowship Slinky in B Major" to *Modern Drummer* in 1994.) He would rarely count along for recording; he has used counting when he has to but has often found that even (or especially) in tougher time signatures, relying on the natural feel has made it easier, while counting made it harder.

Before *The Getaway*, Smith recorded all his tracks playing along to another member, even if it was just the guide vocal. *The Getaway* was recorded with drums alone, then bass alone, then guitar, and then vocals and overdubs.

Performing Outside of the Red Hot Chili Peppers

Longtime Red Hot Chili Peppers producer Rick Rubin favored Smith as a drummer and for a few years used him as a go-to session drummer when the Peppers were not playing. This led to an on-record appearance with the Dixie Chicks, while his known love of 1980s metal music led to the Chickenfoot project with ex–Van Halen bassist Michael Anthony and famed shred guitar virtuoso Joe Satriani. (Satriani would continue to work with Smith, later doing his 2018 solo album *What Happens Next* as a creative collaboration with Smith and Glenn Hughes.)

He became former Deep Purple bassist Glenn Hughes's go-to drummer almost instantly after they worked together. The two became so comfortable that Smith's instrumental jam band where he is the leader, Chad Smith's Bombastic Meatbats, is almost exclusively the other band members from Hughes's band. Smith and Hughes were so close that when Smith's son was born, Hughes became his godfather. Hughes once wrote and published an eight-point list on why a producer should hire Smith in *Drum! Magazine*, where he said that Smith was both "the greatest all-around drummer" and his "closest friend."

Smith told *Rhythm* that his best performance was the one he did with Wu-Tang Clan, a remix of "Wu-Tang Clan Ain't Nuthin ta Fuck Wit," featuring him and Tom Morello. His reasoning was that every time he has ever listened to it, he has felt good and felt the drums were good.

Top Chili Pepper Performances

In 1999 in *Modern Drummer*, Smith picked his own top performances as "Give It Away" because the drums control the track, "Sir Psycho Sexy" for its slow but deep funk, "They're Red Hot" for his fast and sloppy-but-fun playing—which was done entirely by hand without drum sticks—and "Higher Ground" because it took Smith the longest to get the correct feel for, with more than one day dedicated just to tracking the drums. *Blood Sugar Sex Magik* was recorded with only four drum microphones—one on the kick, one on the snare, and two overheads placed in different spots in the room. (*Stadium Arcadium* was recorded the same way.)

In terms of technical difficulty, "The Greeting Song" is arguably the hardest Smith song to perform as played. Smith displayed its subtle difficulties in his DVD *Red Hot Rhythms*: at various points in the song, Smith locks the kick drum (played via single pedal) in with every single note Flea is playing on bass, all while keeping a steady groove.

Drums, Heads, and Setup

Smith has exclusively played a single pedal on the kick drum within the Red Hot Chili Peppers, though he briefly had two kick drums (and two separate kick pedals). He explained to *Modern Drummer* that if he had a double-pedal setup, he feared that he would end up overplaying.

In the 1990s, Smith got his signature bass drum sound via muting it from the inside with a U-Haul packing blanket. Live, he put an impact pad on it but tuned the head so it was very loose. By 2012, he used Remo drumheads and tuned them in a standard way, with the batter side tuned tighter than the crowd side and his snares tuned very tightly.

His setup constantly evolved. For the *Blood Sugar Sex Magik* tour, he used a setup with one snare drum, one kick drum, two mounted toms, and two floor toms. He kept that for *One Hot Minute* and its tour but at various points added the second bass drum that still played single pedal. For *Californication* and its tour, he stuck with one kick drum, one snare drum, one rack tom, and two floor toms—but also simplified it so that his cymbal setup was just his hi-hats, a ride, and a crash for a short while before expanding it to include a full four toms—a ten-inch mounted tom, a twelve-inch mounted tom, a fourteen-inch floor tom, a sixteen-inch floor tom, a twenty-four-inch bass drum, and his signature snare drum. With *Stadium Arcadium*, he went back to one mounted tom—just the twelve-inch—and the two floor toms.

He began to be sponsored by Pearl drums in 1989. For *I'm with You*, he received a custom acrylic drum kit from them with artwork designed by Damien

Hirst in the style of the album cover. On *The Getaway*, he switched away from Pearl—not because he didn't like them but because he felt that if he didn't make a change, he would never have made a change—and had a twenty-four-inch bass drum, a fourteen- by six-and-a-half-inch steel snare, a fourteen- by five-and-a-half-inch auxiliary snare, a ten-inch Remo roto tom, six-inch octobans, a twelve-inch mounted tom, a fourteen-inch floor tom, a sixteen-inch floor tom, and a twenty-nine-inch timpani.

Cymbals

Smith has been a sponsored drummer of Sabian's for decades, primarily playing on AAX cymbals and even getting his own signature line of China cymbals in the late 2000s. In the *Californication* era, after briefly using only a crash, a ride, and hi-hats, he played Sabian fourteen-inch AA Fusion hi-hats, a six-inch cymbal disc, an eight-inch cymbal disc, a ten-inch AAX splash, a twenty-one-inch AA rock ride, a (no longer in production) twenty-and-a-half-inch Chad Smith signature Explosion crash, a fourteen-inch AAX mini China, a nineteen-inch AA China, and a twelve-inch Jack DeJohnette Encore crash. By *Stadium Arcadium*, he used fourteen-inch AAX X-Celerator hi-hats, a ten-inch AA splash, an eighteen-and-a-half-inch Chad Smith signature Explosion crash or a nineteen-inch AA Medium crash, a twenty-one-inch AA Rock ride, a twenty-inch AA Rock crash, a nineteen-inch AA China, and an LP Jam Block and a Pearl cowbell for percussion. This setup would remain through *The Getaway*, though he would gain his own signature cowbell.

That said, Smith played on Zildjian K cymbals throughout *Mother's Milk* and *Blood Sugar Sex Magik*. This can be easily spotted in the *Funky Monks* documentary, as well as the "Suck My Kiss" music video. For years, he intentionally played with the hi-hat loudest and as sloshy as possible; it originated from his time in the 1980s when his drum set was often without a microphone and had to be played that loud in order to be heard.

Chad Smith's Complete Non–Red Hot Chili Peppers Performance Discography

All contributions are drums or percussion.

Pharaoh—*Pharaoh* (1982)
Toby Redd—*In the Light* (1986)
Twenty Mondays—*Twist Inside* (1986)
Second Self—*Mood Ring* (1990)

Anacrusis—*Manic Impression* (1991)
Queen—"We Will Rock You/We Are the Champions (Remix)" (1991)
Session Man Soundtrack (1991)
Twenty Mondays—*Twist Inside* (1992)
Wild Colonials—*Fruit of Life* (1994)
General Clusterfunk—*Starin' Straight at the Sun* (1994)
Honeymoon Stitch—"Day of the Lords" (1995)
Grace of My Heart Score (1996)
Wayne Kramer—*Dangerous Madness* (1996)
Thermadore—*Monkey on Rico* (1996)
John Fogerty—*Blue Moon Swamp* (1997)
Lili Haydn—*Lili* (1997)
Leah Andreone—*Alchemy* (1998)
Fishbone—*The Psychotic Friends Nuttwerk* (2000)
Wu-Tang Clan—"Wu-Tang Clan Ain't Nuthin ta Fuck Wit" featuring Tom Morello
     and Chad Smith (2000)
Dave Navarro—*Trust No One* (2001)
Johnny Cash—*Unearthed* (2003)
Glenn Hughes—*Songs in the Key of Rock* (2003)
Hughes Turner Project—*HTP 2* (2003)
Players—*Clear the Decks* (2003)
John Frusciante—*Shadows Collide with People* (2004)
Glenn Hughes—*Soulfully Live in the City of Angels* (2004)
Glenn Hughes—*Soul Mover* (2005)
Dixie Chicks—*Taking the Long Way* (2006)
Glenn Hughes—*Music for the Divine* (2006)
Glenn Hughes—*First Underground Nuclear Kitchen* (2008)
B'z—*Ichibu to Zenbu/Dive* (2009)
Chickenfoot—*Chickenfoot* (2009)
Chad Smith's Bombastic Meatbats—*Meet the Meatbats* (2009)
Chad Smith's Bombastic Meatbats—*More Meat* (2010)
Paul Oakenfold—*Pop Killer* (2010)
Kid Rock—*Born Free* (2010)
Rhythm Train with Leslie Bixler, Chad Smith and Featuring Dick Van Dyke—
     Rhythm Train with Leslie Bixler, Chad Smith and Featuring Dick Van Dyke
     (2010)
Chickenfoot—*Chickenfoot III* (2011)
Chad Smith's Bombastic Meatbats—*Live Meat and Potatoes* (2012)
The Avett Brothers—*The Carpenter* (2012)
Flea—*Helen Burns* (2012)
Jake Bugg—*Shangri La* (2013)
Sammy Hagar—*Sammy Hagar & Friends* (2013)

Steve Lukather—*Transition* (2013)
Jennifer Nettles—*That Girl* (2014)
The Process—*The Process* (2014)
Rammstein—*Rammstein in Amerika* (2015)
Andrew Watt—*Ghost in My Head* (2015)
Glenn Hughes—*Resonate* (2016)
Tarja Turunen—*The Brightest Voice* (2016)
Tarja Turunen—*The Shadow Self* (2016)
The Lego Batman Movie Soundtrack (2017)
Joe Satriani—*What Happens Next* (2018)

24

The New Slim

Josh Klinghoffer on Guitar

Not Always a Guitarist, Not Always a Chili Pepper

Joshua Adam Klinghoffer was born in Los Angeles on October 3, 1979. His father was a sound technician for films and television. Klinghoffer was not always known as the guitarist for the Red Hot Chili Peppers; he started music by taking drum lessons at age nine because his mother observed he banged around percussively on household items with regularity. He dropped out of high school when he was fifteen with the explicit purpose of developing himself as and becoming a professional guitarist.

The Bicycle Thief

Although he joined the Rock and Roll Hall of Fame at the youngest age for an inductee at thirty-two years old (surpassing Stevie Wonder's mark of thirty-eight years old), his first recognition came as the guitarist for Bob Forrest's 1990s alternative rock group the Bicycle Thief. Having joined at age seventeen, Klinghoffer was interviewed about the Bicycle Thief by *SF Weekly* and described his self-perception as a child as being the "little music dork around the corner, [who] dropped out of high school, and was just playing guitar all day long." His abilities as a multi-instrumentalist were what attracted Forrest to Klinghoffer; soon after, the Bicycle Thief was opening for the Red Hot Chili Peppers on the *Californication* tour in 2000. Klinghoffer became friends with the four Red Hot Chili Peppers of that time and was particularly close with John Frusciante, leading the two to collaborate after the tour's end.

Klinghoffer can be seen making inside jokes with Anthony Kiedis and John Frusciante on the *Greatest Hits* DVD.

Forrest thought of Klinghoffer and Frusciante as two peas in a pod, saying that both lived only for music and film. After Forrest and Klinghoffer signed a record deal with the Bicycle Thief, each got $10,000 in advance royalties. Kling-hoffer spent the majority of his money within eight hours on 100 CDs and an acoustic guitar from the 1940s.

Klinghoffer and Frusciante Collaborate

Smith worked with Klinghoffer and had previously discussed drum parts together on a John Frusciante solo album, *Shadows Collide with People*, where Klinghoffer had actually worked out all of them but Smith was the one to play them. This kind of chemistry with Smith paid off when Klinghoffer joined the band, as Smith remained happy to have another drummer on his side when it came to mixes and drum sounds.

Stay in Touch

Klinghoffer stayed in touch with Frusciante after replacing him in the Red Hot Chili Peppers. After recording *I'm with You* but before leaving for his first tour with the group, Klinghoffer had a phone call with Frusciante to talk about the band. He talked about it with *Rolling Stone*: "I was talking to [Frusciante] about playing with [Flea, Smith, and Kiedis]. . . . He said, 'There's something amazing about getting up in the morning and playing something amazing with your friends.'" (The same article that told this story indicated that Smith ran into Frusciante at a Soundgarden concert around the same time and exchanged pleasantries for the first time since his leaving.)

The Chosen One

It is almost impossible to talk about Klinghoffer's style as a guitarist without talking about John Frusciante. This is because Klinghoffer and Frusciante col-laborated for almost a decade before Klinghoffer replaced Frusciante but also because Klinghoffer mirrored his guitar playing after Frusciante's in the Chili Peppers even when outside the Chili Peppers. *Guitar World* said he possessed "Frusciante's experimental edge and offbeat tonal adventurousness," while his sense of rhythm can equally be compared to Frusciante's.

Similarly, Kiedis first met Frusciante when he was auditioning for Bob For-rest's then rock group Thelonious Monster. (Flea convinced Kiedis to go to the audition with him and poach Frusciante for the Red Hot Chili Peppers, which is exactly what happened.) Kiedis first met Klinghoffer in 1997, when Bob Forrest praised the guitarist as a musical savant. Although it wasn't quite the same—and didn't lead to any poaching—it's still notable that Kiedis met the two guitarists as potential players for the same man.

When it was time to replace Frusciante, Klinghoffer was the only real choice. Flea thought about other guitarists but decided he was really comfortable only with Klinghoffer, having already considered him part of the Chili Peppers family from years of touring as their keyboard player.

Style

Klinghoffer's style as guitarist has been compared—often unfairly—as a less impressive take on Frusciante's sound. They do share certain stylistic tendencies—playing partial chords rather than the full voicings, relying more on rhythm from funk music or from post-punk, and an odd sense of polyrhythmic ability—but their roads have diverged plenty, too. A good example of their common but unusual rhythmic sense is comparing Frusciante's guitar polyrhythm on "Charlie" from *Stadium Arcadium*—Frusciante played in 3/4 while the rest of the band played in 4/4—and Klinghoffer's guitar playing on "Ethiopia."

"Ethiopia" during the introduction and verses is 7/8; during the introduction, Klinghoffer plays in 4/4, creating a polyrhythm that a less apt musician would make sound clashing, but Klinghoffer subtly shades the music so that it feels normal. The song was intended to share a beauty of the band's trip to Africa; the polyrhythm gives it a bit of an African feel. Similarly, the guitar solo is a three-note triplet lick, still happening over 7/8, creating another polyrhythm that doesn't feel disjointed in the hands of the guitarist.

He was a drummer first and thinks of the guitar's rhythms before he thinks of the specific chords or notes, adding to his ethereal style and why his parts often blend and allow for easy overdubbing. He hears the space in the song and asks whether it needs to be filled and whether guitar is the right thing to fill it. This contrasts every other guitarist in Red Hot Chili Peppers history, who were guitarists first.

Klinghoffer himself admitted he preferred to be a rhythm guitarist and not be the lead player or in the forefront. In the studio, this led to more layering—not quite as much as was done in Dave Navarro's day where two guitars were almost entirely necessary if not the bare minimum but more than Frusciante, who typically relied on one primary rhythm track and some overdubs to flesh out the sounds.

Klinghoffer literally learned every song in the Red Hot Chili Peppers' discography after joining the band, including those predating Frusciante, though not all of them have been played live. (He said the hardest one to play was "Snow (Hey Oh)" and more because he had difficulty singing the backing vocals and playing it than just playing it. Nonetheless, that song has been played live in Klinghoffer's time.)

Total Guitar suggested that the two defining traits of Klinghoffer's playing were "creating internal melodies around a single chord"—similar to Hendrix but not as wildly—and blending wah-wah with fuzz over the blues scale—also similar to Hendrix but not as wildly.

In his own words, Klinghoffer's strong suit is not lead playing. He told *Gitarre & Bass,*

> When I listened to the Chili Peppers for the first time I was still a drummer and didn't have any clue about the guitar.... When I started playing the guitar I only played chords.... With every tour or session job I did I learned more and more and expanded my knowledge. Therefore I always tried to avoid playing solos because I never focused on doing it—until I joined this band.... The reason I play less solos is not because I don't like playing them or because I reject them. It's just something I've never really learned to do.

Influences (or Lack Thereof)

Klinghoffer has never named a single guitarist as an influence on him that wasn't a former Red Hot Chili Peppers guitarist. He has stated that his taste in chords and voicings comes from his knowledge and from learning to play every single song he heard growing up on guitar or drums. He has said he loved Brian Wilson and the Beach Boys, Radiohead, and electronic music like Aphex Twin. (He, Flea, and Frusciante briefly had a group with Stella Mozgawa that covered Aphex Twin's ".000890569.") He told *MindEqualsBlown* that he loves Damon Albarn's work in any band and has longed to collaborate with him. Chad Smith compared Klinghoffer's multi-instrumentalism and piano playing to that of Paul McCartney's in multiple interviews. Klinghoffer told the *Winnipeg Free Press* that he was a big fan of Chris Cornell and Soundgarden.

Guitars

In the Red Hot Chili Peppers, Klinghoffer relied primarily on three Fender Stratocasters for live and studio work during the *I'm with You* years. One was originally Chad Smith's, a 1963 with a thick neck; the other two are black and white Stratocasters from the 1970s. *Guitar Player* said he has a 1967 Custom Telecaster that he got from John Frusciante; it was his backup Telecaster, but *Guitar World* stated this guitar was actually a 1957.

After *The Getaway*, Klinghoffer began to use a 1960 sunburst Stratocaster named Dashiell, a 1959 sunburst Stratocaster named Chick, a black 1974 Stratocaster with a hardtail bridge named Gus, a pink custom relic Stratocaster named Monty, and a black 1974 Starcaster tuned to E-flat.

When he played songs that Frusciante used to play on a Gretsch White Falcon, such as "Californication," Klinghoffer used his own Gretsch G6134 White Penguin as an homage of sorts. He has also used less valuable guitars typically viewed as garbage to get weirder sounds, like Airlines or Harmonys. (He played a Magnatone Tornado on "Did I Let You Know.") Most of *I'm with You* was recorded with the 1967 Telecaster and the 1963 Stratocaster.

In Dot Hacker, Klinghoffer has played primarily the 1967 Telecaster, a Fender Starcaster, a Rickenbacker, and a 1962 Fender Jaguar. (He has three Jaguars, one in white, one in black, and a 1964 custom-colored green.) Beyond that, he also possessed a Gibson ES-335 TD, a 1964 Airline Res-O-Glass, a Fender Coronado XII, a Gibson Firebird XII, a 1964 Gibson Firebird V, a Martin 0015 acoustic, a Hagström Futurama, a Gibson SG, and a Fender Bass VI. The Futurama and the Airline guitars were his primary guitars for Beck.

Amps

On *I'm with You*, Klinghoffer played through seven amps going through a radial splitter, trying any number of amp combinations to dial in the right sound. The tracking amps were the same that Klinghoffer has used as his go-to on tour, 200-watt Marshall Majors and Silvertones. Sometimes, he has used Fender Super Sixes and Super Reverbs.

Effects

Klinghoffer changes his pedal board at an enamoring rate. At one point, he was using just a DOD overdrive, the Pigtronix PolySaturator, an Ibanez WH-10 wah, and a custom fuzz from Wilson Effects. His pedal board changes by day on tour, as he has claimed to own more than 100 effects pedals, making an accurate snapshot of his current pedal board impossible. (Despite that, he has often claimed he is trying to get rid of pedals he doesn't use; perhaps one day, he will settle into a final pedal board.) He often made use of a Dunlop Rotovibe in his lead playing.

In Dot Hacker, he used a lot more effects, singling out the Electro-Harmonix Holy Grail, the Boss DD-3, and the Boss DM-2. (As a synthesizer, he praised the Korg MS-20 as his go-to for Dot Hacker.)

At various other times, he has used a Catilinbread CSIDMAN glitch/stutter delay, an Electro-Harmonix Holy Grail Nano, an Electro-Harmonix Holy Grail Reverb, an Electro-Harmonix Cathedral, an Electro-Harmonix B9 Organ Machine, an Electro-Harmonix Deluxe Memory Man, a Death By Audio Interstellar Overdriver, a Boss DD-6, a Boss VB-2, a Boss CE-2, a Boss PS-3, a Boss RV-5, a Boss DS-2, a Tonder Bender MK 1.5, an Ibanez AF201 auto filter, a Robot Pedal Factory Brain Freeze filter, a BS10 Bass Stack, an Xotic Effects SP Compressor, a Wampler Tumnus, a JHS Firefly Fuzz, a Line 6 FM4 Filter Modeler, an EarthQuaker Devices Dispatch Master, and a Misty Cave Echo—among others.

25

His Other Past

Josh Klinghoffer's Music outside the Red Hot Chili Peppers

Perfectionism

As a musician, Josh Klinghoffer was a perfectionist on every instrument, but especially on guitar, he has been known to spend hours chasing perfect tones and be upset with his equipment even after everyone else in the band thinks what he did was just right. Kiedis told *Rolling Stone*, "We'll play a song, and I'll think, 'Fuck, that is so good.' Then I'll look over and [Josh will] be kicking his equipment. He'll hear one itty-bitty thing that didn't go right with his pedals. It felt so good to me. But he wants to get it more correct."

Stealing Bicycles into Touring Forever

Klinghoffer joined the Bicycle Thief at age seventeen, two years after dropping out of high school (for further details, see chapter 24). He played on their lone studio album, *You Come and Go Like a Pop Song*, originally released in 1999 and rereleased in 2001. (Former Pepper John Frusciante played lead guitar on one song from the album.)

After the Bicycle Thief opened for the Red Hot Chili Peppers in 2000 post-*Californication*, Klinghoffer began to receive a ton of offers for session and touring work. Right when the tour ended, he got the offer to go on tour with the Butthole Surfers—who remained one of several groups with which Klinghoffer never recorded but was a live member.

Frusciante

The most interesting and strangest part of Klinghoffer's tale is also the most covered: how he went from Frusciante collaborator to Frusciante replacement.

Klinghoffer began as a friend and musician working on Frusciante's material; beginning with one song on *Shadows Collide with People*, "Omission," Klinghoffer occasionally got songwriting credits, sang lead vocals, or played lead guitar (or all three). The frequent collaborations led to a more equal relationship: the two released one electronic album with equal billing—*A Sphere in the Heart of Silence*—and were equal members in a power trio with Fugazi's Joe Lally: Ataxia. In Ataxia, Klinghoffer was primarily on drums; on other albums, Klinghoffer worked out the drum parts as drummers (including Chad Smith) played them, or Klinghoffer was "just" a guitarist.

Truthfully, Frusciante met Klinghoffer before the other Peppers did: Klinghoffer was recording in the same studio as the Peppers were recording *Californication* in. Klinghoffer was leaving the studio at age nineteen with a guitar in hand, and Frusciante asked what he was working on. When Klinghoffer said he was recording with Bob Forrest, Frusciante knew who Forrest was and asked to hear what they were working on. So began a long friendship.

In the late 2000s, Klinghoffer was a member of a one-off group with Frusciante, Flea, and Stella Mozgawa that did instrumentals and jams, including a rock instrument interpretation of an Aphex Twin song. In this group, Klinghoffer played drums. Other various jams happened; Frusciante went through a similar output with Omar Rodriguez-Lopez in the early to mid-2000s.

While Klinghoffer has insisted he and Frusciante have remained amiable, he has also commented that the relationships are not what they once were, as they were once literally best friends. After his gripes with *The Getaway*, he told *Gitarre & Bass* that he thought it would be odd if he continued talking to Frusciante regularly. He was aware some fans didn't like the new album or his playing on it in comparison to Frusciante's, and he couldn't imagine a scenario where he didn't want to discuss it with Frusciante. He thought it would only hurt their relationship, so he wanted to put more space between them before they maintained regular contact again.

He has also said that only "idiots" compare him to John Frusciante, hinting at just how often it is written about.

Danger Mouse to Gnarls Barkley to Beck

In a stroke of luck, Klinghoffer met producer Danger Mouse of Gnarls Barkley (and future Red Hot Chili Peppers producer) when he was working on a trip-hop album for an artist he loved: Martina Topley-Bird. Klinghoffer did almost everything musically on the album, and Danger Mouse produced it; the two became friends. Klinghoffer was drunk at a Gnarls Barkley show and heard the keyboard player was quitting. He told *Total Guitar*, "I said, 'I think I can [play the keyboard parts].' I woke up the next day going, 'What did you say you would do?' So I became the keyboardist for Gnarls Barkley, and that band also opened for the Chili Peppers."

Warpaint

Warpaint's original drummer, Shannyn Sossamon, left the band to focus on acting in 2007. Josh Klinghoffer filled in for some live shows and recorded one song with the group on drums (on a record that was eventually mixed by John Frusciante). It's worth noting that the drummer who ended up as the full-time replacement for Sossamon was Stella Mozgawa—who drummed alongside Klinghoffer in a group with Flea and John Frusciante (they had two drummers the whole time). Flea originally told Mozgawa she wasn't allowed to drum for Warpaint because he didn't want her to become busy with projects he wasn't involved in.

Sossamon went on to have a successful film career. Frusciante also gave guitarist Emily Kokal a 1955 Fender Stratocaster, a 1966 Fender Jaguar, and an old Martin acoustic. (Kokal called Frusciante a "generous guitar-giver" in *Music Radar*.)

A fun. Favorite

Often overlooked in Klinghoffer's history are the songs he played guitar on for the Format's *Dog Problems*. The Format was two musicians: Sam Means, who has, by and large, laid low since the Format's hiatus, and Nate Ruess, who also became the front man of fun. and has maintained a successful solo career. (It should be noted Means has songwriting credits on every song on fun.'s first album, *Aim and Ignite*, despite not being in the band.) While not the most advanced guitar work, one of the songs became one of the Format's largest hits in "I'm Actual" and foreshadowed fun.'s sound.

Nate Ruess returned to the Klinghoffer well with his solo work on "Nothing without Love" in 2015. Ruess told *SPIN* that Klinghoffer was one of several musicians he worked with on the album who were inspiring but singled out Klinghoffer as someone Ruess wanted to get into the recording studio with more.

Creative versus Following the Leader

Despite his prolific output as a session musician, Klinghoffer has much preferred to be a creative and writing his own music. He was unhappy touring with Gnarls Barkley and Beck, claiming that it felt like he was hiding and that it stunted his own development. That urge to create led to the formation of Dot Hacker, but he was also satisfied in the Red Hot Chili Peppers.

In multiple magazine interviews but especially in *Gitarre & Bass*, Klinghoffer admitted he wishes the Red Hot Chili Peppers would self-produce. He identified issues with Danger Mouse not as anything with the producer specifically but as a problem with all producers: Klinghoffer felt the band could make better choices than anyone outside the band, while the other three Chili Peppers always want an external opinion. (As such, Klinghoffer isn't entirely satisfied with *The Getaway*; the album was recorded drums, then bass, then guitar, and then vocals, and Klinghoffer longed to record an album based on intimate jams produced by the band itself.)

Christina Aguilera

On July 7, 2009, Josh Klinghoffer performed with Christina Aguilera on acoustic guitar as she performed "Beautiful." They did so in a public performance that was recorded for the From Hunger to Hope campaign. The campaign was focused on solving world hunger, particularly for children in poverty. Given the time line, it's likely this was Klinghoffer's last performance on guitar before joining the Red Hot Chili Peppers.

Influences

While Klinghoffer has been quiet to name too many influences on him as a guitarist, he speaks freely about who influenced him as a drummer. On an unofficial Josh Klinghoffer website (verified to be him responding to fan e-mails), he named Ringo Starr, Charlie Watts, Jack Irons, Simone Pace, Elvin Jones, Steve Shelly, Jay Bellerose, Meg White, John Bonham, Brian Blade, and Chad Smith as influences. He has stated that he misses drumming and is hoping to get another project off the ground where he is a drummer—and also noted that he didn't spend enough time focusing on rudiments as a young person but that his drumming improved immensely when he began to play guitar and hear music from a guitarist's perspective, too.

A Complete List of Acts Josh Klinghoffer Has Performed Live With

Christina Aguilera
Beck—guitar (2003)

The Bicycle Thief—guitar (1997–2000)
The Butthole Surfers—guitar (2001)
Dot Hacker—guitar, vocals (2008–present)
Perry Farrell—guitar (2001)
Vincent Gallo—guitar, bass, piano (2001)
Gnarls Barkley—guitar, keyboard, synthesizer, vocals (2006–2008)
Golden Shoulders—bass (2003)
PJ Harvey—guitar, drums (2004)
Red Hot Chili Peppers—second guitar, keyboard (2007–2008), official member
    (2008–present)
Sparks—guitar (2006–2008)
Tricky—drums (2001)
Warpaint—drums (2007–2009)

Josh Klinghoffer's Complete Performance Discography

The Bicycle Thief—*You Come and Go Like a Pop Song* (1999)—guitar
Perry Farrell—"Did You Forget" (2001)—guitar
Tricky—"#1 Da Woman" (2001)—drums
Golden Shoulders—*Let My Burden Be* (2002)—bass
Ataxia—*Automatic Writing* (2004)—drums, synthesizer, vocals
John Frusciante—*Inside of Emptiness* (2004)—drums, bass, keyboards, vocals,
    guitar
John Frusciante—*Shadows Collide with People* (2004)—vocals, bass, guitar, syn-
    thesizers, keyboards, piano, mellotron
John Frusciante—*The Will to Death* (2004)—drums, bass, keyboards, guitar
John Frusciante and Josh Klinghoffer—*A Sphere in the Heart of Silence* (2004)—
    arp string ensemble, guitar, bass, synthesizer, drum loops, drums, vocals,
    piano, production
Golden Shoulders—*Friendship Is Deep* (2004)—bass
PJ Harvey—"You Come Through" (2004)—guitar
Thelonious Monster—*California Clam Chowder* (2004)—guitar
Gemma Hayes—*The Roads Don't Love You* (2005)—guitar, sitar, vocals
The Format—"I'm Actual," "Time Bomb," "Dead End" (2006)—guitar
Bob Forrest—*Modern Folk and Blues: Wednesday* (2006)—guitar
Ataxia—*AW II* (2007)—drums, synthesizer, vocals
Toni Oswald—*A Loveletter to the Transformer/The Diary of Ic Explura Pt. 1*
    (2006)—music, songwriting
Charlotte Hatherley—*The Deep Blue* (2007)—drums
Spleen—*Nun Lover!* (2007)—guitar, drums, organ, strings, percussion

Gnarls Barkley—*The Odd Couple* (2008)—bass, guitar

Headless Heroes—*The Silence of Love* (2008)—vocals, bass, cimbalom, guitar, organ, piano

Martina Topley-Bird—"Carnies" (2008)—bass, guitar, drums, keyboard, synthesizer, songwriting

Neon Neon—"Steel Your Girl" (2008)—guitar, bass, drums, songwriting

Pocahaunted—*Chains* (2008)—drums

John Frusciante—*The Empyrean* (2009)—drums, percussion, electric piano, organ, piano, synthesizer, vocals

Golden Shoulders—*Get Reasonable* (2009)—drums, bass, guitar, mellotron, organ, synthesizer

Joker's Daughter—*The Last Laugh* (2009)—drums, guitar

Bambi Lee Savage—*GJ and the Pimpkillers* (2009)—bass, keyboards, guitar, piano, synthesizer

Warpaint—"Billie Holiday" (2009)—drums

Warpaint—"Krimson" (2009)—guitar

Paul Oakenfold—*Pop Killer* (2010)—guitar

Red Hot Chili Peppers—*I'm with You* (2011)—guitar, backing vocals, keyboards, synthesizer, six-string bass on "Happiness Loves Company"

Dot Hacker—*Dot Hacker EP* (2012)—guitar, vocals

Dot Hacker—*Inhibition* (2012)—guitar, vocals

Sophie Hunger—*The Danger of Light* (2012)—guitar, synthesizer

Josh Klinghoffer—*Bob and the Monster Original Score* (2013)—composition

Red Hot Chili Peppers—*I'm Beside You* (2013)—guitar, backing vocals

The Bicycle Thief—*Rare* (2014)—guitar

Dot Hacker—*How's Your Process? (Play)* (2014)—guitar, vocals

Dot Hacker—*How's Your Process? (Work)* (2014)—guitar, vocals

Tinariwen—*Emmaar* (2014)—guitar, pedal steel guitar

Nate Ruess—"Nothing without Love" (2015)—guitar

Red Hot Chili Peppers—*The Getaway* (2016)—guitar, backing vocals, bass on "The Hunter," piano on "Dark Necessities"

Dot Hacker—*N°3* (2017)—guitar, vocals

Part 3

The Band and Its Own Story

26

Out in LA

Anthony Kiedis's Early Years

His Father's Father

Anton Kiedis was born in Lithuania and moved to America in the early 1900s with his wife, Julia, and their children, George, Irene, and Anton Jr. While on the journey across the ocean, they gave birth to another daughter, Victoria. In 1914, they had their last child together, John Alden Kiedis. John Alden Kiedis moved to Los Angeles after he followed George and Anton Jr. there; but when his wife became pregnant, he moved to the quieter area of Grand River, Michigan.

His Father

John Michael Kiedis was born on December 7, 1939, two years to the day before Pearl Harbor was bombed by the Japanese. (The event spoiled the birthday celebration.) While still married, John Michael Kiedis's parents were in the process of separating: the father tried to save the marriage but had to work double shifts to finance the family, and the mother dated around. John Michael Kiedis didn't take to either parent because of this and ran away from home. He ended up staying with his aunt, Irene, who lived in Lansing, Michigan.

As John Michael aged, his parents got formally divorced. His birth mother, Mollie, got involved in politics, supporting Democrats like Harry Truman. His father remarried a woman named Judy but remained a staunch Republican. John Michael went to Michigan State University, where he met Margaret Elizabeth Noble, age seventeen; John Michael, a twenty-year-old, fell in love with her and married her on July 2, 1960. Margaret went by the nickname "Peggy."

John Michael Kiedis cheated on his wife from the outset but blamed her for slandering him whenever he was caught cheating. He admitted as much in his autobiography. Nine months into their marriage, the two moved to Hollywood, California, with a few friends so that John Michael could pursue acting.

A Son Is Born

There was a rumor that his mother was dating Denny Shookman, and his father flew to her; the two took a bus back to Michigan and conceived their son on February 3, 1962. Less than a month before Anthony was born, his father spent more than a week in jail after acting as a failed lookout for his friend Scott, who was doing crimes regularly: selling drugs and small-time robberies. At 4:30 a.m. on November 1, 1962, Anthony Kiedis was born. He was given no middle name because his two parents couldn't decide: John Michael wanted it to be Courage, while Peggy wanted it to be either John or Michael.

UCLA

John Michael returned to college at the University of California, Los Angeles, where he was a classmate of Kareem Abdul-Jabbar and hung out with Jim Morrison and Ray Manzarek of the Doors before the two dropped out to pursue music full-time. While Anthony was still a young boy, he and his father would prowl the drag strips and look at dive bars as the elder Kiedis sold drugs and pursued acting. The two learned dialogue for the auditions that John Michael had together.

Photos were taken of John Michael and another woman who were hanging out as friends. The photos were given to Peggy; because of his history of cheating, it was the final straw for her. Their marriage ended. Peggy moved to Culver City, California, and Anthony spent time split between his father and mother. John Michael attended class less and less often as he pursued acting and debauchery more and more. When Peggy returned to Grand Rapids on vacation, she met someone else and opted to move back. The young Anthony would spend most of his time in Michigan but stay in touch with his father by mail and fly out for visits.

Quasi-Famous Drug Dealer Blackie Dammett

Now an eligible bachelor, John Michael began to go by the stage name of Blackie Dammett. He also sold drugs to rock bands he began to hang out with; he attended the first Led Zeppelin show in Los Angeles and remained their southern California drug dealer until their demise. Dammett tried cocaine but remained focused on his career as an actor. He briefly tried stand-up comedy.

Once an early preteen, Kiedis returned to Hollywood to spend most of his time with his father. Dammett dated a woman named Connie, who befriended Sonny Bono from Sonny & Cher. The famous husband and wife were in the process of divorcing but kept it under wraps to keep their public image together; Sonny bought Connie a new Fiat convertible and asked to be with her. Connie accepted his proposal and the gift and politely broke up with Dammett on returning to him. Despite this, the two remained amiable; through the high jinks of their relationship, Cher often ended up as Anthony Kiedis's babysitter. Dammett made an attempt at sleeping with Cher that was turned down with a polite smile.

Sex, Drugs, Father, and Son

Kiedis lost his virginity to Dammett's eighteen-year-old girlfriend when he was twelve. This happened after his father suggested the two go for it, and the woman was game. Dammett maintained a misogynist view of women and an inappropriate view of age differences throughout his life; in 2013, he wrote about how he thought Woody Allen's marriage to his former stepdaughter was fine because his ex-wife married a fifty-year-old when she was twenty-one. (He went so far as to call Mia Farrow a "hypocrite" but paid no mind to how Allen pursued the daughter of his then girlfriend.)

His father began to host parties where Kiedis was viewed as a fellow partier and an entertainer. At a party in Malibu, Kiedis accidentally discovered heroin when he thought it was cocaine. (He was still an early teenager.) The same dealer responsible, Kendall Pacios, once gave Dammett more heroin than he could handle. Pacios kept Dammett awake by slapping his face, kicking him, and helping him take a cold shower until Dammett pulled through.

As Dammett pursued acting, the young Kiedis began to as well. He earned small roles as rebellious Vinnie on NBC's *Who's Watching the Kids*, on an *ABC After School Special*, and on *F.I.S.T.* with Sylvester Stallone, among others. In these roles, he was often billed as Cole Dammett as he played off his father's stage name.

Fairfax High School

Anthony Kiedis began to attend Fairfax High, where he'd go on to meet all of the first round of Red Hot Chili Peppers. There, he had shared classes with Saul

Hudson, later known as Slash from Guns N' Roses, and was friends with fellow Fairfax students Demi Moore and David Arquette.

His father often drove him to school, but Kiedis almost always walked home. Kiedis's first friend was Ben Tang, a Chinese boy, and Tony Shurr, a weak teenager. At the start of the school year, Shurr was head locked by someone with big hair and a gap between his front teeth; Kiedis got protective and confrontational and threatened the boy, who appeared to be attacking his friend. The head locker was Michael Balzary, later known as Flea, who established he was just trying to be friendly to Shurr. Kiedis and Flea quickly became best friends.

27

I'm a Little Pea

Flea's Childhood

Birth of a Flea

Michael Peter Balzary was born on October 16, 1962, in Mount Waverly, a suburb of Melbourne, Australia. His father, Mick, took him fishing as a boy. When he was eleven years old, the family moved from Australia to Larchmont, New York; within two years, the young Balzary's parents were divorced.

Jazz in the House

Flea's father returned to Australia, and his mother remarried his stepfather, Walter Abdul Urban. (Urban was born in 1941 and passed away in 2011.) The newlyweds moved to Los Angeles, where Urban hosted jazz jam sessions in their house. Flea started out as a jazz drummer and practiced until age five; as his stepfather idolized trumpeters like Miles Davis, Dizzy Gillespie, and Louis Armstrong, he began to feel a calling to trumpet and took up the instrument of his own accord.

When he was a young boy, his stepfather took him to a performance of Gillespie's, where Flea snuck backstage. Flea ran up to Gillespie and was in awe; Gillespie in turn held the boy for a moment as he talked to other people for a few minutes. It was one of the highlights of young Flea's life.

Violence in the Home

Although his stepfather brought him an appreciation of all sorts of music and helped teach him how to play jazz on his trumpet, the same man was very violent. Flea often slept in the backyard rather than inside because he was scared of what would happen if he stayed in the house. On at least one occasion, his stepfather got in a shoot-out with police. To avoid being home, he often stayed out late and did drugs despite being young and spent a large amount of time in camaraderie and debauchery with Anthony Kiedis.

Urban took the young Flea to jam sessions around Los Angeles that had several noteworthy musicians, including famed drummer Philly Joe Jones of, among other projects, the Miles Davis Quintet. In Flea's autobiography *Acid for the Children*, he spoke highly of his stepfather and placed blame for a large amount of the household violence on Urban's alcoholism.

During this time, Flea began to rob people to finance his escapades even though he wasn't yet a teenager.

An Outcast, a Little Pea

Flea felt out of place due to his taste in music; a high schooler obsessed with only jazz didn't fit in with other kids in the mid-1970s. He was constantly picked on and called a "faggot" almost every day; though he had acquaintances he was friendly with at school, he didn't have anyone he felt he could open up to until he met Anthony Kiedis. He told *Rolling Stone* that the day they met, he told his mother that he finally found someone he could talk to, even though he was thirteen years old.

As Kiedis introduced Flea to rock music, Flea introduced Kiedis to jazz. Flea met a young Israeli named Hillel Slovak, who showed him punk rock. When Slovak needed a replacement bassist, Slovak suggested Flea use his knowledge of jazz but apply it to a new instrument to join Slovak's rock band, What Is This?

28

Green Heaven

Hillel Slovak's Youth

Pure Israeli to Pure Californian

Hillel Slovak, or הלל סלובק in Hebrew, was born April 13, 1962, in Haifa, Israel. Both of his parents were survivors of the Holocaust; they immigrated the Slovak family in 1967 when Hillel was only five years old. The family originally moved to the Bronx in New York City before uprooting again to California, where they would remain for the rest of Hillel's life.

Slovak went to Fairfax High School with Michael "Flea" Balzary, Jack Irons, and Anthony Kiedis, along with future Queens of the Stone Age member Alain Johannes, with whom he would start the band What Is This? (also known as Anthym). Slovak had a younger brother, James, who published a collection of Hillel's art and diary entries in 1999 titled *Behind the Sun*.

The Gift of Guitar

Of those who would become his musical compadres, Irons met Slovak first when both were ten years old. Irons was present at Slovak's thirteenth birthday party, when Slovak received his first guitar as a gift from his uncle, Aron. Irons believed he could spot a different sort of excitement from Slovak the moment he received it.

KISS, Chain Reaction

Irons and Slovak became obsessed with KISS and one year attended school on Halloween in KISS's signature makeup. (Slovak was logically painted as Paul Stanley.) They mimed their parts as a show for friends, but Slovak took his actual guitar work seriously and closely studied Jimi Hendrix.

Their first band was Slovak, Irons, Johannes, and a Todd Strassman on bass doing covers and originals influenced by Queen and Led Zeppelin. The band was named Chain Reaction; it would evolve into Anthym and eventually became What Is This?.

Meeting Kiedis and Flea

Flea and Kiedis hitchhiked to a water park on the outskirts of Los Angeles. They smoked a joint and, after swimming, realized they couldn't get home. After walking around in a search for someone they recognized, they spotted a boy who was also in their geometry class, Hillel Slovak. After a casual conversation, Slovak gave them a ride home in his Datsun B210.

Anthony Kiedis was friends with the other members of Anthym in high school and wore a pin of the band's around school. Slovak, being a member of the band but not knowing Kiedis, politely confronted Kiedis. The two became fast friends when Kiedis realized Slovak was different; the future vocalist typically felt like the leader of whomever he was with but felt like Slovak was the leader whenever he was around. He admired Slovak's visual art and how he brought a calming presence to any situation. He also found as a positive trait just how Jewish and unashamed of it Slovak was. In *Scar Tissue*, he wrote that he knew almost instantly that they would be best friends as long as they lived.

Teaching the Band

Flea has, on numerous occasions, credited Slovak with his understanding and love for post-punk, Jimi Hendrix, and funk. Flea has also made it a point to credit Slovak for teaching him bass guitar; he has done so in numerous interviews and in the band's official oral history.

Personality

Slovak was outspoken about his religion and his heritage as an Israeli, speaking of it often with pride. In *Rolling Stone*, Flea categorized him as "a wild partyer. Before he got carried with drugs, he was a lot of fun. He was really funny and kind of funny looking. Real skinny with a long head and big lips." He was never too successful with women, but he didn't lack confidence either—he just occasionally felt shy when he really liked a girl.

29

Deep Kick

The Group's Teen Years

Disgusting Mini-Games

Flea and Kiedis grew very close and began to create games with each other that no one else was invited to. They were so comfortable with each other that Flea once ate Kiedis's phlegm on a dare. This dare lead to a game they would later play on tour called "Tongue in the Dirt." (The original incident stemmed from when Kiedis hocked up a large, gross piece of phlegm into his hand, and Kiedis looked down and dared Flea to eat it, claiming that if he had any balls, he had to do it.)

Flea's Night Out

Flea experienced his first nightlife experience with Kiedis and his father, Blackie Dammett. He was told to dress fashionably but instead wore the same suit he wore at his junior high graduation, which he then vomited all over after drinking too much beer.

Early Band Shenanigans

While still teenagers but in the Red Hot Chili Peppers, Anthony Kiedis bought several hats and ripped off their original logos. He put "The Red Hot Chili Peppers" on in their place, and it made Flea and Hillel Slovak laugh. They'd do this with a variety of merchandise and dress up in costumes regularly at early shows to help stand out.

Two Boys in LA Proper

Kiedis was hanging out with his father, a drug dealer, but going to high school classes by day. Flea became first trumpet in the high school band and dedicated most of his time to studying music. Kiedis helped the theater department with production. Kiedis heard a lot about Flea's sister, Karen, from him; the first night they met, Kiedis and Karen had sex.

Flea later told *Billboard*, "The music program at Fairfax High was a huge part of my life. I mean, it was the only reason I went to school. Otherwise I would have been a complete ne'er do well pothead. You know, a petty crime-making fuck-up."

Flea and Kiedis smoked weed together; Kiedis would steal pot from his father and get away with it. Once, on a skiing trip, Flea's mother lent him a credit card, but the attendant at the mountain wouldn't accept it unless she were present. Kiedis dressed up in full garb and do-it-yourself drag and pretended to be Flea's mother. The two successfully rented skis and smoked pot on the whole trip.

The Hillside Strangler

Kiedis's father called a prostitute, but on meeting her, he wasn't attracted to her. He offered her cocaine; when the prostitute left, she called the police because she thought Blackie Dammett was the Hillside Strangler, a famous Los Angeles–area serial killer. The police came over and seized Dammett's drugs. Kiedis was fine for a while without his father, as he saved his money from doing television commercials.

Pool Jumping

In Michigan, Kiedis jumped off railways into pools. In Los Angeles, Kiedis adapted the idea: jump off buildings into pools. He and Flea did this together and didn't care if anyone was around; sometimes, the added witnesses added excitement.

The two routinely did a jump from a local five-story building. (They developed a technique for shallow pools: go sideways to let your body flow out rather than down.) Kiedis's father warned him of the dangers of pool jumping, particularly if he were to do it while high, but that didn't stop him.

Kiedis overshot a pool on his block. He landed on his feet but missed the pool entirely; he fell into the pool and went into shock. An ambulance came and took him to the hospital, where he stayed for weeks. He broke his back and still suffered occasionally from the problems it brought as an adult.

Stories like this were referenced in "Deep Kick" from *One Hot Minute*.

Curfew—and Moving Out

After returning from the hospital, Blackie Dammett attempted to impose a curfew on the young Kiedis. At the same time, Kiedis began to introduce Slovak's band, then known as Anthym, and Flea began to practice bass in secret so that he could join the band. Kiedis introduced the band at their shows doing bits stolen from one of Dammett's friends.

Kiedis, Flea, and Slovak became very close and referred to themselves as a gang: Los Faces. Kiedis was Fuerte, Mike was Poco, and Slovak was Flaco. After suffering the wrath of the curfew, Kiedis moved out from his father's home and moved in with his friend Donde Baston.

Someone Sucks Anus

Flea was caught cheating by one of their teachers, Don Platt. Platt also taught Kiedis and had routinely given him good grades throughout the years, but it hurt Flea's chances of getting into a good school. Kiedis asked Platt for a college recommendation letter, but Platt wouldn't do it for someone who associated with Flea.

In response, the two changed the marquee on the front of Fairfax High to say "Dandy Don Platt Sucks Anus." They graduated without being so much as questioned by authorities, and at the end of the summer, they changed the marquee again to say "Dandy Don Continues to Suck Anus."

College

Slovak and Flea did not go to college. Kiedis went to UCLA and studied writing. There, he began to use drugs at an alarming rate, believing he had to do them before he started working like they do in real life. He was still dating his high school sweetheart but ended up cheating on her twice. He sought out heroin and tried it for the first time, though the batch he got was very weak.

Kiedis briefly became homeless and couch surfed at various friends' apartments. Sometimes he'd stay where Flea was staying, and sometimes he'd crash at Slovak's, which was his favorite place. When he got money, rather than saving for a place to live, he'd go on a drug binge. He found a place to stay but began doing heroin more frequently.

At the same time, Keith Barry gave Michael Balzary the nickname "Flea," which stuck for the rest of his life. Now known as Flea, he got an offer to play bass for Fear, the biggest punk band in Los Angeles.

The La Leyenda Tweakers

Kiedis became even more into drugs and dropped out of college during his second year at UCLA to fulfill his addiction to heroin and cocaine.

When both Kiedis and Flea were homeless, Bob Forrest was dumped by his wife. Given the situation, Forrest invited the two to live with him. Forrest himself was a musician, the main brain behind Thelonious Monster. The three started a band: the La Leyenda Tweakers. They received a terrible review in *LA Weekly*.

Forrest introduced them to a Middle Eastern man who was a reliable connection for speed, and they began to use the drug with a higher frequency.

30

Tony Flow

The Band's Formal Beginning

Tony Starts an Act, if Not a Band

Anthony Kiedis was friends with Gary Allen (not to be confused with country singer Gary Allan), a post-punk musician who fronted the band Gary and Neighbor's Voices. Allen suggested that Kiedis, Flea, and Hillel Slovak write one song and open for his band in 1983; the suggestion, according to Kiedis, was primarily because Allen recognized Kiedis's stage potential as a crazed performer. Kiedis believed they took influence from only a few places—the funk of Defunkt, the style of Gang of Four, and the soul of Jimi Hendrix—but relied primarily on the funk side of things solely because it was totally missing in What Is This?, Slovak's other band. Drummer Jack Irons, though friends with all the group, became the fourth member out of necessity and being in the area, not out of Allen's invitation.

Antwan the Swan Song

The first song written and performed became "Out in L.A." Kiedis wrote the lyrics since he wanted to stick to something he knew, hence the introduction to every member and the guitar, a capella, and bass solos. (The studio version includes a drum solo, while the original demo and live versions do not.)

The show took place at the Rhythm Lounge club in front of approximately thirty people on February 17, 1983. Kiedis was sober, but Flea had snorted heroin before playing. Few external accounts of the band's performance exist; Kiedis's account states that the promoter of the show and club ran up to him immediately afterward and asked the band to play again the following week with two songs.

Anthony Kiedis in 1983.   *Photo by John Coffey*

A Second Antwan the Swan Song

The band's second song began with Flea's bass line. Flea had long been working on an impressive piece of slap work, full of muted ghost notes and syncopations at a blistering speed; Kiedis encouraged him to use it as the basis for the band's next work. As the musicians laid the groundwork, Kiedis wrote cartoonish lyrics on the theme of jumping—jumping beans, jumping rope, jumping around.

He included a line about Hillel Slovak's balls, which were abnormally large, and if Slovak became excited, they would form a pumpkin shape in his pants. Slovak had a crush on one Rita Frumpkin, and the lyric changed to reference Slovak's excitement. After the group's second performance, Frumpkin and Slovak hooked up and began a brief relationship.

The second show happened a mere week after the first on February 24, 1983, and also included an attempt to do a choreographed dance introduction set to "Pack Jam" by Jonzun Crew. After Irons couldn't keep up with the dance moves at the show, they bailed midway through and started their two-song set. The failure lead to the song getting a reference in the Chili Peppers' song "Nevermind."

"Police Helicopter"

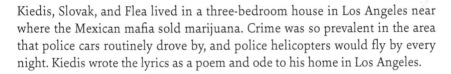

Kiedis, Slovak, and Flea lived in a three-bedroom house in Los Angeles near where the Mexican mafia sold marijuana. Crime was so prevalent in the area that police cars routinely drove by, and police helicopters would fly by every night. Kiedis wrote the lyrics as a poem and ode to his home in Los Angeles.

"Green Heaven"

In the same house in which the band wrote "Police Helicopter," they wrote "Green Heaven." It took them a full twenty-four hours to compose it; it became the highlight of their shows as Slovak ran wild on guitar. Kiedis composed the lyrics as an attempt to bring light to social injustices and contrast life on land with life in the ocean.

Naming the Band

The Red Hot Chili Peppers, in that first performance, went by Tony Flow and the Miraculously Majestic Masters of Mayhem. They went through a handful of other names, including Spigot Blister and the Chest Pimps. Both Flea and 1980s saxophone player (and friend of the band) Keith "Tree" Barry claimed to have come up with the new name: The Red Hot Chili Peppers. (Originally, "The" was part of the band's name; it's unknown at what specific time the band started to go by just "Red Hot Chili Peppers," but it likely has to do with either Hillel Slovak's rejoining the band or his death.)

Moving Out (Anthony's House)

Slovak, Flea, and Kiedis moved into a house together between their second and third shows. Slovak and Flea would practice and write music all day for their various projects—Slovak often working on What Is This? and Flea often focusing on his punk output with Fear—while Kiedis would bounce between everyone and drugs and remain creative lyrically in the new band. Kiedis would especially stick with Flea, who appeared to enjoy writing the chaotic slap of the Red Hot Chili Peppers more than the picking required in Fear. (Fear front man Lee Ving insisted that everyone in the band only down pick, as he considered that the only true punk way of playing.)

By the band's third show, they were commanding a sizable guarantee of $200 and had four (or six, depending on perspective) songs ready to perform: "Out in L.A.," "Get Up and Jump," "Police Helicopter," and "NeverMind." The arguable fifth song was hardly a song at all but still was recorded and eventually released as part of the *Out in L.A.* rarities release "Stranded," a variation of an immature school-yard chant encouraging a person stranded on a toilet without toilet paper to wipe using their hand. The sixth was "She'll Be Coming round the Mountain," a performance of the children's song not altered in any major way.

The gig again took place at the Cathay de Grande, which was considered a real music venue, unlike the Rhythm Lounge, on March 5. Because of lesser attendance, the promoter couldn't pay the full $200, and Kiedis had to shake the promoter up to get more than $40.

Hot in the Press

Beginning with the band's third performance (and first as The Red Hot Chili Peppers), Kiedis and Flea began to appear in *LA Weekly*'s social gossip column, "L.A. Dee Dah." Kiedis attributes this not to their importance but rather because he and Flea were on drugs and clubbing every single night of the week. Nonetheless, they were thrilled, and it is likely that their regular appearances in the weekly column led to some recognition and helped the band build some buzz.

It was at this time that Kiedis met German singer Nina Hagen, whom he began a relationship with and wrote "What It Is [aka Nina's Song]" about. According to Kiedis, Hagen predicted the band would be known worldwide within five years and become the biggest rock group in the world within seven years.

31

Courting *The Red Hot Chili Peppers*

How They Signed to a Major Label

Demoing

Before even thinking of signing to a major label, the Red Hot Chili Peppers recorded a demo with Spit Stix on a budget of $300 for three hours of studio time that included the engineer and the recording tape. The money was paid exclusively by Kiedis. The demos included six complete songs according to Kiedis (but likely was seven) and a few a capella joke ditties: "Out in L.A.," "Green Heaven," "Police Helicopter," "Get Up and Jump," "What It Is [aka Nina's Song]," "Nevermind," and "Sex Rap." The a capella ditties, unreleased until 1994's *Out in L.A.*, were "You Always Sing the Same," "Stranded," "Flea Fly," and "Deck the Halls."

Kiedis claimed in his autobiography that recording had never gone so energetically and so smoothly as in those first demo sessions. Statistically, that was true: the a capella recordings and demos combined add up to nineteen minutes and forty-three seconds of tape, meaning that nearly one-ninth of every moment in the studio led to a recording the band would eventually release.

The band had a few cassettes made and the master tape, so they could continue pressing it if they so desired. They flew out to New York to show their music to promoters and anyone in the music industry who would potentially listen but were, by and large, ignored; Kiedis conceded in his book that their immature tactics and cockiness were likely of no help at all.

Homeless (Again), but with Friends

After returning from New York, Flea, Kiedis, and Slovak were without their previous Hollywood home. Flea and Kiedis moved in with Bob Forrest of Thelonious Monster; Forrest made friends with Flea earlier that year when Forrest played a Defunkt record while deejaying in a club and Flea ran over to tell the deejay that the B-side was better than the side he was playing. Forrest quite literally ran into Kiedis and Flea on the street and offered them a place to stay after the two told Forrest they were homeless.

The Debut of Socks on Cocks

Kiedis had previously used a sock as his only clothing to cover his penis when answering the door to a woman who had a crush on him when he lived with a marijuana dealer. When the Red Hot Chili Peppers played a strip club named the Kit Kat Club, they agreed to do it together to try to steal some attention from anyone who was there to see the strippers. The whole band, including the often sober Jack Irons, smoked weed and were high throughout the performance. It was done as an encore from the start.

It was that same show that had Lindy Goetz, previously the manager of the Ohio Players, in the audience. Goetz wanted to manage the band, who all agreed he could if he bought them Chinese food. He did, and he became the band's first manager as well as a caretaker of sorts: any time the musicians were short on food or drugs, they would hang out with Goetz, get a solid meal, and maybe smoke weed or snort cocaine for one night.

Goetz made it his mission to get the band a record deal.

It was in this era, still in the original lineup, that Flea received an offer to be the bassist for John Lydon from the Sex Pistols' new band, Public Image Ltd. Flea declined it.

Take Me Out to Dinner

Goetz had a sense of humor about the band and an unwavering belief in them. He once told *Artists Magazine* that he discovered the band by listening to their demo tape—a blatant lie—and that he was interested in them because he "thought they were black."

Getting a Lawyer

The Red Hot Chili Peppers decided that if they were to get a record deal, they'd need a lawyer. Eric Greenspan was recommended to them through other musician friends; Flea and Kiedis showed up at his office unannounced, demanded to see Greenspan, and dropped their trousers at the secretary until Greenspan agreed to see them. He then agreed to be their lawyer for the standard 5 percent and remains their lawyer to this day.

EMI Signs Them, and Everyone Leaves a Band

After shows at the Lingerie and the Universal Amphitheater, several record labels began attending the band's concerts and contacting Lindy about a potential record deal. Ultimately, EMI/Enigma offered them a contract, and the band, through Flea and Kiedis, agreed.

However, within a week, Flea received a call that Irons and Slovak had quit the Red Hot Chili Peppers, as the record deal meant they had to decide between What Is This?, who also recently signed a record deal, and the Red Hot Chili Peppers. Flea quit Los Angeles punk band Fear weeks before when Lee Ving kept knocking him for being in two bands and asked if he was going to be in Fear or the Red Hot Chili Peppers. Flea chose to be creative in his own band.

The Hunt for New Chili Peppers

Flea suggested within minutes they could replace Irons and Slovak. Cliff Martinez was Flea's first suggestion as a replacement drummer; Martinez had previously drummed for the Dickies, Roid Rogers, the Weirdos, and Captain Beefheart. Kiedis was most impressed by his being a member of the Weirdos, a hard-core punk band he loved.

Their first audition for a new guitarist after Martinez joined was Dix Denney, who played with Martinez in the Weirdos. Flea and Kiedis went on a European trip together thanks to a gift from Kiedis's father and the whole while had planned for Denney to join. When they got back, it became apparent Denney didn't have the songs memorized. They got along as people, but the band fired him when it wasn't working musically.

They auditioned several guitarists but came up with two finalists: Mark Nine, an art school student who had been in a band with Martinez before, and someone who came off rather uncool named Jack Sherman.

Sherman's connection to the Red Hot Chili Peppers was through his sister; she was connected to the punk and underground scenes, while he was on more of a professional music circuit. Sherman called Flea and arranged the audition; he auditioned without Kiedis present but with Martinez and Flea. Sherman had met Captain Beefheart and his band when Martinez was a member, and Sherman was a Beefheart fan, so he recalled Martinez positively.

It became clear that Sherman was the better player than Nine. After an additional follow-up audition, they offered him the position (asking him to join the band by doing three-part harmony on the phrase "you got the gig"). Sherman had a girlfriend whose ex-boyfriend had also auditioned, but it didn't stop him from accepting the offer. Relatively soon thereafter, it became clear they wouldn't ever get along as bandmates. Sherman did not share much with the band, musically or in terms of personality, but needed the work. He told *The Five Count* that his car was stolen the first week he had moved to Los Angeles and he did not want to play only in cover bands.

With the band's lineup in place, they set off to make their first album.

32

It Starts

The Making of the Band's Self-Titled Record

Choosing a Producer, and Getting Tenser With Him

The Red Hot Chili Peppers had a say in choosing their own producer. One of their first choices was the guitarist for Gang of Four, Andy Gill. The band were fans of Gang of Four (according to Anthony Kiedis—though Flea said a few years later he never liked them), and the four were optimistic that Gill would push them in the right sonic direction. By all accounts, that did not end up being the case.

Gill wanted them to use a beat box. Kiedis interpreted this as a beat box to replace the drumming; Gill has since told interviewers that he was using the beat box as a timekeeper or click track and that they compromised by having Cliff Martinez record a cowbell as a click track to the original beat box versions and then playing to his own cowbell click.

These tensions were worsened by their treatment of guitarist Jack Sherman. Flea and Anthony Kiedis were nasty and rude to Sherman due to personality differences—Flea and Kiedis were punk rockers and rule breakers, Kiedis was a drug addict, and Sherman was more of a clean-cut nerd. Kiedis thought Sherman acted like a patsy for Gill and was easily manipulated, while Gill believed he actively encouraged the band to treat Sherman more like a person who deserved some respect and shelter from the other band members' abuses.

Regretting Gill

The band obviously regretted working with Gill. Beyond that, the band regretted not being better or more mature working with Gill. Dave Thompson reported that four years later, Flea said, "We knew what we wanted. We wanted a raw fucking rocking album.... We should have been asking, 'Can't we try something?' but we didn't know. He was a very uptight Englishman on top of it, so that mix didn't really work very well. To this day, I really regret our inability to deal with Andy [Gill]."

Much like their live show from the time, the Red Hot Chili Peppers had outrageous album art.   *Author's collection*

Flea told *BAM* magazine in 1985 that working with Gill was

> a nightmare. . . . No one was happy with anything, and it was a con-
> stant argument over every little thing. It got to the point where it got
> so emotional that it got way beyond just not liking what was going on
> sound-wise. Andy was calling us names and we were calling him names.
> We called him an old idiot and an old, jaded fool. He called us stupid
> and said we didn't know what we were doing. Everything just got com-
> pletely blown out of proportion.

He felt strongly that Gill had sterilized the wildness that was their whole
appeal at the time of the first record. Flea believed that he wasn't trying to be
anti-polished but wanted to make sure their energy was there and that Gill was
restricting that energy in a way he could not work around.

Gill said at the time that the band was fans of Parliament but not Funkadelic and that Jack Sherman was the one who introduced Kiedis and Flea to Funkadelic in 1984.

Shitting outside the Box

In what has become a famous incident, after a longtime buildup borderline hatred and distrust of Andy Gill and the way the band felt disrespected by him, Flea said he had to take a big shit, and Andy Gill told Flea to bring some back for him. Flea literally pooped in a pizza box; he and Kiedis gave it to Gill as a "shit pizza" to voice their displeasure. Gill was unfazed but displeased; it likely furthered his view that the Red Hot Chili Peppers were a bunch of immature teenagers.

Helldorado

Recorded at Eldorado Studios in Hollywood, the album was done entirely in April 1984. While Gill wasn't on their side; someone else was: engineer Dave Jerden. At the time, Jerden had previously engineered the Talking Heads, David Byrne, Brian Eno, Frank Zappa, and Herbie Hancock; he would go on to produce Jane's Addiction's debut studio album, *Nothing's Shocking*, and its sequel, *Ritual de lo Habitual*, and return to mix the Red Hot Chili Peppers' own *Mother's Milk*, among other outputs.

Jerden was approachable and conversational with the band and with Gill but often got caught in the middle, and it affected his personal health. Toward the end, he had a stomach ulcer and missed a week in the studio. (Similarly, Gill had a cancerous testicle removed during the recording, and during those days without the producer, Flea and Kiedis tried to get Jerden to remake the album in their own style, but Jerden refused.)

Green, but Not Heaven

On the rerelease, the demo versions of songs are notably more energetic and do a better job of capturing the punk energy the Red Hot Chili Peppers were going after. These demos were produced not by Gill but instead by Flea's former bandmate in Fear: drummer Spit Stix.

While "Green Heaven" on the album features no talk box, the demo version with Hillel Slovak on guitar does so prominently. This is perhaps the most major difference other than the tinny drum sounds on the final studio versions: Slovak made prominent use of the talk box in the band's early days, and then guitarist Jack Sherman never used one. (The whole point of the song in Kiedis's view was to lyrically juxtapose the peacefulness of nature underwater and the ruin of man above it, while musically it was there to show off Slovak and his talk box. As such, he was always displeased with the studio recording.)

The other demos include "Get Up and Jump," "Police Helicopter," "Out in L.A.," and "What It Is [aka Nina's Song]"; "What It Is" was never recorded in any other form and is just Flea's bass guitar and Anthony Kiedis's rapping. The lyrics from "What It Is" went on to be used in a song by the titular Nina, Nina Hagen (for more on Hagen, see chapter 12), as well as a few lines pulled into the final version of the *Freaky Styley* song "The Brothers Cup."

Strange Credits

"Baby Appeal" is notable in that both Hillel Slovak and Jack Sherman received songwriting credits for it, being one of the few Red Hot Chili Peppers songs to have more than just four people receive a credit. (Cliff Martinez also received credit, but Jack Irons did not.) "Baby Appeal" was first written after Flea and Kiedis returned from New York City on their trip shopping the band's first demo to promoters (for further information, see chapter 31).

The backing vocals on "Mommy, Where's Daddy?" were performed by Gwen Dickey, better known by her stage name of Rose Norwalt of the band Rose Royce. (She sang lead on disco hits like "Car Wash" and "I Wanna Get Next to You.") Most of the other studio musicians used for the self-titled sessions did not go on or return to prominence, but their trombone player was Phil Ranelin, an experimental jazz musician who had previously played with Stevie Wonder and Freddie Hubbard.

33

Sherminated

Hillel Slovak Rejoins the Band

An Endlessly Terrible Time with Jack Sherman

Although Jack Sherman had some high points—including being the guitarist in the band when they made their first appearance on television in 1984—his time was overall quite tense. Kiedis unplugged Sherman's guitar with his dance moves multiple times, and Sherman always felt it was intentional and took it personally. This led to Sherman taping off his corner of the stage and telling Kiedis it was off-limits and that Kiedis shouldn't enter without Sherman's permission.

Toward the beginning of the band's 1984 tour, Flea was already breaking bass strings at a breakneck pace because of his violent slap bass playing style. The band sat down to discuss whether replacement bass strings could be viewed as a band expense; Sherman was the first (and apparently only, according to Kiedis's autobiography) member to oppose it.

Sex and Drugs

The tour itself was full of cocaine usage from Flea and Kiedis, but Kiedis was using particularly regularly. They went through a roadie, Bob, before adding a second one who was more responsible: Ben. Evidently, Bob spent a good portion of his time chasing cocaine deals on the road for Kiedis. Kiedis admitted in his autobiography that he also was sleeping with different women on the road "more than half the time" even though he was dating a woman named Jennifer Bruce back in Los Angeles. Kiedis wrote more about sex and drugs on the road than the musical performances when talking about 1984 in his autobiography.

Slovak shortly after returning to the band in Philadelphia, 1985.   *Photo by John Coffey*

The Firing

Towards the end of the tour in New Orleans, Flea broke a string onstage, and Kiedis tried to keep the show's momentum going with stage banter. Sherman hated the chatter, and on that night, Kiedis responded by dumping ice on Sherman when he was taking a guitar solo later on. Sherman went to a microphone after the song and claimed it was his last show with the band, and Kiedis responded into the microphone by saying it was the last night he'd have to play with that "asshole" on guitar. People couldn't tell if the tensions were staged or not and took it in stride as an entertaining part of the show.

The New Orleans show was not Sherman's last performance with the group.

At the end of the 1984 tour, Jack Sherman was fired. All of the three other members were present and ended up being in a laughing mood due to their nervous energy—something Sherman came to resent. Flea's first suggestion to replace him was Hillel Slovak, something that Kiedis immediately got behind.

Slovak Brings the Chemistry, Kiedis Does the Drugs

Instantly, the group's creativity picked up, and the overall mood changed. Jack Irons, the original drummer for the Red Hot Chili Peppers, stuck around in the band Slovak had just left, What Is This?, for the time being. He knew before it happened that Slovak would eventually leave, as Slovak was more into the funk of the Red Hot Chili Peppers than the music he and Slovak were playing in their band. What Is This? had grown into a band whose style Slovak did not value.

Slovak, being a longtime friend of Kiedis's, was worried about his drug use despite being a drug user himself. Kiedis's girlfriend, the previously mentioned Jennifer, was more and more into heroin and wanted Kiedis to do only heroin with her; Kiedis preferred to do cocaine when he was using heroin, and it led to an odd amount of romantic tension between them as she policed his drug habits but also facilitated them. He had more or less become dependent on heroin and wouldn't realize it until it was far too late.

The guitarist too was dependent on heroin but did his best to do the drug in secret while Kiedis was far more out in the open. Irons later recalled worrying about the two of them and coped by avoiding thinking about either man. Slovak, shortly before rejoining the Red Hot Chili Peppers, began to trade in the Hollywood underground circle, read William Burroughs, and began to isolate himself more and more, with or without heroin.

Sherman would later return at three separate points: in the recording studio for *Mother's Milk* in 1988 or 1989, to sue the band for harassment and money owed in 1993, and to complain about not being admitted into the Rock and Roll Hall of Fame when three other guitarists were in 2014.

As Slovak helped push the band to become more obsessed with Defunkt and Funkadelic over the winter of 1984, the band began to plot out the producer for their next studio album.

34

Freaky Styley

Making an Album with George Clinton

The Short Search for a Producer

The first potential producer the band looked at was Malcolm McLaren, who previously produced the Sex Pistols and Bow Wow Wow, among others. McLaren went to a Red Hot Chili Peppers band practice and told the group what he envisioned as the keys to becoming the next big thing: simplify music into 1950s rock 'n' roll, make the group's imagery more like hot pink surfers, and make Anthony Kiedis the clear front man and sole star of the band. Flea allegedly passed out from the interaction, and everyone—including Kiedis—was vehemently opposed to the idea.

When EMI asked the band who else they would want to produce the album, George Clinton was their first suggestion. Flea and band manager Lindy Goetz traveled to meet up with Clinton after sending him demos, and Clinton agreed to produce the album, receiving $25,000 from EMI to do so.

Hanging with Clinton

The songs were about 70 percent finished when the band went to Detroit. Clinton had set aside a month for preproduction and hanging out before even attempting to record; he was not worried about finishing the songs as much as setting the tone for the recording sessions. Most of that 70 percent was composed while ex-guitarist Jack Sherman was still in the band.

Sherman received writing credits for "Jungle Man," "American Ghost Dance," "Freaky Styley," "Blackeyed Blonde," "Battleship," "Lovin' and Touchin'," and "Catholic School Girls Rule"—half of the album's final songs. Guitarist Hillel Slovak received fewer credits than Sherman due to two covers—the Meters' "Africa" turned into the Red Hot Chili Peppers' "Hollywood (Africa)" and Sly and the Family Stones' "If You Want Me to Stay" and the interesting decision to give Dr. Seuss sole writing credit for "Yertle the Turtle," even though he did not write the lyrics or the music, just the original story the song was based on. Flea was

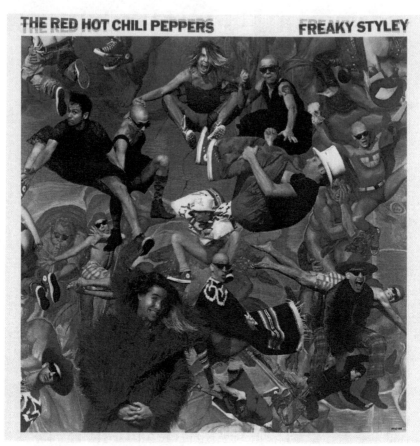

The album cover of the George Clinton–produced *funkathon*.   *Author's collection*

the one who wanted to cover the Meters, but Clinton suggested the band change "Africa" to the band's version of Africa, which was Hollywood.

For the first week of preproduction, the four band members and manager Lindy stayed at George Clinton's actual house; the rest of the time, they rented out a house within a short distance to the studio. Hillel Slovak and Kiedis shared a room, Cliff Martinez and Flea shared a room, and Lindy got his own room. Soon thereafter, Kiedis began to experience heroin withdrawals; Kiedis did not realize it until Flea pointed out to him that his nausea and vomiting were caused by the dope sickness. Despite this, the band immediately spent $500 on cocaine and partied nonstop for the start of their stay.

Crashing Detroit

The band was actually supposed to spend the whole time at Clinton's house, but that changed when Kiedis crashed one of Clinton's snowmobiles and they were all around very destructive. Multiple times, the four band members went to shows and had at least one member start playing another band's instruments while they were between songs and sets; one time, the full band did it, while another time, Flea attempted to replace the bassist at an in-house bar band's performance. The night the entire band did an impromptu Red Hot Chili Peppers set was the same night Hillel got the nickname "Skinny Sweaty Man in a Green Suit" because he wore a green suit but would not stop dancing ridiculously at the club they were at.

Clinton took the band to see Aretha Franklin live, and the only two people to not wear fur coats were Flea and Lindy Goetz.

Moments of Inspiration

The song "Freaky Styley" was meant to be a short instrumental jam between songs, but Clinton was too big of a fan of its groove and insisted they turn it into something more. Clinton came up with the chant for the song in the control booth, while Kiedis came up with the actual titular lyric over Clinton's rhythm stylings. The whole band had begun to use "freaky styley" as their own word for cool or interesting; when it came time to name the album and Martinez asked what it should be called, Kiedis suggested they call it *Freaky Styley*.

For most recordings, Kiedis was set up in the center of the band's room, helping to give him energy that the previous record sorely missed. For the cover of "If You Want Me to Stay," Kiedis was alone, but Clinton was dancing around and singing with him to help put his mind at ease. Clinton had spent a large part of his time mentoring Kiedis, building his confidence, and going fishing with him, treating him like a little brother or an equal, and Kiedis credited Clinton for giving him the confidence to do a good performance.

"Millionaires against Hunger" was recorded at these sessions but was not formally released until the "Taste the Pain" single in 1990 and the B-side collection *Out in L.A.* in 1994.

Look at That Turtle Go, Bro

Clinton's drug dealer, a man named Louie, showed up one day threatening violence if he didn't get paid soon. Clinton appeased him and bought himself time to pay Louie by saying he could make his vocal debut on the album, which he did as the narrator voice, saying, "Look at that turtle go, bro" on "Yertle the Turtle." (It remains unusual that Dr. Seuss got the writing credit for the song.)

Additional Musicians

Several musicians provided backing vocals, including Clinton, Steve Boyd, Shirley Hayden, P-funk guitarist Gary Shider, Joel Virgel, soul singer Pat Lewis, Robert "Peanut" Johnson, Lous "Bro" Kabbabie, and Andre Foxxe. Famed saxophonist Maceo Parker played saxophone; Perry Farrell later named his cat after Parker and wrote the song "My Cat's Name Is Maceo" as an ode to said cat. (Parker played saxophone on that Jane's Addiction song but confronted Farrell and told him that he wasn't Farrell's cat; Farrell explained that Maceo was literally the name of his feline, and Parker responded by upping his fee for playing saxophone.)

Former James Brown trombonist Fred Wesley played on the album and did the horn arrangements. (Clinton received credit for the vocal arrangements.) But the most interesting connection was Parliament and Funkadelic percussionist Larry Fratangelo playing on the album. Fratangelo was literally future Red Hot Chili Peppers' drummer Chad Smith's teacher at this time; the two were bandmates in Pharaoh while Fratangelo did the sessions with the Red Hot Chili Peppers. (For more on Fratangelo, see chapter 23.)

Reception

When the album was finished, EMI flew out a few executives to listen to the album in Michigan. They were unimpressed and remained silent after listening to the entire album.

Despite this (and unlike their first album), *Freaky Styley* actually turned a few heads. *Rolling Stone* even praised it, noting that rock music in general was overdue for racial integration. It didn't lead to their becoming a cultural sensation; they still remained a largely underground but respected band who were known for their drug addictions if they were known at all.

35

Another Change

Jack Irons Comes Back

Back in Hollywood, Back into Heavy Drugs

Although hardly an instant success after *Styley*, the band was happy with it and hit the road hard. They appeared in the 1986 film *Thrashin'* starring Josh Brolin playing "Blackeyed Blonde" with Cliff Martinez on drums despite the fact that by the time of the film's release, Martinez was no longer in the band. (It is also one of the high-quality video recordings of Hillel Slovak out there, where he played a double-neck guitar but used only one neck.)

Around that time, Anthony Kiedis began to mix heroin with sex. He swiftly came to obsess over it, believing that the highest form of lovemaking came from it. Hillel Slovak started using more and more; he most likely felt freer being around the even more addicted Kiedis.

In the immediate aftermath of *Freaky Styley*'s release, the band still played Hollywood shows, opening up for Oingo Boingo another time. The show was notable in that George Clinton had traveled to Hollywood and danced onstage during the Red Hot Chili Peppers' set, and Kiedis made an unprompted anti-drug speech onstage after a large drug binge the previous day.

Drugs Again, on the Road Again, Unsupported by EMI Again

A month after the Oingo Boingo show, the band began a long tour. Kiedis noticed at this time that Slovak was weaker than ever. The two didn't do heroin on the road but compensated heavily with alcohol, particularly Jägermeister. Kiedis's girlfriend almost overdosed while they were doing heroin at Slovak's one night; Kiedis remembered the basic techniques for overdose revival, rushed her into a cold shower, and slapped her to stay awake while Slovak called an ambulance. She survived, but it still did not serve as a truly much-needed wake-up call for either band member.

Kiedis attempted to get clean from time to time, once by Flea's urging. Kiedis tried to dry out at Flea's place; Kiedis eventually moved into the building with his drug addict girlfriend, met a new drug dealer named Dominique, and relapsed.

Despite the respect from critics and heavy work on the road, the band's record label still didn't market the album heavily in the band's mind. EMI did not give the band any money for a music video, and in the MTV age, it prohibited greater success. The band made a music video for "Catholic School Girls Rule" using their own money with help from friend Dick Rude—later the filmmaker for their *Off the Map* DVD—and the fairly blasphemous video got played in music venues only because of its mature but inappropriate nature.

After one leg of the tour, Kiedis discovered that his then girlfriend cheated on him with a friend of his. Despite the fact that Kiedis had cheated on her countless times over the past year, Kiedis broke it off with her and ended his friendship with her affair partner.

EMI Funds a Demo and Selects a Producer for Their Third Album

In between tour legs, EMI gave the Red Hot Chili Peppers $5,000 to record a demo. No one in the band thought making a demo actually cost that much money, so they chose producer Keith Levene from Public Image Ltd because he was a good drug connection. Of the $5,000, $2,000 was set aside for drugs. Flea didn't agree with it, and it's likely that drummer Cliff Martinez never truly knew, but Slovak and Kiedis were all for it. The relationship with Levene wouldn't last; he didn't take much control of the band to get them to be productive and didn't work well with his engineers, often yelling, "Just mash it up! Mash it up I say!" as if it would fix problems, according to Flea's revised *Freaky Styley* liner notes.

In the studio, Martinez saw an early electronic drum kit and became obsessed. The rest of the band sensed his heart was no longer in the Red Hot Chili Peppers, and he was promptly fired by Flea. Martinez took it hard and was not on good terms with the band for a few years but eventually moved on.

That was in April 1986; reports vary as to what exactly happened. Original drummer Jack Irons had already been called by Flea as a replacement, possibly as early as October 1985; he considered Flea's offer, quit What Is This? in January 1986, and joined the Red Hot Chili Peppers instantly in the middle of a studio visit in April. (Kiedis's time line did not agree with that time line, but biographer Dave Thompson reported that Irons's and Flea's did.) When the demos were finished, the band decided on Michael Beinhorn as their producer for their next album, believing him to understand the band while still holding intelligence and a hit maker's ear, as he recently produced the hit Herbie Hancock song "Rockit."

Kiedis Briefly Fired, First Period of Sobriety

Kiedis had been showing up to rehearsals late, forgetting lyrics, and overall not producing at any sort of respectable level. Slovak was also on drugs at the same or greater level, but it didn't stop his ability to write music or jam with the band, while Kiedis literally dozed off during band practices.

At one band practice, the three other members—led by Flea—kicked Kiedis out of the band. Kiedis shrugged it off and binged even more heavily on drugs until the money ran out. A week or so after his firing, friend of the band Bob Forest of Thelonious Monster informed Kiedis that the Red Hot Chili Peppers— still without Kiedis—were nominated for the *LA Weekly* award for band of the year. Kiedis snuck into the award ceremony after doing a speedball; when the band won the award, the three other members accepted it and did not mention the missing Kiedis.

Afterward, Kiedis called his mother in Michigan, was honest with her about his heroin addiction, and made arrangements to go home to a methadone clinic for his first true attempt at rehabilitation. He missed his flight and kept getting high a few times. He was nearly busted by police on the street one day, and after the incident, he flew home to Michigan while still high.

After twenty days in Michigan at the clinic, he went home to his mother's. Flea called him, heard he was sober, and congratulated him; the two caught up and still maintained a friendship. After another few days, Flea called again to ask if Kiedis would like to rejoin the band; Kiedis said nothing more would please him, and he eventually returned to Los Angeles to begin work on what would become *The Uplift Mofo Party Plan*.

36

The Uplift Mofo Party Plan

The Original Lineup Makes an Album

1986: A Year of Touring

The Red Hot Chili Peppers knew they wouldn't release an album until 1987 as they struggled to write new songs with half the band addicted to heroin. From the start of the year, the plan was to tour as heavily as possible. Flea proposed to his girlfriend, Loesha. Around the same time, Kiedis moved in with band manager Lindy Goetz on his return from Michigan.

The Producers, the First Marriage, and More Destruction

Before Michael Beinhorn, Rick Rubin was the band's first choice as producer. The impression Beinhorn got is that Rubin wanted to work with bigger, more successful bands than the Red Hot Chili Peppers, but others have told a different side of the story. Flea recalled Rubin attending a band practice with the Beastie Boys but not connecting at all with him; Rubin remembered attending a rehearsal and said that it musically worked but that drugs had brought an incredibly dark energy to the band.

Rubin later spoke to Kiedis about meeting the band about potentially producing the album for *Interview* magazine. Kiedis said that "it was odd—and remarkable—that we were still showing up and practicing, because both Hillel and I were very involved in pursuing self-destruction and copious consumption of narcotics to the point where you didn't know what was going on when you walked in that room."

Beinhorn felt no shame in being the second choice and quickly went to work on production. They decided to record the album in the basement of the Capitol Records building. Kiedis started out sober and encouraged Hillel Slovak to go

A promotional poster for the "Fight Like a Brave" single.   *Author's collection*

to Alcoholics Anonymous with him. Slovak responded by saying that he wasn't an alcoholic and thus that he didn't have to go.

Ten days before they entered the studio, Kiedis had lyrics for ten songs but hadn't finished the rest.

The Songs

Kiedis wrote both "Skinny Sweaty Man" and "No Chump Love Sucker" as odes to Slovak. ("Skinny Sweaty Man" was a direct reference to an incident from the recording of *Freaky Styley*; for more information, see chapter 34.) Beinhorn ended up helping Kiedis with the group chant chorus to "Fight Like a Brave," a chorus later referenced in the Sublime song "All You Need."

One song that failed to make the album but that was recorded from the *Uplift Mofo* sessions was "Fire." Released in 1988 in the United Kingdom on *The Abbey Road E.P.*, it was the last song to feature Hillel Slovak in the band's studio discography. (*The Abbey Road E.P.* was released by EMI America as a way to introduce European audiences to the Red Hot Chili Peppers' back catalog; EMI didn't release *Freaky Styley* or *The Uplift Mofo Party Plan* in the United Kingdom until 1990.)

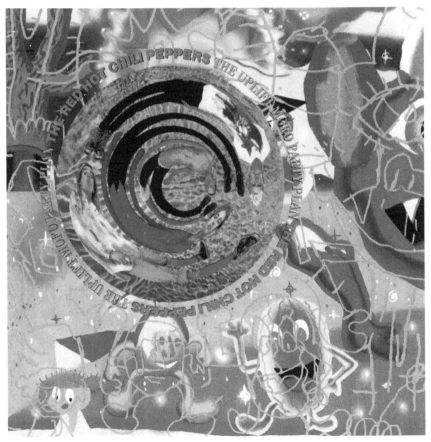

The album cover.   *Author's collection*

End of Sobriety

After exactly fifty days of sobriety, Kiedis thought the time was worth celebrating with drug usage. He planned to smoke weed for a day or two but found himself binging uncontrollably until he did enough heroin to doze off and admit his mistakes to the band. Kiedis chalked up the relapse to the lack of a support system, something he himself contributed to by his own admission, as he (falsely) believed he had to do everything on his own at that time.

Briefly sober again, Kiedis was able to record more singing vocals than usual on the record. Slovak was his vocal producer and pushed him to what both believed were new heights. After the last day of recording, the two celebrated with a huge score of heroin. Kiedis continued to do speedballs in their manager's apartment for weeks after.

A Moment of Success

The Uplift Mofo Party Plan was the band's first album to debut on the *Billboard* Top 200 at number 148. After the label got the band to change the name of the song "Party on Your Pussy" to "Special Secret Song Inside," they worked harder to promote this album than the previous two. It was in this era that future guitarist John Frusciante became obsessed with the Red Hot Chili Peppers and saw them for the first time.

A young Anthony Kiedis.   *Fabio Diena / Shutterstock.com*

Critics were mixed on the album, with some praising it and some tearing it apart. Nonetheless, it has stood the test of time, being the earliest record in the band's discography to go gold. The band's real path to destruction wasn't *The Uplift Mofo Party Plan* but rather the endless touring that took place across the rest of 1987.

Good Times, Boys

The Short High and a European Tour

Tour Mentality

Because of the album's comparative success, the band was able to afford a few luxuries. When it was time to fly the band out for tour, a limousine picked the members up. It fueled their confidence. Inspired, Slovak and Kiedis didn't feel as addicted on the road; they still binged on cocaine, drank a lot, and smoked more than a fair amount of marijuana, but they stayed off heroin for the most part during the 1987 tour dates.

Road Stories

In Texas, Kiedis shaved his pubic hair, and then their merchandise manager tried to sell it in a Ziploc bag for $20. (It didn't sell, but three women gave their panties on seeing the bag.)

They had several tour games. One, dating back to *Freaky Styley*, was called the Truck Stop Vomiting Club. They ate terribly unhealthy food on tour; the Truck Stop Vomiting Club made it a point to have everyone in the band vomit up whatever terrible food they ate at a given truck stop before getting back into their van or bus.

Slovak pioneered a tour game they called the Grizzlers. In it, whenever at a restaurant, each band member would have to rhyme as if rapping when placing their order, and whoever went last would do their line and conclude with "because we're the Grizzlers." (In his autobiography, Kiedis used the example of "I don't know any Chinese, but I've worked with blacks / so give me scrambled eggs with a side of flapjacks / because we're the Grizzlers.")

Tongue in the Dirt came back from their teen years. (See chapter 29.) This time, the band and whatever roadies or girls were around would play catch with a football or a comparable object until someone dropped it. Once dropped, the group would decide whether it was a catchable or an uncatchable throw. If it was something that should've been caught, the receiver got down on the ground and licked the dirt. If it wasn't, the thrower had to. The game progressed to where losing was an honor, and losers took pride in how gross they would get, eating bugs or licking trash cans.

In all of these tour games, Flea was either the leader or the instigator. Slovak and Kiedis were the big partiers; Flea and Irons were more the sober types, but Irons was more like a parent, and Flea seemed to be the party starter or the joker.

A Minor Amount of Fame Finally Stops Kiedis from Road Sex (and Leads to Money)

As the band started to become slightly famous, women started showing up backstage and throwing themselves at the band. (One woman showed up with her boyfriend and showed a tattoo of Anthony Kiedis's name to him right above her vagina; the boyfriend insisted he was fine with Kiedis sleeping with her. She was declined by Kiedis.)

The fame and ease of access ironically led it to be Kiedis's most sexless tour yet. Fame wouldn't always stop him from going for it, but it did in 1987.

According to Kiedis, the band made $3,000 each after the *Freaky Styley* tour. After T-shirt sales and the like, band members made $22,000 each after the *Uplift Mofo Party Plan* tour.

Returning Back to Los Angeles before Europe

With $22,000 in hand each, band members went and did different things. Slovak almost exclusively spent it on drugs and new guitars. Kiedis put down five months' rent for his dream house and moved in with his girlfriend, Ione, who Flea had introduced him to. (Kiedis then drug binged.) The band played Los Angeles rock radio station KROC's festival for the first time. The festival caused a traffic jam that the band got stuck in, causing all of them to have a brief moment where they felt like they were making it.

Kiedis got arrested after he looked similar to the Ponytail Bandit; he was interrogated by the FBI with the previously mentioned Mario and put in the Los Angeles County Jail. Manager Lindy Goetz eventually showed up to bail him out but waited a night after the band encouraged him to do so in an effort to get Kiedis off drugs again.

Slovak's drug use became nonstop and concealed, while Kiedis became more of a binger, going through daylight hours sober until party time started and his cocaine addiction kicked in. Despite Slovak's most likely doing more drugs than Kiedis, Slovak once approached Kiedis and begged him not to die or hurt himself.

Europe

Europe was the clear beginning of the end. In December 1987, the band left for their first tour of the continent. In London on the first show, Slovak almost failed to make it onstage, as he was sick from coping. After a huge effort, Flea and Kiedis got Slovak into the club and played one or two songs, but then Slovak ran backstage, saying he could not play guitar. He cried in his hands. Flea and Kiedis briefly tried to get Slovak back onstage again, but eventually they had to perform, and they performed the rest of the set as a three-piece.

Irons was crazy for his girlfriend at the time. She cheated on him and left him during the European tour, and Irons found out, sending him into a strange sort of mania. Kiedis began to use drugs on the road again, while Flea stayed upbeat and Slovak fought against his weakness. Every night during tour, the band would invite the crowd back to their hotel, with Kiedis giving the crowd Flea's hotel room and Flea giving them Kiedis's.

The tour went fairly smoothly given half the band's drug habits. By the end, their chemistry was extremely tight. Footage from the band on this tour can be seen in *VPro '88*; the year in its name is from its air date, not its recording date.

Returning Back

When they returned to America, they had only a few tour dates lined up. One was at New York University. Kiedis made a deal with Slovak that neither would get high before the show, but Slovak showed up strung out on heroin. It upset Kiedis to the point that, within a week after the show, the band fired Slovak the way it had previously fired Kiedis.

They briefly hired DeWayne "Blackbyrd" McKnight, a black guitarist who used to play with Parliament and Funkadelic, but it wasn't working, and the band swiftly returned to Slovak. (McKnight would return again after Slovak for a short period.) With Slovak back in the band, they played a handful of European festivals, including one with the Ramones where everyone besides Slovak stripped naked and danced to "Blitzkrieg Bop." (Johnny Ramone confronted them after, saying he hated it, while Joey Ramone said he sort of liked it.)

Kiedis took Slovak to one Alcoholics Anonymous or Narcotics Anonymous meeting but couldn't convince him to attend one again. The two discussed trying to do something more positive than simply binging on drugs but always figured it would come after one or two more highs. After the second and final leg of the European tour, everyone stayed in Los Angeles, and Kiedis and Slovak raced to their separate drug dealers. Only one would make it out alive.

38

A Los Angeles Tragedy

Hillel Slovak's Death

Under the Bridge Downtown

The song "Under the Bridge" is about a specific moment of darkness in Anthony Kiedis's addiction where he met a drug dealer named Mario and pretended to be related to him in some way as they went to a Mexican gang area underneath an overpass downtown to buy more heroin. According to *Scar Tissue*, Kiedis's autobiography, that moment happened between tours in 1987. It likely happened shortly before Slovak himself overdosed and is part of why Kiedis has reflected on it as the lowest point in his life.

The Family Finds Out about Hillel's Problems

Slovak worked to conceal his drug addiction from most of his friends and all of his family. Although it was known he was a heroin addict, Slovak did his drugs in private and, especially near the end of his life, isolated himself and hid his use from the world. Nonetheless, one of the Red Hot Chili Peppers' roadies told Hillel's younger brother, James Slovak, about the addiction approximately three months before Hillel passed away.

James confronted Hillel about it, and Hillel admitted he used. Hillel asked James not to tell their mother about Hillel's drug problem; James agreed, though since his brother's passing, he has expressed regret to VH1's *Behind the Music* for not telling his mother about it in his book.

After-Tour Pact

In *Scar Tissue*, Anthony Kiedis wrote about he and Hillel Slovak sharing a dream of getting sober together and discussing one day achieving it. Kiedis also told VH1's *Behind the Music* that he and Slovak had a pact after the tour, believing they would both die if they didn't get clean soon, so they had to sober up for the band. Nonetheless, both went their separate ways and continued to do drugs, Slovak in isolation and Kiedis more publicly. They planned to reconnect in a few weeks but never did so.

Family Efforts

When James Slovak published Hillel's diaries and artwork in 1999, he did very little actual writing of his own. However, he did tell the story of the last things he said to Hillel and how he found out about his brother's death. When Hillel got home after the tour, the two began to speak like brothers for the first time in a long while. He wrote in his book,

> It was all in the open and we were able to talk to each other about his drug problem. A few nights later, Hillel called me, we talked about the heroin because he kept thinking about it. I asked him to please don't do it. "Shooting heroin is like playing Russian Roulette . . . you could die." There was a long pause on the phone and he said, simply, "I know, I love you bro." I told him the same and we hung up. That was the last time I spoke to my brother because he overdosed that night.

VH1 alternatively reported that the phone call took place on the Friday before Hillel's death.

Finding the Body

Regardless of when the phone call was, the band and their manager were unable to reach Hillel throughout the weekend. On Monday, June 27, 1988, police entered Hillel's apartment and found his body on top of a recently finished painting of his. He was smoking a cigarette when he passed—evidenced by a hole burned in the painting from a cigarette still lingering in Hillel's mouth.

After several days, the autopsy came out and confirmed that it was an overdose and that it had likely occurred on June 25. Kiedis found out when his girlfriend told him over the phone but didn't believe it until she told him face-to-face.

The Family Finds Out Hillel Has Died

James Slovak didn't find out about his brother's death until 8:00 p.m. on June 27, 1988—two full days after Hillel passed away. Two friends of Hillel's showed up at his door, asked if they could talk to James, but declined going inside James's home, instead suggesting James go outside for a conversation. James then noticed how pale white the two were, and they told James that Hillel had overdosed and was dead.

When James went to Hillel's apartment, band manager Lindy Goetz already had identified Hillel's body. The younger Slovak went to his Uncle Aron's—the same uncle who bought Hillel his first guitar (see chapter 28)—and told him what happened. They decided that both of them would tell Hillel's mother rather than having one of them do it alone.

James went to Hillel's apartment a week later and took what he considered his brother's valuables. He also took Hillel's drawings, letters, diaries, and paintings, a fine portion of which ended up being published by James as *Behind the Sun: The Diary and Art of Hillel Slovak*.

Flea Finds Out

Flea told *Guitar World* in 2006 about when he found out about Slovak's passing. Jane's Addiction had just finished recording *Nothing's Shocking*, and Flea was hanging out with Jane's front man Perry Farrell. The two watched the Mike Tyson fight that day, but then Flea went home. He was hanging out with his then wife, pregnant with Flea's daughter, when he got the call. He was devastated.

Funeral

Hillel's funeral was held on June 30, 1988—the Thursday after his death and only two days after his family found out. At the time of the funeral, his autopsy was inconclusive about the exact medical cause of death, but according to the *Los Angeles Times*, it was widely known by those close to him that he had overdosed. The funeral and services were held at Mount Sinai Memorial Park in the Hollywood Hills of Los Angeles.

Kiedis did not attend the funeral and left Los Angeles after finding out Hillel died. He went to Puerto Vallarta, Mexico, and stayed in a small house where he kicked heroin cold turkey. On returning to Los Angeles ten days later, he went back to using almost immediately.

On VH1's *Behind the Music*, Flea expressed regret about not being there more for Hillel.

39

A Sea Change

The Peppers Undergo Their First Major Lineup Change

I don't pay attention to the world. I just have the art I like and the music I like and for me that's the whole world.

—*John Frusciante, Guitarist, 2003*

Down One Man Quickly Became Down Two Men

After Hillel Slovak's death and Kiedis's retreat to Mexico, the group laid low. When Kiedis returned, drummer Jack Irons called a band meeting where he respectfully resigned. His stated reasoning differs depending on whose account has retold it, but the basic idea has remained no matter the telling: Irons did not want to be part of an entity or scene where his friends would die so young.

Irons spent months in a deep, dark depression, secluding himself more than anyone else in the band had before. Only twenty-seven years old when Slovak died, Irons would spend time in the hospital from his mental state; the death caused Irons's first bout of clinical depression. Irons disappeared from the music scene until Joe Strummer offered him a series of gigs around Christmas 1988. (Irons argued he hadn't played drums in six months, but Strummer wouldn't take no for an answer.) Flea and Irons kept in touch once Irons stopped secluding himself and began to take phone calls from friends again. Irons later formed Eleven in 1990.

The First New Drummer and Guitarist

It is hard to say whether Irons or Slovak got their replacement first, but within an iteration, the Red Hot Chili Peppers became half African American. The drummer who replaced Irons was D. H. Peligro, former drummer of the Dead Kennedys, who had known the band for years, going back to when the Red Hot

Chili Peppers were fans of the Dead Kennedys and Flea and Peligro discussed punk shows together while Flea was in Fear. (For a more complete history of every iteration of the band, see chapter 13.) For a brief period in the 1980s, Peligro, Flea, and Anthony Kiedis had a joke band together called the Three Little Butt Hairs.

The natural choice to replace Slovak was DeWayne "Blackbyrd" McKnight. Blackbyrd (incorrectly spelled "Blackbird" in Kiedis's autobiography) replaced Slovak once before when Slovak's addiction had prohibited him from proper band practice; McKnight's selection felt natural and easy. Before the band wanted to do any shows or record again, Kiedis wanted to clean up his act one more time.

Kiedis Goes to Rehab Again

Kiedis spent his last $10,000 on going to a California rehab center after he got sponsored by a man named Bob Timmons. Timmons convinced him it might be worth the cost and stayed in touch with Kiedis throughout his rehab and took him to Slovak's plaque in the cemetery. After some discomfort, Kiedis opened up to Slovak's plaque and burst to tears. He vowed not to do heroin after that.

The Permanent Guitarist

After Kiedis left rehab, he remained sober for several years. Peligro was fitting in with the Red Hot Chili Peppers dynamic—already a friend of the band, he knew how to party and how to collaborate creatively with everyone else in the band. McKnight did not fit in so well; he was older than everyone else and was used to following a single band leader, as his primary source of musical experience was playing with Parliament, Funkadelic, George Clinton, and the P-Funk All Stars (though he had also played with Herbie Hancock, among others).

Early Jams Lead to Eventual Songs

Peligro introduced Flea to a teenager named John Frusciante in 1988. Frusciante was obsessed with the Red Hot Chili Peppers and had attended many shows in Los Angeles. He jammed with Flea; the first jam they ever did ended up as the basis for "Nobody Weird Like Me." Another jam from the same session would end up as the basis for "Pretty Little Ditty."

Flea introduced Frusciante to Kiedis, who began spending time with the teenager. Flea invited Frusciante to his house to record guitar on a four-track

Flea was making; after Frusciante nailed the recording, Flea urged Kiedis to have Frusciante replace McKnight. Kiedis didn't need much convincing. Mc-Knight's last show was on September 7, 1988, in Oakland, California, at the Omni. Frusciante's first show with the band was on October 5 of the same year in Tempe, Arizona, at Six Feet Under.

Auditioning

Kiedis literally drove Frusciante to audition with Bob Forrest's group, Thelonious Monster. Kiedis watch Frusciante audition, called Flea to make sure they agreed that Frusciante should be a Red Hot Chili Pepper, and offered Frusciante the Chili Peppers job before Forrest could offer Frusciante the Thelonious Monster job. The members of Thelonious Monster were not pleased.

Kiedis was tasked with firing McKnight. Because McKnight was in south Los Angeles—what felt like an entire world away—Kiedis fired him over the phone. McKnight reacted with anger, repeatedly saying he would burn down Kiedis's house until the call ended.

Kiedis began to clash with Peligro, as Peligro showed up to rehearsals late or drunk and Kiedis was now sober and trying to surround himself with a more sober environment. As they began to write new music for another album, Frusciante told Kiedis that Kiedis could come to him with any musical idea and Frusciante would be happy to work on it with him. Kiedis presented Frusciante the lyrics to "Knock Me Down," and that was the first song by the Red Hot Chili Peppers written in a new method that would become key for the band: Frusciante wrote the melody to Kiedis's lyrics and gave the band the musical framework for the song.

The band did one tour in this lineup that they internally referred to as the Turd Town Tour, playing only the smallest of markets. The tour was seventeen dates in the United States and one in Canada and ended on New Year's Eve 1988. The tour was fun for the group: all four were friends—Kiedis and Frusciante becoming best friends fast—and helped Flea and Kiedis move past their close friend's death.

A New Drummer

The way Chad Smith joined the Red Hot Chili Peppers is the stuff of legend. Peligro was fired in the fall of 1988, probably in November in between tour dates. (Peligro had helped write a few songs on *Mother's Milk*. For more, see chapter 42.) The band had auditioned exactly twenty-nine drummers before Smith and was discouraged by the end of a day's auditions at a rented rehearsal space. A mutual friend of Smith's and the Peppers, Denise Zoom, recommended him to the band, saying the midwesterner ate drums alive. Kiedis and Flea did not particularly believe Zoom's words.

Kiedis saw Smith coming to the audition on the street and thought he wouldn't work at all, as Smith came off as both a metalhead and a motorcyclist—both of which he was. Once it came to jam time, Smith was the only drummer to keep up with Flea and even urged him on, shouting nonsense at Flea and forcing Flea to bring it. Frusciante broke a string during the jam and changed it out as fast as he could. Kiedis was convinced Smith could be the guy.

The band offered Smith the job on one condition: that he shave his mullet and return as a skinhead for rehearsals the next day. Smith showed up but didn't shave it; the band decided that Smith doing his own thing *was* the thing to do and let him join in anyway. At the time, the band thought it was due to a self-absorbed love of his flowing locks; in actuality, Smith was worried about going bald and did not want to speed up the process.

According to biographer Jeff Apter, some sources—including future Mother's Milk producer Michael Beinhorn—believe that Anthony Kiedis and Flea were not entirely sold on Chad Smith on his audition, though all agree it was clear that Smith was the right man for the job from the get-go. It has been stated that manager Lindy Goetz told Smith to be patient, as he would certainly get the job, and that Goetz convinced Kiedis and Flea to hire Smith; this is not the way Kiedis or Smith have told the story in the decades since.

The person who auditioned right before Smith was Chris Warren. Warren left one of his cymbals behind at the audition and later called Flea to get it back. The two struck up a friendship—which led Warren to eventually become the Red Hot Chili Peppers' drum technician. He has also since played keyboard live in the Klinghoffer era of the band.

40

Detroit Rock City

Chad Smith's Pre-Peppers Life

A Midwestern Wild Man

Born in St. Paul, Minnesota, on October 25, 1961, Chadwick Gaylord Smith and his family moved to Michigan when he was still young. The third child of his parents, Joan and Curtis Smith, he was raised in Bloomfield Hills, Michigan. He began to drum at age seven on a set of ice cream cartons that his father stole from behind a local Baskin-Robbins and used a pair of Lincoln Logs as drumsticks. After destroying the ice cream cartons, he got an actual set of drums, though it was a lower-quality set from K-Mart with a tin-like triangle and cymbals.

Both of his siblings played music. His brother Andy, two years older, played guitar and was his first big musical influence, introducing the young Chad to many bands that would become his favorites: Led Zeppelin, Black Sabbath, KISS, the Who, Deep Purple, and the like. Andy was more of a rule follower, while Chad was more of the rule breaker.

Another one of his brothers, Brad, formed Chad's first band: Rockin' Conspiracy. His other two high school bands were named Pair of Dice—a play on "Paradise"—and Northstar.

His father, Curtis, was into country and jazz, and what Smith knew about those genres as a player came from extensive family listening time until the end of high school, where he studied the book *Drummin' Men* by Burt Korall. Curtis was once in the navy and moved to Detroit to work for the Ford Motor Company. He'd often break out his navy suit when playing jazz.

From an early age, Smith was a fan of Detroit-area sports teams, particularly the Red Wings and the Pistons. He was also a fan of the University of Michigan, not Michigan State.

The Teenage Years

Smith lost his virginity at age thirteen to his then girlfriend Jackie, who lived five miles away. They would walk to each other's houses and fool around. (It happened at her house, not his.)

Smith ran away from home at age fifteen for one summer. He spent it smoking marijuana, crashing on friends' couches and living in cars. He adopted a dog that summer, a black Labrador retriever he aptly named Bong. When he came home, his mother sent him to a Catholic school as discipline, and she kept the dog but started to refer to him as "Bo," dropping the last two letters of his name.

Ungainful Employment

Between his teenage and young adult years, Smith was unable to hold a steady job outside of music. He worked for a painting company but was fired when he failed a large order; he had a job at The Gap that did not last long, and he knocked over a vat of maple syrup at a pancake house and was fired. He graduated high school in 1980 and soon after joined a Detroit-area band, Tilt, and began to make $150 a week playing six nights a week, three sets a night. (For further details, see chapter 23.)

Drugs, Alcohol, Addiction

Although he never went as deep as Anthony Kiedis, Smith was a big drinker, and it led to personal problems in his life. By his own admission, alcohol led his first marriage to fall apart. In 1986, he spent a month in jail for hitting someone with his car while drunk. He sobered up in 2008 and quit drinking and smoking entirely, as he felt he needed to do so for his family.

Music

Smith never took tried-and-true music lessons as a child. He did, however, study music in school, playing in his high school's jazz, wind, marching, and concert bands and playing in rock bands throughout high school. His mother was supportive of his practice routine and allowed him to set up his drum set in the house, the garage, and the basement, even supporting it when Smith clearly annoyed his neighbors.

From a young age, Smith knew he wanted to be a full-time musician. He did not go to college and never intended to; instead, he went on the bar circuit and joined as many bands as he could straight out of high school.

In 1984, Chad Smith joined a band named Toby Redd; he joined in time for their second album: *In the Light*. Although not commercially successful, they did sign with RCA, a major label, and opened for Kansas at one point. They also went on several club tours and were playing five nights a week at one point, but their draw as a band never got very high. With their lack of success, Smith moved to Los Angeles shortly before his audition for the Red Hot Chili Peppers. He attended the Musician's Institute for a short while but swiftly stopped.

He can play guitar and piano to various degrees, having once jammed on guitar in the band onstage in Milan for the famous Jam Milan, where Flea played drums. In *Funky Monks*, he can be seen playing a KISS song on piano.

41

I Once Knew John

John Frusciante's Early Life

An Italian Family Tree

John Anthony Frusciante's family came from Benevento, a small town in southern Italy in the Naples region. John's grandfather, Generous Frusciante, moved to America to escape the pains of war. John's father, also named John, was born in New York.

John Sr. loved music, studying piano at the Juilliard School of Music in Manhattan, but lost interest and began to take toward a study of law. He met Gail, and the two dated, wed, and moved to Queens, New York, where John Anthony Frusciante, future Red Hot Chili Pepper, was born on March 5, 1970.

Early Exposure to Music

With his father a Juilliard-level pianist turned strict American judge and his mother a talented singer as part of her church group, the young John was raised in a turbulent, strict, but musical environment as a child. He received his first guitar at age six in New York, but the family moved to Tucson, Arizona, and then Broward County, Florida, soon after. About a year after Frusciante started playing guitar, his mother and father separated.

Gail moved to California and took her son with her. John Sr. would later remarry and have three children and become a respected Broward circuit court judge, known for his evenhanded temperament. The Chili Pepper John has often ominously referenced an unspecified childhood pain but has never given details, preferring to keep it private, most notably in an awkward interview with the *Guardian* in 2003. The elder Judge John told the *Sun Sentinel* that he is "not somebody who's going to tell my kids they should do this, they should do that," preferring a more hands-off parenting approach.

Gail married Lawrence Berkley, a martial artist, in 1979. Berkley was a lover of music, and Frusciante has credited him with supporting his artistic pursuits, always discussing the new bands and music the young boy was checking out.

He also had a teacher named Amed Hughes, who suggested he would end up a famous rock musician, and it inspired Frusciante.

Sports, Punk, and Disco

John loved sports while he was young but remained impractically skinny and thin and did not excel. He became spiteful toward the more athletic children (and once wrote a hateful letter to his baseball coach at age nine); this turmoil served as the basis for his first songwriting done at age nine.

By age ten, he had learned every song on the Germs' album *GI* on guitar by ear. He would listen to the music his mother liked in the car, like Elton John or Kik Dee, and wonder how they made the sounds they did, but he would listen to KROQ and take to New Wave and punk. He still loved classical and the music that Lawrence pushed him to but expanded his own tastes. His mother would tell him to turn off his music and go to sleep, but Frusciante would stay up and tape-record the songs he loved and the songs he wanted to figure out on guitar. At a young age, he got into Kraftwerk and tried to emulate the sound of their synthesizers on his guitar.

First Show, Future Band

John Frusciante attended his first rock concert at age fifteen, seeing the Red Hot Chili Peppers at Perkins Palace in Pasadena, California. He quickly came to idolize Hillel Slovak, learned all the Red Hot Chili Peppers guitar parts to that point and most of the bass lines, and saw the band as often as he could.

Zappa and School Troubles

As Frusciante struggled in school, his mother wanted to continue his education, so she enrolled him in the Musician's Institute of Technology (or Musician's Institute) in Los Angeles. It was during this time that he began a militaristic, formalized practice routine of about fifteen hours a day. He became obsessed with Frank Zappa and hunted down every album Zappa had released—including those out of print—and learned the guitar parts note for note. He learned to read music specifically to read the Zappa guitar book, which was transcribed by noted shredder Steve Vai.

When Vai left Zappa's band, Frusciante heard there was an opening and planned to audition, confident he already knew all the guitar parts. He got as far as the rehearsal studio when he recalled that Zappa had a strict no-drugs policy. Frusciante wanted to be a rock star, do drugs, and sleep with women, and knew he wouldn't be able to do that in Zappa's band; he abandoned the studio without ever auditioning.

At age seventeen, he was smoking cigarettes heavily but heard news that Slovak had overdosed on heroin. He had already been jamming with D. H. Peligro when Peligro joined the Red Hot Chili Peppers. He began to jam with Flea, and once Flea was blown away and Kiedis and Frusciante became friends, it was a matter of time before the still-only-seventeen-year-old Frusciante joined the band.

42

Mother's Milk

The Classic Lineup Starts Off Strong

Pre-Album Rehearsals

The band decided to work with Michael Beinhorn, the first time they would work with a producer more than once, as he had already produced *The Uplift Mofo Party Plan* with them. The band started to rehearse every day of the week, and Beinhorn was a near-daily visitor to prep for the recording of the new album. Flea believed the band played harder and faster in this period than in any other era, according to the remastered album's liner notes.

Frusciante Gets Ribbed

As Frusciante was still significantly younger than the others—just seventeen years old, while everyone else was in their mid- to late twenties—he got playfully picked on by Flea and Kiedis for being young and inexperienced. Frusciante later commented that he took this personally, which later led to some of their issues, but Kiedis wrote in his autobiography that he meant no harm and considered Frusciante his best friend during that time.

The New Basis for Songs

"Knock Me Down" was the first song with Frusciante composing music to Kiedis's lyrics—a composition style that would later lead to hits like "Californication" and "Under the Bridge." Others were still born out of jams, including those from a previous lineup; D. H. Peligro getting writing credits on "Taste the Pain," "Stone Cold Bush," and "Sexy Mexican Maid." The album even featured one song with Jack Irons and Hillel Slovak on it—"Fire," originally recorded for *The Uplift Mofo Party Plan* but first released in the United Kingdom on *The Abbey Road E.P.*

"Taste the Pain" was recorded before Chad Smith joined the band but after Peligro had been canned. As such, on the record, the drums were played by Philip Fisher from Fishbone, who received credits on the album under the name "Fish."

Continuing the style of one cover per 1980s Chili Pepper album (with their debut album playing Hank Williams's "Why Don't You Love Me," *Freaky* featuring both the Meters and the Sly Stone cover, and *Uplift Mofo Party Plan* touching on a wildly funky take of Bob Dylan's "Subterranean Homesick Blues"), the Red Hot Chili Peppers covered Stevie Wonder's "Higher Ground," replacing the distinct octaves of the keyboard with Flea's slap bass. It became their first MTV rotation hit.

Flea's bass line and Frusciante's corresponding guitar part on "Nobody Weird Like Me" came together the first time the two ever jammed together. Their parts for "Pretty Little Ditty" were from a separate jam that came later on the first day they played together.

The first recorded songs on *Mother's Milk* were done at Hully Gully studios in Silverlake. (This definitely included "Taste the Pain" and definitely did not include "Higher Ground" and "Good Time Boys," though beyond that, it is unknown which songs were done where.) The majority of the sessions were done at Ocean Way Recording in Hollywood in February 1989.

Kiedis's New Lyrical Confidence

In this era, Kiedis consciously realized he had previously felt the need to be lyrically busy. He thought that Flea played a very active bass, and Slovak had typically played many notes, too; his reasoning then was that he should match it and rap many lyrics. On *Mother's Milk*, he consciously realized he could write in more of a verse–chorus structure, and he began to focus on doing so.

Several songs are obviously about the Los Angeles Lakers: "Magic Johnson" is about the Lakers player, while the demo of "Salute to Kareem" is meant as an ode to Kareem Abdul-Jabbar.

Production Tension (Again)

On this album, the band and Frusciante in particular believed that Beinhorn wanted to show his idea of his own signature sound and tried to force the Chili Peppers into it. Flea hated it but remained delicate about it in interviews, saying only that things "got a little sketchy" during recording for the album's remastered liner notes. Frusciante fought over it, as Beinhorn's idea was to have crunchy, heavy metal–like guitar sounds, which is not what Frusciante wanted

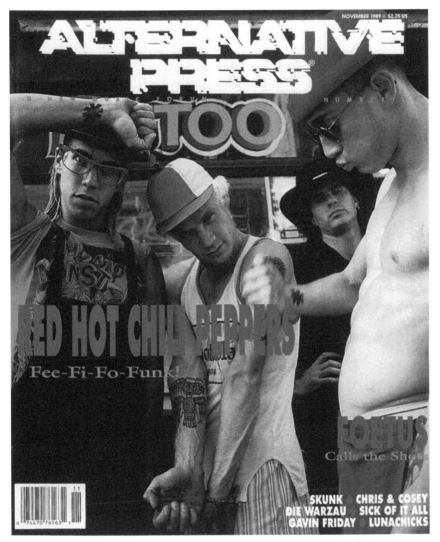

The band appears on the cover of AP to promote *Mother's Milk*. Courtesy: Alternative Press, issue #24, November 1989.   *Photo by Heidi Locke*

at all, having been a fan more of New Wave than of metal. Kiedis sided with Frusciante and thought Beinhorn was too bossy and rude.

The Producer Finds a Hit

Despite this, there were moments that worked between the two. Beinhorn put extra focus on "Higher Ground." Flea had played the bass line the way he did for a long time, but the band had never attempted it as a cover before. Beinhorn had to coach Frusciante into the layered guitar parts, and his confidence in Kiedis helped him sing the song well.

The ad lib at the end of the Chili Peppers version was something Beinhorn pushed Kiedis to do that he did not want to; though it made the recording, it led to a verbal altercation between Beinhorn and Kiedis and effectively ended their relationship forever. Beinhorn was obsessed with having a hit, and (correctly) thought the Stevie Wonder could be it.

The Return of Jack Sherman (and Gang Vocals)

Several songs on the album required gang vocals. Beinhorn had worked out gang vocals with the band before on "Fight Like a Brave"; this time, the band wanted to invite more friends to do it. Beginning with "Higher Ground," the band called more than twenty friends together, many of whom were musicians themselves (though not all), and had them perform gang vocals. Knowing Sherman was still based in Los Angeles, Flea called him up and asked if he would join in the gang vocals. Sherman said yes, marking a brief return to the band though not as a guitarist. (The same group would sing backing vocals for "Good Time Boys" during the same session.)

Endless Touring, Part 1

In March 1989—almost half a year before *Mother's Milk* would be released—the band went on a two-month tour to break in the new lineup. It was during this tour that Kiedis had his incident with sexual assault at George Mason University in Fairfax, Virginia. (For more details see chapter 11.)

Mother's Artwork and Promotions

The band settled on the name *Mother's Milk* for the album. Flea recalled a promo photo from the 1960s of Sly and the Family Stone where Sly held small versions of his bandmates in his arms for the photo, and the Red Hot Chili Peppers decided to do the same with an anonymous woman on their album cover.

Two models were tried out: Kiedis's girlfriend, Ione Skye, and Dawn Alane. Alane was ultimately chosen but claimed she was unaware that she would be on the cover. She did not want her breasts exposed; the record label was notified in time to alter the cover art appropriately but not all of the promotional materials. A poster featuring her nude breasts went to record stores; Alane sued and won a $50,000 settlement against the band and label.

The model on the cover fought to make sure her breasts would not appear on the final artwork.

Author's collection

The band shot a video for "Good Time Boys" they have never formally acknowledged or released officially. It was released as part of a VHS collection, *Hard 'n Heavy Volume 2*. "Knock Me Down" got a video, too, that got some airplay but not a lot; one of the actors in it would go on to direct the video for "Taste the Pain." It was "Higher Ground" and its accompanying music video that got the band mainstream recognition.

Reception

Critics heralded the album, and its sales far exceeded those of their previous albums. Some writers complained about the guitar tones, saying there was too much distortion—something that probably vindicated Frusciante and the band's arguments with Beinhorn—but the consensus still seemed that it was the best Chili Peppers album yet. *Guitar World* called out Frusciante for playing at a level Slovak had not. The album peaked at number fifty-three on the *Billboard* charts, but "Knock Me Down" reached number six and "Higher Ground" number eleven.

Endless Touring, Part 2

Finally selling a good number of records, the band opted to tour in a bus for the first time and brought along a horn section that included their old friend Keith "Tree" Barry and two backup singers who had sung on the record: Kristen Vigard and Vicki Calhoun. Live reviewers noted they still had their punk-rock energy, pointing out crowd surfers and mosh pits; they were playing their largest audiences yet, playing in front of more than 10,000 people in certain parts of Europe.

They began their typical hedonism of tour (but with newfound fame) and found some difficulties. Flea invited a woman to his hotel with the intention of having sex but locked himself in the bathroom when all he could think about were his wife and young daughter back home.

Kiedis was sober and began to play the typical crazy tour games and invent new ones. He came up with "The Job," where band or crew would fill a bowl with something and then be forced to eat it. One of their roadies ate a bowl of money. Kiedis once ate a half a pound of butter for $120. With Kiedis sober, his old relationship dynamic no longer worked; he and Ione Skye broke up, and he began pursuing aimless sex again. He met a woman in Houston, Texas, whom he considered his Houston girlfriend, and he would sleep with her anytime he was single and in Houston.

Kiedis was sleeping with a new woman nearly every night. In Chicago, Frusciante told Kiedis that Smith had an extra bed in his hotel room, so Kiedis took a woman to Smith's room. Smith walked in to find Kiedis and the random young woman going at it, and Smith was enraged. Kiedis would end up having sex with her in a stairway, and the woman would moan loud enough that Frusciante thought other hotel guests could hear her.

Smith, Frusciante, and Kiedis would sleep with and exchange women with each other. Kiedis goes into exuberant detail with this in his autobiography, especially for this era. By all accounts, Flea seemed to be the only one not chasing women or objectifying them at this time, and he struggled with that. Despite that, his marriage was still on the rocks and would eventually lead to a divorce.

A Photographer Joined

Shortly after Chad Smith joined, the Red Hot Chili Peppers hired Tony Woolliscroft as the official band photographer. Woolliscroft remains to this day and has lasted through several lineup changes. In 2009, Woolliscroft released his own photo book of the band from his time with them, aptly titled *Me and My Friends*.

Woolliscroft first heard of the band in Bradford, England, at a friend's apartment. The friend was the drummer for New Model Army, who were label mates with the Red Hot Chili Peppers in the United Kingdom at the time on EMI. His first time shooting them was for *RAW* magazine, but he became friends with the band's crew. He eventually became friends with Anthony Kiedis and Chad Smith, so whenever they needed a touring photographer and could afford one, he became the man for the job.

The Next Record, a New Label

In April 1990, *Mother's Milk* went gold, meaning it sold more than 500,000 records. When EMI threw a party for them as a celebration in New York, other record labels began to contact them. The band's lawyer, Eric Greenspan, noticed they owed EMI one more album, but the band had a personal services clause that voided the contract after seven years. As such, virtually every rock-oriented major label began to pursue them.

They spent time with the founder of Island Records, Chris Blackwell, at his house and talked to him about Bob Marley and reggae. Blackwell admitted he didn't have as much money as other labels. David Geffen and Warner Bros. did. While flirting with Warner Bros., the band reached out to Rick Rubin again, and this time, Rubin agreed to produce the band's next album.

On Halloween 1990, the band agreed to go to a Los Angeles party in matching costumes: naked except for a strap-on dildo. All four did it, and Jane's Addiction played the party. After their set, Jane's drummer Stephen Perkins asked the Red Hot Chili Peppers if they wanted to play; the Peppers went on and performed a cover of the Stooges' "Search and Destroy."

Record label negotiations went on between Warner Bros. and Sony/Epic. Sony upped their contract offer to give each member of the band $1 million, and the decision was made to go with Sony. However, as contract negotiations wore on and days turned into weeks and months, they received a call from the head of Warner Bros. congratulating them on the deal and encouraging them to make the best record they could for Sony.

Kiedis and Flea were touched by that and felt they should go to Warner Bros. Records instead. They contacted their manager; it turned out that Sony had struggled to buy out or negotiate the end of the EMI contract. Warner Bros. was able to resolve that problem in one phone call, and Warner Bros. had the band for what would go on to be their biggest album ever.

43

Blood Sugar Sex Magik

The Band Finds Their Chess Player

Selecting Rick Rubin, a Documentarian, and a Visitor

The Red Hot Chili Peppers had looked at Rick Rubin as a producer before, primarily for *Freaky Styley*, but things did not work out. Shortly before signing with Warner Bros. Records, Rubin and the band met up and decided they would be a good fit; in the band's view, Rubin had mellowed out in his transition from being a Def Jam man based in New York to a vegetarian based in Los Angeles.

Rubin listened primarily to the band's jams and gave suggestions on arrangements and song structures, occasionally guiding the players for fill choices and beats. Rubin helped select the famous mansion that *Blood Sugar Sex Magik* was recorded in; he would eventually purchase it himself, though it once belonged to Harry Houdini. Rubin originally wanted to sign the band to his record label, Def Jam, but was happy to still produce the record.

The band had their friend Gavin Bowden stay in the mansion with them and film the recording sessions. A documentary was made and edited into one hour as *Funky Monks*, though in 2013, a version with an extra eighteen minutes was published on YouTube.

Footage from this filming was used as the music video for "Suck My Kiss." Allegedly, a three-hour version of the documentary exists, but it has never surfaced, and the sourcing of its existence has relied primarily on fan speculation. Bowden eventually married Flea's sister.

The mansion is located on Laurel Canyon Boulevard in Los Angeles. Recording took place over two months; John Frusciante had a small upstairs room to himself, while Kiedis had a larger room on the opposite side of the house where he eventually recorded almost all of his vocals. Flea spent time with his daughter, Clara, there and stayed on the third floor.

Chad Smith slept the first few nights there but bought into the idea that it was haunted and rode his motorcycle to and from the mansion almost every day after the first week. Frusciante and Flea discussed the spirits, too, but didn't feel haunted by them, as can be seen in the *Funky Monks* documentary. Kiedis

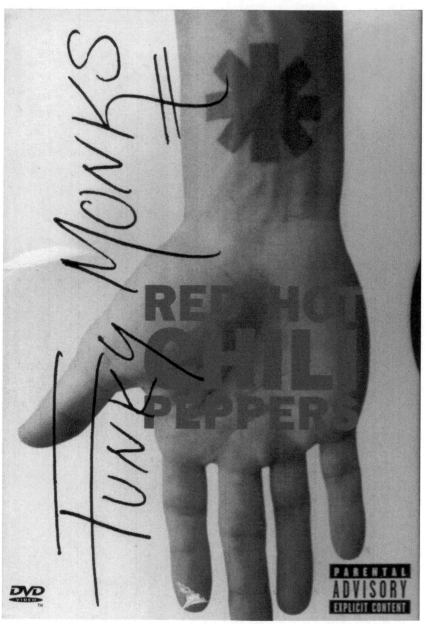

The cover of the DVD release to the making-of documentary of *Blood Sugar Sex Magik*, titled *Funky Monks*.   *Author's collection*

didn't leave at all for the first six weeks but did the final two; Frusciante and Flea never stepped foot off the property until the album was wrapped.

A female friend and fan of the band would visit the studio almost every night, and by the end of the month she had sex with every band member except Smith. The mansion had virtually no security; she was never particularly invited there, but since the band already knew her, she just showed up and they all hung out. She would be a friend when they needed it and have long conversations but also was sexually involved with three different members of the band in short succession.

The album was dedicated to Mike Watt, bassist and singer for the Minutemen and fIREHOSE, not just as gratitude for his musical inspiration but also because they felt that his ethics in self-touring paved the way for what they had done.

Rubin as a Chess Player

Anthony Kiedis has cracked the same joke many times in the press for *Blood Sugar Sex Magik* that "if Baron von Munchausen ejaculated the Red Hot Chili Peppers onto a chess board, Rick Rubin would be the perfect chess player." He made this joke once in *Funky Monks*, once during VH1's *Classic Albums*, and several times in the written press or on television outside of that.

Face/Offs

Rubin valued songwriting over musical chops and hammered that priority into the band. It led to the creation of a game they called "face/off"; whenever the band needed a bridge or another part but had gotten stuck with jamming, Flea and Frusciante would face off and run to opposite corners of the practice space unplugged. After a set amount of time, they would come back and play what they had written in that time as the new part; whoever's was better via the band's democracy would win out, and that would be the song.

"The Power of Equality"

"The Power of Equality" as a Red Hot Chili Peppers song predates the finished product. It was used as a working title for "Johnny, Kick a Hole in the Sky," predating *Mother's Milk*. Rubin supported the lyrics Anthony Kiedis wrote for the song but noted he wasn't into sociopolitical commentary. The drum recording was Flea's favorite, according to *Rhythm*; Smith recorded his drum part on two

The iconic album cover.   *Author's collection*

different drum sets, one overdubbing the first, and they were edited together in postproduction.

"If You Have to Ask"

The song has a rarely seen music video featuring one of Frusciante's first replacements: Arik Marshall. The actual song's guitar solo was played by Frusciante in a single take; the applause heard at the end of the song is from the booth as Frusciante nailed the first take.

"Breaking the Girl"

Frusciante brought in the music to "Breaking the Girl," having the verse and chorus already in place without lyrics. He hummed the melody for Kiedis, who wrote the song about two things: his fairly recent breakup with his then girl-friend Carmen Hawk and his father's treatment of women and how it shaped his view of women and relationships.

Frusciante said his guitar work was inspired by Led Zeppelin's acoustic work, such as "The Battle of Evermore" and "Friends," and Chad Smith said his drumming was his version of Mitch Mitchell's drumming on the *Jimi Hendrix Experience*'s "Manic Depression" in his instructional video. The music video to the song was one of two filmed years later when Arik Marshall was guitarist—the other being the rarely seen video for "If You Have to Ask." The video also has a brief cameo from River Phoenix.

Flea   Chad Smith   John Frusciante   Anthony Kiedis

RED HOT CHILI PEPPERS

A Blood Sugar Sex Magik press scan, gifted to the author from Hamish Duncan.
Photo by Chris Cuffaro

The percussion break was played by all four members of the band across multiple tracks, though not every percussion track was used. The band agreed it needed more, sent a runner to the dump to pick up metallic objects, and came back and recorded several takes under Brendan O'Brien's instructions, changing their proximity to the microphone with his guidance.

"Funky Monks"

Most of the bass lines on the album were recorded with a Wal Mach II bass, but neither of the two that used a five-string bass were; both had a MusicMan Stingray. (The other song requiring a five-string bass on the album is "The Righteous and the Wicked.")

The guitar part featured Frusciante pulling the guitar strings off the neck as if he were slapping and popping like it was a bass guitar. The song was written around a jam that came from Frusciante bringing in the guitar part.

"Suck My Kiss"

The music video for the song features black-and-white footage recorded for *Funky Monks*. It also features footage of the U.S. Army returning from the first Gulf War. The song was eventually Dave Navarro's favorite Chili Peppers song to play live. The Hammond organ on it was played by engineer Brendan O'Brien.

"I Could Have Lied"

Famously written as a brokenhearted note to Sinead O'Connor, "I Could Have Lied" was musically written entirely by John Frusciante. Kiedis wrote an adoring letter to O'Connor after a European music festival in 1989, giving it to her after a brief hangout backstage and just before she hopped on her tour bus. He ran into her in Los Angeles a few weeks later, and she made it a point to tell him that she held onto the loving letter.

This is where the story splits: Kiedis believed they were dating, while O'Connor felt they were having a brief friendship. When it ended, Kiedis was heartbroken, hence the song; he has spoken negatively about its ending to the press in the decades since. O'Connor has said otherwise, telling *My Park Magazine*,

> I never had a relationship with him, ever. I hung out with him a few times and the row we had was because he suggested we might become [intimately] involved. I don't give a shit about the song he wrote. I'm not a Red Hot Chili Peppers fan. I can't bear them, I don't get it.

"Mellowship Slinky in B Major"

Flea played the piano on this song. Frusciante played a fretless Fender Stratocaster during the bridge. Despite its title, it is actually in B Mixolydian, or the key signature of E major. The outro, as recorded, actually went on significantly longer; it can be heard in its original form on YouTube thanks to edits put together from the audio of *Rock Band* play-along tracks.

"The Righteous and the Wicked"

This is another song recorded with the MusicMan Stingray five-string bass. The song is one of the few to not make any appearances at all during *Funky Monks*.

"Give It Away"

Flea brought the riff in, and Chad Smith enjoyed it enough that he was laughing the whole time he played along. Kiedis was inspired by the laughter, and the first words that popped out of his mouth were "give it away, give it away, give it away now." He wrote the song around the energy of that moment, referencing everything from their friend River Phoenix—lyrically used as a literal river—to Bob Marley.

"Blood Sugar Sex Magik"

The song was primarily about Kiedis's sexual exploits with his ex-girlfriend Carmen Hawk. When the band was looking for an album title, Rubin thought it was clearly the best song title, so the band agreed to it as the album title. As can be witnessed in *Funky Monks*, a Warner Bros. employee joked that it was a "diabetic love song," much to Kiedis's dismay, during the recording of the album.

"Under the Bridge"

Other reports have stated that the "Under the Bridge" lyrics date back to the 1980s; Kiedis wrote in his autobiography that it came during the *Blood Sugar Sex Magik* sessions. John Frusciante and Kiedis weren't as close as they once were, while Frusciante and Flea had become closer as they smoked marijuana together constantly. Feeling left out and lonely, Kiedis was driving on the Los Angeles freeway when the poetry to "Under the Bridge" came to him; he wrote it in his lyrics notebook when he got home.

Rubin stumbled on it in the preproduction for *Blood Sugar Sex Magik* and in one of their jam sessions encouraged Kiedis to show it to Frusciante and Smith before Flea showed up. Embarrassed, Kiedis eventually obliged and sang it a capella, changing keys without any musicians to support him.

A day later, Frusciante brought the chord structure and guitar part in. Frusciante brought four different options for it, and Kiedis chose the one he found most interesting. Frusciante and Kiedis performed it once for Flea and Smith, and then the whole band performed it together afterward, with Flea and Smith instantly agreeing on their arrangement.

Kiedis struggled to sing it until engineer Brendan O'Brien joked with him and boosted his confidence. The choir vocals at the end are done by Frusciante's mother and her church group. They were not handed sheet music; Frusciante performed it for his mother and the others, and they figured out the arrangement themselves from there.

"Naked in the Rain"

Despite Flea's stated goal of playing more melodically and fewer notes overall, "Naked in the Rain" features one of his most prominent bass solos. It is one of the songs Flea and Chad Smith cover on *The Rhythm Method* video. Q magazine named it one of their "Songs for Summer" in June 2011.

"Apache Rose Peacock"

Flea played trumpet and tiny piano on "Apache Rose Peacock." The song was born out of a jam and was never played live until the Peppers played a music festival in New Orleans after a hurricane in the mid-2000s.

"The Greeting Song"

The same time that Rubin informed Kiedis he was not into sociopolitical commentary, he told Kiedis he was into songs about "girls and cars." Part of this conversation can be witnessed in *Funky Monks*, when Chad Smith mocks Rubin's exact words by chanting "girls and cars" over and over.

"The Greeting Song" was Kiedis's attempt to fill that void: a song about girls and cars. The Red Hot Chili Peppers have never played it live, as Kiedis decides the band's set list and has always disliked the song, though musically it has a worthwhile performance from Chad Smith's single pedaling on the bass drum. Chevrolet once tried to pay to use the song and its lyrics in advertisement for their cars, but Kiedis didn't feel comfortable with it and declined.

"My Lovely Man"

The song was written as a love letter and good-bye to Hillel Slovak. Kiedis continued to think and talk about Slovak throughout the writing of *Blood Sugar Sex Magik* and told *Rolling Stone that* Slovak remained a key influence. He went through old packages of letters from Slovak, including one he received after five years of a female friend's keeping its possession, and it helped inspire the lyrics.

"Sir Psycho Sexy"

The distinct bass tone of the song comes from a Moogerfooger envelope filter's battery dying. Several pedal boards exist now to simulate the voltage of a battery dying, but at the time, it had to actually be done by placing a battery near the end of its life inside. *Funky Monks* features great rehearsal footage of the band playing it plugged and unplugged. Frusciante recorded the backing vocal "la la's" alone.

The song was banned and deleted from the album in certain parts of the world—mostly Asian countries—for its sexualized lyrics, and in schools that block pornography, it is often blocked to this day. The book *The Stories behind the Song* quoted Kiedis saying it was based on someone the band used to know, but it could be a lie or based on Kiedis himself, as in the same interview he said that Sir Psycho Sexy was currently living on Uranus.

"They're Red Hot"

The song was recorded outside with traffic driving by; the traffic heard at the end of "Sir Psycho Sexy" is actually from the moments before the band started playing "They're Red Hot." Every member of the band did their recording at the same time with no overdubs, including vocals, though the first take was not used. Chad Smith played the drums without sticks, instead using his hands, as can be seen in *Funky Monks*.

The song is a cover of Robert Johnson, the famous blues guitarist whose myth included selling his soul to the devil and who is also the writer behind "Crossroads."

Other Songs Recorded during the Sessions

Other songs recorded at the mansion during this time were "Fela's Cock," an ode to Fela Kuti that would be released as a B-side and on the *Live, Rare, Remix* box, and a few songs that ended up on sound tracks. "Search and Destroy," a cover of a song by the Stooges, was first released on the *Beavis and Butt-Head* television sound track.

"Soul to Squeeze" appeared on the *Coneheads* sound track; it was released as a single and later came out as part of *Greatest Hits*. It had its own music video but came when the band had no guitarist; as such, no guitarist appears in the video. Chad Smith used Paiste cymbals as hand-orchestral crash cymbals on the song and got the sound distinct for them at the bridge by recording to the song sped up on tape, giving the crash a deeper tone when slowed down to its actual tempo. (This can be witnessed in the extended version of *Funky Monks*.)

"Sikamikanico" appeared on the *Wayne's World* sound track after its appearance in the movie, where Wayne Campbell—played by Mike Myers—washes away Toni Basil's "Hey Mickey" by putting a disc in his new CD player that has "Sikamikanico" on it. "Sikamikanico" is played by Flea finger style; he never played with a pick in the Red Hot Chili Peppers until *Californication*'s "Parallel Universe." Despite that, he tried to record it with a pick; he put it up to a band vote, and it was decided that finger style sounded better.

Fans argue over whether another song was recorded, believing that an instrumental appeared in VH1's *Classic Albums* on *Blood Sugar Sex Magik*. That is unconfirmed and possibly a recording from a live show. Two *Jimi Hendrix Experience* covers were recorded in the studio, both eventually released as iTunes bonus tracks: "Little Miss Lover" and "Castles Made of Sand."

Miscellaneous

Anthony Kiedis laid down guide vocal tracks as Chad Smith recorded his drums throughout the album instead of a click track; that practice has continued today. Flea and John Frusciante had a beard contest; Kiedis was to be Frusciante's coach until Frusciante shaved more than Kiedis wanted. (They also had a fart-off, but Frusciante shat his pants.) The band settled who would play synthesizer and piano via coin tosses.

44

The Magik Is Gone

Frusciante Leaves the Band

Frusciante's Brief Post-Album Tenure, Part 1

After *Blood Sugar Sex Magik* was released, Anthony Kiedis and John Frusciante went to Europe to promote it. Flea opted not to go. Kiedis credits this press tour and its repetitiveness as a major factor behind Frusciante's eventual leaving of the band. Frusciante began to use heroin at an ever-increasing rate. Frusciante did not complete the full European promo tour; he eventually ran up a $2,000 long-distance telephone bill in Belgium, apologized, and flew back to Los Angeles by himself.

Kiedis saw the music video for the Smashing Pumpkins' "Gish" and urged Lindy Goetz to get them to open for the Red Hot Chili Peppers on tour. Pearl Jam was chosen for the same tour after former Chili Pepper Jack Irons called and told the band to check them out. Vedder was friends with Irons (Irons would eventually join Pearl Jam) and had worked as a technician for the Chili Peppers very briefly in San Diego. Pearl Jam began to receive heavy rotation on MTV, as were the Red Hot Chili Peppers. As crowd sizes grew, Frusciante isolated himself more and more.

One night on tour, Kiedis missed his vocal cue during "Under the Bridge," and the crowd sang the entire introduction in his place. The record label found out and insisted that "Under the Bridge" be the next single. Flea and his wife were going through divorce, and he began to use drugs at a higher rate than at any other time in his life. Frusciante began to disown popular rock music, finding it pointless, and began to listen to an increased amount of Captain Beefheart and read more William Burroughs, taking to heart Burroughs's belief that every true artist is at war with the world.

When the Red Hot Chili Peppers got to the West Coast, they began to play arenas instead of theaters, and the promoters wanted an opener more popular than Pearl Jam to play. Kiedis was a fan of Nirvana's *Nevermind* and did his best to get them on the tour. In the end, Nirvana would take Pearl Jam's place, but because the Smashing Pumpkins' front man Billy Corgan felt uncomfortable being around his ex-girlfriend, Nirvana front man Kurt Cobain's girlfriend

Courtney Love, the Smashing Pumpkins dropped out and were replaced with Pearl Jam.

The Last Stand

Frusciante was detached from the rest of the band from the start. After the first night of their U.K. tour for *Blood Sugar Sex Magik*, Kiedis had a chest infection and was quiet. Smith was all smiles, but Frusciante left without talking to the rest of the band, and Flea was despondent about his failing marriage. The band's photographer was supposed to get backstage photographs at several events but wasn't allowed to because the vibe in the dressing room was so dark that they wanted no outside figures. The writer for the article in *RAW* magazine noticed this and wrote the headline "The Chili Peppers' Last Stand?" and ran a photograph of Kiedis doing a handstand onstage instead.

Saturday Night Love

Shortly before the band's performance on *Saturday Night Live*, Frusciante's mother and father called Lindy Goetz, urging him to help Frusciante, as they felt he was isolating himself in a dark and dangerous place. Goetz was unable to help, as he felt paralyzed between Kiedis and Frusciante's tensions, Flea's increased drug use, and the band's newfound success. He did his best.

When the band played *Saturday Night Live*, they performed two songs: "Stone Cold Bush" from *Mother's Milk* and "Under the Bridge." Flea wore a lot of makeup, making his face ghost-like. Frusciante was strung out on heroin, reaching a negative apex during "Under the Bridge." The performance was infamous for fans: Frusciante played the introduction in a new way, in what Kiedis viewed as an intentional change to throw Kiedis off but what some fans think is a creative and beautiful take on the song. When Frusciante's time to sing the backing vocals came, he instead dozed off the first two lines and then screamed at the top of his lungs the final two lyrics. Kiedis kicked Frusciante during the performance as a result of this, taking out his anger directly in the process.

Frusciante's Brief Post-Album Tenure, Part 2

After *Saturday Night Live*, they went to tour Europe, then Hawaii, Japan, and Australia. The band began to grow apart as their finances were stronger; Chad was always more of a lone wolf, while Flea and Frusciante separately isolated themselves from the others. Kiedis became close with Jimmy Boyle, a friend of Rick Rubin's, and forced the band to accept his presence when they went to Hawaii. Kiedis got a blow job from a Hawaiian in their hotel hallway late at night while there.

In May 1992, the band went to Japan. In Kiedis's worldview, he thought Frusciante and he had worked out their differences, but Kiedis felt no resolution to them. Frusciante was high almost the entire time. Frusciante told Mark Johnson that he had quit the Red Hot Chili Peppers, and Johnson carried the message to the band, who was already at the venue. Flea, Kiedis, Smith, and Goetz went back to the hotel and pleaded with Frusciante to play the one show to not have to cancel that leg of the tour; Frusciante agreed to one final show and then left the band for several years.

The First Replacement

The band's original plan, formulated when they were still in Asia, was that they'd continue to Australia, meet up with their friend Zander Schloss from Thelonious Monster, teach him the songs and rehearse for a full week, and then continue on. After four days of practice, the others knew it wouldn't work and informed Schloss, who was upset. (For more on this period, see chapter 13.)

The Second Replacement

The band asked Dave Navarro to join, as Jane's Addiction had just broken up, but he declined, choosing instead to be in his band with former Jane's bandmate Eric Avery: Deconstruction. The band held auditions for others and got a wide array of potential band members, including Buckethead, and they decided on Arik Marshall of Marshall Law. Marshall was introverted, but the band carried on and played Lollapalooza and continued a heavy touring schedule. At Lollapalooza, the band dressed up wearing helmets with a giant flame atop them. It foreshadowed the costume they would become known for at Woodstock 1994, and images of it inspired a photo shoot with Chad Smith for *Modern Drummer*. They played the MTV awards with Marshall and won several awards. They went back to Australia to make up for their canceled Frusciante dates with Marshall.

During the Lollapalooza tour, Kiedis's father, Blackie Dammett, went with them. He typically hung out with Ice Cube and his band backstage after Chad Smith drank all of the Red Hot Chili Peppers' beers himself.

On a trip to Asia, Kiedis had a cockroach lodge itself into his ear and make him very ill. Afterward, in South America, they began to headline festivals with Nirvana. Kurt Cobain was reclusive this time around.

While Marshall played every part almost flawlessly, he was not very energetic onstage. The band took no issue with this, but fans and writers commented on it regularly.

The Third Replacement

After that, the band began to work on a new record with Arik Marshall. Marshall was unresponsive when Kiedis reached out about working on new material and seemed to be unavailable anytime someone did actually reach him. The band decided he wasn't the right long-term person as such, and they began another open-audition period, this time leading to Jesse Tobias.

Tobias quit his band, and he began to jam with the band. As they began jamming, it was clear the chemistry wasn't there. Flea was particularly disappointed with Tobias's playing. Chad Smith had been hanging out with Dave Navarro and thought he would be up for joining the Red Hot Chili Peppers this time around. They asked, and Navarro said yes. Chad Smith and Dave Navarro remained close during their time in the band and afterward; according to *Juice*, when the Navarro-era lineup went to Australia, Smith and Navarro got prostitutes together.

45

Jane's Unaddicted

Dave Navarro Joins the Band for *One Hot Minute*

Joining

On joining, Dave Navarro reportedly told Kiedis that he'd heard a rumor that the Chili Peppers fired Jesse Tobias because he was too attractive and stole some of Kiedis's thunder. (This was, of course, a playful lie.) Navarro got guitar picks with the names of each former Chili Pepper guitarist on them, one with his own name and a question mark afterward, as a way of making light of the situation. The band did their best to make Navarro feel like an even partner, but since Jane's Addiction never was, with Perry Farrell earning twice as much credit as all the others in songwriter's rights, Navarro was uneasy at first.

Kiedis's Childish Relationship

Kiedis had an affair with a seventeen-year-old that turned into a relationship. He spoke to *Rolling Stone* about this with pride, speaking of her high school graduation, but wrote with slightly more embarrassment about it in his autobiography. He was over thirty years old at the time.

Kiedis's Relapse and Group Bonding

Kiedis was sober for over five years when he got his wisdom teeth removed in early 1994. Kiedis insisted on local anesthesia and not using narcotics, but after the dentist started, he said he would have to cut it out of the mouth and needed to put Kiedis under, giving him Valium. Such began Kiedis's relapse. When he awoke, he requested Percodan, claiming it was for the pain, but actually he was just beginning another drug binge.

He began to buy heroin and cocaine, leaving his sobriety behind, eventually hitting the point where he was smoking crack but didn't have a lighter, literally using matches to smoke it. He didn't tell anyone in the band.

Everyone in the band bought each other motorcycles, as Chad Smith and Dave Navarro already rode. They named their fake motorcycle gang "The Sensitives" and decided to record in Hawaii for the next record, thinking it would help facilitate creativity. In the end, it had the opposite effect: with so much time to relax and so many other things to do, no one quite focused on music for the time being.

On August 1, 1994, Blackie Dammett gave Kiedis a T-shirt that said "six years clean" on it, even though Kiedis was only a few weeks sober by then. Kiedis felt terrible about it.

Woodstock '94

The album was recorded in several sessions, with the band staying in Hawaii for weeks, then flying back to the mainland, then returning to Hawaii, on and off several times. During one break—over summer, beginning in July—Kiedis maintained sobriety, and the band headlined Woodstock '94. Kiedis was a month sober by then.

It was Kiedis's idea to dress up in crazy costumes to make the event seem even more special, sketching out the idea for giant light bulbs on everyone's head. The costumes made playing difficult, and everyone took off the bulb after one song or less. The band planned their encore to be the *Jimi Hendrix Experience*'s "Fire" as a tribute to Hendrix's 1969 performance at Woodstock. The whole performance was Navarro's first as a Red Hot Chili Pepper.

A Short Relapse

After the concert, Kiedis returned home and relapsed yet again. As Goetz and Flea tried to get Kiedis to record his vocal parts, Kiedis made excuses, including claiming that he had parasites. The lie worked enough that bandmates didn't know he had relapsed.

Kiedis went on a drug binge in front of his sober teenage girlfriend, who told Flea and Kiedis's mother about the relapse. When Kiedis ran out of drugs, he got sober again after having what he believed to be an interaction with a spirit in the form of an elk telling him to get clean. Kiedis was home for Christmas and sobering up again. (He bought his father a car for Christmas that year.)

The Red Hot Chili Peppers perform at Woodstock with light bulb costumes.

Photo by JP Velotti

Making Peace with D. H. Peligro

It was in October 1995 that the band buried any remaining hatchets they had with D. H. Peligro. Peligro had an accident at his home and needed to raise funds to pay his hospital bill; the Red Hot Chili Peppers headlined a secret show helping to raise funds for it. Tony Woolliscroft was the only photographer allowed in, so very few photos from the event are in circulation.

Flea as Composer and Guitarist

Flea's divorce was finalized, and with Frusciante gone and everyone else taking a more relaxed approach to songwriting, he stepped up. Navarro's natural style wasn't that of jamming; this helped fuel Flea to bring more and more riffs in, making him a driving force on the album. As Navarro lost focus, Flea ended up recording several of the basic guitar tracks, leaving Navarro to do all the over-dubs but giving Flea the basic power of half of the song.

After Kiedis's Christmas when he finally got sober, before the band reentered the studio for the final recording sessions, Flea and Kiedis hung out in New Mexico for almost a full week, each day completing the entirety of a new song.

A Canceled *Deep Kick*

There was a plan for another album documentary in the style of *Funky Monks* called *Deep Kick*. It was to be in the vein of Led Zeppelin's *The Song Remains the Same*, with each band member getting a short, fictional autobiographical film sliced into the actual documentary. It was never released, but it is unknown why. It was directed by the same man who made *Funky Monks*: Gavin Bowden. A two-minute clip is available online.

Artwork

The album art was drawn and made by Mark Ryden. Sweetbryar Ludwig did all of the calligraphy for it.

"Warped"

The lyrics were written by Kiedis about his drug relapse as a plea for help. Originally, the song was supposed to have its own music video, directed by Gavin

Bowden. It took place in a giant wooden cylinder and took two full days to shoot. After several shots trying to be mysterious, Navarro and Kiedis kissed as a bit of a joke but also to spice up the shoot. The two ended up making out.

Warner Bros. was upset with the kiss, believing it would alienate their fan base. The band fought against it and insisted that it stay, deciding that if any of their fans were homophobic enough to abandon them, the Red Hot Chili Peppers didn't want them for fans.

"Aeroplane"

Flea played the simple funk guitar. While all of the other songs on the album were recorded with an Alembic Epic bass, "Aeroplane" was played on a Music-Man Sting Ray. It is the only song on *One Hot Minute* where Flea played slap bass. Flea's daughter, Clara, and her classmates were the children's choir for the outro of the song, and they appear in the music video, also directed by Gavin

The *One Hot Minute* album cover.   *Author's collection*

Bowden. It was the band's most expensive music video, meant to be an ode to Busby Berkeley.

Kiedis was disappointed with the shoot; in his autobiography, he claimed there was a record executive from Warner Bros. he considered a "politically correct feminist" who made them tone everything down and its objectification of women. It's unknown how much activity the record label considered inappropriate that they wanted to get away with.

"Deep Kick"

Lyrically, the song is a recounting of Flea and Kiedis's misadventures together, but it includes the notion that there is a drug problem that destroyed a lot of their friends and almost destroyed Kiedis. Flea wrote every instrument and vocal part for the introduction of the song.

Flea also wrote all of the outro and sang that part. He didn't have the last three lines—until much later, as evidenced by a 1995 interview with *Guitar Player* that showed him working on the song when everything else was complete. Lenny Castro, Chad Smith's percussionist mentor, played percussion on "Walkabout," "My Friends," "One Hot Minute," "Tearjerker," and "Deep Kick."

"My Friends"

Flea wrote the vocal melody for the verse of "My Friends." There are two different versions of the video: one in which the band traveled in a small boat across heavy waters directed by Anton Corbijn. Although Corbijn would go on to make feature films like *The American*, the band hated it and cut another one directed by Gavin Bowden. That video may originate from cut footage from *Deep Kick*. Flea had a beard in it, as the footage is from the early sessions of *One Hot Minute*.

"Coffee Shop"

Flea's bass solo in the song is played through an auto-wah pedal at the beginning. Navarro recorded the guitar tracks on it. Its working title was "Baseballs" because the pedal Flea used was a Bassballs pedal.

"Pea"

Essentially a Flea solo song, it was the one song from *One Hot Minute* the band played live when Frusciante rejoined. (Other songs from *One Hot Minute* have been played live with Klinghoffer on guitar.) It was originally titled "The Pea Song." Flea played an acoustic bass guitar in the studio for "Pea."

"One Big Mob"

"One Big Mob" was originally supposed to connect with "Stretch (You Out)," but "Stretch (You Out)" was dropped from the album at the last minute. Stephen Perkins from Jane's Addiction played percussion on the track and on "Warped" and the iTunes extra "Bob." Its working title was "Gang of Four," as they believed the song sounded like a song by that band.

"Walkabout"

Navarro played a Fernandes guitar on it; he told *Guitar* in 1995 that he wanted the guitar to sound "thin" and "bad" on the song. He originally had a hard time playing it because he hated funk music, but it eventually became one of his favorites to play. For a brief period of time, he called it "Crapabout," including in an interview with *Guitar Player*.

"Tearjerker"

Kiedis wrote the lyrics to this song separately from the music, and he did so immediately after hearing that Kurt Cobain had killed himself. He didn't want it to be an obvious ode to Cobain, but it was still about him and directly inspired by him. After finishing the song, the band had ten completed songs and began to enter the studio; Kiedis went to New York and went on another drug binge before attempting to record. Flea composed the vocal melody for the verses. The band never played it live. Keith "Tree" Barry played violin on the song.

"One Hot Minute"

The working title of the song was "Evil." Despite ending up the title song from the album, "One Hot Minute" was never played live. John Lurie from the Lounge Lizards played harmonica on the song.

"Falling into Grace"

The song is the only one on the album to touch on religious themes lyrically. It was one of the songs Flea and Kiedis worked on together right before its recording. It has never been performed live by the band. The chants were done by Gurmukh Kaur Khalsa, a famed prenatal yoga instructor. Former Chili Pepper backup singer Kristen Vigard returned to sing backing vocals on this song.

"Shallow Be Thy Game"

"Shallow Be Thy Game" was released as a single in Australia but nowhere else. Even on the *One Hot Minute* tour, it was never played live in the United States.

"Transcending" and River Phoenix

Flea wrote most of the music on the album, but he also wrote most of the lyrics to "Transcending." It was his ode to River Phoenix, who passed away in 1993 after overdosing at the Viper Room. Al Jourgensen from Ministry was having a performance, with Flea and Johnny Depp as bandmates, that Scott Ian of the band Anthrax, John Frusciante, and Phoenix were attending. Phoenix was also Flea's choice of host when it was time for him to make a bass guitar education video. The two are visibly high throughout the entirety of the video. Its working title was "River."

Other Songs Recorded during the Sessions

During these sessions, the band also recorded "Bob," "Melancholy Mechanics," "I've Been Down," "Let's Make Evil," "I Found Out," and "Stretch (You Out)." "I've Been Down" was written by Flea and was originally released as a solo song by Flea for *The Basketball Diaries* sound track; it had Navarro on guitar and Stephen Perkins on percussion. "I Found Out" was a John Lennon cover recorded for a compilation. "Bob" was the first song the band wrote with Dave Navarro and wasn't released until it was an iTunes bonus track. "Melancholy Mechanics" came out on the *Twister* sound track.

Rehab

After he completed his last vocal recording for the album, Kiedis celebrated by getting high. He felt guilty, and the guilt was compounded by his girlfriend looking for him. After locking himself into a room at a Holiday Inn, Navarro tracked him down by looking at the band's accounting records. He went to the hotel with Kiedis's girlfriend and got Kiedis into rehab at Exodus, the same facility that Kurt Cobain stayed in before his death.

Kiedis learned of Cobain's stay there. It is a volunteer facility where no one is held against their will, but there is a four-foot fence. Cobain climbed the fence and ran away even though he would've been allowed to walk out the front door. Chris Farley, among others, visited Kiedis while there.

Relax Time, Promo Time, and Tour

The band went on one long tour after the album was released. Before touring, Kiedis, Flea, and former drummer Cliff Martinez went on a kayaking trip with their friend Marty Goldberg. Both Goldberg and Martinez were high-quality chefs, and the four ate well the entire time.

Under the stress of the promotional cycle, Kiedis relapsed again. Once on tour, Kiedis cleaned up, feeling like he would be unable to maintain road work while still doing drugs. After the European dates, the American leg was postponed after Chad Smith broke his arm during a baseball game. They were still able to perform on *Late Night with David Letterman*, where the band played "My Friends" and Smith played drums with his arm in a cast.

In between tour dates, Kiedis broke up with his girlfriend and began another drug binge. He smuggled drugs into Mexico to have privacy and solitude when using. When American tour dates picked up, Kiedis fell offstage one night, hit his head on concrete, and passed out. He severely hurt his leg after it got caught in cables during the fall and sang on the rest of the tour with a bum foot.

After playing in New Zealand, Kiedis bought an expensive home there. Navarro and Smith had become quite close, but Flea and Navarro had grown apart. Flea loved to play music all the time, while Navarro wanted to play only when it was for a specific purpose. Kiedis relapsed after another tour leg, then sobered up alone. During one of his many relapses, Kiedis sold a guitar signed by all of the Rolling Stones for a tiny amount of heroin.

Kiedis met Gloria Scott on Venice Beach. Scott sent postcards to Kiedis, encouraging him to continue his battle against drugs and being encouraging. His friends tried to force him into Exodus again, but he didn't want to go; it was mistaken for a suicide call, and he was forced into a hospital. He called the band's lawyer, Eric Greenspan, to get out. One of his friends had called his mom, so when he got out of the hospital, Kiedis's mother was pleading for him to get sober. He pretended to, did all the drugs he had in Beverly Hills, and then flew to Michigan with his mother and got sober again shortly before Thanksgiving.

Dave's Lone Moment in Socks

With Navarro in the band, they put socks on their penises as an encore only once, at the Nassau Coliseum in Long Island, New York, on February 16, 1996. Because the band had backing singers and a second guitarist, it was the largest "socks on cocks" they ever did. The band stayed at a Manhattan hotel afterward, and Flea and Navarro played cards together the entire way back.

No Tensions in Europe

Although things would eventually hit a point with Dave Navarro where they were dysfunctional, it did not come up on tour after *One Hot Minute*. The band was happy to hang out with each other across the tour and were publicly amiable onstage and privately amiable backstage. Rumors floated around that Navarro wasn't getting along with the rest, but at the time, they were mostly unfounded. One *Kerrang* interviewer asked them if the band would break up after the 1996 tour. Each band member, separately, said "yes" with excitement as a way to dismiss the question.

The interviewer didn't get the joke despite their upbeat mood and gave the article the headline "Pretend Best Friends."

Jane's Addiction Reunion with Flea

Flea referred to 1997 as "the Year of Nothing" for the Red Hot Chili Peppers. The band played one festival in July. Kiedis visited the Dalai Lama. He relapsed again but then got sober at a different rehab facility, Impact, in Pasadena, California.

Flea and Navarro recorded with Stephen Perkins and Perry Farrell, both of Jane's Addiction, in their new band: Porno for Pyros. After that, Navarro, Perkins, and Farrell decided to continue on Jane's Addiction; original bassist (and Flea influencer) Eric Avery declined to partake in the reunion. Flea joined as bassist.

Flea would record bass lines on two songs on their compilation *Kettle Whistle* and play bass for the entirety of their first reunion tour. The two songs were "Kettle Whistle" and "My Cat's Name Is Maceo." The tour was featured in the documentary *Three Days*, where Flea can be seen upset that he didn't get a sandwich before a performance.

Radio Free Los Angeles

A presidential election was held in November 1997 with the lowest voter turnout ever at that point. It sparked something in Tom Morello, believing it to be proof that politicians had lost touch with most Americans. With Rage Against the Machine unable to get it going, he formed Radio Free LA: Tom Morello and Zack de la Rocha of Rage Against the Machine with Flea on bass guitar and Stephen Perkins from Jane's Addiction on drums.

They did one performance, covering only Rage songs, but Morello and Flea began to work together. It should be noted that although de la Rocha's vocal

Dave Navarro alone.

Navarro playing with the band he is most known for, Jane's Addiction.

Bruce Alan Bennett / Shutterstock.com

parts remained the same, the instrumentals were changed entirely, being more of a hip-hop jam done by the three musicians. Flea and Navarro were Rage Against the Machine fans and watched Rage play when the two bands headlined European festivals together.

Afterward, the two hooked up with Henry Rollins and Bone Thugs-N-Harmony to record a song for the *Small Soldiers* sound track. After that success, Joe Strummer tapped them to lead the way on his song for the *South Park Chef Aid* album.

A False Start to a Follow-Up Album and the Firing of Navarro

In 1998, the band began to start rehearsing for the follow-up to *One Hot Minute*. Kiedis was now clean but struggling, but Navarro had relapsed. They started to record new material, but most of it never materialized. A tribute to Nusrat Fateh Ali Khan surfaced years later from these sessions called "Circle of the Noose." Several other songs from these sessions ended up as part of Navarro's solo album *Spread*, according to a 1999 interview with *DRUM!* magazine.

The band talked to Navarro and tried to get him to go to rehab, and it ended in an argument where Navarro fell over an amplifier. Navarro told *NME* in

2010, "One [of the reasons I was fired] was [because of] my drug use at the time. The other was musical differences. Anthony says it was because I tripped and fell over an amp while on drugs. I say that he was on more drugs than me at that point. We both had a loose relationship with reality. Who do you want to believe?"

Navarro and the Chili Peppers were quick to agree that it was an amiable split, where things simply did not work out as they should. Navarro told interviewers that they all remained friends but was swift to point out that he *still* hated the light bulb costume idea.

Flea considered giving up on the band but asked Kiedis if he'd be okay with Frusciante as a potential Navarro replacement. Frusciante was in the Los Encinos, a drug treatment facility, after he had given up drugs and had a fire burn down his house. Flea and Kiedis visited Frusciante several times, one time leading to Frusciante randomly doing a split mid-conversation to display his health. One of the final times, the two asked Frusciante if he'd like to rejoin. Frusciante cried, saying he'd like "nothing more in the world," according to VH1's *Behind the Music*.

Smith was asked for his input on Frusciante's joining when Flea asked him over to watch a Los Angeles Lakers game. Shortly after the invite, Flea asked Smith to show up half an hour earlier so that Kiedis could come before the game. While watching television, they asked for his input on Frusciante's joining. He approved.

46

Californication

The Classic Lineup Has a Long Reunion

New Management and Frusciante's Return

At virtually the same time the Red Hot Chili Peppers announced John Frusciante's return to the band to the public, they announced a new manager. Lindy Goetz retired in favor of Q Management, a management company that had the likes of Metallica, Madonna, and Def Leppard on its roster. Goetz chose to leave music management entirely and move to Ojai, California. Goetz and his wife began to focus on the nonprofit organization LaGrange County Animal Welfare Association. Q Management came from Rick Rubin's recommendation.

Navarro's firing was reported on April 3, 1998. Twenty-six days later, Frusciante's return was announced. His first public performance with the band after reuniting was an acoustic twelve-song set on June 5 that had solo performances from Frusciante and Flea in it. A week later, the band did a secret show at the 9:30 Club in Washington, D.C., this time electric; they performed eleven songs, including "Love Trilogy," but no new material.

Despite the April time line given in public, *Rolling Stone* reported that Frusciante had begun to play with the band again in March 1998.

Frusciante's Sobriety

As mentioned in chapter 21, Frusciante spiraled into drug addiction in his years away from the band. While most of the scars on his arms are from drug addiction, some are from a fire that burned down his house. Newly sober, he began to learn guitar again, feeling as though he was nowhere near at the level of playing ability he once was. He had rarely spent any time playing guitar or music since leaving the band, doing solo records for drug money and instead focusing on painting with his creative time.

Kiedis wrote in *Scar Tissue* that he loved Frusciante's playing in this era, as Frusciante still had the creative genius but not the virtuoso skills, and so something simple but beautiful would always come out. Frusciante would play guitar all day in the studio, even when he wasn't recording, then come home and play guitar until he fell asleep.

Flea's Panic

Flea suffered panic attacks regularly while recording *Californication*. He was breaking up with his girlfriend—his first serious one since moving past his ex-wife—and not sleeping well. The previous time he went through a divorce, he turned to drugs; though he attributed the *Californication* time as difficult, he was proud to go through it without resorting to alcohol or drug addiction.

Jamming? No Doubt

A good portion of the songs on *Californication* began as group improvisations from jam sessions. The band practiced in Flea's garage. Flea's closest neighbor was Gwen Stefani, the front woman for No Doubt. She ran into Anthony Kiedis during the preproduction and told him that she listened to the band practice every day because they sounded great. According to his biography, Kiedis accepted the compliment but became more self-conscious since it was the first time he realized people could hear them working out their musical kinks.

Bowie

Before going into the recording studio, the Red Hot Chili Peppers considered other producers. For the third time, they asked Brian Eno if he would produce the band; for the third time, Eno declined. They asked David Bowie, who declined through a politely written note explaining that he had too many other commitments. They asked Daniel Lanois to produce, who also declined because he was set to produce U2, but he let them use his studio for demoing: the Teatro Studio in Oxnard, California.

Flea wanted the album to border on electronica. They reached out to Flood, the producer of U2's *Pop*, and William Orbit, the producer of Madonna's *Ray of Light*, and both declined.

Teatro Sessions, Then a Different Studio

The band entered multiple recording studios at different points in time. One of these studios was Teatro Studio behind an old Mexican cinema. (Iggy Pop also

A poster from the *Californication* era from the author's collection.   *Author's collection*

recorded some albums there.) None of these recordings would become the final versions of songs, but they were officially recorded and unreleased demos of the songs that would go on to form *Californication*. This included an unreleased, almost reggae version of "Californication" and several songs that never saw the light of day, including "Trouble in the Pub," "Boatman," and "Plate of Brown." Fans can hear the leaked sessions online; it makes for an interesting listen to see

The album cover.   *Author's collection*

how the songs progressed from their more jam-like state to the finalized song products produced by Rick Rubin.

One of two recorded jams from those sessions would get officially mixed and released as a B-side: "Teatro Jam." At the actual recording studio they selected afterward, the band laid the basic tracks down—guitar, bass, and drums, with only overdubs and replacement work done—for twenty-three songs in seven days.

Kiedis's Relapse and Vocals

Kiedis relapsed once during the recording of the album during the summer after about six months sober. The band was quick to forgive and support him. Kiedis spent a good portion of time as a "dry drunk," or someone who was technically sober but not going through proper coping mechanisms and who was thus irritable. Throughout his sobriety and relapses, he continued to take vocal lessons with Ron Anderson. Kiedis had previously tried with a few other instructors, including Michael Jackson's vocal coach, but Anderson and Kiedis got along, and Kiedis stuck with him.

Artwork

The artwork is of an orange pool, reflecting the sky and clouds, with an ocean transposed into the background. It was created by Warner Bros. Records art director Lawrence Azerrad, based on a dream that John Frusciante had. (In the dream, fittingly, Frusciante saw a pool that possessed the sky, and the water was where the sky normally was.) Creating the image took about a month. Azerrad took the image from a childhood friend's photography and edited it with Photoshop. The track listing is written in Anthony Kiedis's handwriting.

"Around the World"

Frusciante came in with the syncopated guitar, and the first thing Flea played was his bass line. The two decided that it needed a solo but that the album had enough guitar solos and not enough bass work, so the bass solo became the introduction to it. Flea and Frusciante played an Omnichord for the chorus of "Around the World" along with engineer Jim Scott. It took three people because the Omnichord didn't allow for chromatic notes; they had to slow the tape down for one chord, then speed it back up for the next chord, accounting for how the tape would change the pitch of the recording. Flea did the mental math and figured it out, Scott did the engineering and recording and slowing of the tape, and Frusciante physically pressed the correct buttons for the chords.

Frusciante played a Fender Jaguar through two Marshalls to get his guitar sound on the song. He rolled down the tone knob and volume in the introduction and verse but up during the chorus.

"Parallel Universe"

The song was the first Red Hot Chili Peppers song played with a pick on. (He would go on to play with a pick in several songs on *By the Way* and future albums.) Chad Smith's drum parts were inspired by Larry Mullen Jr., the drummer of U2. Although every song was recorded without a click, *Guitar Player* asked Frusciante if "Parallel Universe" was an exception due to its sixteenth-note

Frusciante rocking out live after *Californication* but before *By the Way*.

groove. (It wasn't recorded to a click.) It came out of a jam in which no one brought in the riff and was born sorely out of improvisation.

"Scar Tissue"

Kiedis wrote the lyrics to the song based around how beautiful he found life with Frusciante back in the band and with himself clean. The Mr. Know-It-All and his sarcasm mentioned in the chorus is a reference to Dave Navarro. The song came out of a jam that started with Frusciante's simple guitar riff. Originally, the solo sections were more jam oriented, as can be heard in the Teatro recording.

Frusciante used his 1955 Fender Stratocaster on the song, as he did on most songs on *Californication*. For the slide guitar leads, he played his 1965 Fender Telecaster.

It was Cliff Burnstein from Q Management, the band's effective manager, who decided "Scar Tissue" would be the first single.

"Otherside"

The song was Frusciante's favorite at the time of *Californication*'s release as well as Chad Smith's mother's favorite. Kiedis's lyrics were inspired by Aleister Crowley and his mysticism; the song is about both Kiedis's drug battle and slipping into and out of the "other" side of consciousness. The bridge section was originally instrumental, but Rubin pushed Kiedis to write a vocal part for it, as he believed it added meaning to it.

Along with "Californication," this song was recorded with Frusciante's 1955 Gretsch White Falcon for the majority of the song. He used a 1961 Gibson SG Custom for the bridge.

"Get on Top"

The main riff was Frusciante's and came after listening to Public Enemy on the way to the studio. Kiedis came up with "cuntzilla" from when he took a drama class and one girl insulted another by using the word. Everything besides the guitar riff was born out of a jam—Frusciante brought in the riff after listening to Public Enemy. The bass guitar part is actually two different bass guitars recorded separately. Frusciante's wah sound is an Ibanez WH-10 on the bass setting. Frusciante's solo was inspired by Steve Howe's solo on Yes's "Siberian Khatru."

"Californication"

Kiedis wrote the lyrics, and Frusciante was assigned to write the music. He wrote several versions, of which only a handful were taught to the band—like the Teatro sessions' reggae version. The final product was likely to have been the final thing recorded by the band; Kiedis wrote in his autobiography that Frusciante brought in the music at the last possible moment. There are several different versions of it out there. (For more information, see chapter 8.)

Frusciante recorded his guitar part on what was then his latest purchase: a Gretsch White Falcon guitar that cost more than $30,000. The guitar solo was Kiedis's favorite on the album.

"Easily"

Rick Rubin and John Frusciante had to fight the other band members to get the song on the album's final listing. The song is, metaphorically, a marriage proposal from Anthony Kiedis to his girlfriend; he did not propose to her in real life, though all the lyrics are directly about them.

"Porcelain"

Kiedis met a woman at an Alcoholics Anonymous meeting who was struggling to get sober. She wanted to get off drugs for her young daughter; Kiedis wrote the lyrics for this song based around that. Smith was trying to imitate what a rock band would sound like in a dirty basement that regularly held jazz concerts. He played a smaller jazz drum kit on it rather than his usual drum kit and played with brushes rather than drumsticks.

"Emit Remmus"

The Teatro version, although a different recording, is at its core identical to the final product, meaning this was one of the first songs finished for the album. The title is "Summer Time" spelled backward. The song was inspired by Kiedis's friendship with Melanie Chisholm from the Spice Girls. Flea's daughter, Clara, was obsessed with the Spice Girls; Clara knew Kiedis was friends with Chisholm, so when Flea told her the Spice Girls might have a surprise at her birthday party, she was elated. Instead, the Red Hot Chili Peppers and their drum technician, Chris Warren, dressed up as the girls for her party in drag.

Contrary to popular belief, Frusciante's feedback on the song is produced by two layered guitars and their natural feedback, not an E-Bow.

"I Like Dirt"

The song came out of a jam in which no one came in with a preexisting part. Smith used it as an example of the great and funky things that come out of the band when their minds are clear to *Modern Drummer*. It was one of their earliest jams in the writing process and one of the first songs they finalized. Smith followed the bass when deciding what to do on his final drum part.

"This Velvet Glove"

The song is about Kiedis's battle with drugs, most notably the line "It's such a waste to be wasted in the first place." He told people from *Kerrang!* as much and that it was about himself personally beyond drugs, too. It was also a song that was born solely from a jam.

"Savior"

Frusciante used many guitar pedals on this song. His delay comes from putting his Stratocaster through an Electro-Harmonix Micro Synth and a sixteen-second delay. It was also inspired directly by Eric Clapton's playing in Cream, just with modern effects over it. The lyrics were written about Kiedis's father, Blackie Dammett, who by that point had been running the band's fan club, the Rockin-freakapotamous, for more than five years.

"Purple Stain"

Flea's bass line never changed, so Smith felt free to go wild on multiple drum takes recording the song.

"Right on Time"

Flea played the impressive bass line with two fingers, inspired by the disco synthesizer bass lines of Donna Summers, such as on "I Feel Love."

"Road Trippin'"

The song was the first completed by the band after Frusciante's return, written on a beach trip by Frusciante, Kiedis, and Flea. (The song only references going on a road trip with two friends—despite that, it was Chad Smith's favorite song on the album.) It was a single and had a music video. Other than "Pea," it is the only Red Hot Chili Peppers song to be played on an acoustic bass guitar. The string section in the song is actually recorded with a Chamberlin. The band wanted John Paul Jones from Led Zeppelin to arrange the string parts, but he sent the band a cost that even the Red Hot Chili Peppers couldn't afford to pay.

Other Songs Recorded

At least twenty-three songs had the basic tracks recorded in the first seven days of studio time, but Frusciante told two interviewers from *Total Guitar* that they had almost forty songs completed.

"Quixoticelixir" was recorded from these sessions with some of Anthony Kiedis's favorite lyrics; it went unreleased until the iTunes release included it as a bonus track. "Gong Li" began as a solo song by Flea and was originally recorded as such; several elements were rewritten and rerecorded by the band. "Fat Dance" and "Over Funk" were also recorded during *Californication* but unreleased until their iTunes bonus track release years later. "How Strong" was recorded and released as a B-side for the "Otherside," while "Instrumental #1" was a B-side for "Scar Tissue," and "Instrumental #2" came as a separate CD available only on the Australian release.

"Slowly Deeply" was recorded for *Californication* but released as a B-side to the *By the Way* single "Universally Speaking" in 2003. Similarly, "Bunker Hill" was recorded for these sessions but came out as a B-side for the *Greatest Hits* single "Fortune Faded."

One song, "Trouble in the Pub," was mentioned in prerelease interviews but never completed. It leaked online in 2015.

Woodstock 1999

The band arrived only three hours before they were supposed to play at the third Woodstock music festival. They once again decided to play Jimi Hendrix's "Fire" after Hendrix's sister said that it would be the first Woodstock to not have a Hendrix song played. The crowd started fires across the board when the song began. The event was widely considered chaos.

Trippin' on the Road and Frusciante's Evolution

After constant touring, Flea talked with the band about splitting the tour into legs. It made tours less profitable but put less wear and tear on his body and emotional mind. The band agreed and said it benefited their own happiness levels. They toured the world with various different openers, including the Foo Fighters, Blonde Redhead, Stone Temple Pilots, Fishbone, Krool Keith, Muse, and the Bicycle Thief—whose guitarist was future Chili Pepper Josh Klinghoffer. The band toured almost nonstop until playing the third Rock in Rio in 2001, a little more than a year before *By the Way* would be released.

Their touring was almost nonstop, with sixty-four shows in 1999 and 107 shows in 2000 before slowing down in 2001 to prepare for *By the Way*. It was during these tour dates that Frusciante's playing began to evolve to the virtuosic state he had prior to his original quitting.

Kiedis's favorite part of the tour was watching John Frusciante and his guitar playing evolve as he came out of his minimalist cocoon and became more of a presence front and center. Although he never did so out of ego, Frusciante began to show off for those who wanted it, slowly asking for more soloing time and opening shows with bold, guitar-based jams rather than following Flea's lead all the time. By the end of the *Californication* tour, Frusciante had gotten all of his old skills back.

Flea had another daughter, who was around four months old when the tour first began. He was beginning to dislike the length of the tours, so he suggested the band break it into three-week-long "legs" with ten days off between each leg. The rest of the band agreed to it even though it meant they would lose a good amount of money, as the band's crew had to be paid for those ten days. Nonetheless, it improved Flea's health and the band's well-being. Flea also suggested that the Red Hot Chili Peppers give 5 percent of their touring income to charity, to which everyone else agreed to immediately.

Chris Rock hung out with the band backstage at a few tour dates, as did Woody Harrelson. Both can be seen talking to the band on the *Greatest Hits* DVD; Kiedis and Rock discuss the rise of Snoop Doggy Dogg as a superstar, while Flea and Rock talk about the greatness of Ghostface Killah's then most recent release: *Supreme Clientele*.

After headlining the Big Day Out Festival in Australia with the Foo Fighters, they came along on tour with the Red Hot Chili Peppers for a while. In Australia, Flea and Frusciante came up with the idea that they should get Mohawks for the entirety of the American tour. Kiedis and Smith were quick to join in, and then the whole crew joined in. Footage of the Mohawk shaving can be seen in *Off the Map*, though the best Mohawk pictures come from Chicago.

The *Californication* Relapse

Kiedis got shin splints right before the band headlined Australia's Big Day Out Festival. He went to a doctor and asked for some sort of painkiller that would help him remain mobile for the performance, specifically requesting something nonnarcotic so that he wouldn't relapse. The doctor originally suggested Advil, but after Kiedis said it hadn't worked, the doctor recommended Ultram, which apparently was not a narcotic. In modern thinking, Ultram is considered a narcotic and an opioid; when the tour ended, Kiedis and his formerly drug-addicted girlfriend decided to try drugs one last time and began a drug binge together as a couple.

Kiedis tried to get the two sober as a couple in his typical route: sobering up in a far-away place, this time in Hawaii. However, with his girlfriend there, both continued to do drugs together each night after swimming in the ocean sober most of the day. Kiedis instead sobered up right before the tour and left for the tour dry.

The Final Well-Placed-Socks Moment

On June 23, 2000, the Red Hot Chili Peppers were set to play the opening of Paul Allen's Rock and Roll Museum in Seattle. (Allen was one of the cofounders of Microsoft.) The band didn't feel they played well at the massive show due to the venue's interesting acoustics and some technical difficulties, so they opted to put the socks over their penises for the final time at this show. It was the first time they had done it since Navarro left and Frusciante rejoined.

47

Almost a Breakup

By the Way and Its Tour

Frusciante Stayed Happy, Flea Did Not

The Red Hot Chili Peppers went straight from three years of touring into the studio to write and record *By the Way*. John Frusciante found himself happy, telling *Total Guitar* that preparing *By the Way* and *Californication* were two of the happiest eras of his life.

Frusciante considered both albums a total band effort, but Flea did not feel the same about *By the Way*. Most of the songs were based on chord progressions or melodies written by Frusciante and not by group jams, and it took a toll on Flea. Flea pushed the band to write funkier songs, but Frusciante's tastes won out as John convinced the band that they had already done a lot to cover the funk sound. Flea began to feel like his voice didn't count.

Years later when promoting *Stadium Arcadium*, Flea told Q magazine that he truly believed Frusciante reached a new level of artistry on *By the Way* but that he incidentally made Flea feel like garbage in the process. Flea originally planned to finish recording the album with the Red Hot Chili Peppers but quit before it was time to tour for *By the Way*. Flea told no one in the band and didn't have a discussion about it until much later with Frusciante at an airport where Frusciante conceded he had been controlling. Flea largely held off on quitting because he couldn't bear the idea of telling Anthony Kiedis he was quitting and resolved his personal tensions only after going into therapy. In particular, it was Frusciante ignoring everyone else's opinions on overdubs that pushed Flea to the limit.

Frusciante's New Guitar Heroes

Frusciante always admired more minimalist guitarists than most. On *By the Way*, he began to name-drop less prominent New Wave guitarists in interviews with *Guitar World* and *Guitar Player*, such as Vini Reilly from Duritti Column,

Johnny Marr from the Smiths, Andy Partridge from XTC, and John McGeoch from Siouxsie and the Banshees.

A New Studio

The band did not record at the famous mansion for *By the Way*. Instead, they recorded at Chateau Marmont on the seventh floor. The Marmont is a famous hotel in Los Angeles where celebrities go for prolonged stays; everyone from F. Scott Fitzgerald to Lana Del Ray lived there for a time. (It is also where the band Death Grips ended up meeting Beyonce Knowles.) Kiedis brought several books to read, including *Gulliver's Travels*, and tried to outfit the band's era with old movie posters from the 1950s. The album was done in Pro Tools and not on tape.

Melodic but Not Punk; Confidence, or Lack Thereof

Originally, the band was going to go for two different styles on the album: the melodic, more "English-sounding" style they ended up going with and heavier punk inspired by the Damned and Discharge. Producer Rick Rubin was not familiar with the bands that John Frusciante had mentioned as his punk inspirations, so they all decided to focus more on the melodic material. Although fans and critics have compared the final sound to the Beach Boys, Frusciante insisted he didn't get into *Pet Sounds* until after recording was finished. The band told *ICE* magazine that they wanted to do a more uplifting sound after the terrorist attacks of September 11, 2001.

During *Stadium Arcadium*, everyone in the band insisted it was their best work yet. During *By the Way*, the band had some doubts. Kiedis told *Meanstreet* that "there are days when I think [*By the Way*] is the greatest thing we've ever done and then there are days when I feel like this is just going to die in the water."

Artwork

The artwork for *By the Way* was done by Julian Schnabel. The woman on the cover is Stella Schnabel, who was Julian's daughter and John Frusciante's girlfriend at the time. Julian Schnabel offered to do the album art, and the band sent him a demo tape of eight songs; he got the general idea of the album and came up with what became the final artwork with no expectation that it would necessarily be used. He also did all the artwork for all of the singles from the album.

The *By the Way* cover is a negative of the original art. The single for "Universally Speaking" is the inversion and thus the original.

"By the Way"

"By the Way" was begun the December after the 9/11 attacks. Frusciante and Kiedis took a Christmas vacation together to St. Barts in the Caribbean and talked about how people acted like the world was going to end, but both could tell it would not. They considered the time a growing pain; one of the songs from that time together was "By the Way."

The song was the first single from the album, released on June 10, 2002, but it wasn't the band's choice; their managers decided it. The band was surprised, as they thought it was too different to be commercially successful.

The music video was directed by Jonathan Dayton and Valerie Faris and had the story of the kidnapping of Anthony Kiedis where the rest of the band then spends the rest of the video saving him. Frusciante had to drive a jeep in the video; he did not have a driver's license and had never driven a car prior to

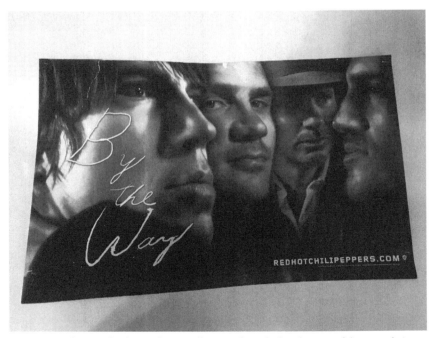

A promotional poster for the *By the Way* album pushing the band's state-of-the-art website.
Author's collection

Another *By the Way* poster.   *Author's collection*

the filming. The song reached number one on the *Billboard* Mainstream Rock and Alternative Songs charts while hitting number thirty-four on the Hot 100.

Despite ending up as the title track, its working title was "Soul Train."

"Universally Speaking"

"Universally Speaking" was released as a single on July 15, 2003, and received a video that acted as a sequel to the "By the Way" video. (The major plotline was the same deranged fan trying to return to Kiedis a book he had left behind in his jeep.) It was performed constantly across the *By the Way* tour but dropped in 2004 before coming back on the *I'm with You* tour. Much like "Can't Stop," the single version has a different mix done by John Frusciante.

The song features a glockenspiel. Kiedis didn't like its inclusion at first but was democratically outvoted, and it remained in the song. The song is also a prominent example of the "face/off" writing game the band played; after coming up with a verse via jamming, Kiedis instantly sang what was the final melody. To get a chorus, Flea and Frusciante went to opposite sides of the garage for a few minutes. When Frusciante played his chorus, Flea knew it was better than his part, and it was the final song's chorus. Flea's idea from the "face/off" became the song's outro.

The negative of the *Universally Speaking* single is the same as the *By the Way* cover.

Author's collection

The version released to streaming services on *The Studio Album Collection 1991–2011* is inexplicably different, missing guitar parts at the chorus with a different orchestration and far more reverb on Kiedis's vocal lines.

"This Is the Place"

Frusciante sings the "ooh-wa-oohs" throughout the song, imitating a synthesizer. This was actually played by a synthesizer in the early versions, as heard in the unmixed early demos of the album. It had two working titles; it was at various points known as both "Drone" and "Wolverine." The song was teased live and played (but not completely) in Austria in 2016 with Klinghoffer in the band.

"Dosed"

The song is a lyrical tribute to Hillel Slovak by Kiedis. It featured many guitar overdubs by Frusciante and was never played live with Frusciante in the band. This may be due to Kiedis; the chorus featured Frusciante singing both the melody and the harmony parts of the first vocal line in the chorus because Kiedis struggled to hear it correctly. Its working title was "The Loop Song." The single release credited Flea for additional guitar work, making this the only known song where Flea played some guitar while Frusciante was a band member.

"Don't Forget Me"

Frusciante played his Ibanez WH10 wah pedal for the guitar to this song. The song is one of the few to come out of a jam session, and when it was jammed, Flea played something similar to the final version. Nonetheless, there was a fill that Flea played in the jam that he couldn't figure out when it came time to record it in the studio; Frusciante recorded the fill on bass guitar for the final track. The incident is one of the noted moments when Flea felt disrespected, though the song remained in the Red Hot Chili Peppers' live set list in the years after.

Kiedis wrote the lyrics about what he believed God to be and the meaning of life.

"The Zephyr Song"

"The Zephyr Song" was the first Red Hot Chili Peppers song since their first album to feature a drum machine. Its working title was "Coltraine." It was released as the second single from the album on August 17, 2002. Its music video was directed by Jonathan Dayton and Valerie Faris and features the outlines of the band playing over an array of kaleidoscopic images.

The song was a common performance from 2002 to 2004 but then disappeared for the remainder of the John Frusciante era. It made its performance with Josh Klinghoffer on guitar in 2016. The working title for the song was "Coltrane."

"Can't Stop"

The single and album versions of the songs have different mixes, with the single being mixed under Frusciante's direction though not necessarily by Frusciante himself. The backing vocals are much louder in the single version.

The music video was inspired by the art of Erwin Wurm, particularly his One-Minute Sculptures. The One-Minute Sculpture series was done by Wurm by bringing people into a room with a series of random objects and giving them one minute to find a position for him to photograph for it to be his art. In the video, Frusciante played an orange Tornado; in reality, he never played this guitar, but he did so because the director, Mark Romanek, directed him to, as it fit the visual color scheme.

The song almost did not make the final cut of the album, as Kiedis struggled to come up with his vocal part for it. In its original instrumental state, it was known as "Choppy Funk."

"I Could Die for You"

Across the whole record, the bass lines were rerecorded after all the overdubs were finished so that Flea could try to play the most melodically sensible thing possible. He originally played the song with a fretted bass but rerecorded it with a fretless one after all the vocals were done. (He was inspired by Paul McCartney, who did that with most of the Beatles bass lines, to do that process.)

The band took pride in its structure immediately, giving it the working title of "The Most Beautiful Chords Ever" in early versions.

"Midnight"

The song was never played live. It featured a recorded string section; this may be why it wasn't played on the *By the Way* tour. The string section was arranged by John Frusciante.

"Throw Away Your Television"

The most bass-oriented song on the album, it stemmed from a jam. It remained a part of their set list throughout the *By the Way* tour and occasionally appeared after that. On the band's official website at the time, the media section was named after this song. Its working title was "Trash Your Television."

"Cabron"

Frusciante was inspired to write his part by Vini Reilly from Durutti Column. Reilly could play flamenco guitar, while Frusciante was not directly familiar with it. He wanted his guitar part to sound more textual than mere chords played to a rhythm.

According to an interview with *DRUM!* magazine, Smith tried several different style drumbeats for the song before producer Rick Rubin added a stereo slap-back effect that changed the whole sound of the drums on the recording. Smith then listened to how it sounded on slap back and recorded the final drum part in the next few takes.

Although Flea played an upright bass on a television performance of this, he still played a bass guitar for the studio performance. Similar to Smith, he couldn't come up with the final bass line and tried many different things. Frusciante suggested that Flea play Frusciante's Vox bass with a capo on, believing the capo would force Flea to see the neck differently. It worked; the Vox bass take is the final bass track. Frusciante also played the song with a capo on the seventh fret.

"Tear"

The song was never played live. Flea played trumpet on it.

"On Mercury"

In early versions, the song was titled "Lemon Trees on Mercury."

"Minor Thing"

Frusciante used a Big Muff pedal for the solo in "Minor Thing." Its working title was "A Minor One."

"Warm Tape"

Frusciante played keyboard on the song. The song's title originates from the keyboard preset he used to play on it, also named Warm Tape. The band played it live a handful of times.

"Venice Queen"

The song was written about Gloria Scott, who helped Kiedis get sober during the *One Hot Minute* era. She was diagnosed with lung cancer, and Kiedis helped put together a benefit to raise money to help her. Scott referred to Neil Young as her higher power, so Kiedis asked Young to play, and he did with his backing band Crazy Horse. Kiedis spells out her name as the chorus to the song.

It was originally going to be titled "Epic" or "Gloria's Epic."

Kiedis recorded vocals separately when the rest of the band had finished (except for Frusciante's backing vocals). The only photographer present for that time was Tony Woolliscroft. He wanted to get an action shot of Kiedis recording vocals, but Kiedis didn't want to fake it, so he invited Woolliscroft into the recording booth as Kiedis recorded vocals for one song. That song was "Venice Queen," so any photos of Kiedis recording vocals during *By the Way* are part of the recording of this song.

The *By the Way* cover.
Author's collection

Other Songs Recorded

"Runaway" and "The Bicycle Song" were recorded during the *By the Way* sessions and went unreleased until they came out as iTunes bonus tracks. "Time" came out on the Japanese version of the album and on the "By the Way" single; "Teenager in Love" came out on the "By the Way" single worldwide and came from the *By the Way* sessions. "Body of Water," "Someone," "Out of Range," and "Rivers of Avalon" were all recorded for *By the Way* but came out as part of the single for "The Zephyr Song." "Body of Water" was written by Kiedis about his then girlfriend—the same who went through the drug binge with him post-*Californication*—and how she always wanted more but her spirit kept him going. Prerelease interviews referred to "Rivers of Avalon" as "New Wave."

"Fortune Faded" began during the *By the Way* sessions but was finished during *Greatest Hits*. (Similarly, one of its B-sides was a song that originated from the *Californication* sessions; another was "Eskimo," recorded for *By the Way*.)

The band recorded a cover of the Ramones' "Havana Affair." Chad Smith said that Johnny Ramone asked them to record it; the band held onto it until Rick Rubin's Ramones tribute album came out. The same tribute album also featured Frusciante's version of "Today Your Love, Tomorrow the World," originally by the Ramones.

"Fall Water," "Goldmine," and "Rock and Roll" have never been commercially released but have rough recordings from these sessions. They leaked online in 2014. Two songs have been referenced in interviews that have not surfaced: "Strumming in D on J," named for what happens in the song (Frusciante strums in the key of D major on a Jaguar), and "Upseen." Those two songs are likely working titles of other songs, as an interview with *ICE* magazine mentioned they only recorded twenty-eight songs, not thirty.

Mixing Issues

John Frusciante talked at length about how he was disappointed in the final mix for *By the Way*. It is because of this disappointment that he led the way on mixing several songs' single versions. Even before the record came out, he took issue with the way Rick Rubin and the mixing engineers were making their record; in a feature with *Guitarist*, the interviewer watched as Frusciante asked that the backing vocals to "Can't Stop" be raised to a higher volume. Frusciante also took particular issue with how Rubin buried interesting and unusual sounds in the mix and instead focused on lead vocals and the core instruments.

Other Potential Producers

Kiedis told *Classic Rock* almost a decade later that the Red Hot Chili Peppers approached David Bowie to produce *Stadium Arcadium* and *By the Way*. (*Californication* was the only album previously reported that he was offered the production slot for.) Each time, Bowie wrote a polite and thorough letter explaining why he couldn't accept the offer.

It's likely that, given Frusciante's issues with the mix on *By the Way*, they searched for other producers beyond Bowie before settling back on Rubin.

Touring by Their Way

Although things improved on tour in terms of tension from where they were in the making of the album, Flea still considered quitting throughout the tour. He would play each show and then isolate himself, still feeling overpowered by Frusciante. It eventually resolved itself midway through the *By the Way* tour at an airport; Flea casually mentioned how he had felt stifled, and Frusciante admitted he wouldn't listen to anyone during the overdub period of the record and took a commanding control that wasn't respectful.

The tour was so successful that family members routinely requested and were granted more than 100 tickets at shows they planned to attend.

A concert video was made from this tour. *Live at Slane Castle* was filmed on August 23, 2003, in Ireland and released on November 17 of the same year. It has three edits that stop it from being a complete performance DVD: Frusciante's cover of Donna Summers's "I Feel Love" featuring Smith and Flea is removed entirely, the full band performance of "Soul to Squeeze" is removed (possibly due to Frusciante breaking a string during the song), and a lyrical flub that causes Frusciante to stop for a moment during his solo cover of "Maybe" is edited out. (The flub is possibly why Flea makes it a point to chant Frusciante's full name and energize the crowd after "Maybe" was concluded.) "I Feel Love" appeared after "Otherside," and "Soul to Squeeze" came after "Right on Time" in the set list.

48

The *Greatest Hits* Sessions

The Tour Pauses for New Music

Tour Pause

Usually, the band would tour for one or two years, then take a short break, and then begin to jam and practice before entering the studio again and start the whole process over. With *Greatest Hits*, the band recorded new songs in between legs of the tour and went straight back into touring right afterward. Smith attributed this as a major reason why all the songs were instrumentally tight and why they could record so many songs so quickly.

The Songs

There is no definitive idea of how many songs were recorded for *Greatest Hits*. John Frusciante reported the band recorded fifteen different songs, while Chad Smith reported they recorded sixteen. Frusciante also stated that of the fifteen recorded, Anthony Kiedis recorded vocals for only nine. This was in the first round of sessions; they had a second series of recording sessions scheduled, but it is unknown whether they went through with them. Frusciante mentioned the plan to record another fifteen songs as if they were a complete album in multiple interviews, including one with *Guitar World Acoustic*.

"Fortune Faded" originated in other sessions but was entirely rerecorded for *Greatest Hits*. It's likely that it is included as one of the fifteen new songs and one of the nine that Kiedis did vocals for, but this is not definitive.

An Unreleased Album

In a fan question-and-answer session on Reddit, Smith said that the Red Hot Chili Peppers would eventually release the "extra album," which is the unreleased *Greatest Hits* songs, as part of a box set. It is likely that this box set would be released only after the band breaks up or enters an extended hiatus.

The bizarre kissing machine on the *Greatest Hits* cover.   *Author's collection*

Song Selection

Part of the band's original EMI contract buyout from Warner Bros. was the nego-tiation of what songs could appear on different labels' greatest-hits packages: on EMI's greatest-hits release *What Hits!?*, "Under the Bridge" was allowed to appear even though it was a Warner Bros.–era song from *Blood Sugar Sex Magik*. In what was basically a trade, "Higher Ground" from *Mother's Milk* was allowed to appear on *Greatest Hits* even though it was Warner Bros.' collection and the song originated from EMI. That is why it is the only song from the era before *Blood Sugar Sex Magik* on the compilation.

Four *Blood Sugar Sex Magik* songs appear (plus "Soul to Squeeze," which was recorded during those sessions), five *Californication* songs are included, and only one *One Hot Minute* and two *By the Way* songs were included. "Can't Stop" wasn't included; it was a larger hit than "Universally Speaking," but "Universally Speaking" made the cut. "Universally Speaking" was the most recent released single from the band at the time, so it is possible that it was chosen in the place of "Can't Stop" to boost single sales.

The two previously unreleased songs were "Fortune Faded" and "Save the Population." "Fortune Faded" originated in other sessions, meaning that at least seven other new songs were recorded with vocals. The knowns of these are "The Bicycle Song" and "Runaway," later released as iTunes extras for *By the Way*.

Two of the known recorded instrumentals are "Starlight" and "50Fifty," which leaked online in 2014. It's likely that three originals that were eventually released on live albums—"Rolling Sly Stone," "Leverage of Space," and "Mini-Epic (Kill for Your Country)"—were recorded for *Greatest Hits*, but this is not definitive.

"Mini-Epic (Kill for Your Country)" was finally released as a live recording from Wales.

Author's collection

Artwork

The compilation's cover is actually a series of photos of an item known as the "Kissing Machine" from the Max Factor collection. Factor was a cosmetician from Poland who experimented in movie makeup in Hollywood in the early twentieth century. The item was sold at an auction on May 15, 2010.

The *Greatest Hits* DVD

Greatest Hits had two versions: the standard CD and another, deluxe edition that had both the CD and a DVD. The DVD had music videos for sixteen songs—this time including "Aeroplane" and "Can't Stop"—and an eighty-one-minute documentary filmed toward the end of the *Californication* tour. Josh Klinghoffer makes a notable appearance in the documentary.

Hyde Park and a Live Album That Never Came Out in America

Greatest Hits was released on November 18, 2003, making it released one day after the concert video *Live at Slane Castle* came out from the band. The band went straight back to touring, eventually recording another live concert, this time an internationally released album that came out everywhere worldwide except America: *Live in Hyde Park*.

Recorded in Hyde Park in London over three dates, the album pulls the best performances chosen from concerts on June 19, 20, and 24, 2004, to form a two-disc performance that includes a Frusciante solo performance of "I Feel Love" by Donna Summers (notably absent from *Live at Slane Castle*), covers of Looking Glass's "Brandy" and 45 Grave's "Black Cross," a duet between Frusciante on bass and Flea on trumpet, and two of the previously mentioned potential *Greatest Hits* songs: "Leverage of Space" and "Rolling Sly Stone."

In the warm-up shows for *Live in Hyde Park*, "Rolling Sly Stone" appeared with different lyrics, though it's likely those were vocal flubs, as Kiedis doesn't sound confident in his first performance of the song. In those warm-ups, they also played "Mini-Epic (Kill for Your Country)." One of those warm-up gigs was released in 2014 as its own live album, *Cardiff, Wales: 6/23/04*. It is notable because it was played between the second and third Hyde Park shows.

After the summer tour of 2004, the band took the rest of the year off and played only a select set of shows in 2005 as they focused on recording what would become *Stadium Arcadium*; they did seven shows in total that year, with the July 2 performance in Las Vegas marking the debut of "Tell Me Baby," "21st Century," and "Readymade."

Scar Tissue: Now a Book

After *Greatest Hits* and *Live in Hyde Park*, Anthony Kiedis's autobiography *Scar Tissue* came out on October 6, 2004. No one else in the band read the 480-page book. John Frusciante asked for a copy from Kiedis three separate times, and Kiedis agreed to give him one each time but never delivered. (Frusciante knew there would be secrets revealed in it and didn't like it, but he didn't hold it against Kiedis.)

Flea tried to read *Scar Tissue* twice but stopped himself both times. The first time, he felt complimented by the mention of their friendship; the second time, he reached the part where Kiedis had sex with Flea's sister. He decided not to read the rest to avoid compromising the music they were working on, as, even though he agreed his sister and Kiedis were perfectly allowed to have sex if they so desired, he didn't want to read about it. Flea told Q magazine in 2011 that he would probably finish reading it someday but that it may not happen until the band is over.

Anthony Kiedis during the Heineken Jammin Festival, 2002.

Fabio Diena / Shutterstock.com

The release caused friction between some band members. Kiedis told *Q* magazine, "I could've revealed a lot more, I really could. It was my first foray into trying to tell the truth about myself . . . and in doing so you have to be hyper-conscious of not telling other people's stories in ways they might not be comfortable with. In retrospect I made some mistakes along the way and I've made apologies for them. . . . It caused a little friction, but I feel like I was forgiven. By most."

Smith didn't try to read *Scar Tissue*.

49

The Double Album

Stadium Arcadium and Its Creation

Love and Happiness

In the two years of writing, practicing, and recording *Stadium Arcadium*, the band was almost entirely in committed relationships for the first time. Chad Smith got married for the second time to his wife, Nancy, who gave birth to a son, Cole, and Flea had a new baby, Sunny, with his then fiancée, Frankie Rayder. John Frusciante was dating Emily Kokal, while Anthony Kiedis was dating a woman named Heather.

Original Intent

The band returned to the same mansion they recorded *Blood Sugar Sex Magik* in. They set out to write and record only twelve songs, as they wanted to make a piece of pop art comparable to *Meet the Beatles*. Kiedis told *The Times, The Knowledge* that Frusciante wrote him a ten-page letter insisting they keep all of that first batch of songs for the record, so Kiedis decided they would opt for a longer album.

They ended up recording thirty-eight songs total, and after no one agreed on a final track listing, they opted to do three albums, with one released every six or eight months. After they realized that by the time the third album would be released they'd be writing new music, they opted for a double album. (Even then, they couldn't agree on a final track listing: the four band members and producer Rick Rubin voted which songs should make the final cut, and the democracy process decided which songs made it and in what order.) The band didn't get mad at each other during the voting process but were constantly surprised by the other members' choices. Some of these surprises can be witnessed on the *Stadium Arcadium* bonus DVD.

The final album artwork.

Guitar Hero Coming-Out Party

On *By the Way*, Frusciante began to add layers of overdubbed vocals and synthesizers. On *Stadium Arcadium*, this happened with guitar parts, both lead and rhythm. Kiedis believed Frusciante was always a virtuoso and a capable rock guitarist but attributed Frusciante's desire to be more in-your-face to hanging out with Omar Rodriguez-Lopez from At the Drive-In and the Mars Volta. The Mars Volta opened for the Red Hot Chili Peppers, and Rodriguez-Lopez and Frusciante became close friends; Rodriguez-Lopez's style of blistering guitar led to Frusciante wanting to be known as a more prominent lead player.

Frusciante's New Influences

While *By the Way* focused on vocal harmonies and post-punk, Frusciante dug into a more diverse set of sounds to influence him for *Stadium Arcadium*.

Rodriguez-Lopez got him playing a more bodacious lead guitar, but Frusciante spent most of his time listening to Electric Light Orchestra, Brandy, Wu-Tang Clan, Wizzard, and Roy Wood for the double disc album. In particular, he noted that Brandy's backing vocal rhythms were just a little off rhythm, and he attempted to do the same with his guitar harmonies.

Original Artwork Rejected and a Deluxe Edition

The band originally set out to use art from Storm Thorgerson, who famously did the cover art for Pink Floyd's *Wish You Were Here* and *Dark Side of the Moon* as well as Led Zeppelin's *Led Zeppelin* and *Houses of the Holy*, among others. The band passed on three different designs of Thorgerson and opted for the artwork that ended up final from someone else. Thorgerson rarely spoke out when artists passed on his work but did so here, as he was offended that they used something so "trite" and "unadventurous," according to his blog (and later reposted by the website *Feelnumb*).

Thorgerson's original designs for *Stadium Arcadium* can be seen online. In the final version, each disc is named after a planet; the deluxe edition's artwork included miniature cardboard planet outlines, stickers, and playing figures as well as a DVD that included a track-by-track commentary on the making of the album.

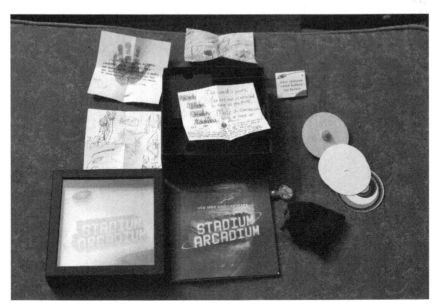

The complete deluxe edition of *Stadium Arcadium*, photographed in the author's living room.
Author's collection

Almost Didn't Make It?

Three songs were not mentioned on the track-by-track commentary of the album; it was filmed before the final track listing was decided and likely covered only the songs that had already been decided to make the final cut. Those three songs were "Torture Me," "Strip My Mind," and "Especially in Michigan."

Recording Process

Recorded at the mansion, the band did a variation of their usual recording process: they didn't lay down basic tracks until Kiedis had finished vocals, and then drums, guitar, and bass were all recorded at the same time, then overdubs and vocal work were done later. They did it song by song rather than finishing all the drum tracks and moving forward. Flea would spend weeknights at the mansion, but everyone else consistently went home. According to an interview with *Total Guitar*, this was because everyone besides Flea lived ten minutes away, and Flea lived an hour away.

Frusciante would often stay in the studio until 5:00 the next morning, according to *Rhythm*. On *Blood Sugar Sex Magik*, *Californication*, and *By the Way*, Frusciante planned all of his solos; on *Stadium Arcadium*, he was deliberately more improvisational.

Flea and Frusciante Tensions Return?

A big part of the interview process for *Stadium Arcadium* mentioned Flea and Frusciante's arguments and issues that happened during the recording of *By the Way*. Even in features where every band member was interviewed, they were all interviewed separately rather than together. *Kerrang!* noted that was by choice and confronted Flea about the notion that some people considered *Stadium Arcadium* an album driven by Frusciante. Flea cussed out the writer and threw a water bottle at his head before returning minutes later to apologize and clarify that he felt like the writer was portraying Flea negatively after he had opened up rather than that he had any lingering issue with Frusciante.

Jupiter: "Dani California"

Frusciante's guitar solo was based around a quoted lick from Jimi Hendrix's "Purple Haze" by design. Lyrically, Kiedis wrote the song as a continuation of a girl named Dani California, apparently the "teenage bride with the baby inside" on "Californication" and the "Dani the girl" from "By the Way." Frusciante wrote the chorus melody when the music was already set by the band.

Its working title was "Wu Tang," as Frusciante came up with the beat for the guitar part, comparing it to the distinct beat that appears across almost all of the Wu-Tang Clan's *Enter the 36 Chambers*. Frusciante was listening to the record almost every day during the making of *Stadium Arcadium*.

The song was released as a single on April 3, 2006. Although its video premiered on MTV, it was one of the first official music videos to get posted by its creators on YouTube. The video was directed by Tony Kaye, who also directed *American History X*; it depicts the band playing the song dressed as though they are from different eras of music, including being depicted as the Misfits, the early Beatles, as a funk band, and so on, before ending up dressed as themselves.

"Snow ((Hey Oh))"

The song was lyrically written by Kiedis about how it was never too late to turn your life around and start anew. It was released as the third single from the album on November 20, 2006. Frusciante came up with the guitar part by playing in a Jimi Hendrix style but picking the strings individually rather than doing the full chordal strums. When they first finished the song, Kiedis's croons of "oh yeah" made the whole band laugh; they repeated that part for twenty minutes or so.

It took a long time for Josh Klinghoffer to be comfortable with singing the harmonies and playing this song live. After the *Stadium Arcadium* tour, it didn't reappear in the band's set list until June 28, 2012.

The song had two music videos, though one never saw the light of day. One, directed by Tony Kaye, was never used; the other, directed by Nick Warham, was a live performance from the band with spliced-in footage of fans waiting outside to go to the show.

"Charlie"

Lyrically, "Charlie" is to be a reference not to cocaine but instead to the human imagination, according to Kiedis. Interviewers doubted him throughout the press process, but Kiedis didn't relapse during *Stadium Arcadium*.

Frusciante plays a polyrhythm against the rest of the band; Smith and Flea play in 4/4 time, while Frusciante plays in 3/4 time.

"Stadium Arcadium"

The title track was written about the spiritual feeling the band felt when playing or attending a gig and when everyone feels as though, together, they are one. The guitar solo was done by flipping over the analog tape it was recorded to and processing it through an EMT 250 digital reverb, then running it again through a high-pass filter on Frusciante's modular synthesizer rig.

"Stadium Arcadium" started with Chad Smith's beat. Smith didn't do his usual warm-up and had been playing the beat for about three minutes when Frusciante arrived and began to jam. Flea and Kiedis arrived later and began to write their parts immediately.

"Hump de Bump"

The song references the basic groove of the 1980s Red Hot Chili Peppers song "American Ghost Dance," hence its working title, "Ghost Dance 2000." At one point, it was also known as "Forty Detectives," when it had a different set of lyrics. Chris Rock directed its music video. The single, the final for the album, came out on April 7, 2007. Its B-sides were the same as the previously released B-sides for "Desecration Smile." Flea played the horns on it and was trying to sound like James Brown's horn section.

"Forty Detectives" started well before *Stadium Arcadium*; Kiedis remembered the groove and urged Flea to keep writing a bass line to keep it. As "Forty Detectives," it had the same groove but a different set of chords. It was recorded in its original state on one of the band member's phones, but the phone deleted it. Kiedis did not want it on the final album, but Rick Rubin and Flea felt very strongly it should be on there and won out. It was one of the final songs to be mixed.

"She's Only 18"

The basis for this song lyrically came when Kiedis found out that his girlfriend Heather had zero interest in the Rolling Stones. He was shocked that they were so popular and renowned, and she absolutely did not care. It was originally to be titled "Only 18." Before lyrics were set to it, it was known as "Funkadelicish to Me"; the working titles were written down on a chalkboard as the band decided which to record. Frusciante was trying to describe it as similar to Funkadelic, but Kiedis thought it was a great way to describe the song.

Kiedis thought it was Frusciante's best guitar solo; you can hear Kiedis's vocal excitement on the recording. It had a different chorus originally before Frusciante wrote a new chord progression.

"Slow Cheetah"

Lyrically, it was written about Kiedis's ex, Yohanna Logan, and how both the good and the bad experiences become a beautiful life moment in the end. He believed she looked like a cheetah.

It was Flea's favorite song on the album.

"Torture Me"

Flea played trumpet on this. He also composed the bass line and brought it in for the band to jam on. It's possible it almost didn't make the final track listing of the album—it was one of only three songs not mentioned in the track-by-track commentary included in the deluxe edition's DVD.

"Strip My Mind"

Its working title was "Early Eighties," as it sounded like it was from that era to the band.

"Especially in Michigan"

The guitar solos on the vinyl and CD versions are slightly different. Omar Rodriguez-Lopez took the guitar solo. Lyrically, Kiedis wrote it about growing up in Michigan.

"Warlocks"

Billy Preston played clavinet on this song. Preston was ill for many years preceding it and hadn't recorded in a long time and was literally bedridden; the band sent him the recording, and he came over and recorded his part, then went back to his bed. It was one of the last keyboard parts he played before his passing. The final studio version is one of the earliest takes; they rerecorded the song several times, but Flea felt it was getting less and less funky with each additional take.

Kiedis wrote the lyrics about the madness of show business in Los Angeles.

"C'mon Girl"

This is one of three songs Kiedis singled out as about the crisis of being in love with his girlfriend Heather. Kiedis believed it was also a note on his failure in past relationships. Frusciante flipped the tape and used his modular synthesizer gear for the solo in a similar manner to what he did for "Stadium Arcadium."

Frusciante wrote almost all of the guitar and bass parts in his girlfriend's apartment and brought them in. He also instructed Smith on what the chorus drum part should be. Flea considered it one of his harder bass lines to play.

"Wet Sand"

This is one of three songs Kiedis singled out in *Rolling Stone* as about the crisis of being in love with his girlfriend Heather, but to *Q* magazine, he said the song was about a man who believed in divine creation and who was arguing with a woman who believed only in evolution. It is possible that was a fight that Heather and Kiedis had.

It was one of Flea's favorite songs on the record. Frusciante wrote all the chord progressions, but Rick Rubin rearranged the song structure on one of the first days of the band's rehearsals. Frusciante also wrote the vocal melody for the outro; Frusciante generally preferred for Kiedis to come up with his own melodies over his guitar parts, but Frusciante sang some random words over his melody; the two words Kiedis took were "wet sand"; all the rest were written by Kiedis.

"Hey"

Kiedis wrote the lyrics about removing something from your life that you depend on that has been hurting you. Its working title was "Light and Jazzy" because Rick Rubin kept referring to it as the "light and jazzy song" they worked on.

The song was one of Kiedis's and Flea's five favorites on *Stadium Arcadium*. Flea brought in the bass line; Smith came up with his drum part before Frusciante had his guitar part. Frusciante played his Gretsch White Falcon on it.

Mars: "Desecration Smile"

The lyrics border on religious at times. During *Stadium Arcadium*'s creation, Kiedis was getting into Kaballah. Although he did not consider himself a fanatic, it did influence his words. Frusciante compared the song to the Eagles, even though he wasn't a fan of the Eagles. It was released as the fourth *Stadium Arcadium* single on February 12, 2007.

It was first performed at the Bridge School Benefit show in 2004 and bootlegged by fans. This early version featured an entirely different chorus and song structure than the final version. Both Kiedis and Flea did not like the original chorus; Rubin pushed them to rewrite the chorus after attending the Bridge School Benefit. Frusciante brought in the new chorus.

"Tell Me Baby"

"Tell Me Baby" was the second single from *Stadium Arcadium*, released on July 18, 2006. The video had aspiring actors and actresses who moved to Hollywood to "make it" telling their stories; for their callback auditions for the part in the music video, the Red Hot Chili Peppers came out and danced or played with the auditionees. The video was directed by Jonathan Dayton and Valerie Faris.

The song came from a jam. It is one of the few slap bass lines Flea played on the record.

"Hard to Concentrate"

The song is lyrically a marriage proposal set to music. It was written by Kiedis for (and about) Flea, as Kiedis wanted to welcome his fiancée to the band's larger family. Smith played the snare drum with the snares turned off and put towels across every drum on the set for the softer sound on "Hard to Concentrate."

Flea wrote the bass line as an imitation of Frusciante's guitar playing. (Frusciante and his use of thirds an octave away was in turn inspired by Jane's Addiction bassist Eric Avery's playing.) Flea wrote the bass line on Christmas Day and failed to help prepare potatoes for his family, as he focused on the bass instead.

"21st Century"

Lyrically, the song was written about the flaws of the future, like global warming, and George W. Bush and his politics, particularly the line "read me the scripture and I will twist it." Flea brought the bass line into the band; Kiedis thought it sounded like the Talking Heads.

"She Looks to Me"

The lyric was originally "she comes to me," which was also its original working title. Kiedis wrote the lyrics about a girl he was dating who had a drug addiction and who admired him as a sober role model; he ended the relationship with her but maintained a fatherly care for her. Frusciante used an Electro-Harmonix POG pedal for the guitar sound.

Flea was originally hesitant about the song, but as they finished it, he became a bigger fan. Originally, the bridge was the chorus and there was no bridge; that part originated from one of their "face/off" games. They then decided it would make a better bridge; Frusciante wrote the new chorus, and the band came up with the modulation at the end. Frusciante was most proud of the outro.

"Readymade"

The song is a tribute to Johnny Ramone, who loved the Red Hot Chili Peppers. Frusciante's guitar riff was inspired by the band Mountain. The guitar solo was inspired by Jimi Hendrix, but more than Hendrix's style, Frusciante admired how Hendrix never repeated himself, and thus Frusciante set out to do a guitar solo that was not in his own usual style.

Smith was particularly proud of the drum track because he got to flip the snare and bass drum beats as the verse went on. Rubin was normally a fan of a simpler drum work; Smith felt like he snuck one by the goalie. Smith was trying to imitate the playing of John Bonham on Led Zeppelin's "Black Dog."

When it was first played live in Las Vegas, fans compared it to Jane's Addiction's "Mountain Song." Frusciante wrote the main riff on bass and brought it in; on *Stadium Arcadium*, Frusciante began to practice bass finger style rather than with a pick. The chorus came from one of Frusciante and Flea's "face/offs." Kiedis was not a big fan of the song.

"If"

It was the shortest song title of any by the Red Hot Chili Peppers. Flea and Kiedis voted for the song to be on the record. Flea wrote the bass line first; in its final form, Frusciante loved it because it didn't sound like any other song on the record. Flea was influenced by Neil Young but didn't think it ended up sounding like him; Frusciante thought it sounded like the folky side of Led Zeppelin.

"Make You Feel Better"

Kiedis wrote this about how the band makes its fans feel better. Flea originally didn't like it but loved it on its final mix. Kiedis believed no one would truly appreciate it until it was finished being mixed, as its initial rough mix was terrible.

"Animal Bar"

"Animal Bar" was originally known as "Neu!" because Flea tried to write it in a Krautrock style like the band Neu. Frusciante used a modular synthesizer on his guitar, taking into account that the artist Bjork said that guitar was boring and that no one ever did anything original; the guitar part on this was one of Frusciante's major attempts to do something different. Its lyrics were about the circle of life; Kiedis came up with the phrase because he had visited a bar in Australia named the Animal Bar, which was located in a dry area that rarely received rain.

The bridge bass line was one of Flea's favorites he ever played. When they jammed out to it, they played it for about three hours over and over.

"So Much I"

This is one of three songs Kiedis singled out as about the crisis of being in love with his girlfriend Heather. Flea brought the main riff in, and the band jammed out to it. Frusciante felt it sounded like Fugazi and let the playing of Guy Picciotto from Fugazi guide his sound on it.

Flea brought the bass line in, writing it on his couch, and the band assembled their parts around it. Kiedis thought it sounded like the Minutemen, while Flea thought it sounded like Blonde Redhead.

"Storm in a Teacup"

The groove in the song was influenced by Public Enemy, which led to its working title "Public Enemy." Frusciante wrote all the parts and was inspired by the same Public Enemy song that inspired *Californication*'s "Get on Top." Flea referred to it as "walking like a sauerkraut" because he found the lyric particularly hilarious.

It was originally one of the band's favorites during the initial vote; when they revoted, Kiedis asked which songs Frusciante wasn't crazy about, and "Storm in a Teacup" was one. Frusciante preferred it when it did not have vocals. Even after the album was finished, Frusciante felt it was the weakest song on the album, as he believed there were B-sides that were far better that didn't make the cut.

"We Believe"

Its working title was "Fela Funk," as it was influenced by both funk and Fela Kuti. The backing vocals were done by children from Frusciante's mom's church. (The children weren't paid for their singing.) Flea learned some theory and came up with the bass line but did not bring it in; as the band jammed, it came out again naturally.

"Turn It Again"

Flea played the horns on it, which made it one of Frusciante's favorite tracks. Its working title was "Talking Heads" because it sounded like a song by that band. Frusciante needed seventy-one channels to record the guitar part for this, using many different cuts and his modular synthesizer board across most of them. Because of how many tracks he used, he mixed the end of the song himself.

It was the only song on the entire album in which every single person's part came straight from a jam, with no revisions later, including Kiedis's vocal melodies.

"Death of a Martian"

Martian was one of Flea's dogs that died before the album was finished. Kiedis wrote the song's lyrics as a tribute to him. Martian was the biggest of Flea's dogs. Frusciante recorded backing vocals when Kiedis's dog Buster passed away; Kiedis informed Frusciante right before recording, and Frusciante got emotional before tracking. Frusciante had two cats, Aztec and Maya, and imagined their loss before singing.

The track used in the final version was one of the live rehearsal takes and not the later studio versions. The outro spoken word was an accident, as Kiedis grabbed one of his poems and felt it worked.

Frusciante used a rotary Leslie speaker to record his guitar part on this song.

Other Songs Recorded and Released

"Joe" was a tribute to Joe Strummer, released as a B-side to "Desecration Smile" along with "Save This Lady," another song from these sessions. "Dani California" got two different CD singles; one had "Million Miles of Water" as a B-side, while another had both "Whatever We Want" and "Lately." "Tell Me Baby" also had two CD singles; one had "A Certain Someone" as a B-side, while the other had "Mercy Mercy" and a live jam edited down to just its guitar solo in "Lyon 06.06.06." "Snow ((Hey Oh))" had "Funny Face," a ska-like song, and "I'll Be Your Domino," a funky song, as its B-sides. The iTunes version included "Permutation," a recording of a live jam that was the introduction to "Californication."

"Hump De Bump" had a single that included the same B-sides as "Desecration Smile," along with the live jam "An Opening."

The band reported that thirty-eight songs were recorded, but only thirty-seven have surfaced. It is possible that they miscounted or that vocals were not finished for all thirty-eight.

The iTunes edition came with a bonus track of "Havana Affair," though that song was recorded during the *By the Way* era.

Sales and Reception

Stadium Arcadium was critically heralded on its release and marked the first true number one album by the band in their then twenty-three-year career. It sold 440,000 copies in its first week.

Its *Rolling Stone* review praised Kiedis's singing abilities. It was nominated for six Grammys, winning four: Best Rock Performance by a Duo or Group with Vocal for "Dani California," Best Rock Song for "Dani California," and Best Rock Album and Best Boxed or Special Limited Edition Package for *Stadium Arcadium* and its deluxe edition. It lost Album of the Year and Best Short Form Music Video.

50

On the Road Again

The Endless *Stadium Arcadium* Tour

On the Road Forever

In less than two years, the band played 132 shows, beginning on May 30, 2006, and concluding on August 27, 2007. It began in Barcelona, Spain, and ended with a headlining performance at Reading and Leeds in England.

Callbacks

On the tour, for the first time in years, the band teased songs from their debut record, *The Red Hot Chili Peppers*. Although they weren't played in full, "Baby Appeal," "Grand Pappy du Plenty," and "Police Helicopter" were all teased. Several songs from *Freaky Styley* actually got played, such as "Catholic School Girls Rule" and "Freaky Styley." Nothing besides "Pea" from *One Hot Minute* was played, though Chad Smith and Flea once jammed out to the "Warped" riff as Frusciante soloed over it in an introductory jam to "Can't Stop."

"Funky Monks" was played twice on the tour, marking the only two times it was ever played. It was played for the first time in Denver, Colorado, after a radio contest in which the biggest Red Hot Chili Peppers fan won the related trivia, the prize of which was that any song one requested would be played that night. The next night, the band played the song again.

Set List

Almost every set began with an introductory jam going into "Can't Stop." "Charlie" and "Dani California" usually followed but were interchangeable as second and third songs. Their regular set typically included a softer number, be it "Desecration Smile," "Under the Bridge," or "I Could Have Lied." Almost every show concluded with "Give It Away" and then a jam as their encore.

After the *Stadium Arcadium* tour, "21st Century," "Catholic School Girls Rule," "C'mon Girl," "Sex Rap," "So Much I," "Stadium Arcadium," "This Velvet Glove," "Torture Me," "Warlocks," "Fortune Faded," "Havana Affair," "Readymade," and "Desecration Smile" weren't played again live.

Openers

For a good portion of the dates, the Mars Volta opened. This included multiple legs of the North American tour and one leg of the European tour. At other points, Dizzee Rascal, Ben Harper and the Innocent Criminals, Dinosaur Jr., Jet, My Chemical Romance, and Kasabian opened. For a while, Gnarls Barkley opened; future Red Hot Chili Pepper Josh Klinghoffer played in that band at the time. It's also notable because one of the *Stadium Arcadium* singles failed to hit number one, reaching only number two, because Gnarls Barkley's "Crazy" held on to the top spot.

Additional Members

The *Stadium Arcadium* tour marked the first time the band had additional musicians tour with them as bandmates since the *One Hot Minute* tour. Marcel Rodriguez-Lopez, also of the Mars Volta, doubled on percussion for the 2006 tour dates.

Josh Klinghoffer, who would go on to replace John Frusciante, joined the band as keyboardist and second guitarist, depending on the song. Songs that included second guitar focused mostly on the ones that had guitar harmonies, such as the final chorus to "Dani California." By the end of the tour, Klinghoffer was treated with respect and joined in on jams on keyboard.

Chris Warren, one of the band's longtime drum technicians, played keyboards when it was required, and Klinghoffer was on guitar.

Occasional Tension

Frusciante began to smoke pot again after *By the Way*. It did not lead to many tensions during the making of *Stadium Arcadium* but may have come to fruition occasionally on the following tour. Kiedis complained about Frusciante being too high a handful of times on tour. One of these shows was in Boston in October 2006; the band ran late as rain delayed their tour bus. On arriving, Kiedis apologized to the crowd for their being late and for Frusciante being high.

Any further tensions stemming from it were never mentioned in interviews.

51

Taking a Break

What the Band's Hiatus Changed

A Much-Needed Break

After doing so many shows in what was essentially a nonstop cycle of recording, promoting, and then touring since *Californication*, the band agreed to a much-needed break. Apart from one recording session for George Clinton where the band helped record a cover of "Let the Good Times Roll"—Frusciante's last session as a Red Hot Chili Pepper—the band did not work together much in the years that followed.

Kiedis took the time to focus on his son, Everly Bear. His autobiography *Scar Tissue* got signed to become an HBO original series, tentatively titled *Spider and Son*. Although HBO produced a pilot, FX bought the rights to it; it has been on hold since at least 2013. (Previously, the Weinstein brothers at Miramax wanted to write a screenplay about Blackie Dammett raising Kiedis in the 1970s. That also didn't pan out, though it inspired Dammett to write his autobiography.)

Kiedis and Smith wanted to hiatus for only one year, while Flea and Frusciante insisted on it being two years. In the end, because of Frusciante's departure, the hiatus lasted three years.

Side Projects

Flea went to the University of Southern California for music, studying music theory on trumpet in the process. He performed with the orchestra and jazz bands and was viewed as a good student by his theory professor. He also joined Thom Yorke's project: Atoms for Peace; there, he met Mauro Refosco, who would join the Red Hot Chili Peppers as a percussionist on tour in the years that followed.

Flea also went to work on his solo album, though it would not come out until after the Red Hot Chili Peppers returned. He played with Patti Smith at various points during the hiatus, too.

Chad Smith started a supergroup in the style of 1980s hair metal called Chickenfoot. Chickenfoot started as a three-piece with Sammy Hagar and Michael Anthony, creating the logo and then the name Chickenfoot. They eventually decided they needed a guitarist, and Hagar recommended shred virtuoso Joe Satriani for the position. The Chickenfoot name remained. They have gone on to do two albums: *Chickenfoot* and the confusingly titled *Chickenfoot III*. When the Red Hot Chili Peppers are on tour, Smith is replaced by drummer Kenny Aronoff.

Smith formed another group, Chad Smith's Bombastic Meatbats, in 2007 but began to play shows and clinics with them more frequently during the hiatus. The Meatbats were Smith, guitarist Jeff Kollan from Cosmosquad, bassist Kevin Chown from Uncle Kracker and Tarja Turunen, and Ed Roth from Ronnie Montrose and Gamma. They originated as the backup band for Glenn Hughes, but when the Red Hot Chili Peppers were off, Smith brought the group together more frequently. They have released three albums: *Meat the Meatbats*, *More Meat*, and *Live Meat and Potatoes*.

Smith played drums on a record by Outernational, a band that was discovered by Tom Morello from Rage Against the Machine. Similarly, he made an album with his son's music teacher: the famous actor Dick Van Dyke.

Smith also acted as a guest editor for one issue of *Rhythm*. He had the magazine interview himself and answered letters from fans.

Frusciante Departs

Throughout the interviews of *By the Way*, including with *Guitar Player* and *Kerrang!*, Frusciante commented that he could one day see himself leaving the Red Hot Chili Peppers again. Smith had told fans and an interviewer that he didn't see the hiatus lasting more than a full year; as it got into early 2009 and the band stayed quiet, fans speculated that Frusciante had quit.

Frusciante wrote that he officially quit sometime in 2008. After some time debating breaking up or thinking that Frusciante might return, the three remaining Chili Peppers decided to continue. They came up with only one candidate: Josh Klinghoffer, who had previously toured on guitar and keyboards for them and opened up for them in the Bicycle Thief. (The band's drum technician, Chris Warren, also played drums in the Bicycle Thief with Klinghoffer.)

Josh Klinghoffer was offered the position on July 20, 2009, when he was at a Los Angeles Dodgers game. He received a call from Flea, and Klinghoffer was surprised to hear the offer; he told Flea he'd think about it and call him back. He didn't give Flea an answer for two weeks; when he finally called Flea back, he accepted the position.

Despite this, the band didn't reconvene with Klinghoffer in the fold until either October 9 or October 12, when they began jamming and writing their new record. (For more information, see the next chapter's section "Brendan's Death Song.") Frusciante made his departure public in December 2009 via a post on his MySpace page, saying that the feelings between the band were amiable. He wrote that no one in the band was angry but that he was no longer interested in making popular rock music and instead felt excited about creating electronic music and mixing it with his guitar.

The Red Hot Chili Peppers understood Frusciante's reasoning for leaving. Kiedis told the *Los Angeles Times* that "John had become disenchanted with being in a touring rock band, which is completely understandable. He's a driven person in the world of music and sound, and he wanted to change gears."

Their first gig with Josh Klinghoffer as the sole guitarist in the band was January 29, 2010, for a MusiCares event honoring Neil Young. They covered Young's "A Man Needs a Maid" at the event. Even though the gig was in January, the band did not issue a statement saying Klinghoffer was the full-time man until February 2010.

A Frusciante Comeback?

Frusciante did an interview with *Guitarist* before he quit that was published after he quit in March 2009. He said the Red Hot Chili Peppers were on "indefinite hiatus" with "no plans whatsoever to do anything—at all."

Smith originally expected Frusciante to return after getting more time off. He told *Drum!*, "I thought he might come around one day and go, 'Yep! I'm ready!' But he never did, and that's fine. He's probably the best musician I've ever known and played with. He's just fantastic and I love him. But we want to keep going."

Changes

After getting out of music school, Flea began to write on piano just as often as he did bass and focused more on melody than on the creation of his bass lines. Klinghoffer was also a drummer in other bands—including bands with Frusciante—and it added a second opinion on drum takes. Their jams changed from being more contrapuntal between Flea and Frusciante to a more funk, choppy percussive style with Klinghoffer on guitar. Klinghoffer was also more understated vocally, staying quieter in interviews than Frusciante.

I'm with You

Josh Klinghoffer Joins the Band

One complaint in life I've always had is that I'll never not be this person. I can't know what it's like to be someone else. How many yous are there? The idea of being one person rather than many. I think I've always tried to make myself as many different mes as I could.

—*Josh Klinghoffer, MindEqualsBlown, 2014*

New Guitarist, Same Producer

In September 2010, the band entered the studio with Josh Klinghoffer on guitar but kept Rick Rubin on as producer. They wrote just as many, if not more, songs than they had for *Stadium Arcadium* but wanted to stick to a shorter, typical length album that time around. The album ended up being fourteen songs because no one could agree on which twelve were best.

The band wrote between sixty and seventy songs, though not all of them were recorded or had completed vocals. They had been writing for nine months before they began recording on September 14, 2010, at East West Studios in Los Angeles. East West was previously known as both Ocean Way and Cello Studios; it was the same location where they previously recorded *Californication*. Recording concluded on March 18, 2011.

Before recording, the four Chili Peppers and Rick Rubin rented out a barn from Al Jardine of the Beach Boys. There, they rehearsed the songs they planned to record and played them for Rubin. After that, they all felt comfortable entering the studio.

Kiedis compared Klinghoffer joining the Red Hot Chili Peppers to eating locally grown farm goods and "local produce.... No trucking, no shipping, no pesticides. Just your own friend from the neighborhood who happens to be a person you really want to play music with."

The *I'm with You* album cover. Some fans thought it implied that Anthony Kiedis was back on drugs.
Author's collection

Learning Every Song

Josh Klinghoffer learned every Red Hot Chili Peppers song ever, including B-sides, before starting to record with the band, as he wanted to know the complete history of the band's guitar feel before injecting his own taste into it. Despite this, he held off playing "Snow ((Hey Oh))" live for several years because he felt uncomfortable singing and playing it.

New Influences

Flea told *Rolling Stone* that the Frusciante-era lineup was more in line with Led Zeppelin, while Klinghoffer's joining turned them into more of a lucid, less riff-based band focused on songs like the Rolling Stones. Because of that, Flea began to listen to the Rolling Stones more. He told *Classic Rock* the three things he was listening to during the composition of *I'm with You* were the Stones, Johann Sebastian Bach, and avant-garde electronic music. Flea also told *Bass Player* that he had become obsessed with J Dilla and Billy Holiday and that his favorite bass player before the album came out was Squarepusher.

Africa

In February 2010, Klinghoffer and Flea traveled to Ethiopia and other places in Africa and jammed with local musicians. Those jam sessions led them to pursue more African sounds and add percussionist Mauro Refosco to the fold for the studio and on tour. (Percussionist Lenny Castro also played percussion.)

Working Title

Anthony Kiedis told *SPIN* that the album had a working title of *Dr. Johnny Skinz's Disproportionately Rambunctious Polar Express Machine-Head*, but the band never planned to truly name it that. Allegedly, Dr. Johnny Skinz was a real person, and he reminisced to the Red Hot Chili Peppers about one of his drug binges and an acid trip where he sold out shows to the moon and stars with a song title of the same name. The band found it funny and held on to it as a working album title until something better arose.

Kiedis later admitted that everything about Dr. Johnny Skinz was a lie.

Klinghoffer came up with *I'm with You* as a title a few days before the album's making had concluded. He wrote it on a piece of paper for Kiedis, who thought it was a brilliant name, and then Flea and Smith immediately agreed to it as the title. It was not a conscious reference to backing Klinghoffer as the full-time guitarist. *I'm with You* marked the first album since *Mother's Milk* to not be named after a song title.

Anticipation

Fan anticipation was high, and music writers added to the hype. It made *Kerrang!*'s "50 Most Anticipated Albums of 2011" list and *NME*'s list of the "60 Most Exciting Albums of 2011," coming in at number fifty-five, before its release. (Flea's album with Damon Albarn that would turn out to be *Rocket Juice & the Moon* also made *NME*'s list.)

Piano

At the university, Flea learned piano for the first time. Josh Klinghoffer, on the other hand, had just come from playing keyboard for Gnarls Barkley. As Flea focused more on writing on keyboard and Klinghoffer's chops never left, the band's sound shifted to include it more. Although this remained true on *The Getaway*, it was particularly true on *I'm with You*.

Flea believed you could stay in playing shape on only two instruments. For this album, he played bass and piano, so none of the trumpet parts were recorded by him. For a while, Flea studied *The Evolving Bassist* by Rufus Reid on upright bass but gave it up when he started to focus more on piano.

Drum Selection

Chad Smith, Rick Rubin, and engineer Greg Fidelman set up Smith's drum set in different rooms at the recording studio with the same microphone setup and played a fast beat and a slow beat, then did the same thing at Rubin's house. They then blindly chose which one sounded best, which was unanimously Room Two at East West, where they tracked all the drums.

Since Klinghoffer started as a drummer, he often wanted the drums mixed louder. Smith appreciated this and thought the drums were his best sounding on a record since *Blood Sugar Sex Magik*.

Art

The album art was done by Damien Hirst, a British artist whose work normally centered around death. He was controversial not only for his subject matter but also for having been sued for plagiarism previously.

Flea's first daughter, Clara Balzary, did some of the promotional photography for the album. The band promoted *I'm with You* with street artwork around Los Angeles that was done by Mr. Brainwash, who was the focus of the 2010 documentary *Exit through the Gift Shop*, directed by Banksy.

"Monarchy of Roses"

The opening song's verse began as a jam between Flea and Klinghoffer and was arranged into a song later. Flea brought in the chorus riff. They talked about how cool a song that started off like Black Sabbath but ended up like disco would be, and this was their attempt at doing so.

Its working title was "Disco Sabbath" because of the hybrid of sounds. The band members were aspiring to make the disco section sound like a Giorgio Moroder record.

The song was the second single from *I'm with You*, released on October 7, 2011, in the United Kingdom but on October 25 in the United States. The music video came out on November 14. The video was inspired by the punk artwork of Raymond Pettibon, who was Greg Ginn from Black Flag's brother. The video was directed by Marc Klasfeld.

The song was played as the opening song at every show on the *I'm with You* tour but was not played again at all after it. It also appeared in a 2011 car commercial for the Nissan Elgrand.

"Factory of Faith"

The lyrics weren't consciously written about anything; they were the first thing Kiedis wrote that fit the music. Once finished, he thought the song was about the process of loving someone and putting yourself out there.

"Brendan's Death Song"

The song was an ode to their friend and Los Angeles nightclub owner Brendan Mullen. (Mullen also authored the oral history books for Jane's Addiction and the Red Hot Chili Peppers.) On the way to the band's first rehearsal with Kling-hoffer, Kiedis got a text saying Mullen had passed. The music originates from one of the jam sessions from that day. Although Mullen passed on October 9, *Rolling Stone* reported it as October 12. One of those two dates was the first time the lineup with Josh Klinghoffer played together.

Mullen was the first promoter who gave the Red Hot Chili Peppers a gig after Flea and Kiedis burst in with their demo tape. The band tried to make it a celebration of his life and not just a death march.

Smith was influenced by Keith Moon for his crazier playing during the end of the song.

It was the album's final single, released on June 11, 2012. Marc Klasfeld also directed this video. The video was filmed in New Orleans and aimed to re-create a jazz-style funeral.

The song was one of three to not feature percussion from Mauro Refosco; it was instead played by Lenny Castro, who previously toured with Boz Scaggs.

"Ethiopia"

Smith's playing on the song was inspired by Frank Zappa drummer Vinnie Colaiuta and Pearl Jam's Matt Cameron. Although it doesn't sound like Ethiopian music, the African trip inspired Kiedis's lyrics. Damon Albarn from Blur started what he called the African Express. Every year, Albarn invited musicians he was friends with to come with him across Africa and jam with locals. Flea got lost in the city of Harar when the bus left without him. He walked around the town for more than an hour in an area in which no one else spoke English.

One person came up to him who spoke broken English and helped him find the bus. Flea told Kiedis the story, and that was what made Kiedis write the song.

The main verse is in 7/8, but the chorus is in 4/4. During the introduction and outro, Klinghoffer plays a 4/4 polyrhythm against the 7/8, while during the solo, he plays a 3/8 polyrhythm against it.

The bass line was written by Flea when he was in Ethiopia.

The song originally had a saxophone part played by jazz artist Joshua Redman that was recorded. Flea previously played bass for Redman.

"Annie Wants a Baby"

Annie was not based on a real person. The song came out of a jam.

"Look Around"

It came from a jam between Flea and Klinghoffer. Flea wrote the bridge part sitting on his porch while he waited for a friend to arrive so they could go surfing. Lyrically, it was written about falling in love with a stripper.

The song was the album's third single, released on January 25, 2012, though it leaked a day early. The video was directed by Robert Hales and gave each band member a room reflecting their own personality, with most of the room's supplies actually coming from the band members. Kiedis's room focused on his son, Everly Bear; his dog; and model Charlotte Free. Klinghoffer's room was mostly empty minus a table and a lamp. Flea danced in his room in his underwear with the woman he was dating at the time: Sandha Khin. Smith's room had nothing more in it than a toilet and a punching bag.

The song was used in a commercial for *The X Factor*.

Money Mark, perhaps best known for his collaborations with the Beastie Boys, played a Hammond B-3 organ on the track.

"Look Around" was released as downloadable content for Rock Band, where it featured a different introductory part.

"The Adventures of Rain Dance Maggie"

The song got two different music videos, one of which was directed by rapper Kreayshawn, who was only twenty-one years old at the time. It was Klinghoffer's first music video in any of the bands he had ever been in. In the end, the video didn't get used. Kreayshawn's video took place in the 1990s and starred Melanee E. Nelson as a woman who was drugged in a club and went on a fantasy trip; Smith played a bouncer, Flea played a bartender, and Kiedis and Klinghoffer played two paramedics in it.

The second video that was released was a performance video on a rooftop directed by Marc Klasfeld.

It was the first single from the album and the only one released before the album came out; it came to radio on July 15, 2011, and was made available for digital download on July 18. It was the Red Hot Chili Peppers' twelfth number one single on the *Billboard* "Alternative Songs" chart, setting a record.

Flea wrote the bass line in his kitchen. Kiedis wasn't sure it would make the album let alone be a single, though it was his favorite song to dance to. "Maggie" was loosely based on at least two actual people, neither named Maggie.

"Did I Let You Know"

Smith was going for an Afrobeat vibe on this song. Engineer Greg Fidelman deadened Smith's toms and gave him a piccolo snare to give it a distinct sound. Fidelman rented every Tama Bell Brass snare he could so that as Smith beat the heads out of shape, he had another one ready to go.

The song was released as a single in Brazil but nowhere else. Mike Bulger played trumpet on it because Flea did not believe himself to be in trumpet-playing shape.

At various points, its working titles were "Lagos" and "Take Me Home," and it originally had the suffix "(This I Know)" after the full song title.

"Goodbye Hooray"

Even though both Klinghoffer and Flea played piano, the piano on "Goodbye Hooray" was recorded by Greg Kurstin. Kurstin later produced some songs by Beck.

"Goodbye Hooray" was the one of two songs on the album to not have additional percussion recorded for it. Its working title was "See You Around."

"Happiness Loves Company"

Flea wrote the song on piano. Klinghoffer recorded the bass line on a Fender Bass VI; he also takes over on bass when they play this song live.

"Police Station"

Greg Kurstin played piano on this song. Kiedis considered "Police Station" an overdue sequel to "Police Helicopter" from *The Red Hot Chili Peppers*. Its working title was "Stolen Stone."

"Even You Brutus?"

The song title is a reference to William Shakespeare's *Julius Caesar*, where Caesar is betrayed by Brutus and delivers the Latin quip "Et tu, Brutus?" Flea wrote the piano part, but it was played on the record by Greg Kurstin.

"Meet Me at the Corner"

Along with "Goodbye Hooray," it was one of two songs to not feature additional percussion in the studio.

"Dance, Dance, Dance"

When Kiedis and Rubin interviewed each other in *Interview* magazine, they talked about their shared love of modern dance music. Kiedis singled out LCD Soundsystem in particular.

The song's composition started with Smith's beat. Flea was listening to a lot of electronic music, so Smith listened to electronic music for a while and then tried to come up with a beat that sounded similar to an electronic groove. Flea loved the beat and wrote the bass line to it, and the song that came out of it was "Dance, Dance, Dance."

Other Songs Recorded, and *I'm Beside You*

Many more songs were recorded during the *I'm with You* sessions. Rather than release them as B-sides to singles, the Red Hot Chili Peppers released the songs as seven-inch singles on vinyl themselves and on digital stores in pairs (except for "In Love, Dying," which was the longest song from the sessions).

The seventeen songs released this way were "Strange Man," "Long Progression," "Magpies on Fire," "Victorian Machinery," "Never Is a Long Time," "Love of Your Life," "The Sunset Sleeps," "Hometown Gypsy," "Pink as Floyd," "Your Eyes Girl," "In Love Dying," "Catch My Death," "How It Ends," "Brave from Afar," "This Is the Kitt," "Hanalei," and "Open/Close." The first eight songs were previously released as an Australia-only bonus disc to *I'm with You*. When all seventeen songs came out on vinyl, the corners of the singles could be connected to form one larger piece of artwork.

"Your Eyes Girl" was originally titled "Mormon Lover," while "Magpies on Fire" was known simple as "Magpies."

Once all the seven-inch singles in the series were released, the band released them as a collection on Record Store Day on November 29, 2013, under the title *I'm Beside You*. The title was a play on "B-side." No songs from the collection have ever been played live in full. The vinyl of it is out of print.

Refosco played percussion on "Strange Man," "Long Progression," "Victorian Machinery," and "This Is the Kitt," while Lenny Castro played percussion on "Magpies on Fire." (Henry Kwapis added shaker to "Never Is a Long Time.") Vanessa Freebaim-Smith added string arrangements and played cello on "Pink as Floyd"; the other members of the string quartet were Alwyn Wright on viola,

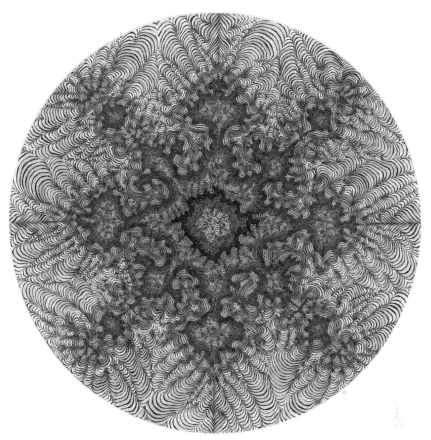

The accompanying B-side collection, *I'm Beside You.*   *Author's collection*

Caroline Campbell on violin, and Kathleen Sloan on viola. Greg Kurstin provided piano on "Never Is a Long Time," "Hometown Gypsy," and "How It Ends."

There are rumors that nineteen other recorded songs are out there, but the
only one confirmed to exist is "Renaissance."

The Album's Reception

The album was met with mixed to positive reviews from critics. *Pitchfork* gave
the album a 4.0 out of 10, while *Entertainment Weekly* gave it an A. Most other
reviews split the difference, not going too negative or too positive. In terms of
sales, it debuted at number two in the United States and number one in the
United Kingdom. The band later conceded that they were let down by its recep-
tion from fans and that that helped lead them to choose a new producer for their
next album: *The Getaway.*

Some well-worn shirts from the *I'm with You* tour belonging to the author.

Author's collection

The *I'm with You* Tour

On one of the first nights of the tour, Kiedis's microphone cut out (or he lost his voice) for one of the choruses of "Californication." It was rumored online that Klinghoffer sang lead on the song when this happened; the truth is that Klinghoffer still sang his harmony part even though Kiedis's lead was not there.

On August 30, 2011, the band played a concert at E-Werk in Cologne, Germany, that was recorded live and broadcast internationally to select movie theaters at 8 p.m. locally. Known as *Red Hot Chili Peppers Live: I'm with You*, it served as a hard-core fan's introduction to Klinghoffer's playing for the group and helped promote the album. It was rebroadcasted on September 1.

They played all of *I'm with You* except for "Even You Brutus?" They experienced technical difficulties during "Did I Let You Know" in the film, so they played it again during their encore. In the film, they also teased "Frankenstein" by the Edgar Winter Group after "Look Around," did a jam between just Smith and Flea after the first performance of "Did I Let You Know," and gave Flea a piano solo after "Goodbye Hooray." Michael Bulger joined them on trumpet. The only older songs they played in the film were "Me and My Friends" and "Give It Away."

The tour was the first that the Red Hot Chili Peppers began to sell official bootlegs at. They had been keeping soundboard recordings since at least the MP3 of each show for $9.95 or FLAC downloads for $12.95, available beginning

The band in the Klinghoffer era, live.   *Sterling Munksgard / Shutterstock.com*

three days after each concert. They've since gone back and released some of the older concerts though not the complete tours as they did with *I'm with You.*

Kiedis suffered a leg injury and required surgery, which postponed the first leg of the North American tour. Klinghoffer broke his foot during the tour but didn't cancel or postpone any shows.

The band continued to avoid songs from *One Hot Minute.* The only two songs from before *Mother's Milk* they performed in full were "Freaky Styley" from *Freaky Styley* and "Me and My Friends" from *The Uplift Mofo Party Plan.* The only *Mother's Milk* song performed in full was their cover of Stevie Wonder's "Higher Ground."

Klinghoffer did solo covers in the same vein that Frusciante used to. Some of the songs he covered included Randy Newman's "Burn On" and the theme to *Laverne & Shirley*: "Making Our Dreams Come True" by Cyndi Grecco.

Bassist Thundercat joined them for one show and played "Give It Away" on November 1, 2012.

Fandemonium

While on tour for *I'm with You*, the band's official photography book, *Fandemonium*, was done in tandem with photographer David Mushegain. It was released November 18, 2014. Kiedis, Smith, Flea, and Klinghoffer all wrote short pieces for the book, with the longest coming as the introduction from Kiedis.

53

Exit Music

Josh Klinghoffer's Early Life

Birth of a Pepper

Joshua Adam Klinghoffer was born on October 3, 1979. Although he was born in Santa Monica, California, his family lived in Canoga Park, California. His home in Canoga Park was extremely close to where Guns N' Roses recorded *Appetite for Destruction*. His parents, Steve and Kathy Klinghoffer, were native New Yorkers; Steve worked in film as a sound technician. The two moved to Northridge, California, in 1987 when the young Josh was starting third grade.

Drummer First, Guitarist Second, Musician Overall

Klinghoffer started out as a drummer before he played guitar or keyboard or sang. He told *Drum!* magazine in 2011 that "my first musical instrument was drums when I was nine years old or so. I had the Chad Smith instructional video as a kid. When I used to go on tour with them opening up, I used to perch myself behind John's amps and hang out with Chris Warren, Chad's drum tech, and just watch Chad like a hawk."

He took lessons for drum set but taught himself guitar and keyboard.

High School Dropout

The young Klinghoffer dropped out of high school at age fifteen to practice and pursue music. By that point, he was also playing guitar and studied Jimi Hendrix, Led Zeppelin, the Red Hot Chili Peppers, and Pearl Jam. His first Chili Peppers album was *One Hot Minute*; he became a Jane's Addiction fan as well.

Flea enjoying the *I'm with You* tour.

Andrea Raffin / Shutterstock.com

Klinghoffer taking over live harmony duties from Frusciante.   *Aija Lehtonen / Shutterstock.com*

Addicted to Music

The first band he was in that signed a large record contract was the Bicycle Thief. Everyone in the band got a $10,000 advance; by the end of the first day, Klinghoffer had spent the bulk of his advance buying hundreds of CDs and an acoustic guitar from the 1940s.

Stuck Being Himself

When asked about becoming who he was, Klinghoffer told *MindEqualsBlown*,

> One complaint in life I've always had is that I'll never not be this person. I can't know what it's like to be someone else. How many yous are there? The idea of being one person rather than many. I think I've always tried to make myself as many different mes as I could.

Famous Murdered Relative

Josh Klinghoffer is a distant relative of Leon Klinghoffer, who was murdered in the *Achille Lauro* hijacking of 1985. Leon's was the only death in the incident.

The hijacking happened when the Italian ship was taken over by four men who represented the Palestine Liberation Front. Leon was in a wheelchair at the time and was thrown overboard after being killed. He may have been chosen as the first hostage to die because he did not remain quiet when the terrorists took his watch and cigarettes.

He was a very distant relative of Leon's, though: either a fourth or a fifth cousin of Josh's grandfather.

54

The Getaway

The Band Comes Back with a New Producer

Producer Selection

Although the band loved Rick Rubin, they felt it was time for a change and to be inspired in a different way. They believed that Chili Peppers guitarists typically found their best footing on the second album in the band and believed that *The Getaway* could be Klinghoffer's *Blood Sugar Sex Magik*, a new sound forged from years in the band, with *I'm with You* being his *Mother's Milk*.

The Chili Peppers ceased playing most of the *I'm with You* songs once they toured for *The Getaway*.

They decided they wanted someone other than Rick Rubin to produce, believing a new producer could help push them into a new sound. Brian Burton, also known as Danger Mouse, was floated as an idea. Josh Klinghoffer had already worked and toured with Danger Mouse; Danger Mouse was half of Gnarls Barkley (the other half being CeeLo Green), and Klinghoffer was part of the Gnarls Barkley touring band at their peak.

Flea's Injury Causes a New Album

The band originally had between twenty and thirty songs written with the intent of recording them the way they usually record: live tracking the basic rhythm tracks, laying down vocals, and then deciding overdubs as a group. Flea then broke his arm snowboarding; the injury caused them to put their recording plans off for nearly six months.

When Flea healed, they had already settled on Danger Mouse for a producer. Danger Mouse pushed them to forget about the songs they had already written and write the songs in the studio his way: the drummer records a track, then the bassist does, then the guitar, then the vocals. He came from a hip-hop background and was used to doing most of the writing in the studio. The band decided to buy in; they kept only a handful of songs from the original set they wrote and wrote an entirely new batch of songs in the studio.

The album cover.

Of the older songs that were kept around, all of them were chosen by Danger Mouse. He did not want to work on anything he wasn't a fan of, feeling he could be passionate about only what he truly liked; the Red Hot Chili Peppers backed up his decision and bought into his production ideas immediately.

As Danger Mouse encouraged them to write in the studio, he'd encourage them to write better than their original ideas. It led to frustration from some band members, especially Anthony Kiedis, who would sing certain melodies and lyrics and Danger Mouse would shoot them down as not good enough.

It's possible the injury helped them choose Danger Mouse as producer. The band stayed in touch during the necessary time off from the accident, and all agreed that they had grown too comfortable in their sound, believing they had gotten predictable and possibly stale.

The Actual Injury, the Actual Accident

Flea's injury was serious, as most of his arm's bone was shattered. He required multiple surgeries and was worried he'd never be able to play music again. It took four months after the accident before he could pick up an instrument again; before that, he tried a handful of times and felt a shooting pain go up his arm.

Anthony Kiedis was present when Flea got injured. The two went on a trip to Montana together, explicitly to snowboard. Flea told *Rolling Stone*, "We were jetting down the mountain, going, like, 50 miles an hour, when I just wiped out. It was like, bam. My arm started swelling up right away. I broke my arm in five places. Big pieces of bone were shorn off."

He was able to snowboard down the rest of the mountain to get himself help. An ambulance took him to the hospital immediately.

Despite the accident and a screw permanently stuck inside his arm, Flea continued to go snowboarding and had returned by the time the album was released.

Drums

Smith used Danger Mouse's drum kit rather than his own, which threw him off for a while. The producer preferred a softer sound than Smith's typical heavy

Flea playing the instrument that was once named after him, instead of his signature jazz bass.   *Sterling Munksgard / Shutterstock.com*

Kiedis brought out the moustache on the *Getaway* tour.

Chad Smith and a typical baseball cap.

Three quarters of the band on the *Getaway* tour.   *Christian Bertrand / Shutterstock.com*

hitting, so he often put towels and or tape on the drums to soften them and help dampen the sound. Smith also played softer than he usually did.

Danger Mouse would instruct Smith on the type of beat since drums were written in isolation. Sometimes, he'd ask for something funky and distinct; other times, he'd ask Smith to lay back.

Other band members would listen to Smith's beats as he was recording them and inform him of the general idea for the song they were thinking so that he could shape his beat with that in mind. That was the most communication Smith received on what would end up being the full song until the album was done.

Smith told *DRUM!* magazine that "[recording separately] did make everybody play differently. When we record together, it's really hard for me to play quietly because we're all looking at each other's faces and inspiring each other. The ones that started with just a drumbeat, they didn't know how hard I was playing. They just heard the sound coming out of the speakers. It was a wide-open canvas to paint on, so actually it was kind of freeing. It didn't have to be aggressive because it was just based on how you hear what you're playing over."

Naming the Album

The album was named after the song, but it stuck out because Anthony Kiedis was a Steve McQueen fan. (McQueen starred in the original film *The Getaway*, though it was remade in the mid-2000s starring Mark Wahlberg and Charlize Theron.) Flea also liked it as an album title because it gave the notion of moving on instead of being stagnant.

Artwork

The album cover was a painting by Kevin Peterson. Peterson already had it painted under the title *Coalition II*. Kiedis felt connected to it, telling KROQ that Chad was the bear, Josh was the girl, Flea was the raccoon, and Kiedis was the raven in front.

Fancy Demos

A demo exists from before the band entered the studio with Danger Mouse. The songs on it include "The Longest Wave," "Goodbye Angels," "Go Robot," "Detroit," "This Ticonderoga," "Encore," and "Outer Space." It was recorded at The Boat in Los Angeles in 2014. Fans came to know these demos as the "Fancy Demos," though they have not leaked online.

"The Getaway"

The song was Kiedis's favorite on the album. He and the rest of the band wanted for it to be the first single. Lyrically, it was written about dealing with heartbreak; Kiedis had gotten out of a two-year relationship in the making of the album.

It was one of the songs written in the studio with Danger Mouse. The producer played synthesizers on the song. Anna Waronker added her backing vocals to the song.

"Dark Necessities"

"Dark Necessities" was the first single; though management and the band wanted a different song, it was Danger Mouse's top choice and eventually won out. *Rolling Stone* compared the song to U2 and old soul music. It was released on May 5, 2016, though the band announced that it would be the first single on May 2. It was the band's thirteenth number one single on the *Billboard* "Alternative Songs" chart.

The music video was released on June 17, 2016. Olivia Wilde directed it. The video was a performance video from the band but also had longboarders skate around Los Angeles as they performed.

Danger Mouse made Smith listen to a psychedelic soul band from the 1960s. Smith did his own take on it and intentionally played less hi-hat than usual; after tracking it, the band picked the best parts of the beat and organized the song. As such, it was also one of the songs written with Danger Mouse.

"We Turn Red"

Smith identified "We Turn Red" as one of his favorite songs in an interview with *Absolute Radio*. Getting the final vocal line took a long time, as it was one of the songs that suffered the most from Danger Mouse pushing Anthony Kiedis to write better.

The song was a lyrical examination of America; the reference to red was not meant as a reference to communism but instead to blood as the color of war and the cost of capitalism. The band became more out about politics in *The Getaway* era; they played a concert where the proceeds went to fund Democratic presidential candidate Bernie Sanders and spoke out about how terrifying it would be if Donald Trump became the president.

Its working title was "The Dirge Song" when the band was writing it in the studio with Danger Mouse. The producer also played mellotron on the song.

"The Longest Wave"

The song was written before going into the studio with the producer.

"Goodbye Angels"

The song was written before entering the studio with Danger Mouse. The producer played synthesizers on the song. It was the fourth and final single from *The Getaway*, released to radio on April 4, 2017.

The music video was made on April 14, 2017, at their show in Atlanta, Georgia. Directed by Thoranna Sigurdardottir, it followed the path of a woman in her effort to get to a Red Hot Chili Peppers show spliced in with performance footage of the band playing live. It appeared in an advertisement for the television show *Animal Kingdom*.

"Sick Love"

Elton John played piano on the song. His lyricist and songwriting partner, Bernie Taupin, also got a songwriting credit; Taupin was not obligated to receive credit on everything John wrote, but he did not write any of the lyrics.

Instead, the Red Hot Chili Peppers came up with the groove and the verse melody and felt it sounded like the Elton John song "Benny and the Jets"; they listed that song's songwriters in the credits. John was in a neighboring studio, so the band asked John to play piano on the song. John said yes, as he was already a fan of the Red Hot Chili Peppers.

John was nervous to meet the band. He did two plays of the song in the studio, the first time going wild in his own style; the second time, he received instruction from Danger Mouse and played the final track. Danger Mouse also added synthesizers to the song.

The song was written before entering the studio, but they expected to change the verse melody, as they feared people would hear it as an Elton John rip-off. The band's former touring percussionist, Mauro Refosco, added percussion to the studio recording.

It ended up as the third single from *The Getaway*, released on December 4, 2016. The music video was animated by Joseph Brett and Beth Jeans Houghton and directed by Houghton. The two slipped a few references to "Benny and the Jets" into the video for good measure.

"Go Robot"

"Go Robot" was management's choice for a first single. It was written going for a Prince-like groove. Anthony Kiedis was friends with Prince when he passed. The song was written before Danger Mouse gave his input. Danger Mouse played the synthesizers on this song. Mauro Refosco also added percussion to the song.

In the end, it was released as the second single from *The Getaway*. The music video was directed by Tota Lee, with production in July; it was released on September 8, 2016. In it, Kiedis portrayed a robot in white paint acting like John Travolta's character from *Saturday Night Fever*. He and the other band members enter a dance contest.

Each band member was credited on a variation of their stage name: Kiedis went by his old acting name, Cole Dammett; Smith went by his first and middle names, Chadwick Gaylord; Flea also went by his first and middle names, Michael Peter; and Klinghoffer was credited as J. K. Dashwood.

For Record Store Day on April 22, 2017, Warner Bros. produced a twelve-inch pictured disc of "Dreams of a Samurai" and "Go Robot," featuring live recordings from the tour that followed the album's release. It was a limited run of 4,750 copies; each copy had a spelling error, writing it as "Dreams of a Sumurai."

When performed live, the song uses two bass guitars. Flea plays one, while the group's tour manager, Samuel Bañuelos III, plays the other.

"Feasting on the Flowers"

The song started with a beat that Chad Smith came up with in the studio with Danger Mouse. The producer played organ on the song. Lyrically, it was a tribute to former guitarist Hillel Slovak.

"Detroit"

The song was written as a lyrical ode to Michigan and Detroit and bands from Detroit in the 1970s. Both Kiedis and Smith spent time in Detroit. Kiedis had bands like the MC5 and the Stooges in mind.

"This Ticonderoga"

The song was written before entering the studio. Danger Mouse added synthesizers to the song.

"Encore"

The song was set in stone before entering the studio. It was the last song on the album to be performed live, finally getting played on April 24, 2017, in Jacksonville, Florida. It was not used as the show's encore.

"The Hunter"

The song was written with Danger Mouse in the studio. The producer added his synthesizers to the song. It is the only song from the album that was not performed live.

"Dreams of a Samurai"

The song was written about ending a relationship with someone too young to be committed to. The synthesizers were played by Danger Mouse. The vocal solo was taken by Beverly Chitwood.

The song was one that Danger Mouse allowed in from the Red Hot Chili Peppers' previous writing session. Flea wrote the bass line first and brought it in for a jam. Danger Mouse still thought it needed a more uplifting chorus; the band wrote the new chorus in the studio together, and the final recording was only the second time they had played it together.

Smith told *DRUM!* magazine that the song was in 10/8, but in *Rhythm*, they claimed it was in 5/4. (The song is factually in 5/4.)

Other Songs Recorded

Fifteen songs were planned for the album, but only thirteen made the final album. The two songs that were cut at the last minute were "Kaly" and "Outer Space." It's possible other songs were recorded during the sessions.

Additional Musicians

The band had a string quartet on "Dark Necessities," "The Longest Wave," "This Ticonderoga," "Encore," and "The Hunter." The quartet was contracted by Chris Tedesco with the scores prepared by Jeremy Levy; the actual quartet had Peter Kent on first violin, Sharon Jackson on second violin, Briana Bandy on viola, and Armen Ksajikian on cello.

Similarly, the band had a choir on "Goodbye Angels," "The Hunter," and "Dreams of a Samurai." The choir was contracted by S. J. Hasman, who also performed in the choir. The other choir vocalists were Alexx Daye, Beverly Chitwood, David Loucks, Kennya Ramsey, Matthew Selby, Loren Smith, and Gregory Whipple.

Reception and Sales

The album debuted at number two in the United States behind Drake's *Views* and number two in the United Kingdom behind Radiohead's *A Moon Shaped Pool*. It debuted at number one in several smaller countries, including New Zealand, the Netherlands, Italy, and others.

Critics were lightly positive with it; the *Independent* gave it four out of five stars, and *USA Today* praised the band for reinventing themselves. The *A.V. Club* wrote, "Kiedis is still more likely to rap about his sexual harassment days than anything profoundly meaningful. . . . The strengths remain in the three musicians behind him; the weaknesses play no more of a role than they always have."

Touring *The Getaway*

The band finally added additional songs from *One Hot Minute*. They learned both "Aeroplane" and "My Friends" from the album; though not everyone else was a fan—Smith continued to refer to it as the "bastard album" to *Rolling Stone*—Klinghoffer convinced everyone to get those two songs and "Pea" back in the set list.

The band added other songs they had never played live before to the set list. Irontom opened for the Red Hot Chili Peppers, and their guitarist, Zach Irons, played second guitar when the Peppers wanted to play "Dosed." Irons was a childhood fan of the Red Hot Chili Peppers and considered opening for them a dream come true; he met the band as part of the Los Angeles scene, and they invited him out on tour. (Irons also took guitar lessons from guitarist John Frusciante when Irons was only fourteen.)

When the band played "Dosed," Kiedis still didn't sing the lower harmony of the chorus vocal's first line. Instead, no one sang it, leaving Klinghoffer to sing it alone. For the ending guitar solo of the song, both Irons and Klinghoffer would play it. The band did it by request from a fan who was ill and passed away a few days shortly after the shows.

Where's Blackie Now?

Blackie Dammett suffered from dementia. Kiedis acknowledged as much during live shows for *The Getaway*, often dedicating "Soul to Squeeze" to his ill father. His father held on and is still alive; his autobiography came out in 2013 even as the disease began to take hold.

Flea and Frusciante Hang Out

On July 28, 2018, Flea and John Frusciante attended the Garca vs. Easter Jr. boxing match at the Staples Center in Los Angeles. The two sat side by side and talked throughout the match. It was the first time the two hung out in public since Frusciante's exit from the band.

55

Where Do We Go from Here?

Looking toward the Future

Frusciante and Producers

The band originally planned to use Danger Mouse as producer for their next studio album, feeling compelled to give him a second shot at production and believing that they would develop more chemistry with him. On December 15, 2019, the band and Flea's official Instagrams confirmed that Josh Klinghoffer was no longer in the group and John Frusciante was returning to his role as guitarist.

Shortly after, Chad Smith confirmed the band was working on a new album with Frusciante, but it is unknown if Danger Mouse would be returning in his role as producer. As of the time of this publishing, fans have reportedly asked the band members and gotten various answers, but nothing has been confirmed by a reputable source other than that Frusciante has, in fact, returned. With Frusciante's return, speculation suggests Rick Rubin's return as producer may be in the cards.

Radiohead producer Nigel Godrich was present in the studio for *The Getaway* and is a bandmate of Flea's in Atoms for Peace. He'd be a likely candidate for a producer down the line.

A Return to Chemistry, with More Quirks

The band was looking toward Klinghoffer's further development as a lead guitarist. With Frusciante's return, a new album will likely be more exploratory in the same ways *The Getaway* and *I'm With You* were: more keyboard and synth sounds, but with Frusciante's stamp taking the place of Klinghoffer's. It is unknown whether Frusciante will play Klinghoffer-era songs live.

Spicy Chili Peppers

Chad Smith now lives primarily on Long Island, sober, with his family. John Frusciante, Kiedis, and Flea still live in Los Angeles, though Frusciante lives a comparatively private life. On *The Getaway*, the band avoided rehashing old sounds and were consciously trying to do something different to avoid getting comfortable. All four band members do not want to become a band performing their greatest hits and only their hits live; they want to keep pushing their boundaries.

Smith himself told *SiriusXM*'s Eddie Trunk,

> We were riding in a van after a gig and Flea was like, "How much longer do you think we should. . . . How do you think we should end this?" I was, like, "I don't know!" I want to make records, I still love making records, but the touring part . . . I don't know if we can continue . . . I don't know if we can continue to do the long tours, the year, year and a half we normally do. That's a good question.

Either they will succeed and make new music that fans enjoy that sounds like a different angle of the same musicians, or they will fail and stop touring shortly after. Either way, tours will likely become shorter in length though perhaps increasing in frequency to compensate.

Kiedis's mother retired after forty years at the same job; 2023 would mark forty years in the same employ for him as a Red Hot Chili Pepper. The smart money is on their continuing until Flea is disinterested in music, which is to say until they're dead.

56

Red Hot Trivia Peppers

Ten Random Facts You Probably Didn't Know about the Band

1. The only thing Chad Smith felt he had in common with the band when he joined was basketball.

Chad Smith rode a motorcycle before the others did and still rides his, while the others mostly do not. But Smith, Flea, and Anthony Kiedis all adored basketball and the National Basketball Association. Kiedis and Flea are huge Los Angeles Lakers fans, having courtside seats since the late 1980s. Chad Smith is a Detroit Pistons fan. When they played pickup basketball, Flea was the best shooter, while Smith had the best interior post game.

2. The band was one of the first to have a modern Internet presence.

Dating back to the 1990s, Flea responded to fan e-mails on the band's official website as Fleamail. It was even a $400 *Jeopardy!* question in 2004 of which the band was the correct answer and the contestant incorrectly answered with Phish. Even before then, the band was ahead of the game: at the 1999 MTV Video Music Awards, the band won the first, last, and only award for Best Rock Website, beating out David Bowie, Jennifer Lopez, Sheryl Crow, Massive Attack, Smashing Pumpkins, and Limp Bizkit.

Before social media established a greater online community, the band had message boards dedicated to them, first on the band's official website, then on the fan-run stadium-arcadium.com website. The author of this book was once a moderator for the official band forum's media section after *By the Way*, accordingly named Throw Away Your Television.

Klinghoffer in concert during the Heineken Jammin Festival. *Fabio Diena / Shutterstock.com*

3. Chad Smith can play guitar, and Flea's first instrument was drums.

Although not well by his own admission. Smith practices guitar and plays it for fun. At one show in Milan, Italy, on November 14, 1999, the band switched instruments for their encore jam: Flea on drums, Smith on guitar, and John Frusciante on bass guitar. The jam was not one of their best moments, but it is something they did at a musical enough level to be enjoyable.

4. They can connect to almost any band in Six Degrees of Separation.

Thanks to a revolving door of guitarists; the extensive session work of John Frusciante, Flea, Chad Smith, and Josh Klinghoffer; an endless amount of touring; and What Is This?'s connection to Alain Johannes, who joined Queens of the Stone Age, they can connect to almost any band within a few jumps. Led Zeppelin? Johannes played for Queens when Dave Grohl drummed, who later played in Them Crooked Vultures with John Paul Jones. Parliament? You could go directly through *Freaky Styley* producer George Clinton or through former Pepper guitarist Blackbyrd McKnight. Wu-Tang Clan? Frusciante played guitar on *8 Diagrams*.

5. Flea plays a vintage Fender Jazz bass because he loves John Paul Jones from Led Zeppelin, even though John Paul Jones didn't always play a Fender Jazz bass.

In a Fleamail from November 23, 1999, Flea wrote that he wanted to play a vintage Fender Jazz bass so he could be "as cool as John Paul Jones." The Led Zeppelin bassist played a similar bass to the one Flea currently uses, a 1962 Fender Jazz, for the early Led Zeppelin records but retired it and switched to a Series II Four String midway through the 1970s. He now has his own line of basses named after him: the Manson E-Bass John Paul Jones Signature.

6. John Frusciante was influenced by three of his future replacements.

Frusciante never listened to *One Hot Minute*, the band's album with Dave Navarro on guitar, but he loved Jane's Addiction and studied Navarro's playing from that era. (He admired Jane's Addiction bassist Eric Avery's playing and adapted it to his guitar style as well.)

Similarly, Frusciante was a fan of Zander Schloss's bass playing in the Weirdos and the Circle Jerks and his guitar work in Thelonious Monster; Frusciante auditioned in Thelonious Monster before Schloss was in the band but came to be a fan of his guitar parts when Schloss was the guitarist from 1992 to 1994. Schloss was the first person to try to replace Frusciante, but the Red Hot Chili Peppers fired him after a week of two-a-day rehearsals.

Frusciante was also influenced by his final replacement: Josh Klinghoffer. The two made an album together credited to both of their names, and Frusciante organized most of the music to his album *Shadows Collide with People*, influenced by Klinghoffer's tastes.

7. Rick Rubin bought the house that the band recorded *Blood Sugar Sex Magik* in . . .

After the success of *Blood Sugar Sex Magik*, Rubin turned the mansion into a studio full-time and occasionally used it as a home in Los Angeles. The original home was built in 1925—Harry Houdini did not actually live there but did live nearby—but was burned down and rebuilt in the 1950s. In addition to the Peppers, Rubin recorded albums with LCD Soundsystem, Maroon 5, and Marilyn Manson there.

8. . . . but he sold it a few years ago.

Brigette and Mark Romanek bought the house in 2014. Rubin was friends with the couple when they were looking for a luxury home. It may still be excessive: it has at least 22 bedrooms in it. The new owners have redone most of the home, from the walls to the kitchen to the floor and electrical wiring.

9. The band's fan club used to get a quarterly magazine.

The Rockinfreakapotamus, the band's official fan club, also had a magazine that came out four times a year under the same name. *Rockinfreakapotamus* was edited by the same man who ran the fan club: Anthony Kiedis's father, Blackie Dammett. Dammett would do his best to answer fan questions or get the band to write something short back and publish fan photos and quips.

10. The band are all fans of—and friends with—Fugazi.

One of the promotional images for *Blood Sugar Sex Magik* featured John Frusciante wearing a bootleg shirt for Fugazi's *Repeater*. The Frusciante lineup covered Fugazi's "Latest Disgrace" as an introduction into "Parallel Universe" at Slane Castle. Frusciante and Klinghoffer also had a band with Fugazi's Joe Lally, Ataxia, that put out two albums: *Automatic Writing* and *AW II*.

When Frusciante didn't release music for a few years after he quit the Red Hot Chili Peppers, he still hung out and played music with Fugazi's Ian MacKaye. MacKaye told *Ultimate Guitar*,

> I think Frusciante's taking [artistry] to a really pure level. Because he's trying to pursue something that only he knows what it is. . . . He is pursuing something that has not yet been made, so therefore cannot be described. So that's just the way it is. And you know, almost once a year I'll see him and hear what he's working and be like "Wow, this is really out there."

If there's ever a full Fugazi reunion, the Red Hot Chili Peppers will be there.

Selected Bibliography

Absolute Radio, May 17, 2016.

Allsworth, Steve. "Cabron." *Total Guitar*, Summer 2003.

Anders, Marcel. "Josh Klinghoffer." *Gitarre & Bass*, November 11, 2016.

Angel, Johnny. "The Red Hot Chili Pepper's Surging Blood Sugar." *BAM*, 1991.

Anonymous. "Singer Convicted of Sexual Battery, Indecent Exposure." United Press International, April 3, 1990.

——. "Cover Story: Red Hot Chili Peppers." *Kerrang!*, June 1990.

——. "HOT LIPS!" *RAW*, November 1994.

——. "Mad, Chad, and Dangerous to Know." *Rhythm*, November 1995.

——. "News Flash: Chili Peppers Poised to Return to Stage." *MTV News*, December 10, 1997.

——. "Red Hot Chili Peppers News Brief." *Rolling Stone*, April 4, 1999.

——. "Red Hot Chili Peppers News Brief." *Sound on Sound*, Summer 1999.

——. "News Brief." *Bassist*, Summer 1999.

——. "By the Way, the Chili Peppers Are Back." *ICE*, June 2002.

——. "Bootsy & Flea." *Bass Guitar*, September 2006.

——. "Interview with Sinead O'Connor." *My Park Magazine*, 2009.

——. "See The Red Hot Chili Peppers Rejected Storm Thorgenson [sic] Artwork for Stadium Arcadium." *Feelnumb*, May 9, 2016. http://www.feelnumb.com/2016/05/09/red-hot-chili-peppers-rejected-storm-thorgensen-cover-artwork-stadium-arcadium.

——. "The Worst Offenders." *TV Tropes*. http://tvtropes.org/pmwiki/pmwiki.php/LoudnessWar/TheWorstOffenders.

Appleford, Steve. "A New Beginning for the Chili Peppers." *Los Angeles Times*, August 7, 2011.

Apter, Jeff. *Fornication: The Red Hot Chili Peppers Story*. London: Ominbus, 2004.

"Article about Hillel." Hebrew interview with Hillel Slovak. Translation provided by *The Chilis Source*. http://thechilisource.com/article-about-hillel.

Ascott, Phil. "Universally Speaking." *Guitarist*, 2003.

——. "Red Hot Chili Peppers." *Total Guitar*, July 2006.

Ballard, Joe. "Interview: Josh Klinghoffer (Dot Hacker)." *MindEqualsBlown*, July 25, 2014. http://mindequalsblown.net/interviews/interview-josh-klinghoffer-dot-hacker.

Bass Player Staff. "The 100 Greatest Bass Players of All Time." *Bass Player*, February 24, 2017. http://www.bassplayer.com/artists/1171/the-100 -greatest-bass-players-of-all-time/61989.

Bogosian, Dan. "It Took Me Some Time to Figure Out How Punk Was Music." *Ultimate Guitar*, May 29, 2012. https://www.ultimate-guitar.com/news/ interviews/ian_mackaye_it_took_me_some_time_to_figure_out_how_ punk_was_music.html.

——. "Red Hot Chili Peppers Add New Flavors to the Old Recipe on *The Getaway*." *A.V. Club*, June 17, 2016. https://music.avclub.com/ red-hot-chili-peppers-add-new-flavors-to-the-old-recipe-1798188149.

Bowcott, Nick. "Cayenne U Dig It?" *Guitar*, November 1995.

Bradman, E. E. "Flea at Your Service." *Bass Player*, August 2002.

Brakes, Rod. "Warpaint Talk Essential Gear, Inspiring Players and Borrowing Guitars from John Frusciante." *Music Radar*, August 17, 2017. https://www .musicradar.com/news/warpaint-talk-essential-gear-inspirational-players -and-borrowing-guitars-from-john-frusciante.

Brannigan, Paul. "Pretend Best Friends." *Kerrang!*, July 1996.

Brown, Harley. "Nate Ruess Is the Happiest He's Ever Been on Solo LP." *SPIN*, May 14, 2015. https://www.spin.com/2015/05/in-the-studio -nate-ruess-solo-lp.

Bryant, Tom. "Red Hot Chili Peppers." *Kerrang!*, May 2006.

Budofysky, Adam. "The Red Hot Chili Peppers: Chad Smith." *Modern Drummer*, December 1994.

California Superior Court. Plainsite.org. https://www.plainsite.org/dock ets/2pvfczfh8/superior-court-of-california-county-of-los-angeles/ jack-sherman-v-red-hot-chili-peppers-et-al.

Cline, Justin, and Dustin Wilmes. "An Evening with the Red Hot Chili Peppers' Jack Sherman." *The Five Count*, July 19, 2014. http://thefivecount.com/ audio-posts/an-evening-with-the-red-hot-chili-peppers-jack-sherman.

Cohan, Jim. "Chad Opens Up." *DRUM!*, 1999.

Cohan, Jon. "Chad Smith & Rick Rubin: In the Studio with the Red Hot Chili Peppers' Drummer and Producer." *DRUM!*, May 2002.

——. "Double Dip of Chad Smith." *DRUM!*, April 2006.

——. "Once a Pepper, Always a Pepper." *Rhythm*, May 2006.

Coryat, Karl. "Flea Jumps in a Different Direction." *Bass Player*, February 1992.

Dalley, Helen. "Red Hot Chili Peppers." *Total Guitar*, August 2002.

Dammett, Blackie. *Lords of the Sunset Strip: An Autobiography by Blackie Dammett*. Beverly Hills, CA: The Spencer Company, 2013.

Darling, Cary. "Born to Be Weird." *BAM*, August 1985.

Di Perna, Alan. "Free Spirits." *Guitar World*, November 1991.

——. "Shock Exchange." *Guitar World*, November 1997.

——. "Resurrection: LA Style." *Guitarist*, September 2002.

——. "Death & Axes." *Guitar World Acoustic*, April 2004.

——. "Funk Brothers." *Guitar World*, July 2006.

——. "Guided by Voices." *Guitar World*, July 2006.

——. "Get the Funk Out." *Guitar World*, October 2011.

Doerschuk, Bob. "Chad Smith and the Road Less Traveled." *DRUM!*, September 2016.

Dunn, Jancee. "Q&A with Dave Navarro." *Rolling Stone*, March 19, 1998.

Edwards, Gavin. "The Red Hot Chili Peppers Rise Again." *Rolling Stone*, April 27, 2000.

Farman, Julie. "Blood, Sugar, Sex, Dickheads." *The Grayish Carpet*, https://thegrayishcarpet.com/2016/04/20/blood-sugar-sex-dickheads.

Fitzpatrick, Rob. *Red Hot Chili Peppers: The Stories behind Every Song*. London: Carlton Books, 2004.

——. "The Band That Couldn't Be Stopped." *The Guardian*, August 19, 2011.

Flams, Robyn. "Chad Smith: Serving Up a New Red Hot Brew." *Modern Drummer*, August 1999.

Flanary, Patrick. "EXCLUSIVE: Anthony Kiedis Talks New RHCP Album." *SPIN*, February 18, 2011. https://www.spin.com/2011/02/exclusive-anthony-kiedis-talks-new-rhcp-album.

——. "Jack Irons: Alt Rock Anti Hero." *DRUM!*, April 2011.

——. "Ex-Chili Peppers Guitarist Feels 'Dishonered' by Rock Hall 'Snub.'" *Billboard*, May 5, 2012.

Flea. *Flea: Adventures in Spontaneous Jamming and Techniques*. Milwaukee, WI: Hal Leonard, 1999.

——. *Acid for the Children*. New York: Grand Central Publishing, 2019.

——. *Freaky Styley* liner notes. EMI Records.

——. *Greatest Hits* liner notes. Warner Bros. Records.

——. *Mother's Milk* liner notes. EMI Records.

——. *The Red Hot Chili Peppers* liner notes. EMI Records.

——. "I'm Flea, ASK ME ANYTHING." *Reddit*, October 30, 2014. https://www.reddit.com/r/IAmA/comments/2ktu98/im_flea_ask_me_anything.

——. *Uplift Mofo Party Plan* liner notes. EMI Records.

Fox, Brian. "Flea!" *Bass Player*, October 2011.

FOX News Live. August 23, 2016, https://www.youtube.com/watch?v=SkGGEuBstwM.

Fricke, David. "Red Hot Chili Peppers: The Naked Truth." *Rolling Stone*, June 25, 1992.

——. "Tattooed Love Boys." *Rolling Stone*, June 25, 2006.

——. "The Radical Rebirth of the Red Hot Chili Peppers." *Rolling Stone*, July 7, 2011.

——. "The Unstoppable Groove of the Red Hot Chili Peppers." *Rolling Stone*, September 1, 2011.

Frusciante, John. *Greatest Hits* liner notes. Warner Bros. Records.

Frusciante News. "John Frusciante Biography," https://www.frusciantenews.com/2013/10/john-frusciante-biography-part-3-red.html.

Funky Monks. Directed by Gavin Bowden. Warner Bros. Records.

Garbarini, Vic. "All for One: Pearl Jam Yield to the Notion That United They Stand and Divided They Fall." *Guitar World*, March 1998.

Gluckin, Tzvi. "Forgotten Heroes: Hillel Slovak." *Premier Guitar*, March 17, 2015.

Goldsby, John. "Exploring Minor 7th Intervals." *Bass Player*, April 2014.

Gore, Joe. "The Red Hot Chili Peppers: Gods of Sex Funk." *Guitar Player*, October 1991.

——. "Inside the Peppermill: Dave Navarro and Flea Reinvent the Chilis." *Guitar Player*, April 1995.

Greene, Andy. "Red Hot Chili Peppers Talk Risky Danger Mouse–Inspired Reboot." *Rolling Stone*, June 14, 2016.

Gross, Joe. "Everything Louder Than Everything Else." *Austin 360*, October 2, 2006.

Grow, Kory. "Hear Red Hot Chili Peppers Lost Navarro Era 'Circle of the Noose.'" *Rolling Stone*, February 4, 2016. http://www.rollingstone.com/music/news/hear-red-hot-chili-peppers-lost-navarro-era-circle-of-the-noose-20160204. Retrieved October 16, 2017.

Hawkins, Elijah. "Gear Rundown: Flea." *Mixdown*, June 21, 2016.

Hemsworth, Ryan. "We Got Ryan Hemsworth to Interview Cliff Martinez about Composing Your Favorite Soundtracks." *VICE Thump*, February 18, 2016. https://thump.vice.com/en_au/article/9avkv3/we-got-ryan-hemsworth-to-interview-cliff-martinez-about-composing-your-favorite-soundtracks.

Hughes, Glenn. "Eight Reasons to Hire Chad Smith." *DRUM!*, May 2006.

Isaak, Sharon. "Former Red Hot Chili Peppers Guitarist Files a Lawsuit against the Band." *Entertainment Weekly*, April 2, 1993. http://ew.com/article/1993/04/02former-red-hot-chili-peppers-guitarist-files-lawsuit-against-band.

Joyce, Collin. "Review: Trickfinger—*Trickfinger.*" *Pitchfork*, April 15, 2015. https://pitchfork.com/reviews/albums/20478-trickfinger.

Kammerzelt, Laurie. "Red Hot Chili Peppers." *Artists Magazine*, 1984.

Kaufman, Gil. "Chili Peppers' Dave Navarro Reacts to Reports of Drug Use." *MTV News*, January 1998. http://www.mtv.com/news/2456/chili-peppers-dave-navarro-reacts-to-reports-of-drug-use.

——. "Red Hot Chili Peppers Sue Showtime over 'Californication.'" *MTV News*, November 20, 2007. http://www.mtv.com/news/1574710/red-hot-chili-peppers-sue-showtime-over-californication.

Kenneally, Tim. "Chilly Pepper." *High Times*, July 1995.

The Kevin and Bean Show. KROQ, May 5, 2016.

Kiedis, Anthony. "Rick Rubin." *Interview*, December 29, 2010.

——. *Red Hot Chili Peppers: Fandemonium.* New York: Running Press, 2014.

Kiedis, Anthony, and Larry Sloman. *Scar Tissue.* New York: Hyperion, 2004.

Klinghoffer, Josh. "Josh Mail," November 22, 2016. http://josh-klinghoffer.org/joshmail/question-leandro.

Klinghoffer, Josh. "Josh Mail: Question—Moritz H," September 2017. http://josh-klinghoffer.org/question-moritz-h.

Late Night with Conan O'Brien. NBC, March 6, 1998.

Lebar, Erin. "Chillin' with a Chili Pepper." *Winnipeg Free Press*, May 27, 2017.

Lee, Dave. "Dave Mail 59." *John Frusciante Effects*, April 12, 2017. http://www.jfeffects.com.br/2017/04/dave-mail-59-superstitions-before.html.

Leigh, Bill. "Flea & Haden: A Rock Star & a Jazz Legend Find Common Ground in Music's Beauty & Depth." *Bass Player*, June 2006.

Manelis, Michelle. *Juice*, Issue 50, July 2000.

McCauley, Ciaran. "Interview with Mike Patton." *Bizarre*, July 2010.

McLaughlan, Jordan, and Louise King. "Rhythm Section: Chad and Flea." *Rhythm*, August 2006.

Mervis, Scott. "A Look Back at Some Wild Nights with the Red Hot Chili Peppers." *Pittsburgh Post-Gazette*, May 10, 2017. http://www.post-gazette.com/ae/music/2017/05/10/Red-Hot-Chili-Peppers-Pittsburgh-PPG-Paints-Arena-Graffiti-Decade-Flea-Anthony-Kiedis/stories/201705080112.

Morgan, Gareth. "Q&A: Red Hot Chili Peppers." *Classic Rock*, August 2016.

Moriates, Chris. "The Red Hot Chili Peppers." *Meanstreet*, July 2002.

Mullen, Brendan. *Whores: An Oral Biography of Perry Farrell and Jane's Addiction.* Cambridge, MA: Da Capo Press, 2006.

My Park Magazine. Retrieved using the Internet Wayback Machine for 2009. http://Mypark.co.uk.

Navarro, Dave. *Instructional Guitar: Dave Navarro*. Milwaukee, WI: Hal Leonard, 2004.

——. *Mourning Son*. DVD. Directed by Todd Newman, 2015.

Neely, Kim. "Anthony Kiedis: Confessions of Sir Psycho Sexy." *Rolling Stone*, April 7, 1994.

Nelson, Artie. "Space Cadet." *RAW*, November 1994.

Nguyen, Dean Van. "Red Hot Chili Peppers' Josh Klinghoffer: 'We Are Already Up to 28 or 30 Songs.'" *New Musical Express*, August 16, 2014. http://www.nme.com/news/music/red-hot-chili-peppers-65-1242786#cSrzdMfHE4KZswLt.01.

Nolin, Robert. "John Frusciante: Broward Judge's Guitarist Son Enters Rock Hall of Fame." *Sun Sentinel*, April 17, 2012. http://articles.sunsentinel.com/2012-04-17/news/fl-judge-rocker-20120416_1_roll-hall-rock-hall-guitarist-son.

Norris, Chris. "Anthony Kiedis: The Pursuit of Happiness." *Blender*, March 2007.

Odell, Michael. "Wonderland." *Q*, May 2006.

Off the Map. Directed by Dick Rude. New York: Warner Bros. Records, 2001.

Perry, John. "Dude, Where's My Carp?" *Loaded*, October 2002.

Phillips, Robb. "Flea & Me." *Bass Frontiers*, March 1998.

Plasketes, George. *Warren Zevon: Desperado of Los Angeles*. Lanham, MD: Rowman & Littlefield, 2016.

Poak, Tom. "Three Men and a Baby." *Classic Rock*, August 2011.

Prato, Greg. "Voodoo Chili." *Guitarist*, March 2009.

Rawlins, Melissa. "Sexual Harassment: Music." *Entertainment Weekly*, December 6, 1991.

Rees, Paul. "Chili Peppers Last Stand?" *RAW*, April 1992.

——. "Red Hot Chili Peppers Won't Be Killed." *Q*, September 2011.

Resnicoff, Matt. "Flea: On Top of the Mountain." *Musician*, January 1994.

Roes, Paul. "California Man." *Kerrang!*, May 1999.

Ronaldo and Mark Ramshaw. "Take It to the Bridge." *Total Guitar*, 1999.

Rotondo, James. "Interview with Guitar Player." *Guitar Player*, November 1997.

Sandall, Robert. "The Red Hot Chili Peppers Are Still on Fire." *The Times, The Knowledge*, April 2006.

Scapelliti, Christopher. "How Eddie Van Halen Helped John Frusciante Score a Wah Pedal." *Guitar World*, April 5, 2017. https://www.guitarworld.com/gear/how-eddie-van-halen-helped-john-frusciante-score-wah-pedal.

Sharken, Lisa. "Red Hot on the Empyrean." *Vintage Guitar*, 2009. http://www.vintageguitar.com/3743/john-frusciante.

Sherman, Lee. "New Blood New Magic: Dave Navarro Joins the Flea Circus." *Guitar*, October 1995.

Simpson, Dave. "Red Hot Chili Peppers: It's Great to Go Straight." *The Guardian*, February 14, 2003.

Slovak, James. "Red Hot Chili Peppers 1986 Hendrix Tribute." *YouTube*, https://www.youtube.com/watch?v=ffGpPy23wMk.

——. *Behind the Sun: The Diary and Art of Hillel Slovak*. New York: Slim Skinny Publications, 1999.

Smith, Chad. *Red Hot Rhythms Method: Chad Smith Instructional Video*. Van Nuys, CA: Alfred Music Publishing, 1993, 2003.

——. "Confidential Chad Smith." *Kerrang!*, September 2000.

——. *Greatest Hits* liner notes. New York: Warner Bros. Records, 2004.

——. *Rhythm*. Summer 2008.

Southall, Nick. "Imperfect Forever." *Stylus Magazine*, December 22, 2006.

Stableford, Dylan. "Kevin Spacey Threatens to Sue Indie Rock Act." *The Wrap*, https://www.thewrap.com/kevin-spacey-threatens-sue-indie-rock-act-over-album-name-27283.

Stadium Arcadium Documentary. New York: Warner Bros. Records, 2006.

Staff of Q. "Singing in the Rain." *Q*, June 2011.

Staff of *Kerrang!*. "50 Most Anticipated Albums of the Year." *Kerrang!*, January 2011.

Staff of *Los Angeles Times*. "Hillel Slovak; Guitarist in Flamboyant Rock Band." *Los Angeles Times*, June 30, 1988. http://articles.latimes.com/1988-06-30/news/mn-7531_1_hillel-slovak.

Staff of *New Musical Express*. "Does Rock'n'Roll Kill Brain Cells?" *New Musical Express*, April 21, 2010.

——. "60 Most Exciting Albums of 2011." *New Musical Express*, January 2011.

Staff of *Rolling Stone*. "Rolling Stone Readers Pick the Top Ten Bassists of All Time." *Rolling Stone*, March 2009. https://www.rollingstone.com/music/pictures/rolling-stone-readers-pick-the-top-ten-bassists-of-all-time-20110331/10-victor-wooten-0230408.

——. "Dark Necessities." *Rolling Stone*, June 2016.

Stratton, Joe. "Interview: Mike Patton of Mr. Bungle." *A.V. Club*, October 20, 1999. https://www.avclub.com/mike-patton-of-mr-bungle-1798208059.

Sullivan, Kate. "Spin Interview with Flea, Anthony, and John." *SPIN*, August 2002.

Swift, Jacqui. "My Son Everly Changed My Life." *The Sun*, August 10, 2011. https://www.thesun.co.uk/archives/music/710709/my-son-everly-changed-my-life-our-relationship-makes-me-forgive-my-father.

Tenreyo, Tatiana. "Flea Says Revisiting His Old High School Sparked His Crusade for Music Education." *Billboard*, September 6, 2017. https://www.billboard.com/articles/columns/rock/7950150/red-hot-chili-peppers-flea-interview-silverlake-conservatory-music.

Thompson, Dave. *Red Hot Chili Peppers—By the Way: The Biography*. London: Virgin Books, 2004.

Thrush, Glenn. "Funky Monks." *Guitar School*, July 1992.

Trunk, Eddie. "ET: Chad Smith." *SiriusXM*, June 22, 2017. https://player.fm/series/the-eddie-trunk-podcast-59879/et-chad-smith.

Vanishing Tattoo. http://www.vanishingtattoo.com/tattoo/celeb-flea.htm.

VH1. "Behind the Music: Red Hot Chili Peppers." 1999.

——. "Ultimate Albums: Blood Sugar Sex Magik." June 2, 2002.

VPro. "Red Hot Chili Peppers: Europe by Storm." Directed by Bram van Splunteren, 1988.

——. "Red Hot Chili Peppers: 1998." Unknown director, 1998.

Weisbard, Eric. "Ten Past Ten." *SPIN*, August 2001.

Weiss, Neal. "Still a Beautiful Mess." *SF Weekly*, December 15, 1999.

West, David. "The Chilis Legend Takes Over Rhythm!" *Rhythm*, Summer 2008.

——. "Chad Smith." *Rhythm*, September 2016.

Wild, David. "As If We Needed One, Here's a Reminder of Dylan's Power." *Rolling Stone*, December 1994.

Witter, Simon. "Red Hot Chili Peppers: 'We Eat Raw Cactuses!'" *The Guardian*, 1985. https://www.theguardian.com/music/2014/aug/06/red-hot-chili-peppers-we-eat-raw-cactuses-a-classic-interview.

Woolliscroft, Tony. *Me and My Friends*. New York: Abrams Publishing, 2009.

Yanick, Joseph. "From Red Hot Chili Peppers to the 'Drive' Soundtrack: An Interview with Composer Cliff Martinez." *VICE Noisey*, July 15, 2014. https://noisey.vice.com/en_us/article/rp5596/from-red-hot-chili-peppers-to-the-drive-soundtrack-an-interview-with-composer-cliff-martinez.

Yates, Henry. "Higher Ground: Josh Klinghoffer Puts His Stamp on the Chilis." *Total Guitar*, July 2012.

YouTube. https://www.youtube.com/watch?v=Fwecdpj-8Fo&t=11s.

Index